PENGUIN BOOKS
FANNY BY GASLIGHT

Famous as *Fanny by Gaslight* came to be, Michael Sadleir, who died in 1957, did not consider himself to be a novelist, but a biographer and collector. He was England's greatest expert on Anthony Trollope; his *Trollope: A Commentary* and *Trollope: A Bibliography* remain standard works. His collection of nineteenth-century fiction and knowledge of the literature and social background of the period were immense and clearly reflected in the entirely convincing back-cloth to *Fanny*. His study of Victorian author-publisher relationships, distribution methods and reading habits culminated in his two-volume *Nineteenth Century Fiction: A Bibliographical Record*, which was based on his own collection. As Managing Director of Constable & Co., he was a well-known publisher. Orange Street was and is the firm's home and Michael Sadleir would wander for hours round those by-ways of Leicester Square in which 'Hopwood's Hades' once thrived.

D1386965

MICHAEL SADLEIR

Fanny by Gaslight

PENGUIN BOOKS

Penguin Books Ltd, Harmondsworth, Middlesex, England
Penguin Books, 625 Madison Avenue, New York, New York 10022, U.S.A.
Penguin Books Australia Ltd, Ringwood, Victoria, Australia
Penguin Books Canada Ltd, 2801 John Street, Markham, Ontario, Canada L3R 1B4
Penguin Books (N.Z.) Ltd, 182-190 Wairau Road, Auckland 10, New Zealand

First published by Constable & Co. 1940
Published in Penguin Books 1981
Reprinted 1981

Made and printed in Great Britain by
Richard Clay (The Chaucer Press) Ltd, Bungay, Suffolk
Set in Plantin

NOTE

FANNY BY GASLIGHT is a *novel*, with wholly imaginary plot and characters. But, because it is specifically dated and the events mainly take place in London, care has been taken to maintain period-accuracy and to give invention a basis of fact.

The institutions and scenes presented as characteristic of London night-life at the dates in question, are entirely fictitious as regards locality and in detailed description. But little is made to occur which, in some form or somewhere, did not actually take place. Similarly one or two of the characters, in themselves imaginary, have life-stories borrowed and blended from those of real people. The manner of speech and the slang used are so far as possible in period; and, although liberties have been taken with London topography (for example there was never a Panton Passage, a basin off the New River or a Larne Circle), Fanny's London is innocent of anachronisms.

Differences in style between the various sections are deliberate. The first section and the last, which tell a tale of our own days, are written as the author wished to write them. Parts One and Three of Fanny's story are told by her in the first person *but written by Warbeck in the nineteen-thirties;* they are therefore modern as to narrative but 'period' as to conversation. Part Two of Fanny's story, told in the first person by Harry Somerford, is more nearly period throughout, because it purports to read as a contemporary account of events which took place during the eighteen-seventies.

M. S.

CONTENTS

INTRODUCING FANNY HOOPER

NOW THAT he had started her remembering, recollections –
like flotsam on a river in sudden spate – came dancing, glid-
ing, bobbing and bumping across her reluctant mind. Some in
themselves were pleasant, even lovely – her first visit to the
Crystal Palace and the new tartan dress she wore; mamma's
prune-mould, with whipped cream piled in the centre, over-
flowing, and dribbling down the smooth, purple-black flutings
of the outside; the brooch from Mr Seymore; mamma's story
told in the firelight of the Becketts' parlour, and the picture it
conjured of a strip of golden sand, of rocks warm in the sunshine and of the deep blue-green of a hidden pool; 'Vandra' or
water-sprite; the discovery of Andrew; the happy carefree
days at Aughton; dear staunch old Chunks; the pagan luxury
of 'Florizel Thirteen'; and finally the climax of them all –
that brief enchanted life with Harry, and the joy of loving and
serving him and seeing his eyes smile.

It seemed that after Harry went she had known no real
happiness, nor hoped for it; but had been thankful for such
intervals of surface contentment, security and excitement, as
fortune brought her. Of contentment there had been little
enough; of security, thanks to Kitty Cairns and dear kindly
little Ferraby, what should have been sufficient; of excitement
(as if excitement mattered!) plenty and to spare. . . . Some
memories, if memories you wanted, were pleasant enough.
Others, however, were horrible – things she had striven and
striven to forget and at last forgotten – only now to recall them
again, as vividly as though they had never been hunted from
her mind.

Why had this man Warbeck asked her to remember? Why
had she consented? 'Don't be a fool, Fanny' she told herself.
'You must have money and he will get you money – just for
remembering.'

But while half of her approved the commonsense as irrefutable, the other half fought desperately against the encroaching shadows of the past. She hated the past, whether it had been sweet or bitter; she was done with the sort of life she had known, almost done with life altogether. Here in Les Yvelines she had found peace for the few years left to her. And he had destroyed it. No – interrupted it only. She could change her mind, tell him that on second thoughts. . . . If she now refused to do what he asked, refused even to think of anything but the daily nothings of her quiet retreat, that peace would come again. 'Without money?' queried the tart voice of commonsense; and to that question no heroic answer came.

She was lying in a wicker chair on a sort of covered platform in a corner of the garden at the Hôtel de la Boule d'Or. It was early afternoon and very hot. The untidy grass was drenched in sunlight and the rambler-roses fell in a matted curtain between the dazzle without and the deep shade in which she sat. There was hardly a sound near at hand, save the burring of a solitary grasshopper in the sunlit garden and an occasional rustle in the pile of dead leaves which lay behind her against the penthouse-wall. From beyond the buildings came the noise of a lorry grinding down the street, then fading in the distance. The old woman lay very still. A cat, full length on a window-ledge a little to her right, lay very still also. The hotel seemed to be asleep; the little town seemed to be asleep.

*   *   *

Sleep came easily – and not only on hot summer afternoons – to the threadbare town of Les Yvelines-la-Carrière. Halfway between Versailles and the western fringe of what used to be called the Ile de France, it lay at the foot of an escarpment which marked the boundary of one of the more westerly of the chain of forests surrounding suburban Paris. Thus to the east of Les Yvelines and partly to the south, rose a steep, tree-crowned ridge, while flat fields and marshy meadows stretched west and north.

The place was very poor. Apart from a saw-mill, in forlorn

competition with better equipped rivals for favours of the Eaux et Forêts, no industry survived; for the great quarry which gave the town half its name had been abandoned many years ago, and was now a sinister amphitheatre draped with weeds and ivy, scooped out of the hillside and already half-hidden by encroaching trees. The inhabitants, therefore, lived on agriculture; collected for sale fallen timber, cêpes, wild strawberries and lilies of the valley from adjacent areas of the forest; and thus contrived to live a frugal, apathetic life in a place which – though barely forty miles from Paris – was seemingly forgotten.

For not even the dubious benefits of tourism came plentifully to Les Yvelines, though it had things to show as good – or which would have been as good, with money to spend on repairs and advertising – as many far more famous places. Once it stood on a high road; but in those days motors were scarce and travellers made careful calculations about train journeys. Then, in the nineteen-twenties, a new big motorroad was driven across the plain to northward, which missed Les Yvelines (awkwardly hidden under the barrier of hills) by six miles, and took its tourists with it. Now only very determined lovers of antiquity or persons genuinely in search of solitude found their way to Les Yvelines – with results delightful to such as hate motoring sightseers, but sadly unfavourable to the town's economy.

The Boule d'Or – except for a squalid tavern near the station (a very minor station on a branch-line and a mile from the town) – was the only hotel Les Yvelines possessed. It was an old-established house, whose age was now more evident than its establishedness. But although the widow Bonnet had neither cash nor incentive to 'modernize', she maintained with the stubborn pride of a true ménagère the standard of her simple cooking and the comfort of her beds, and saw to the casual but adequate sweeping of her tall, carpetless and sparsely furnished rooms.

On this hot June afternoon the Boule d'Or showed no more sign of life to the street than to the garden. The flat four-storey façade, once grey-washed, now cracked and streaked with brown and deeper grey, rose sheer from the narrow pavement. On the ground floor, the rusty paintless shutters were closed; before the main door hung a curtain of striped canvas, which, being only a year old, seemed unsuitably blatant in its vivid colouring. Two dusty trees in tubs, placed on the doorstep, threw into almost vulgar relief the green and orange brilliance of their back-drop. The name of the hotel, in spaced letters of tarnished gilt, clung unsteadily to the wall under the second-storey windows.

The street in which the hotel stood was the main street of Les Yvelines, inasmuch as it prolonged from the south the one-time turnpike, debouched into the irregular space in front of the church, turned the left flank of that beautiful but crumbling building and, crossing a wide square bordered with low houses, divided by a stream and centred by a walled pond, passed out through an untidy suburb toward the station and the new arterial road.

It was called Rue Neuve, which – considering there was not a house in it of later date than the mid eighteenth century and many far older – bore pathetic testimony to the longevity of the town, and emphasized, a little distressingly, its decayed old age.

*   *   *

Into the empty silence of this Rue Neuve broke, first the chuff-chuff of a small car and then the car itself – a little Peugeot, driven by a coatless young man in a beret. At his side sat a girl with a mop of yellow hair. The car came from the direction of the church and slowed uncertainly as the street narrowed. The young man spoke to his companion, gesturing with one hand toward the hotel. She did not trouble to follow his gesture, but merely smiled. Her eyes were heavy with contentment, and the smile said: Anything you like. I don't care.

The car stopped at the Boule d'Or and the young man got out. He wore pale trousers with a belt, a white singlet and canvas shoes. Pushing the gaudy curtain aside, he stepped into the shadows of the hall. The girl sat motionless in the car, gazing in front of her, seeing nothing. In a few minutes the man returned accompanied by a plump maid in an overall, who seized the small suitcase from the dickey and opened the door for the girl to alight. They disappeared into the hotel. The young man got into the car again and drove it slowly into a tunnel-like gateway which at the far end of the hotel façade gave access to the so-called garage.

Ten minutes later the old woman in her wicker chair behind the matted ramblers heard voices in the garden. The sound was welcome. Any intrusion of the present kept reverie at bay. Lying there alone with the hot silence all about her – faces, hands, rooms, sounds, even smells from the past crowded and jostled intolerably. Now she could keep them away – if only for a few moments – wondering who was coming, perhaps watching them when they came. Chance was kind. A young man and a girl with yellow hair came slowly into view. They were manifestly French. His arm was round her and she leant drowsily against him. Here and there in the neglected wilderness of garden stood chairs and tables. The new-comers chose places in a patch of shade, across the garden from where the old woman sat but well within her view. The plump maid brought a tray with glasses and siphon, poured menthe-Vittel, smiled encouragingly and stumped away. The visitors sipped their drinks, and then, as though flung together by invisible hands, were in one another's arms. For a few moments they sat, pressed close one against the other. Then the girl turned slightly and, with her arms round his neck, slid backward on to his knees. He bent to her mouth, and as the kiss clung her arms whitened with the effort of crushing her lover's face against her own. When at last he raised his head, she let her arms fall limply, and lay a moment with closed eyes. Her ripe wet lips were parted, her breast rose and fell, and one could almost hear the beating of her heart. He sat looking down at her, a tiny smile of adoration creasing his lean dark cheeks. Then he bent again and, lips almost touching hers, whispered into her mouth. She faintly nodded, lay a second longer in happy relaxation before swinging herself quickly to her feet. With a vigorous movement she ran her fingers through the shining mass of her hair, shook it back and stood waiting. The young man rose and picked up the tray. Side by side they moved toward the terrace-door of the hotel and passed out of the old woman's sight. As they passed, the sunshine lighted the contents of their two glasses to a livid golden green.

She stirred uneasily in her chair. Her ally, the present, had cruelly and uncannily betrayed her. Those two young things – so much in love, so fiercely happy in the refuge they had found – might have been phantoms from that portion of the past she dreaded most. She had not cried for years, yet now she felt the tears pricking her eyes. With a veined and wasted hand she touched the neat white hairs which lay smoothly under her widow's bonnet. 'Oh Harry, Harry...' she muttered, and her head fell forward on to the pleats which ridged the bosom of her dress.

*   *   *

An hour or two earlier on this same day – shortly after one o'clock, to be precise – Gerald Warbeck was eating his lunch on the bank of one of the several solitary and reed-grown *étangs* which occur here and there in the forest above Les Yvelines. He had started from the hotel about ten o'clock, carrying in his rucksack some bread, two slices of galantine, two tomatoes, a piece of Gruyère and a bottle of Vin Rosé. He wore grey flannel trousers and a short-sleeved sports jumper. A thin linen jacket was tucked into the strap of his rucksack, and on his head he wore what he pleased to call a Panama hat. It was darkish yellow and rigid in its shapelessness. All the same it might have been a Panama, once. It had belonged to Warbeck's Uncle Oswald.

Gerald Warbeck was in his early forties. He had a high colour and reddish hair. Until he reached the shade of the trees he wore sun-spectacles, and these – perched fiercely on his prominent nose under the aggressive brim of Uncle Oswald's hat – gave him an air of stubborn determination. Actually (as

became evident when spectacles and Panama were laid aside)
he was neither stubborn nor determined, but a mild, rather
intelligent man who, because he was more interested in de-
viations than in conformity, minded his own business and
wished others would mind theirs.

By trade Warbeck was a book-publisher, who did a little
writing on the side. He was seldom shocked by the things
which shocked the British public, but often found either painful or disgusting things in which that public took delight.
Consequently his taste and theirs were apt not to coincide.
Further, his instinct for novelty outran the normal; and he had
not even yet learnt to make allowance for the reaction-time –
seven to ten years – which was common form among his com-
patriots when faced with any new idea in the practice or
appreciation of matters of the mind. As a result, he published
books far ahead of any possible acceptability, failed to sell
them, and was duly chagrined when, years later, his competitors published others of similar character and got away with
them. Further again, he refused to admit that political conviction justified any author in distorting the truth or lapsing
from literary integrity – a prejudice which lost him many
opportunities of profit, but in return won him no particular
esteem.

Finally, because he was interested in too many kinds of
things, he could not think day and night of one job and nothing
else; and, being one-third author to two-thirds publisher, was
not without sympathy for writers' grievances. These short-
comings placed him at a disadvantage vis-à-vis single-minded
sloggers, who knew that sticking to a last meant getting in
first, and usually did so.

But despite these handicaps, Warbeck made as much of
a living as he wanted, enjoyed as much of his work as he
inclined to do, and secured each year a short spell of perfect contentment by going off on his own and leaving no
address.

One such spell was now in progress; and today, when after
walking steadily for two hours and a half he had reached the

étang, he placed his sack and stick on a mossy bank, found a comfortable seat against a tree trunk, lit a pre-lunch cigarette, and told himself that this indeed was happiness. The scene before him had beauty, but also a remote serenity which was magically anodyne.

The *étang* was an elongated mere, perhaps half a mile in length, but nowhere more than a hundred yards in width. It was pinched to a sort of waist in the middle, where a forest-track crossed it on a low flint bridge. Bullrushes, flags and other reeds grew thickly round the shores; and already yellow iris flowers were starring their greenery, over which dragon-flies of iridescent blue hovered and darted. Beyond the reeds the water was so overgrown with floating pondweed that clear patches were few. There was no wind in the trees, no ripple on the surface of the mere. Warbeck sat motionless, revelling in the dapple of sunshine on the opposite trees, the sweet woodland smell, above all in the silence. He felt part of another world or, if this were indeed fairyland as it appeared to be, that he was dreaming. He wished the dream to continue; and was glad to find that it persisted, even after he ground out his cigarette and unpacked his lunch. Only gradually, as he ate, did actuality step back into his consciousness. He welcomed it, for he found that he was now ready for it and prepared to consider its problems with interest. It was as though his brief excursion into another sphere had soothed and refreshed him.

Naturally the first subject to present itself was that of the remarkable old lady at the Boule d'Or, and the strange progress of his acquaintance with her.

He had arrived at the Boule d'Or a week ago. It was his first visit to Les Yvelines, a place he had several times tried to fit into a preconceived itinerary, but always been compelled to miss. It was characteristic of Les Yvelines not to march with other places on a tourist's route. Everything about it was just a shade awkward; and in nine cases out of ten it had to be skipped – as Warbeck had skipped it. This year, however, he had determined to get there and, to prevent any possibility of deflection, would make it his first objective after Paris.

Eventually he had driven out from the city in a taxi, which he had picked up near the Montparnasse Station after a brief and heart-breaking study of the available train service.

And already he had stayed a week.

Certainly the place had justified itself. The hotel was just the kind of hotel he most enjoyed – out at elbows and a little uncertain as to sanitation, but with the faded dignity of a house with traditions, an easy friendliness of direction, excellent food and drink, and the sort of fundamental peace which at times he feared had altogether vanished from the world.

The town was no less rewarding, with its knot of narrow streets; its jumble of ancient houses propped crazily one against another; the desolate stretch of trodden earth beyond the church, planted with two long rows of dusty planes beside the sluggish stream.

As for the church of St Etienne itself, it was an enchanting medley of styles, each almost perfectly represented, all harmoniously slipping into tragic but lovely ruin. The west front was Late Decorated at its most exquisite; but where the elaborate tracery had perished or been deliberately smashed was makeshift cement, and some catastrophe to the rose-window above the main doors had been remedied by planks, nailed across the opening and brushed with creosote. The south transept had a renaissance interior, faultless in proportion and detail and reasonably preserved; the north should have had the same, but the work had never been completed, and the delicate carving of medallions and pilasters faded off into rough stonework of a later date, which did not aspire to ornament and only just achieved utility. The nave and chancel were simple Gothic of the fifteenth century. Poverty had prevented paint; and the pillars, walls and roof were naked stone or plaster and greying wood – in places stained green with damp, generally discoloured and probably unsafe, but spared at least the niggling patterns and hideous colour-scheme of provincial catholicism. To crown all, across the Gothic and the renaissance, the eighteenth century (presumably during some spurt of local prosperity) had scrawled its grandiose signature.

It had filled the west end with a huge organ-loft, whose front
and curving stairs were tempests of baroque carving; at the
corner of the north transept it had erected a monstrous pulpit,
which swung upward in a spiral from a luscious base to a
canopy in the form of a gilded shell. The once polished wood
was dull and cracked; the gold a dim survival of itself. But
still the spiral flung its curves to heaven, and the flamboyant
piety which had created it stood side by side with earlier
pieties, facing a common ruin.

Oddly enough the best preserved and most coherent feature
of this dilapidated hybrid of a church were the windows. Of
mid sixteenth century date, they pierced the clerestory in
series along both sides of the nave, and with boldness of design
and graceful naïveté depicted scenes from the Old and New
Testaments. Attracted by their liquid colouring, Warbeck had
studied them in detail, and discovered among them a rendering of the Garden of Eden. The composition demonstrated in
words of one syllable the desire of man for woman, and was of
a kind unusual in a sacred (or indeed in any public) edifice.
This flash of candour delighted him; and was duly registered
in that corner of his memory reserved for anything eccentric,
pathetic, sinister or abnormal, which might come his way.

Seeing that to these attractions of Les Yvelines itself could
be added the miles of forest-walks which lay within easy reach,
this year's holiday would in any event have ranked high among
Warbeck's experiments. When lavish chance produced the
ultimate bizarrerie of the old lady at the hotel, it shot ahead of
all its rivals. Never, he told himself, will you have such luck
again. Go very carefully and make the most of it.

The afternoon of his arrival – was it indeed only a week
ago? – he had encountered the widow Bonnet in the hall, as he
was wandering out into the town. His previous meeting with
her having been a purely professional affair of room and terms
and formal courtesies, he took the opportunity to seek a better
acquaintance. She was a small, demure grey-haired woman,
very quiet in manner and simply dressed in a black frock
sprigged with white. Her face was pleasant but worn with

anxiety and a little melancholy. She received Warbeck's polite greeting with a bend of the head and a faint smile, and would have passed on into her office if he had not made some friendly remark about the interest and antiquity of Les Yvelines. Yes, she agreed, it was an old place and lovers of old places found it attractive. 'But they are few enough' she added with a return of her sad smile, 'and we are off the track of modern life.'

Warbeck felt slightly embarrassed. Was this a gentle lament which called for condolence, or an implication that people of his sort were of no great use to a hotel and would gladly be exchanged for motorists or commercial travellers?

'I am sorry' he said lamely. 'I suppose it is difficult, when one has to cater for uncertain guests.'

'Oh, monsieur, I am not complaining. I have lived so long in Les Yvelines and grown so settled in my ways that I should not be happy anywhere else. But I was afraid you might find it too quiet and my hotel – well, not up-to-date in its appointments.'

'I assure you, madame' Warbeck spoke with the emphasis of conviction – 'that I am the least up-to-date of living men and the Boule d'Or – so far as I have seen it and with an excellent déjeuner fresh in my mind – is precisely the sort of hotel I usually seek in vain.'

The rather stilted diction and the genuine warmth of this red-haired, large-nosed Englishman appealed to Madame Bonnet.

'Thank you, monsieur' she said. 'I shall try to fulfil your expectations. The garden is pretty' she went on wistfully 'though I wish you could have seen it a few years ago. My husband was alive then and kept it in better order than is possible today. So few young men stay in Les Yvelines; and the old ones, who might come and do the garden, get older and fewer every year. But even overgrown, it is pleasant to sit in. I like to take my coffee there in the summer, if there are not many people staying – and there seldom are.'

'You have people now? . . .'

'A couple last night, but they left early. And of course Madame Oupère.'

'Madame . . . ?' queried Warbeck. 'And why of course?'

She smiled almost gaily.

'Pardon, monsieur. I am stupid. How should you know? Madame Oupère is an old English lady – very old – who has lived here now for several years. I do not know why she came or why she has stayed. Some sorrow probably, and in any event not my business. But without knowing anything about her or indeed becoming at all intimate with her (for she keeps her counsel), I have grown quite fond of her. I think we all have.'

Warbeck felt a twinge of curiosity. His instinct for a queer story stirred in its sleep and opened one eye. Also he was glad that this nice widow had a permanent pensionnaire.

'That is interesting' he said. 'I do not think I saw her at déjeuner.'

'No, she does not as a rule come down until the afternoon. She is old, as I said. My niece Léontine looks after her as well as she can – takes her meals upstairs and helps her. But you will see her at dinner. . . .'

After a few more generalities, Warbeck took leave of his hostess. As he strolled down the street, he found himself looking forward to a sight of the old lady from England who had lived alone in Les Yvelines for several years. He wondered what her surname really was.

* * *

They two were alone in the salle à manger – Warbeck at a small table near the buffet, Madame Oupère across the room at another small table by the window. She was a quaint enough little figure to satisfy any amateur of oddity. On her head was a close-fitting cap of white muslin, tied with a black-velvet ribbon which finished in a large bow halfway between crown and forehead. Her snow-white hair, parted in the centre, swept tidily to left and right and back over her ears. She wore a gown of black satin, very plain, with a touch of white lace at her throat and wrists. Her tiny hands were innocent of rings, save for a plain gold band on her left hand; round her neck she wore a single string of pearls.

From this severe – almost puritan – setting an impish little face threw out its challenge. It was a lined face, of course; and below the high cheek bones wrinkles tugged at the corners of the mouth. But it remained the face of one who had not lost her capacity for merriment and cheerful cynicism, who still – through a pair of bright black eyes – could see the funny side.

Throughout the meal Warbeck covertly studied this re-markable little person – a process of some delicacy because, so far from ignoring his presence or shrouding herself in the aloof dignity dear to the British who encounter their kind in foreign lands, she was unabashedly studying him. The more he looked at her, the more he liked her looks. A Londoner himself, he could respond to what were surely a Cockney gaiety and a Cockney impudence in the tilt of a nose, in the long humorous mouth and in the flicker of mischief in the eyes. He was wondering how the inevitable acquaintanceship would begin, when she pushed back her chair, threw her napkin on to the table and prepared to leave the room. He bent over his dessert, feeling that to watch her even surreptitiously would be in-trusive. He heard her steps tapping toward him on the plain polished floor – steps surprisingly brisk and firm – and was more apprehensive than surprised when they stopped by his table instead of passing onward to the door.

'Young man' she said abruptly, in a voice perhaps more unexpected than anything else about her – a deep contralto voice disturbing but delicious in its shadowy luxury – 'You are an Englishman.'

Warbeck rose clumsily to his feet and stood in the awkward position of one who, unable to push table and chair apart, must droop inward at the knees, pretending to be upright.

'Yes' he replied. 'Yes, I am.'

'I am English too' she said. 'If an old woman asked you as a kindness to take coffee with her . . .'

'I should accept with pleasure. . . .'

She gave him a quick, almost a coquettish smile and moved away.

'In the garden' she said, as she left the room.

He sat with her in the garden while the twilight faded. Night fell, and the evening primroses hovered like huge white moths. The scent from a group of nicotines lay heavy on the air. The darkness was faintly lit by indirect reflection from the hotel. Here and there in the high wall a lighted window shone; from the glass veranda which gave on to the garden came a muffled gleam, and through the glass the plump little maid and another youngish woman, presumably Léontine, could be seen clearing the dining-room. Warbeck could see little of his companion who was sunk almost out of sight in a low wicker chair. He was grateful for the darkness which thwarted vision but left the listener free, for Madame Oupère was a siren to the ear. She talked a good deal in that low thrilling voice, asking questions, praising Madame Bonnet and her niece, re-tailing anecdotes of small events in Les Yvelines and of the idiosyncrasies of passing guests. But of herself she said almost nothing. Her name, he discovered, was Hooper. As he had guessed, she was London-born and London-bred.

Clearly it was impossible for Warbeck to question her; and he realized, when at last he rose to take his leave, that he had told her a great deal about himself and learnt very little in return. She bade him goodnight in a friendly way and thanked him for his company, concluding:

'Would you please tell Léontine, as you pass the bureau, that I would like to go upstairs?'

Warbeck had found a problem after his own heart, and for a while he lay awake devising explanations of old Mrs Hooper. When he awoke next morning he devised some more. They were all incorrect.

*   *   *

The acquaintance ripened rapidly; but although Warbeck now felt quite at his ease with his new friend, he was little better informed as to her personal history. Piecing together such indications as she let slip, he surmised that she had known not only many places, but many kinds of life; that she was no reader, having a fund of worldly knowledge gained at first hand, but little of what – in his faintly pedantic way – he called 'cultural background'. She tended to flippancy, especially with regard to the established conventions and castes of her own and other countries, while her occasional comments on restriction-mongers – national and international – were hostile even to savagery. Warbeck began to suspect that the mutual sympathy which each had clearly felt at their first meeting was in fact based on a fierce individualism common to them both – a suspicion which an incident of their fourth day of friendship tended to confirm.

About six o'clock in the evening, as he came downstairs, bathed and changed after a day in the forest, he met Mrs Hooper in the covered veranda. He had an English weekly paper under his arm and was bound for the café on the Place St Etienne, where he liked to sit for an hour before dinner. 'Good evening, Mr Warbeck. You are going out?'

'Only down to the café by the church.'

'May I come with you?'

'Of course.'

The request surprised him, for he had never seen her leave the hotel and had assumed – without the least reason – that she was semi-invalid. But as they walked down the street, he noticed that she stepped securely for an old woman, and also that several of the people they met saluted her. Clearly she was a figure familiar in Les Yvelines.

Settled in the café – a homely place with a very small apparent clientèle – she accepted a cigarette and asked for absinthe. Tasting it, she pursed her lips and twinkled across the table at Warbeck.

'Not the stuff it was' she said. 'They've taken the life out of it – as out of most other things.'

'You have been a frequenter of cafés?'

'Cafés . . . divans, as we once called them . . . all manner of places. Not sitting outside, you know. In my day that would have been indiscreet. But inside ... upstairs ... in rooms. ...'

Casually Warbeck picked up the English paper.

'I was reading here, just before I came downstairs, about raids on clubs and cafés in London – catching them out selling drinks after hours, you know. It angers me, this monstrous system of dressing up cops in evening clothes to catch poor devils out.'

Mrs Hooper nodded vigorously.

'We are all in leading strings nowadays. Our spirit is broken and even spies are honourable, when working for righteousness. They ought to be lynched. And they would have been in the old days. I'd like to have seen...'

She broke off and sipped her drink.

'Never mind ... I've seen plenty ... Stupid to want to see anything more. ...'

He took a chance.

'Tell me some of what you have seen. ...'

She picked up her glass, and, as she put her lips to it, looked quizzically at him over the tilted brim. Replacing the glass on the table, she turned her head and stared across at the crumbling church-front.

'Shall I?' she mumbled, half to herself.

He said nothing. He had dared. It was for her to punish or reward.

'How do I know ...?' she began, and broke off abruptly; then shrugged her shoulders and fixed him again with her bright derisive eyes.

'I like you, Mr Warbeck. I like your big nose and your funny tufty hair. Also you are kind. You are big and some-times clumsy, but I think you are gentle as well as masculine. Women – even old women – like that mixture, as I daresay you have found out for yourself. But I do not know you *inside*, do I? You may have dislikes, prejudices, principles, which I would wish to respect. ...'

Again she broke off, and began playing with the white

muslin cuff which sat demurely at the wrist of her simple black dress. Warbeck smiled at her.

'Thank you for liking me and for not wanting to ruffle my feathers. But I am sure you need not be afraid. I have my feathers. But they ruffle principally at hypocrites and brutes, and you do not seem to me either of those.'

She considered his words carefully.

'Brutal? No, I don't think I have ever been that. As for hypocrisy, I have worn a mask most of my life, but I had to – at least I thought I had to. And yet I am still nervous of offending you. Let me ask you this – what in a year's time will you remember most clearly of that church there?'

'The Adam and Eve window' he replied.

She flashed him a look, mock-scandalized. 'Oh, Mr Warbeck!' she said, and her little face creased dangerously.

After a few moments she chuckled.

'I will tell you my story – or as much of it as you care to hear. It is not much of a story in itself; but I have known all sorts of people and seen all sorts of things, and so much of what I used to know has disappeared. Also you may be able to help me – for I am in a difficult position. . . .'

'Anything I can do. . . . Does the story start after dinner?'

'As you wish' she replied. 'Shall we go back now? I am hungry.'

*   *   *

That evening and the following day, and the day after that, the story of Mrs Hooper, or rather her souvenirs, gradually accumulated. She was capricious as a teller of tales, sometimes talking readily enough, at others saying she was tired, or could not think of anything worth recalling, or insisting on retracing her steps and correcting some earlier inaccuracy. One evening, when Warbeck put a casual question, hoping to launch her on a stream of reminiscence, she said:

'I'm not in the mood tonight, Mr Warbeck. There's something on my mind which I want to tell you.'

'Please' he replied. 'Go right ahead.'

She gave a little laugh.

'I'm almost shy about it. I don't like bothering you with my private affairs, but I have no one else to consult. So here goes. Well, to put it bluntly, I am broke. (Don't be afraid. I'm not going to touch you for a loan.) When I came here about five years ago, I reckoned that I had enough money to live on for ten years and that I was not likely to need all of that. But two misfortunes occurred. The first was the failure of an American investment in the crash of 1929. The second has only just happened.

'There are some dwellings in one of the poorest parts of East London, of which I own a share. I have regularly received rents from them – not very much, but useful to have. These dwellings have now been condemned. The agents who transmit the rents have sent me the Council Surveyor's report, and a very terrible thing it is. It makes me almost ill to think that for years I have been taking money from people living in such conditions.

'You see, I never went to the place. The share which is now mine was left me years ago by a dear friend who was one of the earliest philanthropists in the building of what were called Model Dwellings in the slums. He built this block, which at the time was thought a wonderful place; and so long as he was alive and interested in the dwellings, a decent orderly lot of people lived there. Forgive this long story; but I must make my dilemma clear.

'Well my old friend died, and the ownership of the block passed into a number of separate possessions – of which mine was one. We new landlords were strangers to one another, scattered all over and mostly ignorant of or indifferent to our responsibilities. Control came to be exercised mainly by a firm of agents and rent-collectors, and by one or two of the part-owners, who took pains to keep in touch. I am afraid these people thought of nothing but how to make more money from the property.

'The dwellings are in a district which has been closely built up for many many years and has hardly any open spaces.

Being fairly close to the centre of things, house-room is in constant demand, because working-folk can live there within easy, and therefore economical, distance from their jobs. The district has in consequence always been badly overcrowded. Evidently the men who were now managing our block of dwellings saw in this overcrowding the chance of collecting more rents. At any rate they allowed division and sub-division of flats, and took as tenants any who could pay.

'I do not try to excuse myself. I noticed my rents increased somewhat; but I was too busy with my own affairs to wonder why or to trouble to inquire. Even now I have learnt most of what I am telling you from the Report, and, by putting two and two together, have guessed the remainder. One thing is quite clear from the description – that the place deserves to be pulled down.

'The agents, when they advised me of the Council's decision, urged me to join with other part-owners in demanding higher compensation than was offered. This I cannot and will not do. After reading what that place is like, I would like to refuse to take any compensation at all. But if I do refuse, I shall starve; for I have practically nothing else left.

'What am I to do, Mr Warbeck? That is what I want you to tell me.'

'Are the other owners standing out?'

'I have no idea. I suspect that the wish to do so originates with the men who have let the property get into this abominable state; they hope by writing round to get the rest of us carelessly to agree.'

'You know of no one who could go into it for you – a firm of solicitors —?'

She made a grimace.

'I have no solicitors; my bank is in Paris; I have no friends and I am too old to go to London myself.'

'I could make inquiries for you, when I get back' said Warbeck, doubtfully. 'Go and see the agents or something but I'm not much good at that sort of thing. What amount of compensation is actually offered?'

'My share would be about two hundred and fifty pounds. As a capital sum equivalent to what has been bringing in eighty or ninety pounds worth of rent per annum it is, of course, just comic; but then we had no right to extort anything like that amount from such a pigsty.'

'And you would prefer not even to take the two-fifty?'

'Immeasurably – if I could survive without it. I should *take* it, and then give it back to the Council; for if I refused it in advance, some of my charming co-owners would swallow it themselves. But it's no use thinking of that, I fear. I *must* have the money; and it frightens me to think how I shall get on if the payment is long delayed.'

'Let me sleep on it, Mrs Hooper, and see how things look tomorrow.'

Next day he said:

'I have an idea, which would enable you to do without your compensation money altogether.'

'Oh, Mr Warbeck, how wonderful! How happy that would make me!'

'Wait; you may hate my idea. It is this. There is a story in what you have been telling me. It wants filling out and arranging; but it might interest many people. Would you allow me to make a book of your memoirs and pay you for them?'

Her face clouded.

'Oh, I don't think I should like that – making money out of people I have known – and out of my own feelings and sorrows. It is different just telling you. Besides, you could not pay me enough to solve my difficulty; it wouldn't be worth it.'

'Please, Mrs Hooper. I have thought this over carefully and am quite serious. I will prepare the book, subject to your approval, and publish it; and because I believe something good could be produced, I will pay you three hundred pounds for it in advance – now, if you wish. Then you will have your compensation – and a bit over – and can make your restitution when the matter of the dwellings is settled. As for your not remembering, I am sure that, if you try, lots more will come to mind. You shall talk; I will make notes, and afterward I will write it out. I have a good memory for anything which interests me. Please think it over.'

She sat motionless, evidently turning the suggestion over in her mind. He had noticed before that she was a person who listened to what you said and gave it her attention. Not everyone did that, and he welcomed the trait as part of her fundamental honesty.

'Yes' she said at last. 'I will think it over. It is good of you to suggest it, and I would love to give that money back. To-morrow evening I will have decided.'

'Then that is agreed. I shall be out walking all day to-morrow, and look forward to seeing you at dinnertime.'

*   *   *

'Tomorrow' was now today; he *was* out walking, and supposedly looked forward to seeing her at dinnertime.

Did he in fact? Most certainly. As he thought back over the course of his friendship with this strange solitary woman, he felt no regrets at the offer he had made to her. He had spoken on impulse, and three hundred pounds were three hundred pounds. She might, of course, refuse; but this he doubted. Of course, even if she consented, the story might be starved of material or he might handle it dully or clumsily. Conversely, it might be far too rich in incident and philosophy of an un-marketable – even an unpublishable – kind. Well, those were normal risks enough, and if the book *did* come off . . .

He looked at his watch. After three o'clock! The sunlight had changed its slant, and now shone full and hot on the heather and birch-saplings to his right. Soon it would find him also. Taking out his map, he planned his homeward walk; then knocked out his pipe, crammed the debris of his lunch into a hole in the ground, and clambered up the slope to the path. As his steps died away on the trodden sand and leaves of the woodland track, the raucous chatter and bark of a frog split the silence. Farther down the mere other frogs replied, their raised throats swelling and throbbing among the pond-weed. The din mounted, crashed echoing against the banks of trees, and died away as suddenly as it had begun. Over the irises the dragon-flies, like tiny lengths of neon-blue, still hung poised a moment; then whisked away on soundless wings.

PART ONE

Told by Fanny Hooper

PANTON STREET

I

I WAS born in the late 'fifties – in 'fifty-seven or 'fifty-eight, no matter which – on the second floor of a house on the south side of Panton Street, and therefore within a stone's throw of the Haymarket on one side and of Leicester Square on the other. This house was my parents' place of business as well as their home. The ground floor was a licensed premises and therefore public; the first, second and third floors and the attics were private and residential. The building was tall and narrow, but of considerable depth, running back to a passage which in those days connected Oxendon and Whitcomb Streets. In consequence the upper floors, which for years were 'home' to me, were awkwardly elongated and far from uniformly lit. The stairs were curiously broad for a house of no particular pretension but rather steep and very dark. This was because, after their first flight, they climbed up the middle of the house, so as to thrust the rooms to north and south, the only two directions from which daylight could be obtained. Over the well of the staircase was an octagonal skylight, through which – except for a few dazzling weeks each year, after Chunks had performed the hazardous job of cleaning the sooty panes – filtered a strangled gleam. The best rooms, looking on to Panton Street, only got sun in the late afternoon; those behind, although facing south, got none at all except on the attic floor, because only a few feet from their windows rose the virtually blank wall of the house across the passage. That blank wall of grimed yellow brick was so inescapable a part of my infant universe that it never occurred to me either to resent it or to wonder what it was. Later, when I made the acquaintance of its other side, it was too late for resentment and the focus of my curiosity had shifted.

The most important section of the building, because it represented my parents' livelihood, was of course the tavern which ran from front to back at street-level. Beneath it was a still larger area, put to purposes of its own. Gold letters on a green ground, displayed on a board which ran the whole length of the Panton Street façade and blossomed in the middle into an ornate escutcheon, declared that here was THE HAPPY WARRIOR, and that the proprietor William Hopwood was licensed to sell Wines, Spirits and Beers. Below the signboard was a wide expanse of frosted window, with at its extreme left two doors. Of these the larger and more magnificent gave access to the tavern, while the other opened on to a narrow passage which ran to the foot of the stairs leading to our private quarters.

I now realize (using, I suppose, some uncorrelated childish memory) that the huge ground glass window of THE HAPPY WARRIOR differed from its kind in two respects. First, it was absolutely blank. No white appliqué lettering spoke of 'Cigars', 'Billiards', 'Pyramid' or 'Pool'; no wire blinds carried a painted promise of the diversions to be found inside. Second, it showed no light, even after dark. The tavern might be brilliantly lit, but the window from outside was black as brickwork. The main door was as laconic as the window, not even carrying a brass plate to ensure that passers-by knew it for an entrance to a public bar. Only one notice was affixed to any part of the building, and that had been tampered with. At the back of the block, on Panton Passage, was a door from which stairs led down to the basement. Over this door was a projecting board, which had originally read

HOPWOOD
SHADES

Some wag had painted out the first letter of the second word

and added it, with an apostrophe, to the first. The new version
had never been challenged and

HOPWOOD'S
HADES

remained, begrimed and out of centre but tacitly approved
and, by the time I began to take notice of the life about me, a
phrase of general usage.

William Hopwood was as far from the typical publican of
caricature as can be imagined. He was of medium height, very
thin and with a long sallow lúgubrious face, which a drooping
black moustache made more doleful than ever. Actually he was
not a melancholy man at all, but cultivated a mournful taci-
turnity as other men have cultivated a monocle or a languid
drawl or a heavy geniality – in order to set off his peculiar
form of humour. This expressed itself in an elaborately sarcastic manner of speech, and probably reflected a secret pride
in his educated accent and lavish vocabulary. He had been
personal servant to Mr Clive Seymore – now an important
figure in the Government Service – and had not only travelled
extensively with his master, but, having been treated more as a
confidant than an employé, had made good use of his opportunities for self-improvement.

It might seem strange that while still a youngish man – he
could not have been much more than forty when I was born –
he should have exchanged agreeable and aristocratic service for
tavern-keeping in the heart of London's turbulent night-life. I
believe that to those bold enough to question him he would explain that he wanted to get married and have a place of his own.

My mother was several years his junior – a cheerful round-
faced, bustling young woman who looked exactly the farmer's
daughter that she was. I came to know that her parents were
prosperous folk, who occupied a large farm on the fertile East
Riding plains not far from Selby. They were the tenants of Mr
Clive Seymore's father – Sir Everard Seymore of Aughton
Hall – so that no doubt William Hopwood met his future bride
while attending Mr Seymore on a visit to his home.

I was an only child and was thrown into my mother's company more closely than is usual even with only children. Living 'over the shop' as we did, Mrs Hopwood's domestic job was on the spot, and the shop being what it was and she being liable at certain times to have to take her share of supervision, the making of outside acquaintances and their entertainment at home were almost impossible. So she made a companion of her little daughter, who learnt from her to laugh at vexations, to have no great opinion of herself, and therefore not to sit in judgement on others but leave the world to go its way.

My mother's closest friend – almost her only one – was a Mrs Beckett, who was the wife of an antiquarian bookseller in Chandos Street, and had a little girl not much older than I. Mr Beckett was in a good way of business, acting as 'buyer' for several gentlemen of wealth and position and at the same time carrying a considerable stock of good quality books, bought for his own account. Because his duties took him frequently from London to country houses and to country sales, and because he was a considerate and rather uxorious man, he engaged a qualified assistant to look after the shop in his absence, and did not – as so many of his kind were used to do – leave the responsibility to his wife. She, therefore, was more of a lady of leisure than most tradesmen's wives and, being very fond of my mother, used that leisure to pay us frequent visits. A slow-moving, Junoesque woman, with a large oval face, a clear olive skin and eyes like sleepy velvet, she contrasted so strikingly with my vivacious little mother that even as a small child I relished seeing them together. Lucy Beckett and I would play with our dolls in a corner of the living-room, while Lucy's mother sat at the table sipping a glass of stout, and my mother ran to and fro between parlour and kitchen, chattering and laughing, as she kept an eye on her cooking in the intervals of ironing or mending or making clothes. Occasionally – but very occasionally – we would visit the Becketts in return, and if, as sometimes happened, Mr Beckett was at home, he always joined us for tea and greatly impressed my youthful mind by his assiduity in handing food to his wife and to my mother, carrying cups for replenishment, arranging footstools and cushions, and generally putting himself out to make the ladies comfortable. Nothing of this sort ever happened at home. William Hopwood took his breakfast and sometimes his midday dinner with his family (from five o'clock onwards he was either out or downstairs, and presumably supped in the tavern for I neither saw nor heard him until next morning) but during a meal he never stirred from his seat, leaving it to his wife to bring him food, remove his used plates and fill or refill his cup or glass. After he had finished, he would slew round in his chair, pick his teeth and read the paper, while my mother cleared the table and washed up.

Possibly this trifling difference of behaviour between the rarely seen Beckett and the familiar Hopwood was the first unrealized challenge to my normal childish assumption that all households resembled our own. In any event, as I grew older, I began to notice a lack of fundamental intimacy between my parents. I did not of course put it like that to myself. Probably I merely noticed that my mother got little response to her lively conversation, and that, while she would rattle on about her doings and mine (very ordinary doings they were), he seldom volunteered any information in return.

Not that he was unkind to either of us. Indeed in his aloof ironical way he treated us with indulgent generosity. But he seemed to shut off, even from his wife, what must have been the chief preoccupations of his mind. This also I was led to notice by comparing him with Mr Beckett. Whenever we were at the Becketts and the bookseller was present, he would continually turn to his wife with this or that detail of his business – telling her where he had been, whom he had seen, what he had bought or hoped to buy; asking her opinion how to treat a difficult client, consulting her about some suggestion of his assistant's, discussing the merits and demerits of a new messenger boy. But in my presence my mother was never thus confided in. For all we heard of the proprietor's business, Hoppy's might have been a dwelling-house and nothing else, except that, when for some reason he wished my mother to take charge of the desk downstairs, he would state briefly her hours of duty, and perhaps leave a message or two to be given to acquaintances who might be expected to come in. For a short while I assumed that, because my knowledge of what went on in Hoppy's was so limited, my mother's was equally so. But then one night I heard them talking in their room (it was below mine and the floor was a single one); and the talk went on so long that at last it flashed across me that possibly the subject was avoided on *my* account, that *I* was not supposed to hear how Papa spent his time. This, as can be imagined, set me thinking hard. But try how I might, I could not understand why, if Lucy was allowed to listen to her father talking of his work, I was not.

The cumulative effect of these – to my childish mind – inexplicable reserves, was to invest 'downstairs' with the lure of forbidden ground, and to create without much delay an inclination to trespass.

It was queer how quickly – once the idea of forbidden ground had set its glamour on Tavern and basement – my whole attitude to those places changed. That they were strictly out of bounds for me I had always known and never thought to question; nor had it ever occurred to me to disobey my mother even to the extent of peeping inside. But now that curiosity was aroused from another direction – now that I suspected that, not only certain rooms in the house but also an element in my parents' lives were being kept from me, I felt a desire and then a determination to investigate.

II

I was, I suppose, about seven years old when I was taken by my parents to the Crystal Palace. The expedition entailed much preparatory discussion, as well as generous provision by William Hopwood for clothes for my mother and myself. Outings of any kind were very rare, and this was so clearly a super-outing that by the time the day arrived I was in such a flutter of anticipation as to be almost sick in advance with excitement and worry about the weather. But the appointed day was bright and mild and, after an early breakfast, we set off in company with Mrs Beckett and Lucy for the Victoria Terminus of the Crystal Palace Railway. My mother carried a large string bag full of sandwiches, cake and needlework; Mrs Beckett carried a satchel of plaited straw with similar bulges; William Hopwood, Lucy and I carried nothing at all save, in his case, a malacca cane with a fine ivory knob, in ours tiny parasols in careful harmony with our frocks. At the age of seven a girl-child hardly notices the clothes of her contemporaries, and how poor Lucy was dressed I have completely forgotten. But my own tartan frock, broad sash, white cotton stockings and gloves, shiny black boots and tiny saucer hat are still as vivid as ever, while the crowning embellishment – the silk parasol of a tartan identical with my frock – actually survives to this day.

We travelled by omnibus to the terminus, caught the desired train, and reached the grounds of the fabulous Palace about eleven o'clock. Hardly had we passed the turnstile, when a man hailed William Hopwood – a tall, fresh-faced man in a check suit, who wore his billycock hat at a jaunty angle.

'Hey there, Duke!' he shouted. 'Who'd 'a thought of seeing you here?'

Hopwood shook the stranger by the hand and, turning to my mother and to Mrs Beckett, said in the mock ceremonious manner he loved to adopt:

'Permit me to present Mr Mark Cunningham, who – not being blest as I am with the delights of domesticity – does not know a family outing when he sees one. Mark, my boy – my wife and Mrs Beckett.'

Mr Cunningham bowed and showed his teeth.

'Your servant, Duchess. And yours, ma'am. And these young ladies are, I suppose, the reason for my friend Hopwood's truancy.'

He pinched my cheek (a familiarity I have never ceased to resent), patted Lucy on the shoulder and strolled alongside of us up the broad pebbly path. Before long he dropped behind with Hopwood, and the two men soon left us, to go into a bar.

'Why did he call you Duchess, mamma?' I asked, as soon as they had disappeared.

'Some of your father's friends call him Duke' she replied.

'Why? He isn't a duke, is he?'

She laughed.

'Not quite, darling. But he has a gentlemanly way with him. I suppose that is why.'

The day wore on. We bought ginger-pop at a stall and ate our sandwiches in the sunshine. We wandered under the vast arcading of the Palace, staring at statues and costumes in glass cases and models of engines and triumphs of ornament in porcelain, gilt and ormolu. We went on the tiny railway and fed the ducks on the pond and stared at the crowds. During the afternoon Hopwood reappeared, gave Lucy and me a shilling each for sweets or what we would, settled his wife and her friend on a comfortable seat, and wandered off again. In one part of the Palace grounds was a children's play-park, with swings and see-saws and sand-heaps, a maypole with ropes and rings, a 'bumble-puppy' and even an asphalt space for roller-skating. Lucy and I found our way there and soon made friends with a family of two boys and a girl, who were playing about under the eye of a nurse-maid. One of the boys seized a chance to occupy the bumble-puppy and proceeded to instruct me in the unfamiliar game. It was great fun hitting the ball in its string-bag so that it wound tightly round the pole, but not such fun when – rashly looking away – I failed to remark the counter-hit and was struck smartly on the head by the swinging ball. It knocked my hat off and bruised my ear and the game ended in tears and some confusion. But when composure returned, there returned with it a memory of what had so fatally distracted my attention. I had seen our new friends' nurse-maid walking away with a young man; and, sure enough, now that her charges were ready to return to her, she was nowhere to be seen.

So far from being dismayed, the two boys leapt at the

opportunity for adventure. They told us that, living in Sydenham, they had often been to the Palace, and knew a backway into the organ-loft which dominated the smaller of the two concert-halls – that used at night. True, they had been caught the first time and forbidden ever to go there again: but Ada had vanished and we should have plenty of time to make the expedition and rejoin her at an agreed rendezvous by the time she was likely to reappear.

'Ada has been off before with a young man' the elder boy explained 'when we were here alone with her. And they stayed away – oh, a long time. And she fixed a meeting-place. Usually mamma is coming to find us, and then Ada stays with us. But today mamma is out calling, so do come on!'

Rather apprehensive, but unwilling to seem lacking in enterprise (in particular to be less daring than the boys' little sister), we scuttled across the grounds to the Palace, and followed our guides to a region of passages and closed doors which even to the mind of a child had the flavour of 'out of bounds'. The boys tiptoed along, peeping round corners and behaving with the extravagant secrecy of a game of Indians. At last they stopped at a narrow doorway, from which a steep spiral staircase led upward into darkness. I was now frankly scared; but it was too late to retreat, nor could I ever have found my way back through the maze of corridors. So, clutching Lucy's hand, I crept up the stairs and, a few seconds later, was leaning on a balustrade looking down on the projecting platform used by the orchestra with, beyond it, the gloom of the concert-hall.

The afternoon light was dimming; and the silent place, with its rows of empty seats and distant corners full of crouching shadows, was eerie and menacing. I felt the beginnings of fear, and was only a little consoled to see that both Lucy and our new girl-acquaintance were in the same plight. Meanwhile the boys were clambering silently about the steps and bench of the organ itself, which towered horribly above us, the tall pipes rising to what seemed a vast height before they were lost in darkness. I stared at them fascinated. The vents, curving in a wavy arch from left to right, looked like mouths; and as I crouched against the balustrade I seemed to see them leer at me, as though the pipes were a regiment of elongated and malevolent hobgoblins, only waiting a signal to bend downward from above and seize upon me with their hideous tentacles.

Wrenching my eyes away I turned toward the hall. I was staring downward, trying to master the fright which threatened to choke me, when I fancied that from somewhere underneath the loft there came a sound. It was a cautious, scratching sound, and curiosity for the moment made me forget my fear. The orchestra platform did not stretch the whole breadth of the hall, but left a space to either side which ran under the organ-loft to (presumably) the passage from which we had climbed the spiral stair. Something was afoot below me, in the invisible space to the left of the platform. Immediately afterward there was a sharp click, and the darkness below the loft changed from black to grey. Instinctively I realized that a door had been opened and that a faint light from the passage was filtering into the hall. The grey faded to black again. The door had closed, but silently and with no sound of latch. A man's figure (it was now too dark to see more than the moving shape) was slipping soundlessly down the gangway to the left of the hall. Almost too frightened to breathe I watched him disappear into the gloom at the far end. In a few moments, to my even greater alarm, he came into dim sight again, creeping back the way he had come. By chance the others in the loft were making no noise — the girls because they were too scared to move, the boys as part of a private game of their own which required silent progress between two given points. It struck me that the man in the hall would not be pleased if he discovered us and that, to prevent him doing so, I must warn my companions. By good fortune one of the boys was within reach. I caught him by the arm and with a finger on my lips jerked my head toward the hall. He was quick to understand and, attracting the notice of his brother (who had crawled silently on to the organist's seat), repeated the gesture. The second boy slipped carefully to the floor between the bench and the console. But unluckily he alighted on one of the pedals, and the next moment from above our heads an unearthly sound – half-shriek, half-groan – tore the silence. I saw a momentary blur of white as the stealthy intruder raised his head toward the loft; then he ducked and scurried out of sight into the passageway by which he had entered. As for us, we fled in wild panic down the spiral stairs, colliding at the bottom with a man who came running along the passage from the right. He dashed through us and raced onward round the corner. But I saw his face and recognized Mr Mark Cunningham.

* * *

Retribution for our truancy, when at last we came together with my mother and Mrs Beckett, was too severe to permit any speculation on the recent past. Our three acquaintances had vanished, and I was shocked to realize that Lucy and I were suspected of having invented them. There was no question of waiting for the fireworks now. Tired and scared we were dragged to the station in disgrace, promised a good whipping when we got home, and denied even a stick of chocolate. There was no sign of William Hopwood.

During the journey I was too cowed even to sulk. When at Charing Cross Lucy was firmly led away by her mother to her share of expiation, I did not dare to wave her farewell. If, on reaching Panton Street, I hoped for reprieve, I hoped in vain. I was whipped with an efficiency which, despite hunger, rage and tears, impressed me, for my mother who had hardly ever lifted a hand to me showed herself more than competent. I was then given a cup of milk and put to bed, where soon enough I cried myself to sleep.

Next morning appetite and the heedless buoyancy of youth had driven yesterday's transgression from my mind. Cheerful as ever, I hurried to breakfast. But when I found both my parents at the table and saw that they merely nodded to me coldly, shame and apprehension returned. A bowl of porridge was put in front of me which I tried to enjoy, although the silence of my elders made me increasingly uneasy. The porridge finished, a large slice of bread and dripping was provided, which also I consumed, but with bowed head and much nervous foreboding. I did not dare to glance even at my mother; and it was almost a relief when, as I popped the last piece into my mouth, William Hopwood spoke.

'So Miss Fanny Hopwood was pleased to see the Crystal Palace on her own? It was nothing to her that her poor mother was driven half wild with anxiety, or that her father – who has now and again to attend to the trifling business of earning his living and hers – should waste an hour looking for her and so miss seeing some friends. Oh, no! All that was unimportant, so long as Miss Hopwood herself was happy. And now, miss, pray tell me what you were doing, so that at least we may have the consolation of sharing your pleasure in retrospect.'

I was nearly in tears and, unwisely seeking to hide my face in the large cup of milk which was the ordained finish to my breakfast, yielded to the preliminary sob (often a severe one) just when my mouth was full of milk and my nose was almost touching the level of the liquid. Half the contents of my mouth went down the wrong way, the other half sprayed in every direction. I drew some more milk up my nose, dropped the cup in terror, and was left – a sputtering and choking misery – surrounded by a chaos of my own making. My mother jumped up with a cry of dismay and began mopping up the mess. The paroxysm of choking passed, but left its usual legacy – the hiccoughs. I have always been frightened of hiccoughs, ever since as a tiny child I had heard someone say that they could last for days and days and finally kill you. So now to humiliation and a sense of guilt was added the fear of death. Between the three I sat as though frozen to my chair, waiting for the next hiccough.

Suddenly Hopwood spoke again:

'I am waiting, Fanny. If your rendering of a milk-geyser is over...'

My mother interrupted.

'Let her be, William. I must clean her up to begin with, and when she's calmer she'll tell me what happened. Come along, Fanny. You are a very naughty little girl to make such a mess.'

By the time we returned to the parlour, Hopwood had dis-appeared. On the table lay the newspaper. My mother, with the obvious intention of distracting my mind from the recent catastrophe, began turning the leaves, talking as she did so.

'Let us see if we can find anything exciting, shall we? A fire in the docks ... looks like war between Prussia and Austria; how those foreigners do quarrel to be sure.... More speeches, Lord Derby and Mr Gladstone of course.... Hullo! What's this? Listen, Fanny. A diamond necklace stolen at a Crystal Palace Concert – snatched from the neck of a well-known Society woman as the audience were crowding out after the performance – thief escapes by emergency door – usually locked but lock tampered with – robbery apparently planned – accomplice suspected among Palace staff. Well, did you ever? If we'd stayed later we might have seen the excitement.'

She was so eagerly scanning the report of the theft that she forgot to remember why we had come away early. From her disjointed summary of the facts I gathered that the necklace, snatched near the main exit, had apparently been handed to someone waiting to receive it; and that either the snatcher or the receiver had slipped back against the out-going crowd and got away through a door to the right of the platform which, according to the Palace authorities, could only be opened with an official key.

'Oh, mamma!' I burst out. 'I saw him – saw the man who opened the door!'

As I poured out my story, she stared at me in amazement; but when – with a budding sense of the dramatic – I ended by disclosing whom it was I had seen, she tightened her lips and sat for a moment with downcast eyes drumming her fingers on the table. Then she got up with her usual housewifely briskness.

'I must get on with my work. We'll go out to the market soon. And Fanny, keep what you've told me to yourself. Absolutely to yourself. Do you understand?'

'Yes, mamma' I replied meekly, a little dashed yet impressed by the seriousness of her tone.

III

Perhaps the consequences of my adventure at the Crystal Palace damped for a while my ambition to explore nearer home. In any event it was nearly three years (in fact a couple of days previous to my tenth birthday) before I undertook my great trespass into the preserves of William Hopwood – if indeed one can describe as a 'trespass' the chance consequence of a bouncing ball.

When I was eight years old, I was sent to a small private day-school in Bedford Street. I only attended in the mornings, and was expected home for dinner punctually at one-fifteen. Before very long – in the manner of the solitary child – I had developed a mild game which consisted of varying my route to and fro within the narrow limits possible to me. One day I would go by this street and return by that; next I would go a third way and come back by yesterday morning's route taken in reverse direction; next there would be a further variation, until all the changes had been rung and I started again. Naturally I got to know in minute detail every house, shop, grating, curb and crossing on each route and could to this day describe any or all of them with complete fidelity. Also I made friends and enemies, through meeting at stated intervals some grown-ups I liked and others I feared, as well as children with whom I exchanged either grins or scowls. But somehow (this again was characteristic of an only child) I was not anxious for intimacy or for company on my way. I made up all kinds of stories about dark entries and bricked-up windows and empty spaces behind hoardings. I pretended the inhabitants of different streets belonged to different nations, and imagined them at war with one another or paying state-visits. In short, the buildings and their incidentals were much more interesting to me than the actual people who used them and, as I could not have played my imaginary games if I had a companion, I was not sorry to be alone.

Certainly there were other games in which fellow-players would have been a help; but even these I was content to enjoy

alone. Also I soon found that from the point of view of such
games-on-the-way, the different routes had different possibilities which, of course, added to their attractions or their
unpleasantness. One or two involved busy crowded thorough-
fares which required all my attention to avoid being run over,
splashed with mud or chased by horrid boys. Others had qualities of menace or particular spots of which I chose to be
scared. Others, however, were neither difficult nor frightening,
and offered quiet interludes where one could bowl a hoop or
play ball or even (at the right season of the year) perfect one's
skill with a whip-top. The most peaceful (though not perhaps
the most salubrious) lay along Orange Street and Hemmings
Row and then through Taylors Buildings to Bedford Bury.
But the rules of my self-imposed system were unbreakable;
and I never allowed myself to take any walk – pleasant or
otherwise – out of its turn, while I was further bound by
strange sub-rules, such as that which never permitted the use
of Panton Passage (behind the Warrior) save on a return
journey.

One day I was due to go by Whitcomb and Dorset Streets,
past the National Gallery, over the broad crossing to St
Martin's Church and then by Adelaide and Chandos Streets to
the right-angled alley called Bedford Court. This was a horrid
way. Trafalgar Square was dull in comparison with narrow
streets which offered entertainment on both sides, and I seldom had the time to spare to cross to the south side and watch
the pigeons; it was a bad crossing to St Martin's; I hated
having to pass Beckett's Bookshop in Chandos Street without
calling in; finally, though for no particular reason, I had decided that the first section of Bedford Court was sinister and
mysterious. Indeed, the only alleviation was the mouth of the
Lowther Arcade, into which (if I contrived to have a few
minutes in hand) I could slip and gaze enraptured at a toy-
shop window. But on this morning, to make up for an unpopular 'there', I had one of my favourite 'backs' – that which
gave me New Street, Cecil Court, right down Castle Street
to Orange Street again and home by Panton Passage. In

preparation for this delightful walk (hoops being out of season), I took a ball with me, for there were ample stretches of quiet pavement and one long trafficless strip where games could be played without fear of interruption or disaster.

We got out of school ten minutes early, and I made such good going that I reached the eastern end of Panton Passage only a minute or two after one o'clock. The walls of this narrow passage were, as I have said, blank and windowless until some distance above street-level, and I had a fancy to devise a new and rather complicated ball-game which necessitated bouncing the ball forward and sideways so that it struck one wall at an angle, cannoned off toward the other and was intended to end its zigzag course by hitting a drainpipe which ran down the wall from which it had started. The process needed an accurate adjustment of force and placing, and several times I had to go flying down the passage to retrieve the ball, my school-satchel bouncing against my hip, my hair streaming out from under the little pork-pie hat which was my workaday wear. But at last I threw correctly. The ball ricochetted deliciously from south to north, then south again – and hit the drain-pipe fairly and truly. I felt a thrill of victory which the next moment turned to alarm, for the angle at which the ball struck the pipe threw it so straight across the passage that it disappeared into the doorway over which projected the sign of Hopwood's Hades. When I arrived on the scene I understood why it had vanished. The door was open, and a flight of steps led down into darkness. I listened but could hear nothing. Creeping down the steps, I found at the bottom a short passage (in which my ball lay) and at the end a door slightly ajar, behind which a light was burning. I listened again. All was still. Pushing the door open, I found myself in a small square room with a brick floor and white-washed walls. There was a row of pegs to the right, a short counter – half-bar, half-paydesk – facing me, and a few plain chairs and benches piled one on top of another. In the extreme left-hand corner I saw the lower steps of a turning staircase leading to an upper floor. A lighted gas-bracket whistled on the wall opposite me, over a second door which evidently led to a farther room. The excitement of exploration drove caution from my mind. Through the second door I went on tiptoe, and stood amazed. I was in a long vaulted cellar brightly lit by flaring gas, with a raised dais at the far end on which were chairs and music-stands and some large instrument swathed in baize. A curtain-rod ran right across the cellar in front of the dais and heavy curtains hung to right and left. But what astonished me most were the rich furnishings of this apartment and of the alcoves and other rooms which opened off it. There were, I think, four alcoves in the right-hand wall – each with its lesser curtain-rod and dark red curtains looped back with yellow cord; while openings in the left-hand wall seemed to give access to full-size rooms which I decided to examine later. For the moment there was enough in the main hall to hold my attention.

The place was in some disorder, with furniture pushed to-gether and rolls of carpet lying on a bare floor; but I could see that, when set straight, it would be a scene of comfort and elegance. On the walls were occasional mirrors and a crowd of pictures. I began a careful examination of these, and noted two racehorses at full stretch, three pairs of boxers with fists at the ready and knees more widely flexed than in view of their very tight breeches seemed altogether prudent, a girl with nothing on dabbling an uncertain toe in a sunk marble bath, several hunting scenes and some miscellaneous groups of ladies and gentlemen in eighteenth-century costumes. Suddenly a bucket crashed against a table and a hoarse voice called out:

'And ow did *you* get in, if I may make ser bold?'

An untidy bundle of a woman, holding a mop in one hand and a pail in the other, was fixing me with a small bright eye. Wisps of grey hair straggled from beneath her dirty cloth cap; her hands were large and red.

'Please ...' I stammered 'I ... I was looking for my ball...'

'We ain't got no balls ere and kids ain't allowed. Out yer go double quick and don't let me catch yer ere again.'

I edged nervously nearer the door and was about to make a dash for it, when the opening was filled with a second, but this time a reassuring figure. It was Chunks, the big doorman from the Warrior, and he stared at me in astonishment. The moment she saw him, the horrid old woman began screaming that the brat had sneaked in when she wasn't looking and wanted a clout on the ear to teach her what trespass meant. Chunks roared her down:

'Shut yer mouth, mother! This ere's the guvnor's kid, and if you lay a finger on er you'll learn something.' He turned to me. 'Miss Fanny, you've no call to be in this place. Come along, I'll take you ome.'

To my surprise, instead of making for the passage by which I had entered, he led the way to the staircase in the corner of the ante-room. It twisted two or three times and brought us to a small room, plainly furnished with a writing desk, some shelves full of ledgers and a few chairs.

'The govnor's office,' said Chunks, seeing me gaze about in evident uncertainty. 'Through ere's the tavern.'

Pushing open a door, he brought me for the first time in my life into the licensed premises which underlay my home.

We had entered the tavern from the back, and found ourselves in a narrow area, between what I soon realized was the wall separating the Warrior from our private staircase and a high two-tier desk, rather like a presbyterian pulpit, which stood out into the main room, its rounded prow dominating the public hall. In the wall to the right were two doors, one small one leading to the staircase, the other – a double swing-door – giving access to the kitchens, where the patrons' food was prepared. I had known there were kitchens beyond the stair-well, for the staff entrance was in its far wall and I had often smelt savoury smells and heard the clash of pots and pans; but I had never troubled to think why kitchens were there or where the food went with which they were so busy.

Chunks was preparing to push me through the small door leading to the stairs; but I meant to make the most of this opportunity and, slipping past him, ran out into the main tavern and looked eagerly about me. What I then saw was, of course, only a fraction of the description which follows; but it is simpler to complete the picture while I am at it, though in fact it be a composite one, observed over a period of visits.

From where I stood (looking, you understand, away from the high desk and toward Panton Street) I saw a large open room, as wide as the big ground glass window which formed the tavern's frontage and more than three times as deep. The light was very dim, because the space immediately inside the window was partitioned off from the main room by mahogany walls which rose solidly from floor to ceiling. Consequently the only daylight came from double half-glass doors in the extreme right-hand corner, which served as entrance to the tavern. Even these doors could only be reached from the street by passing through a vestibule, which was occupied, during their hours of duty, by the six feet of brawn and muscle known to everyone as Chunks. You can imagine, therefore, that with no daylight save that which filtered through the vestibule and then through a pair of glazed doors, the place would have been in darkness had not a gas-jet been burning in the centre of the ceiling.

As for Chunks, his business was to scrutinize all who came and, when necessary, to hasten those who would not go. If a stranger entered, Chunks would direct him to one of the small tables near the door, where he was well under the eye of the high desk and within reach of door-man's discipline. Habitués, on the other hand, would be greeted with gruff friendliness, relieved of a wet coat or a package, and left to make their way to whatsoever seat they fancied.

But I am still staring about me at the exciting Warrior, still in the throes of my first sight of a public house. These, with reinforcements from later experience, are the impressions I received.

The walls of the main tavern were lined with looking-glass; from the roof hung several chandeliers, while brackets sprouting from the pilasters between the mirrors carried further gas-jets. Tables of small or medium size, with marble tops and heavy wrought iron bases, were ranged along the walls. Each had its water-carafe and drinking-glass, its cigar-cutter, its ashtray and its tiny vase of tooth-picks. The guests sat on fixed divan seats, all tarnished gilding and stained crimson velvet.

The centre of the room was clear, save for an eight-sided reading desk on which were fixed the sporting papers. At the inner end of the tavern rose the round-ended desk. The upper of its two tiers was for old Vellacott, Hopwood's confidential clerk and book-keeper, or, when she took the duty, for my mother. The lower tier, on a level with the floor, was the recognized place for 'treating' the Warrior's proprietor. The ceremony is quaint enough to look back upon, but at the time I never thought of it as in the least unusual. From one of the tables would come the sharp clattering tap of pewter upon marble. One tap – a potman hurried for the order: two taps – the call was for some other guest, every person took heed and, if the signal were for him, acted accordingly. But if the summons were repeated thrice, my father would rise from whatever seat he might momentarily be occupying, bow with dignity to the gentleman who 'beat' for him and then make his stately way toward the lower desk. There he would be joined by his guest-turned-host, drink would be chosen and supplied, and the two would gravely clink their glasses or touch tankards, pledge one another and stand awhile in low-toned conversation.

'Beating for the Duke' was a well-known procedure among the flash habitués of the Warrior. Not only was it in itself a pleasing ceremonial, but it provided good opportunity for confidential talk. The desk was isolated and well out of hearing of the nearest table; the upper storey was sufficiently high for a tall man to stand and talk to the Duke and wear his hat and still be overtopped by three feet of panelling. Further, if the upper desk were occupied at all, it was occupied by someone in whose discretion everybody had perfect confidence. To those, therefore, who had gaming plans to make, tips to receive or perhaps more intimate ambitions to express, a few moments' conversation with my father in this remote but public place were of considerable advantage.

You wonder perhaps why, when privacy was urgent, such conferences could not be carried on in some other room. The reason lay in one of William Hopwood's most obstinate principles. He held it to be the duty of a tavern-keeper never to leave his public premises during the hours of real business. He was always to be seen in the great room of his tavern at any moment between nine pm and two am. I came to understand, as I grew older, that the custom had also its practical advantages. It was a great thing in those days to have, between the hours of nine and two, a more or less permanent alibi. Not only was it known that the Duke was always there, but even when for one reason or another he was constrained to absence, there were plenty of good friends to swear that they had seen him at his post and to possess at least the force of probability behind their words.

'The hours of real business' were rightly interpreted by Hopwood as those of late evening and early morning. There were, of course, in those days no closing hours to speak of, but the Warrior, though technically 'open', hardly saw a soul until seven o'clock. At about that hour a few steady customers came for their chop or steak, while the tavern did not really fill up until some three hours later. Tradition forms quickly in places of public call or entertainment, and only a greenhorn would have tried to use the Warrior for a midday drink or have expected the grill to be at work before the evening. That is why, on the occasion of my first visit, the place was totally deserted.

There was once an inquisitive Inspector of Police who, being new to the district and on the trail of malefactors, ventured to question Hopwood as to what he and his Warrior did all day, calling attention to the contrast between the gloom and lethargy of the tavern until dusk and the lights and crowded gaiety of after-dark. He also expressed curiosity as to the obstinate darkness of the façade. The Duke, with patient suavity, waved his hand at the partitioning which kept the place in deep twilight even when the sun was shining.

'A poor publican' he said 'must cut his coat according to his

cloth. The astute official mind has only to appreciate the
darkening effect of these ill-considered partitions to grasp
immediately why the Warrior is happier at night. No one likes
to eat or drink by gaslight in the middle of the day. Consequently my quiet and very respectable clients go elsewhere at
noon but take their supper here.'

'And what are the partitions for?' demanded the policeman.

'They constitute three small private rooms' replied Hopwood 'which are at the disposal of my patrons who desire a
game of cards or a private talk on business or personal matters.
They were in existence when I took possession, and I have not
cared to spend money removing them.'

'I think I'll look inside' said the policeman.

Hopwood, wearily polite, shrugged his shoulders. 'As you
wish' he said; and drawing a key from his pocket, he unlocked
a door in the main partition. The policeman observed that the
window side of the cubicle was walled with wood as solidly as
the other; he noted the mechanism of the inside lock; he surveyed the furnishings. For a moment he stared thoughtfully at
the lugubrious Hopwood. Then his mouth creased into a slight
smile and he suggested that a pint of porter would not come
amiss. Chatting of this and that he drank his beer. As he set
down the tankard he said 'What card game do they mostly
fancy – Old Maid?'

Hopwood drew himself up.

'I do not understand you, sir. Or, if I do, I could wish it
otherwise. Your superiors should have told you that this is a
house of call for gentlemen only.'

The officer took his leave. Better men than he had tried to
jump the Duke, and failed.

IV

A few days later and it was the evening of my tenth birthday. There had been a small tea-party – Lucy and her mother,
two other school-acquaintances and actually William Hopwood in person. The sugared cake with the ten small candles

and plates-full of various festive trifles had been largely demo-
lished, and neither tears nor temper had marred the happiness
of the meal and the games which followed it. When the visitors
had gone, my parents sat awhile talking. Hopwood was in an
unusually amiable mood, and suggested to my mother that he
take her, one day in the following week, to see the marvellous
Slack-Wire Walker at the London Pavilion. He then looked at
his watch and exclaimed at the lateness of the hour.

'My word! After seven! I must go, my dear. Oh, and by
the way – it is unpardonable not to have mentioned this before
– Vellacott begged off for tonight, from nine to twelve. His
sister is ill. Could you, my love, do me the great favour ...'

My mother looked at him doubtfully, then at me.

'If you had told me.... I don't like leaving the child
alone....'

'I know, I know!' William was almost humble. 'All the
excitement of this young lady's advancing age drove the
matter from my mind.... I have no real excuse. Dear me,
what *is* to be done?'

I sidled over to my mother and twitched at her hand.

'Whisper!' I said.

She bent her head, and I made my outrageous suggestion.

'Fanny!' she cried. 'I never heard such a thing. Certainly
not.' Then she laughed. 'How's that, William? The puss says
she will come too!'

I ran towards him.

'*Please*, papa! I *will* be good. *Please* let me come – just for
a little while – as a treat!'

After slight demur they agreed. The party-spirit was, I
suppose, still at work.

I was forthwith packed off to lie down for a couple of hours
and, contrary to my intention, went to sleep. Roused and tidied
at about nine o'clock, and almost breathless with excitement, I
accompanied my mother downstairs and followed her timidly
into the high desk.

To reach the upper desk you climbed a steep narrow stair
like that of a pulpit, for its floor was quite seven feet above

that of the tavern, and once there I could see little enough,
even on tiptoe. But peeping over the side I managed to see the
huge area of the tavern, and the chandeliers, and here and
there a hat. How astonishingly different it looked, brightly lit
and alive with sound and movement, from the echoing and
gloomy place I had seen not many days before! My preliminary survey sated curiosity for the moment, and for ten minutes
or so I was quite happy crouched out of sight on a footstool at
my mother's side, revelling in the confused noises of talk and
laughter and watching the spasmodic glare of the gaslight on
the white plaster immediately above the desk. But as time
passed, the restlessness of youth overcame shyness. I had been
listening with wonder to the metallic taps that sounded now
from this corner, now from that; to the hum of voices rising to
cries, falling to murmuring; to the potmen's scurrying feet. I
had been watching the cigar-smoke curl into view beyond the
high barrier of desk that fenced me in. I now wanted dreadfully to study the whole scene in detail. Three ringing blows in
quick succession startled me. For the moment I held my
breath. Dared I do it? I glanced at my mother. It was now or
never. She was leaning away from me, talking downward to
some acquaintance who stood beside the pulpit. Noiselessly I
slipped from my seat.

The floor of the upper desk was, as I have said, about seven
feet from the ground. At this level a wide ledge ran along the
side of the pulpit. When it reached the curve of the front, it
was partially broken by a carved pillar, beyond which, round-
ing the prow, it broadened out and became a sort of canopy
overhanging the lower desk. On to this ledge I crept, my
fingers pressed against the woodwork, my small body crouched
and tense. Steps were crossing the tavern toward the desk, but
luckily from the far side. I heard papa's voice and the sounds
of scraping feet. A potman was summoned. He took an order
and, hurrying to execute it, turned the desk corner and saw me
balanced on my ledge. Being something of a friend of mine,
when I laid a finger on my lips, he winked and went quickly on
his way. It seemed a long time before he was back again bear-

ing two tankards on a tray. I began to feel cramped. From
where I crouched I could see two tables that stood against the
tavern-wall parallel with the desk-side. By a lucky chance they
were untenanted. Ahead of me the projecting pillar blocked
my view and hid me from the room's length. Suddenly a man
spoke; it seemed the voice came from beneath my feet.

'Now see here, Duke, there's a young fellow yonder who
came in with me. He's from the west country and carries a lot
of money. If I were to give him a flutter at Patty's say two
nights hence and you were to tip the wink to the coppers—'

Obscurely I was thrilled. The words meant little, but instinct told me that this was eavesdropping and conspiracy and
romance. I edged a little nearer. The speaker resumed:

'That was a nice bit of work with the Frenchman – in
Corders Alley. There are only two bolts from Patty's and I'll
take care which is used. It's worth while, Duke.'

Hopwood replied.

'The Clipper is jailed. I've no one to send.'

The other voice dropped.

'No one?'

A moment's silence, then Hopwood:

'There's Bat Perkins of course.'

'Ah! Good idea. Why not use Hetty and then Bat at the
end?'

'Is Hetty below?'

Mumbled words I could not catch. Then papa once more:

'Very well. But you must make it Thursday. And I must
know by tomorrow if Hetty has got hold of him. Then I'll
arrange. About half past two is the best time. You'll need to
pay the peelers well. They think nothing of asking five hundred
nowadays. I don't know what things are coming to. Old
Barney had trouble only the other day.'

'That will be all right. No need to trouble yourself over
that. Have a good look at the fellow. The name is Westerly.'

Hopwood grunted, and again instinct came to my help. I
began a hasty retreat along the ledge and was soon back at my
mother's side, breathless but thrilled. The escapade had lasted

a few minutes only. No one had seen except my potman-friend. My mother was still talking.

*   *   *

The sequel to that evening's conversation I heard long after-wards. The rich young pigeon from the west left half his pocket-book in Patty Webster's gambling hell; the other half he lost on the way home and, with it, nearly lost his life as well. The place was raided and the gamblers fled; Westerly went stumb-ling along down a dark passage between Red Lion Square and Southampton Street. They found him the next morning, still insensible and stripped to his shirt. There was something of a fuss, for old Sir Edward Westerly was a great man in Somer-set. The police showed awkward curiosity and in unexpected corners. Who started the idea, for example, that Duke Hop-wood was mixed up in the affair at all? Rumour – the kind of rumour that went round the underworld – said that the raid had been 'arranged', and then too little paid. Someone had split. There were questionings. But in the end nothing was proved. Admittedly young Westerly had visited the Warrior some days before the outrage. But he had not spoken to the landlord or even known which was he. On the night itself the Duke had been as usual in his own tavern. It was believed that a girl called Hetty had been intimate with the youth; but she could not be traced and, as the world knew, women were ex-cluded from the Warrior. The matter dropped, for want of the clinching evidence which could only have been given by a little girl of ten.

V

I am now nearing the end of the first period of my life – that connected with Duke Hopwood and his Warrior. I will therefore round off the description of that ingenious man and his ostensible place of business. Both were remarkable phe-nomena whose like will not be seen again. Their proceedings, therefore, deserve such modest record as I am able to give them.

My exploit as eavesdropper, just related, was the only experience in any way dramatic which befell me during my occasional visits to the tavern in its hours of activity. I suppose I was present there another half dozen times in the years following, and nothing whatsoever occurred, either in the way of disturbance or conspiracy, to vary the monotony of regular business. I have often been told by those who used to frequent the Warrior in Hopwood's days that it was in fact a notoriously well-conducted house. It stood in the heart of London's most rowdy and dissipated district. All around it were dance-halls, glittering restaurants, saloons, sporting cribs, brothels, dubious hotels and night-houses of every kind. Obviously it acquired merit from the contrast it presented to its neighbours; and in realising the value of that contrast and skilfully maintaining it, Hopwood showed how clever a man he was.

In organization and internal fittings, the Warrior was half-way between the old English rough and tumble hostelry and the luxurious Saloons and Divans, which had begun to flare in fashionable London during the 'fifties, and by 1870 were West End common form. Hopwood had the wit to see that, by retaining a certain old-fashioned simplicity and at the same time giving his clients cleanliness, bright lights and comfort, he could give his house an individuality which would certainly help its good will and might also, if necessary, serve as witness to character.

The wide floor of the main tavern was neither carpeted nor strewn with sawdust, but was of polished boards, with strips of drugget along the edges and round the newspaper stand. Spittoons and receptacles for cigar-ends were plentiful; and any new-comer who, mistaking the tavern for an ordinary public-house, spat on the floor or ground out the butt of a cheroot with his heel, was quickly and sternly called to order. Billiards were impossible, for there was no table. Dancing was equally impossible, seeing that women were barred. There was neither card-room nor music. Naturally among the patrons were several pugilists and numerous amateurs of the fancy; but Hopwood strictly forbade sparring-matches, even of the friendliest kind, stating that the Warrior was a place for quiet refreshment and pleasant conversation, and that the comfort of those who wished to sit and smoke and talk was paramount.

Of course, as in all licensed premises at that time, much liquor was consumed and cases of drunkenness were frequent. But the Duke's regular drunks were not quarrelsome or otherwise obstreperous; and when, as occasionally happened, the wrong sort of drinker strayed in and tried to interfere with other guests or began to play the rowdy, Chunks had him in the street in no time and Hopwood, leaning against the lower desk, would make a graceful apology to the company for their unpleasant experience.

Mention of the Duke's 'regular drunks' reminds me of a little scheme of his, which I know for certain was put into practice once, and may for all I can tell have been worked several times.

There was an individual who came virtually every night to the Warrior and sat for three solid hours drinking hot gin-and-water. He was in his sixties, an untidy miserable-looking creature, in an old tail coat and one of those elongated Trilby hats which is almost a top-hat but not quite. This he kept on his head the entire evening. I believe he had been a solicitor, but was struck off the rolls for some misdemeanour and thereafter dragged out a forlorn and seemingly half-starved existence in a garret behind Leicester Square. He was always alone, and would bring with him an ancient brief-case stuffed with papers, which he would carefully sort out and, having selected one tape-tied bundle, would turn it through with absorbed attention, making notes in the margins, nodding to himself and occasionally chuckling or exclaiming under his breath. All the time he sipped his toddy, tapping for another glass as soon as one was nearly finished. His name was Lamb.

I have spoken of Mr Lamb as half-starved; and he certainly looked it. But he always had money to pay for his drink, and it was clear that the Warrior was not his only house of call. Perhaps he soaked at home. It was more evident every month that a prodigious consumption of spirits was wearing him down. He grew shakier and more slobbery, and his eyes became permanently glazed. He was a revolting object; yet even to Chunks (who told me all this afterward in his own picturesque vernacular) there was something pitiful about him.

It appears that Hopwood made it his business to inquire into Mr Lamb's private affairs. He found that the old man was a complete solitary. No relations were known to exist, and apart from a few tap-room acquaintances he had no friends. A plan already formed in the Duke's mind was then put into operation. He was in close – if left-handed – touch with a certain doctor. This man was fully qualified and in open practice; but there were incidents in his life which had involved him with the underworld and certain persons with whom – in order to keep these incidents secret – he dared not quarrel. One such person was Hopwood. When, therefore, the landlord of the Warrior called upon him and requested that he write in proper form a medical report on the physical condition of one, Matthew Gregory Lamb, aged sixty-three and residing at Number Two Pepper Court, Leicester Square, and further that he endorse an application for a Policy on the life of this individual to the amount of one thousand pounds, the doctor had no option but to submit. The application and the report were sent to the Insurance Company by Hopwood. The policy was issued to Hopwood and the first year's premium paid.

Shortly afterward, instead of, as hitherto, merely shaking hands and leaving the old man to his imaginary work, he began to linger by the table and talk with him. Then he took a chair, called for drinks on the house, and showed increasing friendliness. Gradually by this means he enlarged the nightly consumption of his besotted client, encouraging him at the same time to mix his spirits and to dilute them less. In four months Lamb was dead of cirrhosis of the liver, a fate which surprised no one, so completely was he known to have been a slave to alcohol. Hopwood collected the insurance, and the Warrior maintained its excellent reputation as a quiet and well-conducted house.

These facts would never have come to light at all, had not

the doctor, when Hopwood was overwhelmed by the trouble which finished him, revenged himself on his blackmailer by betraying them to the police.

Of course my mother knew nothing of the incident or that monstrosities of the kind were ever part of Hopwood's activities. She was certainly aware that half her husband's life was spent on the wrong side of the law. The Crystal Palace episode implied her consciousness of his share in a robbery; and that police regulations were flouted, alike in the Warrior and on the floor below, must have been obvious to her. But anything even indirectly related to a crime of violence she could not have tolerated. The Duke would have denied that his treatment of Lamb could be so described. He would – I think sincerely – have distinguished between hastening an inevitable end while giving the victim pleasure, and the deliberate infliction of pain on a helpless fellow-creature. But the Duke's conscience was a strange one, and my mother was incapable of sharing its subtleties.

VI

Before attempting to indicate what may – not unsuitably – be called the 'basement half' of Hopwood's existence, I must mention an episode destined to prove of great importance to my future career.

I had now been transferred from the school in Bedford Street to the care of a scholarly cripple, who took a few individual pupils in his quiet rooms in Golden Square. His name was Clements, and he believed in the humanities rather than in scientific fact. He took infinite pains to give me a background of taste and understanding; and thanks to his training, though I have always been an ignorant person in the sense of having no learning, I possess intuition and a feeling for atmosphere.

Returning home from school one afternoon at about five o'clock I found a visitor in the parlour with my mother. He was of medium height, slight in build, quietly but expensively dressed in a grey swallow-tail coat with trousers of the same material.

When I burst into the room, they evidently broke off an interesting conversation, for they turned and for a moment gazed at me in silence. Then, with a curious constraint, my mother said:

'A little less noise, darling, though I am glad you have come. Put down your satchel and say how-do-you-do to Mr Seymore.'

I was not a shy child and had a good look at the stranger as I crossed the room to greet him. How much I then noticed and how much was learnt from later experience, I hardly know; but in fact I saw a man of about forty years of age, clean-shaven, with dark hair already greying at the temples. In his face was breeding and melancholy, but his eyes, though tired, smiled easily. I remember remarking at once the handsome signet ring he wore on his left hand.

Rather to my surprise, he took both my hands and held them. 'Already a different Vandra' he said, half to himself and staring steadily at me. Then more loudly: 'Well, my dear, you have become twice the girl since I saw you last, and I don't expect you remember me at all.' To my mother: 'She is going to do you credit, Mrs Hopwood. I hope she behaves as well as she looks.'

My mother smiled.

'She is a good girl on the whole, though apt to dawdle in the streets or go exploring. We call her Fanny.'

'Fanny, eh? I see; a good contraction. Perhaps she will spell it with a V, when she grows up. So you want to see round the next corner, do you, Fanny? Perhaps when you are bigger, you will be able to. Travel is a pleasure and an education, but perhaps the best part of it is coming home again.'

He spoke over his shoulder to my mother:

'How does the schooling go? I think you told me Mr Clements had taken charge of her. He is an excellent man and a good teacher.'

'She is well beyond me in learning' laughed my mother 'and

full of talk about her classes. Mr Clements says he is pleased with her. You like your lessons, don't you, Fanny?'

The visitor was still looking at me with a persistence I began to find embarrassing. Muttering something about liking lessons very much, I retired behind my mother's skirts.

'I must be off, Mrs Hopwood' said Mr Seymore. 'It has been a pleasure to see you again, and now that I am at home I will venture to call in from time to time. I am particularly glad to have had another sight of Fanny. In the hope that I might do so, I brought a little present for her. Will you allow her to have this brooch? It is pretty, and she will set it off well when she is a grown girl.'

'Oh, Mr Seymore, it is beautiful! Look, darling, at this lovely brooch. But is it not too fine for her? I don't think I ought to accept it.'

'Nonsense. It is hers by rights, for the sake of the colour alone. Look at the deep blue-green and the glittering crest of white – a rock-pool and beyond it the breaking waves. Please keep it for her, and on her eighteenth birthday let her wear it, and think for a moment of the man who gave it her.'

My mother had thrust a little case into my hands while he was speaking, and had then abruptly turned aside to the dresser, where she began fidgeting with her workbox. I opened the lid of the case, and on a bed of dark blue velvet saw a large stone of a rich peacock blue-green, surrounded with a circlet of tiny diamonds. The whole was mounted on a plain gold pin.

The beauty of the thing moved even my childish mind to excitement. I had never seen anything like it, and was wholly ignorant of jewels or their value. But this was so manifestly something fine, so absolutely *itself*, that I could only stare at it in astonished delight. Suddenly I heard my mother's voice behind me.

'Say at least thank you, child!' she said, so sharply that I fell suddenly from ecstasy to alarm. I began to stammer a clumsy speech of thanks, but Mr Seymore interrupted.

'It is enough that you like it, my dear. Let your mother keep it safe, and mind that you always love her and look after her. Goodbye.'

And stooping, he kissed me gently on the forehead.

On the chair were his hat and cane. He held these in one hand while he shook hands with my mother.

'Goodbye, Mrs Hopwood. Please remember me to your husband.'

She opened the door for him and, closing it behind her, left me alone. I took the brooch to my usual corner, and sat and just looked at it. In one light the stone was a deep liquid green, in another a rich blue; always it hovered between the two. I wondered what it was called.

'Who is Mr Seymore, mamma?' I asked, when my mother returned. 'And when did I see him before?'

'He is a gentleman whom both your father and I have known for many years. But he has been abroad lately and therefore not come to see us. You were only a scrap when he was last here – too small to remember. He has done us many kindnesses. Now give me your brooch and I will lock it away for you. It is probably worth a lot of money, so tell no one about it. We do not want thieves in here.'

VII

'Hopwood's Hades', no less than the Warrior, set itself certain standards which it was the queer pride of the proprietor most obstinately to maintain. The place – to put it brutally – was a gambling-hell, a drinking-den, a house of assignation, a theatre of obscene burlesque, even – within the limits of its accommodation – a knocking-shop. Practically nothing was too scandalous to be tolerated; virtually no taste too wanton to be catered for. But Hopwood's idea of service to his clients was based on a fundamental honesty between himself and them. Consequently he never took their money without – to the best of his capacity – giving what was wanted in return; he never permitted his girls to 'roll' a client or to pick his pocket, nor tolerated bullies hanging about the entrance to Panton Passage in the hope of holding up a drunken reveller on his way home. The various swindles practised in other night-houses were unknown in Hades. The champagne was real champagne, not the mixture of gin and cider, with a gill of new ale and a teaspoonful of carbonate of soda, which – corked and well shaken – was frequently sold at champagne price in the dives about Piccadilly and the Haymarket. There was no business with 'dead men' – the system of adding two or three extra bottles to the empties ranged against the wall when some wealthy customer was entertaining a young woman. The billiard-room was free from sharps, and a spectator could make side bets without wondering whether his obliging neighbour might not be in league with one of the players.

No one, however much he may disapprove of the Duke's way of life, can deny him a certain genius. He realized – as few impresarios of vice have ever had the sense to realize – that never to cheat on the side was the best way, for one pandering to debauchery, to collect a permanent and really good class clientèle, to encourage lavish expenditure and to persuade authority to turn a blind eye. What in the way of crookedness or even violence went on *outside* either the Warrior or Hades he did not mind. He had arrangements with more than one Madam, and took his share of very dubious earnings without a qualm. He would help to trap a 'pigeon', and ask no questions as to what had befallen him, provided it was not on his own premises. But from the very first he had determined to make his personal clients trust him, and rely with absolute certainty on the discretion and fair-dealing of his establishment. I believe that for two or three years he had a hard time; for the wrong sort of wealthy pleasure-seekers presumed on his system and turned the tables by cheating *him*. But gradually it got about that 'Hades' was something special in the way of night-houses; and when it had become the favourite haunt of a few of the unchallenged aristocrats of dissipation, the undesirables dropped out and the place was 'made'.

I have already described what a little girl saw when, by mistake and during cleaning time, she penetrated Hopwood's

Hades. What follows – namely how the place looked late at night and in full swing, what sort of people one saw, what sort of things were going on – I owe to a one-time habitué who later became my close friend.

Naturally what I have said about Hopwood's principles and general practice is also at second-hand. But it has an element of originality, in that it was picked up from odd remarks and from gossip of all kinds, had to be put together, and could be flavoured with an occasional personal memory. Not so the facts about Hades. The place was closed down while I was still almost a child and, save for that one chance trespass, I was never there in my life. I am glad, therefore, to acknowledge to my kind friend this description of its interior, which is not the only thing for which I am grateful to him.

* * *

You must please imagine yourself a man about town, with money in your pocket and a fancy for a night of pleasure. It is early in the year 1870.

You find a congenial companion with similar inclination, and after a leisurely dinner at the club you look in at the Alhambra. You are purposely too late for the strident variety with which the programme opens, but in easy time for the Ballet which concludes the first half and is followed by a long – a very long – interval. This interval is one of the main features of the show, for the huge basement canteen is open to any of the audience who think a visit worth while. You are luckier than you know, because later in this very year the canteen will be closed to all save members of the company. You wander down after the ballet, pick up a couple of dancers and buy them champagne. They are cheerful young women, still wearing their scanty ballet costumes and with plenty to say for themselves. Nearly an hour passes in telling stories and gossiping about the crowd of swells and chorines who skirmish and lounge and laugh in the long, bare but well-lighted room. It is now nearly time for the notorious Can-Can, and you prepare to return to your seats. The ladies wish to say thank you for their wine, and each, with an arm round your neck or his, puts unmistakable provocation into her kiss. She probably ventures other familiarities, and certainly asks softly if you will be near the stage-door when the show is over. You thank her, but much regret that tonight is impossible. Then you take your leave and hurry upstairs.

The Can-Can is very near the end even of its period of revival – a revival marked by an exaggeration of every suggestive quality. There is also a Can-Can being danced at the Lyceum, as part of Hervé's *Chilperic*, and plenty of folk are deeply shocked by that, but it is a mild affair compared with the one at the Alhambra. Indeed the famous dance, as presented at the Alhambra by the 'Parisian Colonna' troupe, has become so outrageous that by October of this same year the place is to be deprived altogether of its dancing licence. You are, therefore, just in time for the final extravagances of a decadence; and certainly you get your money's worth in the way of whirling legs, glimpses of ivory thighs, and breasts that accidentally-on-purpose shake free from their flimsy covering. The provocative capacity of this degenerate Can-Can is terrific, and can only be believed by those who have seen it danced with shameless abandon. Tonight you can almost feel the rising excitement in the auditorium, as the music clashes and the writhing half-naked girls riot on the stage. As the audience crowds toward the doors, after the last curtain has fallen and the tempest of applause and animal shouting has died away, the eyes of men are bright and hungry and there will be no lack of business 'on the line'.

The cool air of the Square is pleasant after the feverish heat of the theatre, but the noise and turmoil are clamorous. Dense crowds move to and fro. Beggars line the curbs, street-women pluck at your elbow as you pass. You are wary of pickpockets, for every man who jostles you may be a thief, and at midnight in Leicester Square only greenhorns carry their money in a coat-pocket or show a watch-chain, a tie-pin or a jewelled stud. The centre of the Square is still an untidy waste, with cheapjacks' booths and heaps of rubbish and gangs of urchins screaming and dodging among the crazy shacks and piles of garbage. In a dark corner behind a closed marionette theatre a drunken clerk is fumbling a harlot. Four or five young men with linked arms are swaying down the middle of the street, shouting the chorus of the gibberish song which had swept the town in 1869:

> *Jamsetjee ma jabajehoy*
> *Jabbery dobi porie*
> *Ikey Pikey Sikey Crikey*
> *Chillungowullabadorie.*

Round the square are lighted entrances. Next door to the Alhambra is Brooks' 'Hall of Justice', where, in direct succession to Renton Nicholson's famous entertainment, you may hear Judge and Jury and see the *Poses Plastiques*. The Eldorado is just closing down; but gin-palaces flare, and here and there a gas-jet shines discreetly on a descending stair, leading to some basement where is a sing-song, and drink and girls are cheap.

Having made your way round the square you turn southward, and are soon at the door of 'Hades' in the narrow gloom of Panton Passage. The stairs are adequately but not brilliantly lighted, nor is there any outside bracket to throw a gleam on to the projecting nameboard. It is one of the attractive illogicalities of 'Hades' that it only announces itself in daylight when it is not open. At night, unless you know it is there, you will pass it by. But the Duke wants no casual trade and the regulars need no sign-posting.

At the bottom of the stairs is a closed door, which at a knock is opened by as ugly a customer as could be found even in Seven Dials. He is an ex-pugilist called Grabbett, and his orders are only to admit visitors up to a certain number, take their coats and hats, and to keep very close on their heels until they are ready to pay their entrance and go inside. Once he knows you, you have the freedom of his bleak square domain, off which is a wash-room and out of which (as already recorded) rise the stairs to Hopwood's office. At night these stairs are shut off by a door flush with the wall and papered to match it.

Behind the small counter which guards the inner rooms is another formidable figure. This man is dressed as a flunkey, with powdered hair and gold-cords and all the rest. There are three or four alternative bruisers who occupy this post; but by tradition they are all called 'Jeames'. Jeames can be out of his lair in a flash in case of trouble, and with equal ease can bar the entrance to Hades until his job as box-office has been done. Not only are the number of admissions limited, but it costs a sovereign just to get into Hades; and in these respects also Hopwood's dive is highly individual. The great majority of night-haunts do not care how much they crowd their patrons and they charge no entrance, but make up for it by fleecing the visitor when he gets inside. In Hades one is never fleeced and can be sure of comfortable sitting room and space to move about. These considerations are amply worth the risk of being turned away and, if admitted, the entrance charge.

Taking your ticket from Jeames, you pass through the big door and find yourself in a semi-circular space walled in by heavy velvet curtains which fall from ceiling to floor and run on two overlapping rods. Beyond the curtaining you can hear voices, perhaps music; but your immediate business is with yet a third official – also in flunkey's garb, also of alarming physique, but in this case answering to the name of 'Henery'. He takes your ticket, gives your coat a final brush and, drawing one curtain slightly towards him, allows you to sidle for a couple of yards between two walls of crimson velvet into the main hall of Hades.

This long vaulted room has a rich red carpet on the floor. There are small tables with gilt armchairs, sofas, great palms in pots, lamps on torchères. The furniture is arranged with skilful casualness, suggesting a drawing-room rather than a place of entertainment. Men and women are sitting about, drinking and talking.

In the right wall are four deep alcoves – large enough to

accommodate a supper table, several chairs, and a broad sofa strewn with cushions and fitted with a headboard only.

Probably one or two of these alcoves are occupied, and one perhaps has heavy curtains already drawn closely across the entrance.

About the main room waiters in dress-clothes move hither and thither. Against the wall sit a few solitary girls. They have none of the anxious absurdity of the wallflower nor do they thrust themselves on a new-comer with the pert rapacity of a dame de maison. If, when you have chosen a seat, you walk over and invite one of them to join you, she will accompany you with graceful amiability; but you are not expected to do so, for in Hades you are only expected to do exactly what you want.

There are now signs that something is to happen on the small stage at the far end. The curtains have parted; the orchestra strikes up, the footlights go on and the lighting in the hall is lowered. Two smartly dressed comedians do a cross-chat act, full of topical references and scandalous allusions to Royalty, to prominent members of Society, to reformist clergy-men and to politicians. One of them then sings a popular song, while the other arranges a few pieces of furniture to suggest a lady's dressing-room. Very soon a beautiful girl steps on to the stage, muffled in a smart evening cloak. She and the comedians carry on a conversation as elegant as it is suggestive, until she bids them goodnight as she is going to bed. One after the other the men go out. The violinist begins a soft sensuous tune, and the girl starts – unconcernedly but with the skill of an artist – to undress.

Hades made a speciality of this disrobing act, which ended, not with a last-minute disappearance behind the scenes, but with an unselfconscious descent from stage to auditorium. In Hades, when the last rag of clothing had been removed (or shortly before, if she thought well), the girl would step down from the stage and for a short while mingle with the audience. As she left the stage the hall-lights would go up and the stage be darkened. She might stop at a table and accept a glass of

champagne; she might kiss an old friend on the top of his
head; she would wave to acquaintances. My informant declared that it was wholly delightful to see the lovely naked
creature stroll serenely down the hall. Hopwood's girls could
not only strip without a qualm, but let themselves be seen
stripped under a top light and at a distance of a few feet. They
were also pleasant, well-spoken girls who, although they lived
by their bodies and made no bones about it, could behave
decorously and, in public, were always so treated.

This charming spectacle was the more effective because in-
discriminate nudity was not permitted in Hades. There was
never more than one naked beauty to be seen at any one time
(and only that at intervals) and, in decreeing that this should
be so, Hopwood gave yet another proof of his instinctive taste
as a purveyor of entertainment.

The brief stage interlude being over, and the performer
having retired to put on an evening gown and reappear as one
of the ladies of the establishment, you may desire to wander
into the card-room or the billiard-room both of which lie to the
left of the central saloon. Or (for your man-friend has probably gone his own way by now and you are free to please
yourself) you may prefer to choose an agreeable companion for
a protracted supper.

Supper will be served in the open-hall or in an alcove, as
you elect. If you decide for the former, you will now and again
have music to listen to and things to look at on the stage – a
transparency of a dance of nymphs or a singer. During the
meal you make your plans; for it is now after two o'clock and,
whether it be love or sleep or both that you are after, morning
is bound to come. If the girl pleases you, you can go home with
her; if that is too much of an undertaking (and you are not
already in an alcove) you can go upstairs to – of all places –
one of the famous cubicles immediately behind the Warrior's
Panton Street façade.

This arrangement was the crowning triumph of Hopwood's
malicious humour. It enchanted him to contrive that the most
equivocal of feminine activities could be performed in a tavern

where no women were allowed. A second staircase led up from behind the stage of Hades into the extreme westerly corner of the Warrior's frontage, and gave access to the first of the three cubicles. This had no door into the tavern, but only one into the second cubicle, which in its turn opened only into the third cubicle and also gave no direct access to the tavern. The third and last cubicle (the most easterly and the one nearest Chunks' vestibule and the Warrior's main entrance) was the only one with a door into the public-house. This door had a spring lock operated from within and no outside handle. Unless, therefore, you had a pass-key, you could only reach Cubicle Three by traversing Cubicles One and Two.

Admittedly this arrangement gave the occupants of the cubicles little privacy among themselves; and if there were a vacancy beyond where you were, new clients had to pass through your tiny room to reach it. But nobody minded about that. After all, everyone was playing the same game.

*   *   *

Plenty more could be said of Hopwood's Hades, of what went on there, and of the celebrities and notorieties who frequented it. But enough has been told to show that the place was at once outrageous and recherché – which, provided you grant its premises, is as good a testimonial as could be given. Certainly it fulfilled its purpose almost to perfection, and so far as I know nothing has taken place. The sad thing is that it came to disaster thanks to its very distinction, though I suppose, the British being what they are, that was inevitable. In England it has always been both difficult and dangerous to flout simultaneously the virtuous and the vulgarians. Moralists hate you for making attractive what they please to call 'vice', while perverts, sadists and rakes of the merely bestial kind bitterly resent your refusal to pander to their tastes. Of this double offence Hades was guilty; and in order to make clear what occurred and why, it is necessary once again to revert to William Hopwood himself.

In addition to his determination to play fair by his patrons, that remarkable man had two other impregnable principles. Though deeply involved in the organization of prostitution and deriving handsome profits from its exploitation, he refused to take part in any undertaking which permitted cruelty as an element in sex-traffic, and he was resolutely opposed to the victimisation of young children. This latter abomination was terribly widespread at the time of which I am speaking, and indeed continued to be so until the late 'eighties. A direct outcome of the misery in which a large part of the population lived, the sale of little girls was a regular proceeding in slum districts of every large city. In Hackney and Dalston and about Mile End Road, were recognized buyers who would give three to five pounds for a likely 'mark' of ten or twelve years of age, and arrange for her transfer to one of the West End houses. There were also men who, through a network of agents, drew up lists of prostitutes, and by threats rather than money obtained options on any female children which might be born to these luckless women. Such children were destined from babyhood to follow in their mothers' profession, and, as girls under age fetched high prices in certain fashionable brothels, they were launched on the game at the earliest profitable moment.

To anything of this kind Hopwood was savagely opposed. If any one of the Madams to whom he sent customers were proved to have allowed her house to be used for purposes known to be barred, he struck her permanently from his list. A client of Hades, inquiring for a recommendation on these lines, was liable to be spoken to more harshly than he expected. Naturally this procedure made him many enemies; and it was one such enemy who brought about his downfall.

You may well wonder what the police were doing to leave unmolested such a place as Hades. In the 'sixties of last century, the police – especially those responsible for the night-areas of London – were not the disciplined and virtually incorruptible force they have since become. Bribes were a matter of course, and the houses paid annual tribute according to their status and size, as well as providing free service on demand.

Hopwood no doubt paid some dues also; but, owing to his methods of conducting business, he was more of an asset to the police than a liability, and for reasons of their own they found it convenient to leave him alone. Hades was never a centre of disturbance; it was also a haunt of certain very well-known folk, whose reputations had to be safeguarded. The police knew that for the Marquis of — or Lord — or General Sir — to be publicly involved in a night-house scandal would bring on their heads trouble far greater than any merit they could hope to acquire by convicting a restaurant or brothel-keeper of an offence against by-laws or public morals. So long as these (and other) eminent gentlemen frequented Hopwood's Hades, they could be presumed safe, socially under cover, and in a position to enjoy themselves without risk of being found out. Somewhat, therefore, as the authorities will still appear to overlook cafés and lodging-houses where criminals or spies are known to congregate because at least, while there, they can be pulled in if necessary, so Hades was never raided or even cautioned, but rather valued as the safest place in town for prominent persons who wanted a night out.

Now it chanced in the year 1870 there began what is now called a 'purity drive'. Religious bodies, Morality Committees, congeries of earnest parents, temperance fanatics and genuine social workers combined to bring pressure on authority 'to do something about London'. The Refreshment Houses Act of 1865 had imposed a closing hour of one am. But although it had made impossible the survival of frankly 'all-night' establishments (from the most luxurious to the most humble), it had remained very much of a dead letter so far as were concerned the cafés and taverns which wished to continue business until three am. Publicans and night-house proprietors contrived to evade it by closing their main door and leaving another open, or by turning out the façade lights, or simply by purchasing exemption from the police on the spot. But during 1870 public agitation forced the powers-that-were to show an effective zeal for reform. It was decreed that the Closing Act should be more strictly enforced. There was a temporary banishment from the pavements of Regent Street, Pall Mall, the Opera Colonnade and Waterloo Place, of the low-grade foreign prostitutes who accosted men with such persistent shamelessness as to make those streets intolerable to ordinary citizens. Orders were given for the final suppression of the astonishing scenes in the neighbourhood of Waterloo Road, where were certain side streets in which girls, even in broad daylight, sat at open doors in nothing but a chemise, called to men, and often, before going indoors, danced with them to the music of barrel-organs. Other measures followed. There was the withdrawal (already referred to) of the Alhambra's dancing licence. Baron Grant came forward with his plan to make the centre of Leicester Square into a public garden, and once for all to do away with the rat-infested rubbish-heaps, the insanitary hovels, the pockets and hillocks of filthy trodden earth, as well as the opportunities which they provided for petty crime and casual indecency. Consideration had even to be given to a concerted attack on the now decadent Cremorne Gardens, which had become so noisy and disreputable that the people of Chelsea demanded their abolition.

These were typical features of the 'clean-up' of 1870; and it was largely due to the alertness of authority in the cause of social discipline and purification, that in the autumn of the 'reformer's year' Hopwood's scruples made for him his last enemy.

I must explain that the Duke never appeared in Hades before two o'clock in the morning, and often not at all. He had an excellent maître d'hôtel, with a reliable staff, and it was part of his policy to be personally identified with the Warrior rather than with its smarter but more questionable auxiliary. One night, as ill-luck would have it, he came down from his office a little after two and found a struggle going on in the square ante-room. Grabbett and the Jeames of the moment were trying to eject an obstreperous but very powerful reveller, and the process produced a clatter and a disturbance which enraged the proprietor.

'What the devil is all this!'

Hopwood's voice was not loud, but it had a mordant edge which bit into mere noise and fury as sharp teeth into cheese. The two employees released their hold and the captive swung round with a snarl of fury. He was a huge man, with shining black hair, a heavy moustache, long arms like an ape and the thighs and shoulders of a coal-heaver. He was fighting drunk and, when he saw Hopwood, lurched toward him with his great hands curved like claws. Grabbett and Jeames made to seize him once again, but the Duke waved them back. Without flinching he stared the angry giant in the eye, and with a tiny bow said quietly:

'Good evening, my lord. Can I be of any assistance?'

Perhaps there was a sudden recession of the fumes of alcohol, perhaps the level glance and calm civility of his vis-à-vis daunted him; in any event the big man stopped dead, dropped his hands and stood glaring at Hopwood from under his dishevelled mop of hair.

The sudden silence was broken by a faint rustle, and from behind the coats and cloaks which hung against the wall opposite to where the landlord stood, there emerged a figure so fantastic that for a moment the Duke was thrown off his guard. It was a shrimp of a child, with staring eyes set in a face which showed the dead pallor of fright even under smears of rouge and kohl. On the forehead was an angry bruise. Instead of being dressed in a child's frock or (as would have seemed more likely still) in rags and tatters, the little creature wore a grotesque parody of a grown-up evening dress. Made of a white taffeta striped with pink, sleeveless and with a deep décolletage, the garment hung by two straps on the meagre shoulders and fell forward over the child's flat chest, exposing it to the navel. The waist was tightly laced and a full skirt swept backward over a regulation bustle. Arms like matchsticks hung forlornly downwards. The hair was elaborately piled high on the back of the head, and on several skinny fingers flashed rings – showy theatrical jewellery, with imitation stones of fabulous size.

This astounding apparition for a moment diverted Hop-

wood's attention; and in the instant of his looking away his
opponent sprang at him. They were on the floor, with two
great hands tightening on the landlord's throat, when Grabbett, seizing a chair-leg which he kept at hand in case of real
emergency, brought it down on the back of the assailant's
head. The grip relaxed, the two servants dragged the huge
man from on top of their master and flung him against the
wall, where he lay unconscious, his head lolling forward and
blood trickling over his ear and on to his shirt-front. Hopwood
struggled painfully to his feet, feeling his throat. He was badly
shaken and, stumbling to a chair, for a few moments sat in a
white sweat. Jeames had run for brandy, and it was not long
before the Duke was sufficiently revived to remember what
had happened. Again his eyes fell on the shrinking child, with
her painted, tortured face, her bruised forehead and her horrible finery. She was crouched against the coats, hugging one
of them to her chest, and now and again whimpering gently
like a terrified little dog. Hopwood with an effort choked down
the sickness which still threatened to master him, and
wrenched his wandering wits into some sort of control.

'Well, Grabbett' he said at last – his voice was unsteady but
slowly strengthening, 'what is the meaning of this, and why is
that child here?'

The ex-pugilist was never an articulate man, and the problem of giving a coherent account of a series of unusual events
was almost too much for him. But, prompted by Jeames, he
managed to convey to his employer what had occurred. About
half an hour previously his lordship had arrived, bringing the
child with him. He had already been drinking heavily, but was
in full command of himself and produced the money for two
entrances. He explained that he merely wished to take the
little girl inside for a few minutes, in order to win a wager
from Colonel —, who had laid him a hundred to twenty that
the joke could not be played.

Hopwood interrupted to ask how much the porter and
Jeames had been paid to swallow this damned nonsense. The
question caused considerable embarrassment. The two men

hung their heads and mumbled that his lordship had been here before and seemed to be telling the truth; that they were close at hand in case of need —

'Leave that at present' snapped the master. 'What next?'

About ten minutes after the preposterous pair had disappeared into Hades, the maître d'hôtel had come rushing out in great excitement. Grabbett and Jeames must come at once and assist Henery to eject the big man. He had gone into an alcove and ordered a bottle of brandy. He must a little while afterward in some way have hurt the child, for with a frightened cry she dashed out from the alcove, tripped over her long skirt and fell screaming to the floor, knocking her head against the carved foot of a console-table. When members of the staff pulled back the curtains of the alcove, the man was lying back on the sofa, waving the brandy and shouting with laughter. The rest of the story was struggle, and they had got the brute as far as the ante-room when Hopwood had appeared.

The Duke, who was now almost himself again, got up and walked over to the little girl. Putting a hand on her shoulder, he said gently:

'There, my dear. You need not be frightened any more. I will see that you are taken care of. Has the child a cloak?' he demanded, and Jeames disappeared into the saloon returning with a gaudy velvet cape, trimmed with imitation fur.

'Wrap it round her, and take her to Mrs Bellew. Tell her she must put her to bed and find some sensible clothes. I will see her in the morning. This place is closed for tonight, Grabbett. No one else may come in. Say nothing to those inside about me being here. Let them think what they like. And now' (with a return to his usual sarcastic manner) 'for our noble friend, I think we will start by throwing a bucket of water over him.'

The bulky figure was already showing signs of movement, and when a pail-full of cold water had doused his head and shoulders, he came back to some sort of consciousness.

'Get up, my lord' said Hopwood. 'Grabbett, help him up and keep hold of him.'

The man was raised to his feet and propped against the wall. Still half-dazed, he muttered in his heavy moustache and his eyes wandered vaguely from side to side.

'Your lordship will listen to me for a few moments and then you will go and not come back. I do not allow children in here, nor drunken blackguards either, however grand their quarterings. My servants will have orders never to admit you again to any premises of mine; and if I have the least suspicion that you are interfering, even indirectly, with my affairs, I shall know how to set the story of tonight's little frolic circulating round the clubs and maybe in other places as well. Now get out!'

*   *   *

Thus may be reconstructed (and I think with fair correctness) the encounter between William Hopwood and Gerry Manderstroke, which had such tragic consequences. The matter was never actually proved; but I am convinced that what happened was the result of it. As I came to know only too well, revenge was sweet to Gerry and no rebuff ever forgotten.

VIII

In any period of persecution – whether it be placarded as a purge essential to the attainment of liberty, of national safety, of justice for the workers, of racism, of religion, or of social purity – the denouncer will seize his opportunity for venting a personal spite. The clamour for a London clean-up rose steadily throughout the year 1870; and as the appetite for victims grew among moralists and police alike, numerous informers helped to feed it. Probably therefore Hopwood, aware of what was happening all around him, was not greatly surprised to receive, late in December, a familiar but this time rather agitated visitor from the district police-station who, with apologies, reported that a complaint had been lodged against the Warrior on the ground that the premises were used for immoral purposes. The police had no option but to make inquiries, though they knew as well as Mr Hopwood that the charge was ridiculous. Unfortunately the complainant had gone above their heads, and used such powerful influence that the Home Office had insisted on a strict investigation. Only with difficulty had the speaker found an opportunity to slip round and pass the word. The search was to take place forthwith. 'It will, of course' he added with a wink 'be confined to the Warrior.'

Ten minutes after the friendly policeman had gone, two civil officials and two constables entered the premises and demanded the landlord. Hopwood was quietly courteous. He listened to the terms of the warrant and shrugged his shoulders with calm resignation.

'To pretend to understand the reason for this charge would be absurd' he said. 'But I welcome the visit of you gentlemen, which enables me to demonstrate once for all that the whole affair is ridiculous. Where shall the investigation start? Do you wish to see my private quarters upstairs? I believe my wife is at home and will, I am sure, give you every facility.'

The search-party, who had entered on their task in a mood of truculence, played into the Duke's hands by deciding forthwith to examine his so-called 'private quarters'. Sternly on their guard against any attempted deception, they invaded my mother's domain. I remember their coming, for it was just before Christmas and my holidays had begun.

Hopwood preceded them and called my mother from the kitchen: 'My dear' I heard him say, when she joined him in the passage, 'these gentlemen wish to go over the house. Suppose you first show them the parlour. Let them see anything they wish. I will wait for them downstairs. I have some accounts to go over.'

As soon as my mother brought the three men into the room (one of the constables had remained on guard below) even I was conscious of their embarrassment. I now understand that they had not expected so obviously a domestic setting, nor a Mrs Hopwood so manifestly candid and gentle and respectable. Nevertheless they made a show of searching the parlour, turning over my school books on the corner table, opening the cupboards by the fireplace and examining the windows for

signs of extra shutters or sliding frames. They followed my
mother into the kitchen and I heard them clump upstairs. I set
the parlour-door ajar in order to miss nothing of their leave-
taking. By the time they had once again collected in the passage, their leader was awkwardly apologetic:

'You must forgive us, Mrs Hopwood' I heard him say. 'We
have our orders, which I fear have disturbed you. Thank you for
your courtesy, and do not bear us a grudge for doing our duty.'

They went downstairs a good deal more quietly than they
had come up.

According to Chunks (whose story this once again becomes)
when they met Hopwood in the tavern, they were almost
cordial. He had emerged from his office when he heard them
coming; but his greeting was as correct and docile as ever.

'All satisfactory upstairs, gentlemen? That is good. Now for
the Warrior itself. If you would be so good as to follow
me . . .'

They visited the kitchens and back premises; they viewed
the office with its simple desk, row of ledgers and shelf of
catalogues from provision-dealers and wine and spirit mer-
chants. They walked all over the main tavern. They climbed
into the high pulpit. As they approached the main entrance,
the senior official (who by now felt that he had been made to
look a fool) was preparing to take a hasty and almost affectionate leave; but his officious colleague nudged him and pointed
to the solid wall of panelling which masked the window.

'Ah yes' the chief man said pompously, for he was torn
between anxiety to be gone and dislike of being corrected by a
subordinate. 'What – ah – lies behind this panelling? Perhaps,
if we are not troubling you too much . . .'

The Duke gave his standard explanation of the purpose of
the cubicles, and with his key opened the only door. Chunks
told me that he almost chuckled to see the flourish with which
the boss flung back the door and stood aside for the inquisitors
to enter, for he himself had used the interval between the
warning and the raid to make the easy changes which could
transform the little rooms into places for a game of cards or a

quiet business talk, to conceal the stairhead in the innermost cubicle, and to leave in each a gas-jet burning low. But then the thing happened which was for many days to drive all thought of chuckles from his mind. The men had walked through to the last cubicle and, turning on their steps, had regained the first one. Chunks, ready to usher them out through his vestibule, was standing near the partition door so that he could see into the little room. Opposite the door the corner was sloped off to make a tall cupboard, panelled exactly like the rest of the room and marked only by a key-hole. This key-hole caught the still suspicious eye of the junior official and he went up to it and tapped it with his nail. Chunks (and naturally Hopwood also) were still undismayed. The cupboard was not to their knowledge ever opened, save for a weekly dusting out, and contained only a broom, a dustpan, and a long-handled swab for the outer windows. The Duke began to say something to this effect and that he believed the key was in the drawer of his desk, when the pertinacious visitor, drawing some keys from his own pocket, slipped one into the keyhole so that it caught inside the edge of the lock, and pulled. The cupboard was not locked at all. The door swung open, and there in the half-darkness of the dim gas-lit room could be seen a naked body hanging from a hook. They lifted it down. It was the corpse of a little girl, and showed the hideous marks of brutal flogging.

*   *   *

At the moment, the horror of this abominable discovery drove speculation as to whys and wherefores from everybody's mind. Hopwood himself, between terror and astonishment, was utterly tongue-tied. They asked him to accompany them to the police-station, and he went in silence. There was no evidence against him, and had he kept his nerve all might have been well. But unluckily, in the cab on the way to the police-station, he suddenly took the notion to try and escape. He made a dash for the door; there was a struggle, and he and one of the constables rolled out of the cab into the street.

Hopwood, apart from a few bruises, was unhurt, but the constable's head struck the kerb in falling, and he died a few hours later. My mother never saw Hopwood again.

IX

This is *my* story, and I am bound so far as possible to keep it to its subject. Hitherto – unavoidably – I have had to tell many things which at the time they happened I could not possibly have known; but from now onward I shall try to speak almost entirely from my own experience. For this reason I will not trouble the reader with many details as to the reactions outside my own home to the grisly discovery in the Warrior. I have been told that the staff, alike of the Warrior and of Hades, were at once horrified and indignant. The Duke had always treated his people well, while admiration for his cool cleverness and for its material success had gradually convinced them of the rightness of his peculiar principles. Being, therefore, profoundly shocked by the nature of the crime which someone had fathered on their boss, and furious that he should even have been suspected of complicity, they were eager for vengeance.

In the absence of any direct evidence implicating Hopwood in the crime, he was arrested for manslaughter of the constable. His supporters knew this for a subterfuge, and that the Guv'nor was to be sacrificed on the altar of moral indignation. From the moment of his imprisonment there started to move through the corridors of the underworld a set of ill-equipped but angry men, forlornly hoping to discover how and by whom the dead child had been planted on William Hopwood.

The breaking of the news to my mother was contrived with a delicacy which, to those who have never known the rough loyalties of Chunks and his kind, may seem surprising. When the Duke was taken away, the only people on the premises were Chunks and a pot-boy, whose business it was to clean the tavern in readiness for the evening business. This lad Chunks dispatched immediately for Mrs Beckett, while he himself remained on duty to receive the crowd of police who would certainly take possession as soon as Hopwood had been charged. When Mrs Beckett arrived, he told her briefly what had happened; and I can see her now as she walked into the parlour with her usual stately slowness, and, hearing that my mother was in the inner room, passed on and shut the door behind her. In a very few minutes I heard a low cry, followed by a curious yammering. It was an eerie, frightening sound; and, without stopping to think of anything except that my mother was in distress or danger, I rushed at the door in order to go to her. It was locked. I beat on it with my fists, crying for mamma. Almost at once the key clicked, the door opened, and Mrs Beckett surged into the parlour. The continuous wavering cry which had so unnerved me – it sounded a mixture of confused chatter and mere animal lamentation – swelled louder, then dulled again. Mrs Beckett put an arm round my shoulders:

'Fanny, my dear child, your mother has had a bad shock and is very unwell. I shall stay here and look after her. I want you to listen to me carefully and do just what I say. Run upstairs and pack just what you need for a night or two; then go round to Mr Beckett's shop and tell Lucy you are to stop with us for a little while and will sleep in her room. As you go out from here, tell Chunks to send for the doctor. It is nothing serious, so do not be frightened; but it is better you should not see her at present. Tomorrow or perhaps this evening.... Now run along like a good girl. I must get back to your dear mother.'

Without giving me a chance to ask questions or to demur, she went back into the other room and I heard the key turn once more.

*   *   *

Next morning I was allowed to walk round from Chandos Street and see the invalid. She was lying in bed, looking pale and exhausted; but she was perfectly herself and greeted me with her usual gentle fondness.

'Come and give me a nice kiss, darling. You were a very good girl to obey Mrs Beckett so quietly. I am better now and will soon be about again. But I must tell you at once that your papa has been taken by the police who suspect him of something he has not done – something it was not in his nature to do. You will learn more about it sometime; but I want you always to remember this – that William Hopwood's wife (who of all people was able to judge) knew – *knew* I say – that he could not *possibly* have had any share whatsoever in the crime of which they suspect him. Promise me, Fanny, no matter what bad things you hear of him, that *you* will never believe him capable of this monstrous thing.'

I had not the smallest idea what she could mean, but was deeply impressed by her manner.

'Yes, mamma' I said. 'I promise you that.'

She lay back a few moments on the pillows, and then suddenly began to cry in a pitiful silent way. Her eyes remained open and fixed on the ceiling, while the tears streamed down her cheeks. With my handkerchief I wiped her white, weary face.

'Mamma, don't cry! Dear mamma, please don't cry! I will stay with you and soon you will be better.'

The tears gradually ceased. She groped after my hand, smiled faintly and turned her head toward me.

'Thank you, darling' she murmured. 'So long as you stay with me . . . I am sorry to have been so silly.'

I bent over her and, my hand still in hers, laid my cheek on her forehead. So we stayed in silence, and the ticking of the clock made a queer cross-beat with the pulse which I felt throbbing in her temple.

*   *   *

It is not easy to remember in their right order the events of those days of bustle and misery – days the more restless and unhappy because it was Christmas, when all the world except ourselves seemed carefree and jolly. My mother made a quick recovery and soon joined me at the Becketts. No words can do justice to the charity of those good people toward the unhappy Mary Hopwood and her bewildered daughter. They never hesitated to sacrifice their Christmas peace and much of the comfort of their home in order to rescue us from Panton Street. Clearly it would have been terrible to have had to live on over the Warrior, with police in charge, doors barred and every corner of the tavern and its basement ransacked and wrecked, while huge crowds of curious and often angry sight-seers surged about. Yet that, but for the Becketts, we should have been forced to do.

It was not long before I learnt the main facts of what had happened. In spite of every investigation there was no shred of direct evidence against Hopwood to justify a charge of murder, and he was brought up for the lesser offence of the manslaughter of the constable. The papers, however, with material for scandal volunteered or in their files, ran the story with lurid headings. When Hopwood was committed for trial, they daily published portraits of him, some drawn in the magistrate's court or on his way to gaol, others born of pure imagination, but all giving to his long mournful face a savage twist of criminality which was wholly false. They delighted in the revelations of the prisoner's enemies, of whom several (like the doctor who had signed Lamb's death warrant) found satisfaction in unsavoury disclosures. They exclaimed with horror at the discoveries made in Hades and sought gloatingly for still spicier details. When these were unobtainable they made them up.

The Duke's trial came on early in 1871. He was well represented, and his counsel pleaded passionately that the circumstances in which the constable had died could not justify a charge of manslaughter. But from the first the prisoner's position was hopeless. What with the triumphant shouts of the reformers and a mob stirred to fury against a presumed child-murderer (even though not charged with the offence), Hopwood had become a public enemy and the crowd roared for his blood. I was told afterwards that he sent despairing appeals to several of his most influential clients to testify on his behalf. They were asked, in order to meet the innuendoes made against him, to confirm his absolute refusal ever to admit children to his premises. But the frequenters of Hades were afraid to advertise their knowledge of the place; and though one or two sent offers of financial help, no one would stand up in court and admit acquaintanceship with so unpopular a man. Only Mr Seymore, just back in England after a sojourn abroad, volunteered to appear as witness to character. But as he had never entered either the tavern or basement of the Warrior, and as his knowledge of Hopwood was admittedly not up-to-date, it was considered useless to call him.

The prosecution made all the play possible with the secrets of Hades, now dragged into open view. Although the place was innocent of any signs of torture or cruelty, there were peculiar pictures on the alcove walls, queer arrangements of mirrors in other rooms, as well as on and about the stage, gambling properties and a dozen other proofs of licentious illegality which, with officialdom and the public in their present mood, were sufficient to declare a man guilty of every crime in the calendar.

In the end, the Duke was found guilty, sent to penal servitude for seven years and disappeared into the darkness of a convict prison. He was too broken to survive for long, and I learnt later that in a year or two death set him free.

*   *   *

Certainly Hopwood was not by ordinary standards a good man. But he had great talents, and in his way helped more people than he harmed. Thanks to him many men forgot their troubles in real if transient enjoyment, and some women found more comfort and less misery than they would otherwise have known.

*   *   *

It must have been before the trial that Mr Seymore paid his second visit to my mother, for I remember his using the words 'whatever happens' when urging her to leave London for a while and go back to her old home. But various people came several times to Chandos Street to see her – Vellacott, and a lawyer and one or two kindly acquaintances; and I cannot now say exactly when they came nor was I told what they came about, save that money-matters were discussed and that Hopwood's affairs were in confusion. With Mr Seymore's visit, however, I was directly involved. He had been closeted for a long while with my mother in the Becketts' parlour before she came to the door and called for me. He shook hands with me as though I were grown up, and spoke with kindly gravity:

'How do you do, Fanny. Sit down, please. I want to talk to you. I have been telling your mother that this dreadful business will make life very unpleasant for her if she stays in London. It is always uncomfortable to be closely connected with a public scandal, and vulgar curiosity will set folk staring and talking, if nothing worse. I am of opinion that, whatever happens to Mr Hopwood, she should go away – and as soon as possible. Also I think that you at any rate should use another name. This may be only necessary for a time; no one can tell. But to be labelled "Hopwood" at this moment will merely invite vulgar intrusion or worse. Her family name is Hooper, and I have suggested that you become Fanny Hooper, until we see how things turn out.

'As to what is to happen immediately, your grandparents and uncles in Yorkshire are willing for her to go back to her old home, and I want you to help me persuade her.'

Appealed to thus seriously I tried to respond in mature fashion:

'Let us go, mamma' I said. 'You will get quite well again and we shall be happy together.'

'Yes, darling' she replied, though to my astonishment her eyes were full of tears, 'we should be very happy. But ... but ...'

Mr Seymore laid his hand on her arm.

'Let me explain to her, Mary.'

I had no time to do more than notice his use of her first name, for he turned to me and his steady eyes compelled my whole attention.

'The reason for your mother's unwillingness is that she will have to be separated from you – at any rate for a while. You will hardly understand why it is so; but she has now very little money, and you must begin learning how to make your own living. This would not be possible on a farm in Yorkshire, but I can help you to make a start in London. Will you now be a brave girl and for your mother's sake tell her she can safely leave you, and that you will work hard? Soon perhaps you will be together again.'

I stared stupidly at him, while my mind struggled to grasp the full meaning of his words. As gradually I understood that my mother was to go far away and leave me alone, not only in London but in some strange place full of strange people, I felt a sob of fright and wretchedness rising in my throat. But Mr Seymore was still looking at me, with an earnest appeal in his sad brown eyes, and I knew that I must play up to the standard of adult self-control which he was forcing upon me. With a great effort I swallowed down my fear and, squeezing one of my mother's hands, very tightly, mumbled:

'I shall be all right, mamma – until you come for me.'

Then I ran out of the room before my self-mastery gave way.

*   *   *

It was the night before my mother was to leave for Yorkshire. Her box was packed, and only a bundle of wraps lay open to receive the last-minute oddments before her early morning start. I had cried so much during the day that I was beyond tears, and just sat silent and miserable by her side. The Becketts, dear thoughtful people, had all gone out after our high tea, knowing that we would rather be alone.

My mother got up abruptly from her chair and began pacing to and fro between the table and window. It was a raw foggy evening; the curtains were closely drawn and the gas unlit. The only light in the room came from the large coal fire. The flames wavered brightly on the ceiling, and flashed and died on the tall mahogany bookcase, behind whose glass doors Mr Beckett kept his special treasures. As suddenly as she had risen, my mother came back to her armchair and took me on her knee. I snuggled down against her soft breast and, as she put one arm around me, I felt for the first time for days really in safety and at peace. She began to speak in a low steady voice; and before I had time to lose my sense of comfort and security, I was caught up in the excitement and interest of what she was saying.

'You are nearly fourteen now, darling, and things have happened which none of us could have foreseen. So I am going to tell you a story which I should not otherwise have told you for several years. It is a story which a child of your age will not altogether understand; but I will make it as simple as I can, and you must trust me for the bits which are too difficult.

'I am going tomorrow to the farmhouse in which I was born and lived as a girl. It is an old house in Yorkshire and built in the middle of fertile plains which are among the best farmlands in England. The house and the many fields and woods which my father farmed, belonged – and still belong – to Sir Everard Seymore, who lives a few miles away. He is a fine old gentleman, well-liked in those parts, for he seldom leaves home, treats his tenants and servants well, and is always interested in local happenings. This Sir Everard has one son called Clive, and at one of the tenants' dances (every year in Sir Everard's park there was a fête which began with sports and games for the children and ended with a dance in a big marquee put up specially in a flat field near the Hall) I made Mr Clive's acquaintance. He was at that time what they call an Honorary Attaché in the Diplomatic Service, and spent much of his time abroad. But it happened that just then he had three or four months of leave. He seemed to me the most wonderful young man imaginable. He treated me with great politeness – just as if I were a girl of his own kind – talked amusingly about all the places he had seen. And he looked – oh, he looked exactly as I thought a gentleman *ought* to look and very few did – very few, that is to say, of those I had seen.'

She fell silent for several seconds and, glancing up at her

face, I saw that she was staring into the fire and that her lips were gently twitching. I felt her arm tighten round my body; but when she spoke again, it was in the same soft and level voice.

'I am afraid I danced with him several times that night and next day he rode over to our place; and the next day I met him by chance in a lane where I had told him I always walked of a morning — ' She broke off, with a nervous little laugh: 'Silly girl, wasn't I, to pretend it was by chance, seeing that I told him? And told him purposely.... Well, so it went on in a secrecy that made it lovelier still, and the happiest weeks of my whole life were the weeks of that beautiful summer. He was happy too, I am sure of it. A woman can always tell when the man she loves is happy, because that makes her happy. You will find that in due course, my darling – and the opposite. But men are different; they do not always know. Remember that, or you will suffer when you need not.

'When September came, the thought of his going away began to press down on me. To make matters worse, my parents suddenly declared we were all going for a week to Filey – thinking, poor dears, that we should enjoy a few days at the seaside. I was in despair. There were only three weeks left of his time at home; and I must spend one of them in a horrid boarding-house miles away from him, surrounded by a family, who, much as I loved them, seemed by comparison dull and tiresome. Next time I met him I poured out my troubles. But he only smiled, and said he knew Filey well, and would meet me under the South Cliff at nine o'clock the evening after our arrival. And so he did; and told me of his plan.

'A little way along the coast was a secluded cove, with cliffs rising all round and a little sandy beach. Except at very high tide, right under the inner cliff and partly behind the strip of sand was a deep pool – it filled a basin in the rock and the tide flowed in and out of it by a side channel. To that cove in the sunshine of next day he and I went. And the next day, and the next. It was hot still weather, and those hours on the warm sand beside the wonderful blue-green water of the rock-pool were the most perfect things that will ever happen to me or could happen to any girl. I took my sister partly into my confidence and so managed to slip away without worrying my parents. Not that they would have worried much; for they had the easy tolerance of country-folk. But I was sensible enough to realize that, for his sake, we must keep our meetings quiet.'

She paused, and I could feel her heart beating against my side. Then she continued, half to herself: 'Lovely, lovely.... At any moment since, I have been able to see, as though they were right in front of me, our patch of dry soft sand, the rock-walls quivering through the heat and beyond the mouth of the cove the lazy summer sea. And through and over any other sound I can hear the distant splashing of the waves, the rattle of pebbles sucked down by the retreating water, and close at hand the beating of his heart.'

Again she fell silent. I knew that she was deeply moved, for her whole body trembled and it seemed that a sort of excite-ment ran right through me, cradled as I was in the curve of her shoulder.

'That is why, when you were born, he wanted you called Vandra, to mean "water-child" or "water-sprite". By that time I was married to William Hopwood and the name would have been too fanciful for the likes of us. So we shortened it to Fanny.'

'Oh mamma! ...'

For a moment I could say nothing further. I wanted to cry and to laugh, to hear more and to be left to think over what I had already heard. At last I murmured:

'What a lovely story! Do you remember Mr Seymore say-ing I must spell it with a V? And what he said about my brooch?' Then, purposely a little impish: 'Is this Mr Sey-more's name Clive?'

She merely nodded, adding with a gentle simplicity that impressed even my ignorant mind:

'He is your father, darling, and thank God for it. But nobody knows. Only the three of us know.'

'Did papa know?'

'I had forgotten him, poor man. Yes, he knew. So I suppose there are really four who know.'

'What will Mr Seymore do with me, mamma?'

'He is taking you to his home in London. He married a few years ago and has now settled in the West End. I believe you will be taught to help with the sewing and perhaps wait on her ladyship.'

'Who is she?'

'She is his wife. He married an earl's daughter, so she is called Lady Alicia Seymore.'

'Is she nice?'

'I am told so, my dear, but I have never seen her. I hope she is – for his sake.'

For quite three minutes we did not speak. Then my mother, with a sudden reversion to her usual brisk tone, brought us back to ordinary life.

'Bed-time, darling. Jump up and run along. We must be up early tomorrow.'

When Lucy crept into our room some little while later, I pretended to be asleep.

x

Several weeks passed after my mother had left and before Mr Seymore sent for me. The Becketts had of course been informed of the arrangement, and in their warm-hearted way told me to regard their home as mine, to stay till I was fetched away, and thereafter to come and see them whenever I was free to do so. Naturally during these weeks of waiting, with my mother away and the first agony of loneliness passed, I turned to Lucy for companionship, and for the first time began to see her (and myself) with a certain awareness of our respective characters and appearance.

Lucy Beckett was an exquisite child – almost the idealized young girl of the Christmas Supplements. Her hair – so pale as to be more nearly silver than gold – was soft and plentiful; her face was oval, with eyebrows perfectly arched and a short straight nose. Maybe her chin was a thought too long; but the beauty of her full lips, which curved enchantingly into a slow sweet smile, obscured this trifling fault and even justified the slight overweighting of her lower face. At thirteen she was already shaping for womanhood. Her arms were formed and rounded, her legs had lost their childish chubbiness and narrowed sweetly from calf to ankle; her breasts were half-grown and she had the beginnings of a waist, which she was careful to emphasize so far as was possible with the clothes bought for her. That she was very conscious of her beauty is not surprising; and I claim a little credit to myself for feeling no jealousy when I suddenly realized how much lovelier she was than I and how much more mature. Indeed, so far from being jealous, I delighted in the discovery of her beauty, and, I suppose, made my innocent contribution to the vanity which was later to lead her into such strange paths. I loved to help her to alter a frock, to sew on new ribbons, to give some fresh quirk of colour or shape to a flowered hat. At night I would brush her gleaming silky hair for her, standing behind her chair like a proper lady's maid and smiling at her reflection in the glass, which smiled back in happy complacency.

My ministrations gave her an especial pleasure because Mrs Beckett – who, although a devoted and kindly mother, was shrewdly conscious of her daughter's failings – carefully discouraged the child's interest in clothes, rebuked her for looking at herself in shop-windows as they walked about, and tried so far as possible to prevent her reading romantic fiction of the kind which taught that a girl only needed beauty to live happily ever after. My admiration was of course poor thin stuff in comparison with what might have been and surely would be; but Lucy found it much better than nothing, and her affection for me became daily more eager and demonstrative.

No doubt my suitability as confidante and companion would have seemed less complete had I, even on different lines, possessed anything in the way of rival charm. At no time in my life have I ever been thought a serious competitor by the Lucys of this world, for such attractiveness as I could claim

was that of expression and vivacity rather than of looks, and
your real beauty ranks these as very second-class allurements.
Seeing, therefore, that even in my prime I could not aspire
higher than this, you will believe that as a shrimp of thirteen I
did not aspire at all. Sometimes, after feasting my eyes on the
ripening comeliness of my friend, I would sneak an opportunity to look at myself. The result was almost comic. I saw a
brown-haired, rather sallow little oddity, with a small three-
cornered face, in which were two very large dark eyes, a tilted
apology for a nose and a wide straight mouth. The hair fell in
a thick pig-tail halfway to my knees and, when spread about,
was certainly rich and vital; but it seemed a very ordinary
colour, and the olive of my skin was equally disappointing in
comparison with the cream and roses of Lucy's fairness. At
this time, also, I was nearly as flat-chested as a boy, my arms
were still bony and my shoulders lean and sharp. Perhaps because there was no possible comparison between Lucy's prettiness and my plainness, I accepted defeat without resentment
and devoted such instinctive coquetry as I possessed to her
further adornment without any thought for my own. Mrs
Beckett must have noticed this, for I remember one day that
she took me out to try on a bonnet trimmed with fur which she
had seen in a shop and thought would suit me. So it did; and
for once I felt myself smart in my own right. The little hat – it
was more a turban than a bonnet – sat pertly sideways on my
thick hair and, in addition to its fur trimming, had a large and
shining pin shaped like an arrow which transfixed the material
and gave the whole a final touch of rakishness. Lucy was enthusiastic when she saw it and, after trying it on, admitted that
it became me better than her. But all the same two days later
she borrowed the pin to enliven a hat of her own, and if her
mother had not noticed it and made her give it back, I doubt if
I should have had a chance to wear it again.

                    *   *   *

It happened that throughout my stay in Chandos Street Mr
Beckett was at home. The morning he always spent in his

shop, coming upstairs for his dinner and leaving his assistant in charge. In the afternoons he returned downstairs, but often went out on business or to pay a visit to friends in the trade. We had a sort of high tea at a quarter past six, by which time the shop had closed.

Mr Beckett had recently engaged a new assistant and congratulated himself on his good fortune in securing so superior and intelligent a man, after a series of muddlers and fools. In her hospitable way Mrs Beckett had suggested that the treasure be encouraged by occasional invitations to join his employer's family at their evening meal. The bookseller gladly agreed, and within a few weeks of his arrival the new assistant, whose name was Walkinshaw, had become a frequent guest.

He rapidly became also a favourite subject for giggles and speculation between Lucy and me. He was about thirty years old, and somehow or other we discovered that he kept company with a German girl who served in a big German pastry-cook's shop just off the Strand. He was a heavy-faced secretive-looking man, with thick hair of a surprisingly golden brown, which already receded somewhat from his high forehead but was crisp and cheerful. This freshness of colouring was in strange contrast to his lugubrious manner and rather lowering expression. Also he had an unlucky and very violent twitch at the corner of his mouth, which from one angle made him seem to grin; from another to bare his teeth in anger. This twitch was very irregular; and to the fascination of any small physical infirmity was added the excitement of wondering when it would happen again. Lucy and I, with the cruel silliness of youth, would change places at tea in order to judge the effect of the sudden distortion from different angles. Afterward, with explosive giggles, we would decide on which side the German girl preferred to walk and what happened if the twitch came while he was kissing her. Talking of him, we called him 'Walkey' or 'old Jerks'.

Mr Beckett had good reason to be pleased with Walkinshaw, who was not only a conscientious worker but showed a personal interest in topography, at that time a branch of anti-

quarian book-selling both active and profitable. Employer and
assistant would sometimes discuss business at meal-times, and
their conversation would inevitably drift to County Histories,
to So-and-So's Antiquities of Somewhere, to the whereabouts
of certain copies of rare works on the Abbeys of this county or
the memorial sculptures of that. We found fresh cause for
merriment in Walkinshaw's pre-occupation with ruins and
tombstones and such-like melancholies, for his voice and
manner were gloomy in the extreme, and we liked to pretend
that his idea of a rousing holiday was to prowl round a cemetery
or sit in sombre contemplation among the debris of a crumbling church. As for what Walkinshaw thought of us, we never
troubled to consider. He took no notice of us beyond ordinary
civility and as, except at tea, we hardly ever saw him, the odds
were that he never thought of us at all.

XI

Because I have spoken mainly of Lucy and of the foolish
jokes we shared, it must not be thought that during these
weeks I had forgotten the last evening with my mother and the
story she had told me. The mood of ecstatic half-reverie into
which she had fallen had stirred me deeply at the time, and
became, whenever I recalled it, more and more moving. In my
ripening imagination the episode between her and Mr Seymore came to represent romance; and romance, at the age I
had now reached, seemed the most wonderful thing in the
world. It never occurred to me to question, either on her
account or my own, the suitability of what had happened, nor
was I aware (or concerned to wonder) what in fact had taken
place. It was enough to have seen someone I loved swept back
despite herself into a state of radiant happiness; and I was
wholly content to rejoice that she had had this lovely – if
uncomprehended – experience, and that I was directly involved in it. Inevitably Mr Seymore also was touched by the
radiance which now shone from the past. That he should be
my father mattered little, for I had no knowledge of the im-

plications of paternity; but that he should have shared and in some way provoked incidents, the very memory of which could so transfigure my mother, mattered a great deal. From what I remembered of my two glimpses of him, I tried to create a personality as well as an appearance; and it says a good deal for the combined powers of instinct and sympathy, even in early adolescence, that the Seymore I imagined was a reasonable approximation to the Seymore I later came to know.

Every night, after Lucy and I had been stopped chattering by Mrs Beckett and a little later had of our own accord stopped whispering, I would lie on my back and think about my mother and Mr Seymore. I loved to recall the gleam in her eyes as she had talked and the warmth which had crept into her voice. I pictured – with a wealth of faulty detail – the lanes, fields and woods near Aughton in which she and Seymore had wandered, and the tiny hidden beach in the cove at Filey, with pale sand like warm silk in the sunshine and silent pool in the basin of rock beneath the cliff. There was neither curiosity nor embarrassment in these romantic visions. They lulled me into a happy serenity, and, when I was lucky, I fell asleep before they faded. But there were other times when I could not help worrying about the future. I wondered what life in Mr Seymore's house would be like, whether he himself would fetch me, and, if not, how I should have the courage to face a strange place full of strange people. More than that: once there, how should I be treated? In the security of Panton Street – before the crash, when the Hopwood household seemed safe from the sufferings considered natural to poverty – I had heard things said about 'slaveys' which showed that their lot was regarded as necessarily a miserable one. I recalled one story my mother had been told (and repeated in my presence to Mrs Beckett) about a wretched little 'general' who had been so brutally treated by the landlady of a boarding-house that she had run away and drowned herself off Hungerford Bridge. This and other half-remembered horrors would sometimes crowd over me, till I lay there shaking with fear. But I was fiercely determined not to make a sound. Were I to wake

Lucy I should be forced into explanations of which I should be terribly ashamed. I believe that, without quite knowing it, I was at this time deeply humbled by the catastrophe which had overwhelmed my home, and perpetually frightened of being abased before Lucy. That Mr and Mrs Beckett should pity me I did not mind; they were part of my mother-group and therefore on my side. But Lucy, fond though I was of her, represented the potential cruelty of my own kind and the rivalry which is always latent between girls of an age. So, when the nightmare dread of what might be coming seized me, I forced myself to suffer in silence. They were grim struggles, but they taught me a control which has since served me well.

One morning I came to breakfast after a broken night. I had had the 'terrors' worse than usual the previous evening, and, although I had finally slept, it had been uneasily and restlessly. As I entered the room Mrs Beckett looked up from a letter she was reading and began:

'Well, Fanny dear' – she gave me a quick glance, and went on, with barely a pause and picking up an envelope from the table – 'here is a letter for you from your mamma. Eat your breakfast first and then you shall tell us all how she is.'

I knew she had been going to say something different, but was too anxious to get to my letter to wonder what it might have been, and obediently ate the little I wanted. By the time I had read my mother's cheerful and affectionate sheet and reported what she had to tell, I felt almost myself again. Lucy and I cleared away as usual, and were preparing to help Mrs Beckett with the washing-up when she said to her daughter:

'Lucy, I promised Mrs Alderson I would help her one day this week re-cover an armchair. Run round and ask her if I could come this morning – in about half an hour. If I don't go today, I may not be able to fit it in. Fanny will do all the drying for once.'

Lucy skipped away willingly enough. The Aldersons lived only a few houses away; but even a tiny outing on one's own was better than washing-up.

For a few moments after the street door had slammed behind Lucy, we worked in silence. Then Mrs Beckett said in a matter-of-fact voice:

'Mr Seymore is now ready for you, Fanny. He is sending for you this afternoon. So we must pack your trunk. He writes such a kind letter I am sure you will be happy there. As soon as we have finished clearing up, will you go and be getting your things together? I will not be long with Mrs Alderson and then I will help you.'

Thanks to the skilful and considerate way in which the news had been given, the dreaded moment – now that it had arrived – could be met with fortitude. With passable calm I managed to reply:

'Is he coming himself?'

'He does not say, my dear. But I should doubt it.'

*   *   *

At four o'clock a cab drew up at the Becketts' door. My tin-trunk, carefully corded, was hoisted on the roof. I was embraced by Mrs Beckett, kissed by Lucy, patted on the head and given half a crown by Mr Beckett, and even treated to a twitchless smile from Mr Walkinshaw. With a little hold-all in my hand I climbed into the vehicle. It was already dusk outside and the interior of the cab was dark and musty. No one else was there.

'You know where to go?' I heard Mr Beckett ask the cabman.

'Yes, sir, I know. Upper Belgrave Street. And all paid. I'll look after the little miss, never fear.'

The horse swung slowly round toward the west and was soon clumping over the setts of Trafalgar Square. I sat upright, clutching my hold-all in one hand and Mr Beckett's half-crown in the other. I was numb with apprehension. Better not try to imagine what would become of me; better fix my attention on the immediate surroundings. With my mind deliberately empty of foreboding, I stared out of the window into the damp cold of the late afternoon.

UPPER BELGRAVE STREET

I

A WEEK or two in Mr Seymore's house were sufficient to remove my fears of ill-treatment, starvation or need for flight. I was certainly scared of some of the servants, and the large house now and then contrasted so vividly with the modest but familiar comforts of Panton and Chandos Streets that I had to fight hard to keep myself from breaking down. But I had the sense to realize that my personal forlornness was one thing and general staff discomfort another, and that so far as working conditions were concerned the Seymore servants, I myself least of all, had nothing of which to complain.

My complete ignorance of normal domestic arrangements prevented me at first from appreciating the unusual nature of my reception. When after a drive of some twenty minutes the cab drew up at a tall cream-coloured house, with a heavy-pillared porch and ornate area railings painted in black and gold, the driver got down from the box and put his head in at the window.

'Stay where you are a moment, my dear, and I'll tell 'em we've come.'

In the fading light I could see him open a gate in the railings and slowly disappear below the level of the pavement. For a few minutes nothing happened, and new fears crowded upon me. What if the cabby had forgotten all about me and I were left there till it was quite dark? What if the horse ran away? What if some vagabond climbed on to the box and stole my trunk? Fortunately none of these things occurred. In due course the big front door opened noisily and the cabby re-appeared, followed by a short, round elderly woman, wearing a black frock and a black silk apron and with a white cap on her silvery hair. While the trunk was being lifted to the ground, this lady (as I called her to myself) opened the cab-door and greeted me with brusque geniality.

'Now then young woman, out you get! Cabby will bring your box straight upstairs.'

She turned and bundled into the house, across a large hall, through a baize door, down a corridor and up some stairs. I scurried after her, much too anxious to do her bidding to take in any details of my surroundings. We climbed three flights (I could hear the cabman snorting far below as he toiled upward with my trunk) and turned to the left down a long passage. At the end was an open door, at which my guide stopped.

'There!' she said a little breathlessly. 'It's a slip of a room for a shrimp of a girl and I am next door, so no monkey-tricks, *please*.'

It was indeed a tiny room, with a small bed, a washstand, chest of drawers and a chair. On the floor was a strip of carpet, laid on linoleum. The window was warmly curtained and the walls covered with a gay-flowered paper. A naked gas-jet burnt over the washstand, and underneath it a small mirror was fastened to the wall. I put my hold-all on the bed and looked timidly round for the old lady: but she had returned to the stairhead and I could hear her admonishing the cabman as he clumped toward the top.

'*Nearly* there now, cabby, nearly there. Mind you don't bump the corners on the wall. I don't want crumbs of plaster all over the place, if *you* please. This way – in here – put it on the floor in the corner – that's the ticket. Much obliged to you I'm sure, and here's a shilling for yourself. Go out through the basement, mind. I only used the front-door to save you another flight. Goodnight and *thank* you. . . .'

She shepherded the man back to the stairs, and what with his want of breath and her volubility, got him started on the descent without saying a word. The next moment she was back in my room.

'Take off your outdoor things and you shall have a cup of tea. Plenty of time to unpack afterwards.'

I obeyed, and she led the way two doors down the passage

to a pleasantly furnished sitting-room with a bright fire, a kettle singing on the hob, and a general air of lived-in cosiness. Shutting the door (a red curtain on a brass rod hung over the inside and matched the window-curtains, table-cloth and mantel-drop) she came straight up to me, took me by the shoulders and swung me round to face the gasolier which hung from the centre of the ceiling.

'Now let me have a look at you.'

She studied my face from every angle in sombre silence, and I bore the long and formidable scrutiny as best I might. Then, as suddenly as it had begun, the ordeal ended. She muttered 'Yes ... yes ... well, who'd a' thought it', and turned to make the tea.

By the time I had drunk half a cup and eaten a slice of cake, I felt so restored in spirits that for the first time I ventured a remark:

'If you please, ma'am, will you tell me your name?'

She looked up at me with a sudden start of interest.

'Say that again, child!' she commanded. 'Say it slowly and clearly.'

Mystified and a little alarmed I did so. She stared at me a moment and I heard her murmur 'Well, I never ... the voice, too....' Next instant she was her former dominant self, and answered my question in what I came to know was her usual manner.

'My name, miss, is Mrs Heaviside and don't let me catch you calling me "Nanny" as one of those saucy chits downstairs tried to do till I boxed her ears. Your name, though you may not know it, is Hooper in this house, just as cook's is Mrs Blashfield and the butler's is Mr Croggon and the head housemaid's is Miss Ramage and her ladyship's maid is Miss Carver, and Mr Seymore's gentleman is Mr Olley. As for the rest of them they are just Ward and Bellamy – those are the footmen – and the girls are Kershaw and Minton and Gover and Peake and Smith, and a set of chattering sillies into the bargain though good enough girls in their way. What else do you want to know?'

'Is Mr Seymore at home, ma'am?'

'He is not, nor her ladyship either. They return the day after tomorrow, by which time, Hooper, you will have learnt your duties and got down to work good and proper which I daresay is what you have never done in your life yet.'

'I have been at school' I said timidly, 'and helped mamma all I could.'

Mrs Heaviside suddenly smiled, and her large red face which had seemed so forbidding while she was managing the cabman and during the earlier stages of our queer tea-party, broke into a hundred friendly little wrinkles and her very eyes seemed to change expression.

'I'm sure you did, my dear, and you mustn't mind me. I rattle on like the talkative old fool I am, and get out of patience sometimes with the goings-on of girls nowadays. When I was a young girl my mother would have taken a stick to me for half the pertness of some of these minxes. But I hope you'll grow up different – like your mother, mayhap, who —'

In my excitement I actually interrupted:

'Oh, ma'am, do you *know* my mamma?'

Mrs Heaviside seemed to check herself.

'Ay, I knew her a little, long ago' she said quietly, then hurried on: 'But we can't sit here gossiping, you know. You must unpack and then see some of the others, for, though you will sleep here near to me, you will take your meals in the servants' hall and during the day work where you are told to. Run along and put your things away; then come back and I'll show you some of the house and find Miss Carver.'

Quarter of an hour later I was standing outside Mrs Heaviside's door, hearing voices within and wondering whether I dare knock. But the sound of footsteps mounting the stairs decided me. Better be scolded by one whose name at least I knew, than be found hovering in the passage by a complete stranger and be stared at and perhaps questioned.

Bidden to enter I slipped into the room, closing the door carefully behind me. Mrs Heaviside was sitting in her arm-chair by the fire, and on the hearth-rug, with his hands clasped behind him, stood a tall, bald-headed man in a black tail-coat and striped trousers. Neither of them took any notice of my entrance, and the man, evidently continuing a conversation, said in a deep, rumbling voice:

' — not that kind of household at all. If you think, I said to him, that Mr S. does not know one port from another you are greatly mistaken; and, as for bribery and corruption, I said they are foreign words to my vocabulary and to that of everyone here.'

He smacked his lips together at the conclusion of this remark and blew through his nose three times, so vigorously that his nostrils were fiercely dilated and went white at the edges. Clearly he had disposed of his antagonist to his own complete satisfaction and to that of Mrs Heaviside also, for she nodded vigorous approval and said:

'I hope he took *that* back to where he came from! The impudence of them! It only shows what passes for gentry nowadays and the sort of thing that really common servants get up to.' Without a pause or even turning to look at me, she went straight on: 'Hooper, come here! This is Mr Croggon, Mr Seymore's butler. Mr Croggon, this is the child I told you of.'

I bobbed him a curtsey. For his part he surveyed me solemnly, and after a nod of greeting cleared his throat:

'How do you do, Hooper. You have come to a good situation, where all you have to do is to work and be respectful to your seniors. Being – ah – a female, you will naturally be subject to Mrs Heaviside, our excellent housekeeper, rather than to me; but there may be occasions when I shall desire you to do this or that, and I shall expect to be obeyed.'

'Oh, yes, sir' I said. 'Certainly, Mr Croggon.'

Again he nodded, and drew a large gold watch from his waistcoat pocket.

'It is considerably after six o'clock. I must be going now, Mrs Heaviside, and look forward to resuming our discussion at supper. Goodnight, Hooper. You seem a well-intentioned girl and I hope will do us credit. We are not unreasonable, I be-

lieve, and treat our staff kindly; but we have our standards —
oh, yes — we have our standards.'

*   *   *

My first few weeks of domestic service, apart from a second
and a very different encounter in Mrs Heaviside's sitting-
room, were passed in forlorn bewilderment. I had to find my
feet, and the process was as painful as it had to be. More than
once I cried myself to sleep; several times I lost myself in the
labyrinth of floors and passages. Worst of all I had to meet the
rest of my fellow-servants, and suffer that torment known to
every young solitary thrown into a new society and new surroundings — the torment of hanging about with nothing particular to do and facing three times a day the ordeal of com-
munal meals. Not that the others were in the least unkind to
me; they just behaved, when all together, as though I were not
there. Unless she sent for me, I hardly saw Mrs Heaviside at
all; for she took meals with Mr Croggon and seldom appeared
below stairs save on managerial and important business. Miss
Carver, Lady Alicia's maid, and Mr Olley, the valet, also took
their food apart, in the basement sitting-room specially provided for Mrs Blashfield — the cook. The kitchen-meals, therefore, were attended by the junior servants only; and it was
natural that two young footmen and five girls should have
plenty to say and laugh at and quarrel over, without troubling
to bring a child-outsider into their circle. Nevertheless meals
were for some time a miserable experience for me, and I
should have eaten even less than I did and hurried away still
sooner, or gone farther and avoided some of them altogether,
had I had anywhere to hide myself except my tiny bedroom.

My working hours were officially spent partly in Miss
Carver's work-room near Lady Alicia's bedroom on the second
floor, but mainly in the sewing-room with Peake. Miss Carver
was small and desperately refined. She had a neat figure, and
dressed so far as possible in the manner of the traditional
soubrette of French comedy. Her high heels clacked busily

over the parquet-floors; her ribbons fluttered and flounced; she made considerable use of French expressions and had numerous mannerisms which I suppose were imitated from those of Lady Alicia's friends. But the Parisian ensemble was damaged by the poor woman's intensely British face and mincing precision of speech. It was a shut-in, righteous, pale-lipped sort of face, with no gleam in the eyes and no real merriment behind the smile. Her voice and vocabulary were equally shackled – the former by a tight gentility of accent, the latter by the trammels of suburban elegance. One may give the lady credit for her desire to be ladylike and for her impregnable virtue; but these admirable qualities blend oddly with gaminerie, and as a gay coquette poor Carver was a failure.

Peake, on the other hand, though even more British than Miss Carver, had twice her liveliness, because she was content to be lively in the British way. She was a plump dough-faced girl, with a loud laugh and an utterly commonplace, often vulgar, mind but with plenty of good nature and the cheerful lack of imagination typical of Britons in every class. Peake was the first of the servants to take any individual interest in me and my concerns, probably because I spent long hours alone with her in the sewing-room, struggling with the household linen, counting the laundry, darning, sorting thread and wool, and generally devilling for her. After asking where I came from, where and who my parents were, and whether I had any brothers and sisters (questions which required a certain evasiveness of handling), she treated me to facetious comments on the household to which we both belonged. The housekeeper – whom she always called 'Nanny' or 'old Heavitail' – had been with the master for years and years. She was a Gorgon and no mistake. I ventured that she had treated me kindly, though certainly her manner and appearance were alarming. Peake suddenly laughed in her harsh and common way:

'You're under Nanny's wing, aren't you? Not old enough to sleep upstairs like the rest of us and pick up things you didn't ought. Never mind, dearie, you'll learn all right – just as we all do.'

Wishing to turn the conversation, I asked about the master and mistress.

'You'll never see em, me dear. Why I ardly do. Not but what e's a gent, Mr Seymore. Quiet and all that, but always nicely spoken and keeps isself to isself. Er ladyship's more dangerous, though she is such a midget. You wouldn't believe the temper she as under all that la-di-da. My word, what a temper! She breaks out at Carver sometimes fit to smash the winders. But I'll say this for er – she *is* smart, and pretty as pretty, and clothes enough to dress a regiment. You peep over the stairs at er one day, when she's dressed up to go out. Lover-ly she looks! And once when they ad a big party ere I met er in er ball-dress and jools – just down there on the stairs – and – oh my – what wouldn't I give for a chance to wear them things!'

So Peake would rattle on, never forgetting to keep me in my place by stressing the impossibility (save on the merest chance) of my having a glimpse of my employers or even entering the rooms in which they lived.

*   *   *

I have said that one incident cheered the disconsolate monotony of my time of probation. It occurred in the late afternoon of my third day in Upper Belgrave Street. The second housemaid put her head round the door of the sewing-room and said sharply:

'Hooper, Nanny wants you. You're to go to er room at once.'

Peake looked up from her work with a broad grin. 'What you bin up to, duck? Goin to be put across Nanny's knee, or sent to bed without yer supper? I'm ashamed of you. Run along and get it over.'

Once again a man was standing on the hearth-rug of the housekeeper's room, but this time it was Mr Seymore and Mrs Heaviside stood a little behind him. As soon as I appeared, he came quickly forward, took me by the shoulders and looked at me with an affectionate smile.

'My dear Vandra, I am delighted to see you. You must be happy here, if only for your mother's sake. Have you news of her? I must write to her now that I have seen you.'

He did not seem to expect me to reply, for he turned to Mrs Heaviside and continued:

'Is she a good girl, Nanny? I am sure she means to be, and certainly she could not be in better care.'

Mrs Heaviside was all smiles and wrinkles, as I had once before – if only for a moment – seen her.

'It's early days yet, Mr Clive' she said 'but I've heard no complaints so far.'

He walked over to her and put his arm round her massive shoulders. 'Dear old Nanny, what should I do without you; what should I ever have done without you?'

He was looking almost boyish. From my last sight of him I remembered the fatigue in his eyes and the hint of pre-occupation in his kindly manner. By comparison he now seemed carefree and serene.

'Get along with you, Mr Clive, and before the little girl too! I'll be telling some of the scrapes you got yourself into if I'm not careful, and then where will discipline be I'd like to know.'

He hugged her playfully and let her go.

'Nanny' he said gently – and his manner was once again restrained and thoughtful – 'I want to talk to Fanny for a few moments. Will you be a dear soul and lend me this room? Only for a few minutes, I promise.'

She smiled at him fondly and walked to the door.

'As it happens' she said 'I have a number of things to see to, which ought to have been done long ago. Gossiping here with you, Mr Clive, makes hay of my duties.' Then added, with a quaint return to her usual garrulous severity: 'You, Hooper, when Mr Seymore has finished with you, go and clear up the sewing-room and, mind you, don't forget the gas. After that have your supper and go to bed. Sitting up till all hours never did young girls a bittock of good that I heard, and though you may forget there is tomorrow, *I* don't!'

The door closed behind her.

*　　*　　*

'Now, Vandra, come and sit beside me on this sofa. I am going to talk to you as though you were a grown-up person (as you soon will be) and I am sure you will do your best to understand.'

He settled himself in the angle of the single-ended couch, so that by half turning he could see me perched primly at his side. He made no attempt – and for this I was consciously grateful – to pat my hand or stroke my hair in any way to act the genial adult conversing with a child. I felt immensely serious and deserving of every confidence. This man, already my ideal of a gentleman, was going to treat me as an equal. Certainly I was prepared to agree to everything he said, but I meant to look very judicious while doing so.

'I know' he began 'that your mother told you a story about herself before she left London. It was agreed between us that she should do so. I am quite sure that it has made no difference at all to what you feel for her; but I want you – just in case, when you get older, you hear things said which might incline you to blame her – to promise me that you will always love and respect her. She is one of the best women who ever lived, and if you and I can agree about that, we shall have at least one secret to share between us always.'

He fell silent. How strange that he should adjure me to champion my mother, almost as she had bade me stand up for William Hopwood. I glanced at him sideways to see whether he was expecting me to make some reply. But he was staring into the fire with a half-smile on his lips, and I realized that he was back in the same past whose memory had so deeply affected my mother. The thought excited me. I felt that quite suddenly he had become part of me – part of my mother and of me; and I think that in that moment what had been liking and admiration turned, with the fierce singleness of a child's emotion, into love. I could not have spoken, even if I had wanted to; so I just sat motionless and waited.

Very soon he spoke again, in the low, clear voice which I had remembered from my very first meeting with him – a dusky, melodious voice of a kind seldom heard, and – I confess it – an inheritance of which I am shamelessly vain.

'When the trouble came – the trouble over your – er – over Mr Hopwood – I decided, as you know, that your mother must leave London, at any rate for a while. But to send you also to a farm in Yorkshire would be to deny you the chance of learning what must be your life – that is to say, life in a big city. The old days of secluded country prosperity are nearly over; we are all industrial and commercial nowadays. I had hoped, by having you well-taught, that you could have become a teacher or gone to work in some charitable or business institution when you were old enough. With a home and parents behind you, it could have been arranged. But the tragedy at the Warrior wrecked everything – your girlhood included; and it seemed necessary that somehow and somewhere you should grow a new personality so that no one could connect you with what had happened. That is one reason why I brought you here. Another is' (he gave me a quick smiling glance) 'I wanted you and me to become acquainted. I have been out of England so much since you were born, and seeing that I was responsible for the meeting between your mother and the man she married ...'

He broke off for a moment: then went on, as though half in argument with himself:

'Not a bad fellow, Hopwood; not really. And he treated her well. Is not that so, Vandra? He was kind to you both?'

'Oh! yes, sir' I said. 'I'm sure we always liked him.'

To my surprise he laughed.

'I'm glad of that at any rate. Well, do not think too hardly of him' – adding – 'or of any of us for that matter.'

Again he paused, and his next words explained his hesitation:

'What I have to say now is difficult to say, and may be difficult for you to understand. *Try* to understand, my dear, and if you cannot do so at once, try again tomorrow. This is my home where I live with my wife. She is a good wife and I am very fond of her. But she would not like to hear the story your mother told to you or to know who you are or why you are here. As I do not wish to give her pain, I shall tell her nothing – save that you are a young girl recommended by Mrs Heaviside to help in the house. Mrs Heaviside is one of my dearest friends. She was my nurse when I was a child, and ever since has been the person in whom I have most readily confided. Because she loves me, she will love you; but you must play your part. I want you to do your best here, to work hard and to seek to please those who are over you – in particular my dear old Nanny. When you are older, I will try to get you the start in life your mother and I would wish you to have. Until then – even if the days are long and the work dull – I beg you for her sake to do your very best. Will you, Vandra?'

The lump in my throat refused to dissolve. I was determined not to cry; but speech was impossible. Blindly I stretched out a hand, and he took it in his cool lean fingers.

'Will you, Vandra?' he repeated.

I nodded desperately – and by a miracle my voice (or half of it) returned.

'I promise' I whispered. 'But it will be easier if I may see you sometimes.'

He gave a low groan, which at once frightened and thrilled me:

'Oh! my dear...' he began; but checked himself and assumed a brisk amiability which cheated me – child though I was – as little as it cheated him. 'Certainly you shall see me. We might sometimes have tea together up here if Mrs Heaviside allows us.'

The next moment he was standing in front of me.

'Goodnight, darling' he murmured. 'Goodnight and God bless you.'

His lips touched my hair and I felt his fingers caress my ears. As he left the room, I began to cry; and I was still crying – from sheer happiness – when Mrs Heaviside returned and with mock ferocity drove me to my duties.

II

I lived in Upper Belgrave Street for nearly four years. A lot of things happened during that time – including my own passing-over from childhood to young womanhood – which seemed very important to me personally. But as most of them would not be of great interest to anyone else, I shall select and reject with an eye on the future alone.

By the end of six months I was an accepted member of the Seymore household, and after a year in the little room next to Mrs Heaviside, was moved to the top floor, where I shared a bedroom with a seventeen-year-old new-comer who had re-placed the former kitchen-maid. This girl's name was Clara Williams. She came of decent country stock from the Welsh marches and was a gentle, rather yielding creature, whose soft sing-song voice and quiet ways were in agreeable contrast to the strident cockneyism of the other junior servants. We soon made friends and, with the housekeeper's permission, took our every third Sunday on the same day. This Sunday outing was the only one long enough to be of practical use. Frequently we had an hour in the afternoon, and took a walk in the park or did some small errand; but every third Sunday freedom began after dinner and lasted until ten o'clock in the evening. The Becketts allowed me to invite Clara to Chandos Street for tea and supper, and she in return took me to her equivalent of home – the house in Lupus Street, Pimlico, where her father's brother lived and did business as a builder and decorator.

Lucy Beckett had recently been admitted as an apprentice into an old-established dress-making business near Hanover Square. She thoroughly enjoyed her new occupation, with its variety of incident and crowd of new acquaintances, and was full of stories of what happened in the work-rooms, of the marvellous silks and satins, of the impossibility of pleasing some customers and of the money owing by others. No doubt most of the gossip was untrue; but it made amusing chatter, and whether we believed it or not was of no importance to anyone else. Clara and I in return romanced gaily enough about the visitors to Upper Belgrave Street and Lady Alicia's furs and the grand display of plate when people came to dinner. Mrs Beckett would sit on the sofa, her workbox at her side, and smile tolerantly at our jabbering; then we would all have an enormous tea, and after that had been cleared away, Mr Beckett would take his wife to church and leave us girls alone.

Then, I need hardly say, our heads drew together, and talk turned to boys and men and love-affairs generally. Of the three of us Lucy was the most enthusiastic and far the best informed on this exciting subject. Personal beauty predestined her to coquetry; and her work in the dress-shop gave her many more opportunities than were open to Clara or to me of hearing whispered scandal and exchanging secrets with her kind. As I remember them, her revelations were in fact elementary enough; but they seemed to us wonderfully grown up and enlightening, and we were quite content to take Lucy at her own valuation – as a girl of experience well on the way to being an accomplished woman of the world.

Lucy's obvious qualifications to be an expert in love caused me no jealousy. I took her greater prettiness contentedly for granted, and came to regard 'love' as her speciality, and to rely on her for information about it. Naturally, like all young things, I was sexually curious. I responded, with a vague sense of adventure, to giggling jokes and to hearsay reports of various goings-on. But I did not feel that I was personally involved or at present likely to be; and although I pretended to be thrilled by stories of squeezes in the dark, and what the boy in the counting-house had whispered to Lucy as they walked down Regent Street together, I was really playing up to the conventions of girlish excitement rather than being genuinely moved. Clara, I fancy, was as little affected as I: and certainly when we two were alone, we hardly spoke of such things. But then Clara had a calm unhurried nature; she was of the type that does not go out and look for experience, just waits for it to happen.

Among the other young servants at Upper Belgrave Street

there was a good deal of facetious inquiry about outside en-
tanglements, and in the house itself outbreaks of clumsy gallantry and horseplay. There was even one rousing scandal
which ended in the dismissal of a housemaid and a footman.
But these jokes and incidents affected me (and I think Clara
also) even less than Lucy's whispered confidences. She at least
was my contemporary and her formulas were mine: but the
affairs of people in their twenties, even though they lived
under the same roof, were something quite alien to me, and I
had sometimes to work hard to show sufficient response when
Peake, over her sewing, regaled me with stories of her own
adventures and those of her room-mate.

As time went on, I was gradually promoted from the odd-
jobbery of the sewing-room, and sent to work for two or three
hours on end under the rule of Miss Carver. It was during one
such interlude that I had my first sight of my mistress. Miss
Carver, after setting me to mend some lace-bordered hand-
kerchiefs, had gone downstairs to take her mid-morning cup of
tea. I was concentrating fiercely on a job requiring an extreme
of neatness, when the door of the room was flung open and a
high clear voice cried:

'Carver! What did I do with ... Hullo, and who may you
be?'

I had automatically stood up, and saw before me a little
woman no taller than myself, dressed in a riding habit and
bowler hat.

'Miss Carver is downstairs, ma'am' I said. 'Can I do anything?'

She surveyed me with a pleasant if slightly satirical
smile.

'I don't know. Presumably you can do *something* or you
wouldn't be here. Actually I'm looking for my riding gloves.
That fool Carver always hides them somewhere fresh.'

By a lucky chance I had noticed, on entering Miss Carver's
room that morning, that a corner of a glove was sticking out of
a loose armful of clothes which had, I supposed, been brought
from the mistress' bedroom to be sorted and tidied away.

Crossing the room I pulled it out and saw its fellow crumpled beneath it:

'Are these them, ma'am?'

She nodded, took them without a word of thanks, looked me over quizzically and said:

'And now kindly tell me who you are.'

'I'm only Hooper, ma'am.'

The little lady threw back her head and laughed like a girl.

'O dear! "Only Hooper"! You'll be the death of me. That's enchanting. I find you toiling at my horrible handkerchief, which I tore deliberately at dinner last night because that detestable old pig Sir Isidore would talk with his mouth full; you find my gloves which Mademoiselle Toquée for some astonishing reason wrapped up in my chemise – and after all that you are "Only Hooper"! Listen to me, my dear' – and she skipped forward to within a foot of me, thrusting her face close to mine – 'I'm an infuriating, selfish, inconsiderate, untidy little beast; but when I *am* nice, I'm damned nice. And I think I would be nice to you if I got a chance. Will I?'

Bewildered by the torrent of words and uncertain whether the lady was making fun of me or not, I could only stammer:

'Thank you, ma'am. I'm afraid I don't —'

'Goodness gracious, nor you do!' she interrupted. 'Why should you? I also must introduce myself. My name is Seymore.'

'I'm sure I beg your pardon, me lady. I've not been here very long and . . .'

'Don't apologise, child; for the Lord's sake don't apologise. And go on saying ma'am. I hate all that "me lady" rubbish. What do you do here, Only Hooper – just sewing?'

'Mostly, ma'am, though I help Mrs Heaviside a little and I hope Miss Carver will teach me cutting out and fine laundering and —'

She made an impatient little movement with her hand.

'Yes, yes: that will do.' I saw that she had hardly listened to what I was saying. Her rather forced merriment had changed to thoughtfulness, and she was looking searchingly at me.

'There's something about you I can't quite make out' she said slowly. 'Almost as though I'd seen you before. And you don't look quite the ordinary maid. Did Mrs Heaviside engage you?'

'Yes, ma'am.'

'Would you like to help Carver keep me in order?'

'Oh indeed I should, ma'am.'

'Then you shall. I'll see about it at once. Heavens alive! —' pointing to the clock on the mantelpiece: 'Is that right? I'm supposed to be at Albert Gate at twelve o'clock. I must fly. Goodbye, Only Hooper, we'll be great friends, I can see – if only we get time!'

She flicked out of the room, and in a few moments I heard her riding boots clacking across the marble floor of the hall.

* * *

With the trustfulness which still remained to me from childhood, I believed that the Lady Alicia would remember our conversation and her half-promise to make me a second personal attendant; and oddly enough my trust was not abused. By a more normal being I should almost certainly have been disappointed; for fine ladies of an impulsive disposition are apt to make a kindly gesture from sheer good-heartedness and then forget all about it. But by a somersault of probabilities this mad-cap madam – of all people the most likely to default on what, after all, was not even a promise – was better than her word. That very evening she sent for me. She was lying on the sofa in her boudoir, wearing a negligée of flame-coloured silk.

'Come in, Only Hooper, and sit down on that little chair. We are now both of us off-duty and can relax for a few minutes. What have you been doing all day – working away, I suppose, while I have been enjoying myself with all the biggest bores in London. I want you to brush my hair for me. Is hair-brushing one of your accomplishments?'

I got up from the edge of the chair on which I had uncomfortably propped myself, glad to have some kind of occupation to cover the embarrassment caused by her familiarity. But she waved me back.

'Not here, silly, and not yet. Tell me about yourself. Where do you get those eyes from? You'll be a torment to the men before you're much older. Oh, the poor child is blushing! My dear Only Hooper, you mustn't mind what I say. I'm a privileged nuisance to everyone — '

There was a perfunctory knock at the door and the next moment Mr Seymore entered:

' — including my poor husband!' she finished triumphantly, and once again tilted her head and laughed like a ten-year-old.

He glanced from her to me, and as I rose respectfully I saw his eyebrows mount for a fraction of a second and sink again.

'What's this about your poor husband?' he asked good-humouredly, as he crossed the room to kiss her hand.

'Nothing, my pet, nothing but my usual silly chatter. But you must make the acquaintance of Only Hooper. For once old Nanny has found a maid I like. Only Hooper, this is your master.'

It was an absurd situation, and I could see that Mr Seymore was as flummoxed as I was. Perhaps of the two my problem was the easier, for I had only to bob and curtsey and slip from the room. But before I could reach the door I heard him call to me:

'Please do not go, if her ladyship needs you.' And to his wife: 'My dear, I must go and dress. Nanny will be as delighted as I am that her latest recruit promises so well.'

He went quickly from the room, leaving me with my unconventional mistress.

*   *   *

The Lady Alicia, at this early stage of my acquaintance with her, was a fascinating creature. She wore her dark hair in the fashion of an earlier age – with a mass of curls falling on each side of her vivid little face. It was a roundish face, with wide mock-innocent brown eyes under skilfully-arched brows, an impertinent nose and two of the freshest red lips I ever saw. They were the genuine thing in 'dewy lips' – a poetical cliché I have rarely seen matched in fact – and their smile was dazzling. She smiled a great deal, showing two rows of white even teeth and wrinkling up her nose as she did so. Her bodily movements were as lively as her features and her expression. She was not tiresomely restless, but one felt that every joint and muscle was ready for instant action, so that even when lying still she suggested something vital and simmering.

To my inexperience she was the most stimulating specimen of young womanhood imaginable; and I felt a mixture of excitement and insecurity at the thought of serving her. Certainly the task would never be dull; but I had an instinct that her gay familiarity might quickly turn to sarcasm or to cruelty, while at the back of my mind I was uneasy at her being Mr Seymore's wife. No man could desire anything more delicious to look at, or expect in his partner more buoyancy and charm. But there was a gentleness and reserve about Mr Seymore – a sort of deliberate self-withdrawal out of consideration for others – which I feared Lady Alicia might fail to appreciate and therefore abuse. In an obscure way I felt I wanted to protect him against being bruised by an intelligence less sensitive and more selfish than his own – only, next moment, to tell myself not to be silly, but to be grateful for the good luck which had brought me so kind and spirited a mistress.

Does it seem extravagant to claim ideas of this sort for a girl of my age? I can only say that they were in my mind. I believed I understood Mr Seymore and I knew that I loved him.

*   *   *

He lost little time in 'regularizing' our encounter in Lady Alicia's boudoir. Next day, when I was tidying a work-basket for Mrs Heaviside, he came quickly into the room, clearly knowing he would find me there.

'You seem to have captivated my wife, Vanny. Not an easy

thing to do, for she is a critical person and judges others by her
own standard of quickness and cleverness. I am so glad – for
both your sakes. And for my own. Anything you can do to help
her will be worth doing. Some people are like sunbeams and
can light a whole room by just entering it. They should be
relieved of the small cares we more ordinary mortals have
to cope with, so that they are free to shine as widely as
possible.'

I murmured something suitable, and he smiled at me and
left as abruptly as he had come.

*   *   *

Quick and clever she certainly was; and in her cleverness
was composed the rarer quality of tact. Of her skill in managing human beings I had immediate experience when – to my
considerable relief – I found that Miss Carver, so far from
resenting my invasion of her territory, welcomed it. It appears
that on the morning after I had first brushed my mistress' hair,
the latter had spoken to her maid with the most flattering
consideration:

'Her ladyship' Miss Carver told me, with airy relish, 'is
good enough to appreciate my mastery of what I may call *la
finesse de mon métier*. "You are a specialist, Carver" she said
"and specialists should be relieved of routine." *Your* duty,
Hooper, is therefore to wait on her ladyship in a menial
capacity – to fetch and carry, as it were – while I provide the
coups de grâce so necessary to female elegance.'

Put more simply, this meant that Miss Carver was finished
with drudgery and had become an artist. In effect, it left her
plenty of time to study the fashion-papers, devise new
methods of hairdressing and do the elaborate needlework she
loved to do, while laying on me the thousand and one tiny jobs
involved in serving a volatile, careless and desperately untidy
woman, who was always late for something, because she preferred to live in a rush and never started to get ready until the
last moment. Not that I felt ill-used. It would not have mattered if I had; but I genuinely did not. I have always had a

mind for detail and a quick orderly way of dealing with a confusion of tasks; also I was young and strong and liked running about. So the arrangement pleased everyone.

Despite my forebodings, I saw little sign for a long while of any bad temper on my mistress' part. She was sometimes impatient, and had the unreasonableness of all untidy people, who expect others to know where they have left things; but her vivacity seemed inexhaustible, and in a moment irritation would turn to laughter, as some new scheme or absurdity flashed into her mind. One thing I discovered very soon – that she was devouringly though unaffectedly vain of her own beauty and grace. It was not Lucy's kind of vanity – self-sufficient and purring to itself – but the sort which loves to share its exuberance with others. The process of beautifying Lady Alicia was a revelation to me, who had never imagined that a face and a body could receive such enraptured attention. And she liked to have me there while the ceremony was in progress; for without an audience or someone to appeal to, it would have lost half its charm for her. After her bath she would wander about the room with nothing on, examining every part of herself in the numerous long mirrors which lined the walls. There were creams to be applied, and local massage and lavender-water and powders. Then the feet and hands must be cared for, and finally the face, neck and shoulders. While I brushed her hair, she worked on her face in the mirror or polished her nails. It was then time for Miss Carver, who tripped daintily into the foreground and thenceforward took command, while I scurried about removing the debris of the earlier stages of madam's toilet.

III

Time passed, and I grew so thoroughly into the routine of my new life that Upper Belgrave Street came to represent home for me. The old Warrior days slowly frayed into shreds of childish memory. At increasingly long intervals I had letters from my mother. Her father was now a widower, and I gathered that she was fully occupied keeping house for him and her brothers, had little time for writing and could not possibly get away. At any rate she never suggested coming south to see me. But once Mr Seymore went to Aughton to visit his father and brought me back news of her and messages and a warm cloak which she had made for me.

Shortly after my sixteenth birthday – in the early summer of 1873 – dear Mrs Beckett went out on a warm but stormy morning in a thin dress, was caught in a sudden shower and drenched to the skin. Next day she had a feverish cold which turned to pneumonia. Three days later she was dead. I knew nothing of this until I received a distracted note from Lucy, saying her father was stunned by the tragedy and could I come and help her? The grievous news, and my natural wish to do anything I could to help a family who had been such good friends to me, sent me straight to my mistress. I was too wrought up to recollect that junior servants go to their seniors for leave and not to their employers, or that I was asking a considerable favour, or that I might provoke questions difficult to answer.

Lady Alicia was writing letters when I burst in upon her and, half in tears, blurted out a request for two days of freedom. She looked up from her desk and stared at me so coldly that I felt a chill of panic in the pit of my stomach.

'Say all that again please, Hooper, and stop blubbering. It makes you look hideous and I can't understand a word you say.'

With a great effort I controlled my voice and stated what had occurred.

'Here is Lucy's note, ma'am, in which she begs me to come. She is all alone, ma'am, and my oldest friend, and they were always so kind to me. . . .'

Tears choked me, and I stood crying with my eyes open, because too much in awe of Lady Alicia to cover my face with my hands. She sat there, watching me with a contemptuous frown. She made no attempt to take Lucy's letter, which fell from my hand on to the carpet and lay there, forlorn and crumpled. When at last she spoke, it was in a clipped hard voice which I had never heard her use.

'Let me get this clear. These – what ever-their-name-is – were always so kind to Hooper and one of them called Lucy is Hooper's oldest friend and therefore Hooper wants to walk out of her daily work for two days. Is that correct?'

'Oh, ma'am—'

'Silence!' she snapped 'and don't call me ma'am! Haven't you yet learnt how to address people properly? When were these worthy persons kind to you?'

'I lived with them, me lady' I began – and suddenly realized the awful blunder I had made in coming to her at all. I stopped short; but it was too late.

'Oh, you lived with them. I see. In London. Ring that bell by the fire-place.'

In a daze of misery I obeyed, and stood wishing the earth would swallow me up while in silence she waited for the bell to be answered. When a footman appeared she said:

'Tell Mrs Heaviside to come here at once.'

As the housekeeper entered the room, she flashed a look at Lady Alicia and at me. I saw the corners of her mouth tighten. With a bob of the head she waited respectfully to be spoken to.

'Heaviside, I believe you told me that Hooper had come from the country.'

'Yes, me lady.'

'How then do you account for her having lived with tradespeople or something of the kind in central London?'

'Surely not for very long, me lady? She stayed with a Mr and Mrs Beckett just before coming here, because she had things to buy and needed a little time to grow accustomed to London. The Becketts were old friends of her parents. But she *is* a country girl, me lady, as I told you.'

Lady Alicia sat for a few moments tapping her teeth with her penholder.

'Give me that note' she said to me suddenly.

I picked it up and she read it carefully.

'No address. Where is it written from?'

'Chandos Street, me lady, near Charing Cross.'

'And you want to go at once?'

'I felt I ought to, me lady.'

'Well, you must ask Mrs Heaviside. It is her duty to manage the female staff and see that I am not inconvenienced. That will do.'

She turned back to her letter-writing while, trembling with fear, I followed the housekeeper from the room. I knew that Mrs Heaviside would have plenty to say, and I was not disappointed. Once in her sitting-room, she broke out into such a fury of anger that I thought she might actually strike me. What had possessed me to go to Lady Alicia? Had I no grain of sense or slightest feeling of gratitude toward those who had done the most for me? And if I thought I had heard the last of it, I was very much mistaken. Her ladyship never forgot what one wished her to forget, and if she suddenly decided to dismiss me, what would happen then – not only to me, but to the others who knew the truth?

So she stormed on, and I had no word of excuse to offer. I merely stood and hung my head and felt the savage scolding beat me like a stick. And yet, despite the misery and dull suffering, I could not help noticing her indirect references to the real cause of my being in the house. Never before had she said a word which could possibly relate to my encounter with Mr Seymore – in her presence and in this very room – or the common knowledge which underlay it. Now, however, under stress of anger, there was tacit admission that we three were in a conspiracy together. Curiously enough this comforted me; and by the time she had worked off the worst of her indignation I had regained some degree of self-control and was able to apologize. Most humbly I begged her to forgive me. I had behaved very, very foolishly, and would never again be so selfish as to forget all she had done. If I was to suffer for my folly, I would bear my punishment alone and tell any lies to avoid involving others with my trouble. I suppose my sincerity was evident; for Mrs Heaviside spoke kindly to me at last. She said that the only important thing was to spare the master distress; that I had better get away to the Becketts at once and return in good time next day, by when she would try to discover how seriously her ladyship had taken today's unlucky incident.

*   *   *

When I reached Chandos Street I found the shop shuttered. Lucy, looking lovelier than ever in a plain black dress, opened the house-door and whispered that her aunt Mattie had arrived to take charge, that the funeral was that very afternoon and that her father was a little better. The regent-aunt was the sister of the dead woman and not unlike her in build and appearance; but it was soon clear that she lacked the calm forcefulness of Mrs Beckett and that Lucy's attitude toward her was one of sullen dislike. Mr Beckett I did not see until the funeral, to which of course we all went. The poor man was waxen-pale and seemed only half awake. As we stood by the open grave, he clung to his daughter's arm as though stupefied. Mr Walkinshaw was at the cemetery. He did not speak, but greeted us with a deep and dismal bow. When at last we had returned home and drunk a cup of tea, Lucy and I retired to our old bedroom for a talk. The reaction after my hours of strain showed itself in sudden levity.

'Oh, Lucy, I must laugh at something and it shall be Walkinshaw. He was in his element, wasn't he? He ought to be a professional mourner. I'm sure he'd make more money than as a bookseller.'

Lucy smiled absently, but did not reply, and I could see that her mind was full of other things. Fancying that it would help her to forget her grief if I chattered on for a while, I began describing my dreadful interview with Lady Alicia and the subsequent trouncing from Mrs Heaviside. I did not repeat the mistake of betraying a secret which was not mine to betray, but attributed the whole trouble to my having stupidly gone over the housekeeper's head to the mistress and so offended them both.

'So you see, my dear' I concluded 'I have been through quite a deal to get here, and I'm sure I hope you are suitably glad to see me!'

'Oh, I *am*" she cried 'far gladder than you can guess.'

'Poor darling' I soothed her. 'It is dreadful for you; and if *I* feel I have lost one of my dearest friends, what must *you* feel?'

To my surprise, she replied quickly:

'Oh it isn't that — ' then corrected herself: 'At least it *is*, of course, but not *only* that. . . .'

Glancing at her I saw her eyes were dry and queerly strained, and that she was sitting bolt upright on the edge of the bed as though rigid with some nervous suppression.

'Lucy!' I said. 'What is the matter?'

She swallowed hard, and I could feel her gathering herself together to say what she meant to say. Suddenly it came:

'I must leave here. I can't stay, now that mamma is dead.'

I stared at her in astonishment.

'Can't stay here? What *do* you mean, Lucy? Where will you go?'

'I'll find somewhere to go. The main thing is that I can't stay – and I won't. I hate Aunt Mattie, who is a muddling old fuss, and – and – well, I had a horrid thing happen to me the other evening. You are the only person I can tell about it, for papa – poor darling – would only lose his head and do something silly. Besides' she added inconsequently 'I want to get on in life.'

'Lucy' I said severely, 'what in the world are you talking about? Pull yourself together, please, and start at the beginning.'

She laughed, with a swift and rather disconcerting return to her normal ease of manner.

'I don't know which beginning to choose. This end or t'other. This perhaps.' She sat silent for a moment smiling oddly at her own crossed feet, and I noticed with half my mind how balanced and 'finished' she looked, with her pale golden hair beautifully dressed, her perfect skin and the graceful droop of her shoulders. Then she spoke:

'This end is Walkinshaw, whom you thought funny a little while ago. I don't think him funny and this is why. A few evenings ago – the second day mamma was ill – I came in as usual from work about six o'clock. As I walked along the passage to come upstairs, the door from the shop opened and old Jerks looked out. 'I was listening for you, Miss Lucy' he said. 'The doctor is upstairs with Mr Beckett, and would you please wait down here till they are finished.' I followed him into the shop which was half in darkness, for although it was still daylight, only the gas over the desk at the back was burning and the books in the window keep out the light. I asked how mamma was, and he said she was not at all well. By this time we were near the desk, behind the big book-case which cuts it off from the shop. A big square book was lying open on the table by the safe, and, seeing it was illustrated, I bent over to look at the pictures – as much to pass the time and relieve the awkwardness of waiting in the shop as because I wanted to see it.

'And what do you think, Fanny? It was full of pictures of girls without their clothes – not statues, you know, or classical pictures or anything all right; but just Girls – like us. Next minute Walkey seized me from behind, put his hands over my chest and began to kiss the back of my neck. It was dreadful, Fanny!'

'What happened then?'

'Well, naturally I wrenched round, but before I could get free he was kissing me on the mouth like a mad thing. His eyes were all bright – and, oh, greedy. But I went on struggling and at last he let me go and I said: 'How dare you! My father...' and he merely laughed and said Mr Beckett was much too worried about his wife to listen to a hysterical girl who could prove nothing, and anyway what about...'

She broke off abruptly.

'What about what?' I said.

Her eyes swerved away.

'Oh nothing' she said carelessly. 'I don't remember anyway.'

'Come along, Lucy' I insisted. 'What about what?'

'Oh' (reluctantly) 'some silly nonsense about the week before.'

'What happened the week before?'

'Good heavens alive, Fanny, what a plague you are! I only let him kiss me one evening in the shop.'

'*You let Walkinshaw kiss you?* A creature who can't even keep his mouth still!'

She pouted.

'I wanted to see what it felt like. But that didn't mean ... well, anyway ... I wasn't going to have him messing me about, as I showed him – the dirty beast!'

'How did you show him?'

'I smacked his face and ran out!'

For a few moments I considered this unconvincing story. Then I said (perhaps rather priggishly):

'You *are* a pig, Lucy! You've been flirting with him, I'm sure you have. I should have been terrified. Men are so funny; I don't understand them a bit.'

She glanced at me under her eyelashes and giggled. My remark seemed to give her back the confidence which, for all her nonchalance of a few minutes earlier, she had nearly lost.

'Why should you, poor innocent?' she said derisively. 'Perhaps one day ...' And she flung herself back on the bed and hummed a little tune, swinging her pretty legs.

Immediately I felt abashed and inferior. But a strain of doggedness in me and a long standing affection for my friend kept me on the track of our original argument.

'I am afraid I was unsympathetic' I said quietly. 'Naturally I am very sorry you had such a nasty experience. Now tell me from the other end – why you cannot stay here, because you want to get on in life.'

In an instant she was transformed from a mocking enemy to a confiding intimate. She sat up and leant forward, elbows on knees.

'Yes, Fanny; and here you can help me. In Henderson and

White's one of the workroom supervisors has been specially nice to me. The other day she walked part of the way home with me and said she was surprised I did not go to one of the dress-shops where they had live girls to show off the dresses. They won't do anything of that kind at Henderson's – too old-fashioned. She told me the money was better and a girl made all kinds of acquaintances. When I showed interest, she told me she had a friend in Neldé's in Brook Street – very smart – and would speak to her about me. Well, she did; and I went to see this other woman and I'm going there very soon.'

'But Brook Street is no farther from here than Henderson and White's.'

'You *are* stupid, Fanny. If I go to Neldé's and get more money I can share rooms with a friend and so get away from Aunt Mattie and that nasty Jerks. I could never have gone into lodgings while mamma was alive. She wouldn't have heard of it. But *now* I can. Aunt Mattie will look after papa and be glad to be rid of me.'

I had an unpleasant feeling that poor Mrs Beckett's death seemed to her daughter a release rather than a grievous loss; but it was not my business to challenge Lucy's feeling for her mother, so I merely said:

'And how can I help you? It appears to be all settled.'

Lucy came over to the armchair in which I was sitting and, perching on the arm, rubbed herself caressingly against me.

'If you could get Lady Alicia to come to Neldé's and buy some dresses, it would help me enormously. She is well known for her smart clothes and ... and ... a girl who brings a fashionable customer gets all kind of advantages. Dear Fanny, will you try to do this for me?'

I almost laughed; but she was so serious I kept a grave face.

'If Lady Alicia ever consults me as to where to get her clothes, I will suggest Neldé. But it is only fair to warn you that up to now she has not been within a mile of doing any such thing, and after this morning's upset will certainly never think of it.'

'But if she *does*, you won't forget?'

'Oh, no' I replied sincerely. 'I promise you I won't forget.'

* * *

When I got back to work the following morning, everything seemed more or less normal. Miss Carver greeted me with elegant gravity and hoped I had been able to bring a little consolation into the *maison de douleur*. She added that in her view we poor mortals are here today and gone tomorrow, and must therefore be prepared for anything.

When Lady Alicia rang for me, I set my teeth and, inwardly trembling but outwardly calm, entered her presence. She was a little cool and made no reference to my absence or the cause of it; but her general attitude was friendly enough. Mrs Heaviside, whom I did not see till the afternoon, merely said that nothing further had transpired and that sleeping dogs had better lie. The third housemaid, who had done my duty the night before, reminded me that I owed her at least half a day, and if I thought to get off it I was badly mistaken. Thereafter life went on as before.

I thought a good deal of my conversation with Lucy Beckett and how different she was becoming from the girl I had known. It shocked me that her mother's death affected her so little – or rather that it affected her in the way it did. No mother could have treated a daughter more wisely or more unselfishly than Mrs Beckett; but all that seemed to have remained in Lucy's memory were the restraints which had been put on her liberty and the obstacles which a mother's prudent affection had set in the way of youthful exuberance. Over the adventure with Mr Walkinshaw I pondered deeply. I knew nothing of masculine desire, save what could be gathered from novel-reading or deduced from the general atmosphere of 'a girl cannot be too careful' in which my generation was brought up. But instinct told me that Lucy, to feed her own vanity, had been playing with fire, and now blamed on someone else the fact that she had burnt her fingers. Obscurely I felt that the young bookseller – however wrongly he had behaved – would never have attempted to interfere with his employer's daughter without some kind of encouragement. It was my first experience of the meanest of all feminine traits, and little though I understood what had happened, I was even then disgusted with Lucy's behaviour.

There remained the change-over from Henderson and White's to Madame Neldé's. The former was, I knew, a highly reputable concern, with a first-class clientèle and a reputation for treating its employees with severity but justice. It was an expensive shop; but the people who dealt there were well-to-do, and I had always understood that for good quality, material and workmanship and for dignified and restrained design Henderson and White were as reliable as any firm in London. Of Neldé I knew nothing but the name; and as soon as opportunity offered I looked through the pile of fashion papers which lay in Miss Carver's room and read the advertisements and paragraphs in which the shop and its wares were described. Ignorant though I was, I could see that Neldé frocks and lingeries were essentially 'smart'. Indeed by comparison, creations by Henderson and White and their chief competitors looked slightly monotonous. I asked Miss Carver her opinion. She admitted to admiration of the elegance of Neldé productions, but expressed disapproval of their ostentation and of the kind of people who wore them. I gathered that Neldé's clientèle was largely *parvenu* – consisting of the wives and daughters and *autres choses* of the new rich who at this period were invading society. Casual and innocent I asked whether Lady Alicia ever went there, and was primly reproved for even suggesting such a thing. Miledi, said Miss Carver, was much too *comme il faut* to deal in such mixed company.

None of this seemed to have much bearing on Lucy and her change of work. It was obvious that the life spent in showing off beautiful clothes would appeal to her love of self-adornment, and to want to earn more money was perfectly natural. All the same I had a faint suspicion that there was something more in the affair than a mere transfer from one job to a better one. 'A girl makes all kind of acquaintances' the overseer at

Henderson's had said. How would that help? I could see that a clever show-girl might get to know some of the rich women who came to buy; but what could they do for her beyond being friendly and increasing her commission on sales? The problem baffled me and I gave it up, merely deciding that, if I were in Lucy's place, I would far rather come back every evening to a comfortable home than live with another girl in frowsty lodgings. But she thought otherwise, and it was her affair, not mine.

IV

The new pattern of Lucy's existence did not immediately deprive me of my nearest approach to a home in London, because she planned to return to Chandos Street for Saturday night and most of Sunday, and I could still go there for my free afternoons. But I found on my very first visit under the changed conditions that without Mrs Beckett the place was not the same. Aunt Mattie did her best, and Mr Beckett, who in his gentle way was always glad to see me, made me specially welcome; yet the household had really disintegrated, with Lucy nearly as much a visitor as I and, in the place of her mother's shrewd serenity, the flustered mass of Aunt Mattie's self-distrust.

On this particular Sunday Lucy seized on me the moment I arrived and hurried me into her room.

'Fanny, what *do* you think's happened? Walkey has run away!'

'Run away? Nonsense. Why should he run away?'

'I don't know *why*, but he has – ten days or more ago – Daddy is in a great state. Someone came to the house-door to ask something and Daddy was upstairs, and when he went into the shop, the man who-ever-he-was had left, the place was empty. Walkey had been there half an hour earlier, because Daddy was in the shop with him. Now he's gone – with his hat and stick and some odd belongings he kept in a drawer, and has never been seen or heard of since.'

'What a silly thing to do' I said.

'Silly! I should think it was, with a week's money due, the very next day. Daddy kept thinking he'd turn up; but he hasn't, nor sent a word of any sort.'

'Has Mr Beckett got someone else?'

'He's trying to now. He didn't like to start getting someone at once, in case Jerks came back.'

'Well' I said 'he hasn't, so that's settled. What a nuisance for poor Mr Beckett! Anyway I hope the new man won't be quite so attractive to his employer's daughter —'

She threw a cushion at me and we talked of other things.

It was an eventful afternoon, for hardly had we sat down to tea, when there came a ring at the street-door. I was nearest the stairs and ran down to see who was there.

Standing on the pavement was an immense and familiar figure – a man with the shoulders of a bull and a large purple-red face, on top of which, considerably too small, perched a brown bowler-hat.

'Chunks!' I cried. 'Chunks, by all that's wonderful! Oh, I *am* so glad to see you, and where *have* you been all this time?'

Jumping the two steps which raised the door above street-level, I flung my arms round as much of him as they could contain, knocking his hat askew and even causing him to sway on his feet. I felt his big hands close under my arms and myself being lifted bodily into the air. He set me down, still holding me firmly, and beamed at me, while a slow chuckle began rumbling upward from his stomach to the heavy folds of his cheeks.

'Bless my soul' he wheezed. 'It's Fannikins erself, *and* grown into a fine young lady. Eh, it does me good to see you again. Let me ave a look at you, me dear.'

He swung me to the left, then to the right, then turned me completely round to see my back hair, and finally, releasing his grip of my body, took me by the hands and shook them up and down so vigorously that my arms ached.

'Chunks!' I panted. 'For pity's sake let me go! You can't behave like this in the street. Please!'

He dropped my hands at once, took off his hat and began mopping his bald head, over which a single lock of hair was, as always, carefully combed fanwise from right to left.

'Do come in' I said. 'Mr Beckett will like to see you. And I want to know why you've never looked me up all this time.'

'No, me dear' he said. 'I won't come in – not now. It's you I want to see, and they told me you'd likely be ere today. If not, I would ave left a message with my address. I didn't know ow else to find you except through Becketts.'

'Have you been here before, then, looking for me?'

'Was ere a matter of two weeks ago and – but that can wait, with all the other things I ave to tell you and questions to ask and such. When can you spare a little time for a chat, eh? – somewhere where we'll not be disturbed.'

'Where are you living now?' I asked.

From the pocket of his reefer coat he extracted a rather grimy bit of paper and handed it to me.

'I was goin' to leave this for ye' he said. 'That's where I am, and a cosy little place enough though ardly the neighbourhood for smart young gels.'

On the paper in very blunt pencil was scrawled:

Joe Box (Chunks)
Jolly Bargee, River Row, Lower Street
Islington

'Joe Box! I never knew you were Joe Box!' I exclaimed gaily. 'And a public with the same initials! I believe I like you better than ever now, Chunks – I beg your pardon – Mr. J. B. of the J. B.!'

He gurgled hoarsely.

'Get along with you, Miss Imperence, teasing yer old friend! And why shouldn't I ave a name like other folk – like Miss Fanny Opwood, for example —'

The shadow of the past fell suddenly over my cheerful nonsense and reminded me that I also had much to tell him.

'I am Fanny Hooper now' I said quietly 'and had almost forgotten I was ever anything else. I'll tell you why when we meet again. As for when that shall be, my next free Sunday is today three weeks.'

He made no comment on the first part of my remark, save to cock an eye at me and then nod his head solemnly. Muttering 'Today three weeks', and with much grunting and wheezing, he disinterred from an inside pocket a large notebook, the pages of which he began to turn with a laborious thumb. 'That'll be the tenth' he said, and made a note in his book. On the tenth, he declared, he would be at Hyde Park Corner at any time I said and we'd go to Rosherville Gardens and have a good talk and enjoy ourselves.

'Lovely' I cried. 'I'll be there at two o'clock sharp in my best bib and tucker, and you'd better know my address in case anything goes wrong. Give me the book and pencil and I'll write it for you.'

I gave him a parting hug, and was watching him lumber round the corner of Bedford Street, when I heard Lucy's voice from the doorway:

'Heavens alive, Fanny, what *are* you up to? We waited and waited, and I began to think you'd been kidnapped or something.'

'I've had a visitor' I said primly.

'You can't have a visitor out in the street, silly, and why didn't she come in – or' (suddenly interested) 'perhaps it wasn't a she?'

'Please yourself, Miss Curious.'

'Fanny, don't be a pig! Do tell me what's been happening.'

'Well, if you *must* know, I've been invited by a gentleman friend to spend a whole afternoon and evening at Rosherville.'

'Fanny! How exciting! When? Who is he?'

'Aha, that *would* be telling, wouldn't it?'

'Beast! I shall shake you. No, Fanny, you might tell me.'

After teasing her a few moments more I asked her if she remembered Chunks in the Warrior days. She nodded.

'Well, that's him.'

'Oh, that fat old man!' she exclaimed contemptuously. 'What a fuss about nothing!'

* * *

Three weeks dragged by and the day came at last. I slipped away from table before the others had finished, made myself as presentable as I knew how, and was out of the house ahead of time. As I reached the corner of Grosvenor Place I could see Chunks on the pavement outside Apsley House. He looked very grand, even at a distance, and as I got nearer I took in one by one the details of his costume. He wore a white top-hat, swathed round the brim with a muslin scarf loosely knotted at the back; a black coat with short tails and wide silk lapels; a crimson rose in the right-hand button-hole; a fawn waistcoat; a black satin cravat spotted in white and embellished with a large gold pin in the shape of a horse-shoe; tight fawn trousers with very large dark red checks, and shiny black boots. I never saw anyone so splendidly dressed for the Derby who was not going to it. Probably to strange eyes he appeared vulgar and absurd; but the mere sight of him made me warm with affectionate pleasure and, while I dodged the traffic in Knightsbridge, I determined to play a small joke on him. I slipped into the Park, crossed the carriage-roads on the north side of the gateway and came out again immediately behind him. Coming quietly up from the back, I put my hand through his arm and said demurely in his ear:

'Good afternoon, sir. Shall we take a little walk?'

He was very startled, especially as he did not immediately recognize me with my hair in a chignon and a hat like a small boat tilted over my forehead. But next moment his round red face lighted up:

'Well, I never!' he chuckled 'and oo taught you to pick up old men in the street, I'd like to know? It's into a ansom with you, my pretty minx, before ye get up to any more mischief.'

Laughing gaily, I hugged his arm as we walked towards Piccadilly.

A hansom to London Bridge through the leisured Sunday

streets; a train just caught; and in due course we were on the famous terrace of Rosherville, with the gardens at our feet, beyond them the lazy river, and in the distance the Tilbury marshes, their dreary levels broken only by the square fort and the cluster of buildings round the station. Our first business being to talk rather than see the sights, we found a quiet tea-place and settled down.

First of all he asked for my news. I gave him a rapid account of what had happened to me, suppressing all mention of Mr Seymore having visited my mother, but indicating that I was in service in the house of a gentleman of this name, and that my mother had advised me to call myself Hooper.

When I had finished, he shook his head and patted my hand:

'Eh, Fannikins' he sighed. 'It makes me sad to think of yer poor mother and the Warrior and ow it all ended. But it cheers me to see you well and appy, and not too grand a young lady to welcome an old friend. You were a merry little kid and now you're a pretty girl and still merry.'

'You know, Chunks' I said 'no one ever called me Fannikins but you. Nor ever will. Do you remember how I used to climb up you, singing:

> *Oh Mister Chunky!*
> *Here comes Fanny the Monkey.'*

He smiled his heavy creased smile.

'Ay, and you dug your little knees into me good and proper.'

'And do you remember' I went on 'how you used to lift me up so my head touched the ceiling and then suddenly swoop me down to the floor? And holding me in one hand, how you swung me right round in a circle and shouted "Now for the big bump!" but always put me down quite gently?'

'Dearie me' he said. 'That's all gone by now and won't come again. But you and me are always friends, Fannikins; don't forget that. While old Chunks is alive, e's on yer side. So, if ever life treats you bad or you want someone to take yer part, you've only to come to me. There is several I know as will

stand by you for the old Warrior's sake and with them and me
– doin it for *your* sake and yer mamma's also – you'll come out
all right.'

'Dear Chunks' I murmured, squeezing his huge hand. 'You'll
make me cry if you talk like that. But thank you from my
heart. I won't forget.'

There was a short silence. Then he cleared his throat with a
harsh roar, and began humming and hawing and shifting in his
seat.

'What's the matter, Chunks?'

'Just this, me dear – that I ave things to tell you and don't
know ow to say them.'

'Say them anyhow at all, you old silly. I only want to listen.'

With an effort he began to speak:

'Ow much do you know about the end of the Warrior? Not
much, maybe. Well, there are some things you ought to know,
and if I tell em clumsily and frighten or shock you, blame it on
stupid old Chunks oo did his best.'

'You won't shock me' I said 'and I don't mind if you do.'

He then proceeded to tell me a lot of the things I have
already mentioned. He told me about the existence of Hades
(did I recollect when he had found me there and brought me
upstairs?) but few details; about the cubicles behind the main
window of the tavern – but again few details; about the police
raid and what they found in the cupboard.

'From that moment' he said 'I swore to myself to find out oo
it was sent the guvnor to his death – for dead e is, a matter of
twelve months ago, and of a broken eart. Well, now I think I
ave found out – at least I ave me suspicions. And if ever I can
prove em there'll be a reckonin.'

I had listened to his story, absorbed and horrified.

'Tell me' I whispered.

'First of all I run into the doorman of the basement place –
ex-boxer called Grabbett. We got talkin of the old days and
who could've ad a grudge against the guvnor and e recalled a
quarrel and a fight early one mornin between Mr Opwood and
a drunken lord. The quarrel was about a kid girl oo this ere

lord ad brought with him into Ades one night. Mr Opwood
allowed none of that. E was very particular in is way. That set
me thinkin, and I asked myself ow that other kid's body they
found later could've been got into the cupboard on the Warrior
floor. It couldn't ave come up through the basement, for
it could never ave passed the doorman, specially after the
fight. Therefore it must've been smuggled from the Warrior
itself. And then – rememberin's funny – I thought of somethin
else. There used to come to the Warrior a youngish man who
bet on orses igher than e could afford. E sometimes won, but
more often lost; and I was told that at one meeting e ad lost
more than e could ever pay. Certainly we saw no more of im
for quite a while. Then one evenin to my surprise e turned up
again, not a bit down in the mouth, carryin one of them big
boxes they use for them large size violins – what are they
called?'

' ''Cellos' I suggested.

'That's the thing – 'cellos – a 'cello case e ad, and freer with
is money than ever before. They told me e boasted of avin got
a job in some orchestra and ow well e was doing. E came in
several times after that, always with the case and always
standin treat to whoever e was with.

'An' I remembered another thing about this same cove.
Early on, before e came a cropper over the orses, e used to go
to the side seats arf-way up the big room. But when e began
comin again as a musical gent, e sat at one of the small tables
along the partition I was tellin you about, puttin is case down
against the wall if you take me, so it was out of the way of
other folks comin and goin.

'This give me an idea and I thought some more, and I
recollected that one evenin not long before the smash I'd gone
out on some errand for the guvnor, and one of them chaps
from downstairs ad taken my place. I wasn't away more than
an hour, and after I'd been back on duty some little while, out
comes my fiddler gentleman with is at at an angle and wishin
me goodnight gay as a cricket. I must've noticed at the time e
ad no case and yet not noticed, because it come back to me

when I thought about it all, and I set myself to find the chap oo ad been on the door. I found im at last (name of Sturt, doin ostler e is now at Endon) and asked im what e could remember.'

'But Chunks, he couldn't possibly remember, weeks or months afterwards, any one man coming casually into the Warrior!'

'Ah. But you wait, Fannikins. It was long odds against im rememberin, that I grant you; but our gentleman ad a funny thing about im, like you don't often see, and that made me ope Sturt might've noticed im. And e ad, and was sure that when the bloke went into the public e was carryin is case, because Sturt offered to look after it for im, like we did with strangers, and he said no.'

He paused triumphantly; but when I made as if to speak, he held up his hand.

'One moment, me dear. Let me finish. I worried the ole thing over in the light of what Sturt said and I'd seen, and saw ow the trick was worked. Someone had paid this chap – and paid im well – to come regler to the Warrior with is 'cello so everyone ud get used to im. On an agreed night the door from the cubicles would be opened from the inside, the chap would've put is case down across the door on the outside – with the table in front of it, if you understand – and easy as wink the bag would be drawn through the door and in it the poor kid's body all ready for stringin up. See?'

This grievous story shocked me badly, and for a few minutes I could only sit, feeling bruised and frightened. But I pulled myself together, for he had clearly more to say and I had promised him not to give way. With an effort I said:

'Oh, how *horrible*! That such things can happen.... And why should anyone do such a wicked thing to poor papa? And what was there funny about the man with the bag?'

'As for one' replied Chunks solemnly, 'the lord oo got knocked out by the guvnor for bringing a *live* child into Ades wouldn't forget, and it would suit is kind of blackguard mind to take revenge with a dead one. As for two, this Mister

Fiddler ad a twitch in is face – a real fierce one too, like he was screwin back is lips and snarlin. Once you seen it you couldn't forget it. Like Sturt didn't forget it.'

I stared at him, struggling to arrange the thoughts which tumbled over one another in my astonished mind.

'A twitch. . . . I've seen a man like that . . . often . . . in Beckett's shop . . . and he vanished suddenly a month or so ago.'

'Vanished it is, Fannikins, and I'll tell you for why. You're on it right enough. That's the villain, that very chap oo was at Becketts till a month or more ago. The time I went there to inquire after you, while I was waitin in the street for Mrs Who-is-it to find Mr Beckett, I appened to glance through the window of the bookshop and there inside the shop was the very man. I saw im plain as I used to see im in the Warrior, but unluckily e also saw me. I whipped out of sight quick but it was too late. E'd seen me and I knew it. I couldn't do any-thing. I'd no proof except me own certainty, and e'd deny ever avin eard of the Warrior if I challenged im. Why should Mr Beckett or anyone else believe me against im? They'd think I'd invented the ole story. So I come away and done the only thing I could do – put a sharp boy on to keep an eye on our friend and find out all e could. But two days later the chap give im the slip and never been seen since.'

I digested this amazing coincidence in silence. I wondered if, by discreet questioning at Becketts, I would be able to find out how Walkinshaw had come there and where he had lived. Then I remembered the German girl and their alleged walking-out. I mentioned this to Chunks, who wrote down the name of the pastrycooks in his famous notebook and said he would make inquiries. It was not very hopeful, but better than nothing.

'What about the lord?' I asked finally. 'Do you know who he is?'

Chunks nodded.

'Ay, I know who e is safe enough. Is name is Manderstoke.'

*   *   *

We had long finished our tea, and I was exhausted by the strain and loathsomeness of Chunks' grisly tale.

'I can't stand any more horrors today' I said. 'There is more I'd like to know about what happened after papa's arrest and about what you've been doing. But not now. Let's walk about and have a look at everything.'

And we set off to explore Rosherville.

For those who never saw this – to my unsophisticated eyes – enchanted place, I must explain that it was originally a large chalk quarry. The steep cliffs were skilfully planted with all manner of rare trees and shrubs; paths and rough staircases led in and out and up and down; caves were lit with rows of gas-jets, and flower-beds blazed with various colours. Right along the crest of the long cliff ran the Terrace. At one corner rose a Tower, only built a few years before my first visit, with battle-mented top and a gallery high up, from which the whole panorama of river and countryside could be seen like a map. The flat bottom of the vast quarry was given over to amuse-ments. There was a bear-pit; a dance-floor with a bandstand in the middle; a maze; a baronial banquet-hall; fortune-tellers' booths; bowling greens and all manner of other side shows.

But the real popularity of Rosherville lay in its kindness to lovers. There were bowers and alcoves in every corner, secluded seats and lonely paths between hedges of flowering shrubs, and after dusk the place assumed a new and exciting life. Fairy-lamps twinkled round the dance-floor and among the trees; the band played, and eager crowds of young people flocked into the gardens for their evening of gaiety and romance. With the fading of daylight the very air seemed to become charged with yearning and tenderness. Whispers and laughter floated out from the shadows, while the summer breeze rustled the tree-tops.

Nowadays, when the despised Victorians are labelled as tyrannical and prudish, the freedom of Rosherville would simply be disbelieved. But I can assure you that the sweet-smelling luxuriant gardens were for lovers to use as they wished, and with no one to interfere save to prevent rowdiness or breaches of the peace. I know what I am saying; for though naturally my afternoon and evening with Chunks had a special justification of their own, I went more than once later on, and was grateful to Rosherville as much for its indulgence as its beauty.

In order to be back in time I had to leave about eight o'clock. But it was dark enough by then for the gardens to have assumed their evening garb; and the magical effect of lights and gaiety, with mysterious shadows cloaking a hundred happy privacies, completed the cure of my lacerated mind. I was now not only soothed and content, but vaguely expectant. Of what I hardly knew. A last-minute incident might have told me; but not until later, when no telling was needed, did I see its significance. At the time, though I stirred in my sleep, I was not yet awake.

On our way to the main gate Chunks and I passed through a coppice of small trees, in the centre of which – just withdrawn from the path – was a pillared summer-house. The white columns glimmered in the semi-darkness; the interior lay in deep shadow. Suddenly the ray of coloured light, which by a device in the Tower could be thrown over adjacent areas of the gardens and was considered one of the prettiest of the many marvels of Rosherville, struck through the branches of the trees and for an instant lit every corner of the tiny temple. In that moment of illumination I saw, as plainly as though in broad daylight, a girl lying limply in a man's arms. Her head was thrown back and her eyes were closed; the shoulder I could see was bare, and a slim white arm swung loosely by her side. Of the man only a head of dark hair was visible, for his face was buried in her throat.

v

If I have seemed to neglect what was inevitably the most important element in my life at Upper Belgrave Street – my relations with my father – it is because their development was so gradual and so indefinite that it can hardly be described in words. The position was inherently a delicate one. Only Mrs Heaviside was in the secret; and the three of us had to conduct our campaign of discretion on two fronts. If Mr Seymore was unable to give any sign which might betray the situation to his wife or friends, it was equally important that my fellow-servants should not think me more intimate with my employer than my work justified. Fortunately, having slipped into an intermediate position in the household – half auxiliary-lady's-maid and half general factotum on the upper floors – I was expected to divide my time between Miss Carver and the housekeeper and take orders from both. It was easy for Mrs Heaviside to arrange that I should be at her disposal from after midday dinner until six o'clock, and I regularly spent this portion of the day (apart from the hour of freedom permitted three times a week) in or about her room.

Lady Alicia, unless she were entertaining, seldom spent her afternoons at home. She would drive out to do shopping or to visit an exhibition or to pay calls, returning between six and seven to dress for dinner – a ceremony which demanded considerable preparations and, in its early stages, my personal attendance.

I learnt that Mr Seymore's official work did not as a rule keep him in Whitehall much after four o'clock. It had been his custom to go from his office to his club and stay there until he had to come home to dress. But he now made an occasional practice – on afternoons when his wife was out – of coming home earlier and spending an hour in the housekeeper's room, either with the two of us or with me alone. He was careful not to do this with any regularity, and that he should now and again like to go and sit with Mrs Heaviside caused no surprise to Mr Croggon or Mr Olley, for everyone knew she had been his nurse and a second mother to him. Nor did they – as conventional men-servants might well have done – despise him for his familiarity with one who, though he had known her for years, was still an employee. The butler, for all his pulpit manner, was a kindly, simple soul, and the valet had been Mr Seymore's personal servant for many years and thought his

master could do no wrong. There was some quality in the
Seymore family (as I discovered when I went to Aughton)
which enabled them to treat their servants with friendly informality and still retain their respect. In consequence the
Yorkshire household, and that portion of the London one over
which Mr Seymore ruled, were contented and harmonious to a
degree rare at any time.

Of the pleasure and benefit I myself had from the time
spent with my father I find it hard to speak. The slight
awkwardness there had at first been between us – embarrassment on his part and timidity on mine – soon disappeared. He
greeted me, whether the housekeeper was there or not, as any
man would greet a daughter of whom he was fond. After inquiring into my doings he would talk freely of his own, of
events in the great world, of amusing or interesting things seen
or heard. I did everything I could to train myself to intelligent
listening. I never failed, at some moment during the day, to
get hold of the newspaper and read the sort of news of which
he would be likely to speak. If he mentioned a book, I asked if
he could lend it to me, and read it with devoted care in odd
minutes and after I had gone to bed. I had to come to some
understanding with Clara Williams about night-reading; but
self-education was a good deal in the air at that time, and she
not only accepted my aspirations with placid approval but
even began to share them, bringing back from her uncle's
house cheap textbooks on architecture and odd numbers of the
trade journals taken in and read by builders. There now seems
something a little comic in the thought of two domestic
servants still in their teens, reading away by candle-light under
the slates of Belgravia. But we were both deadly serious, and –
as girls will, when they are determined to improve their minds
– found real satisfaction in fuddling our brains and spoiling
our eyes.

Now that the masks were down, I was naturally on different
terms with Mrs Heaviside. She maintained her briskly auto-
cratic manner during working hours, calling me 'Hooper' and
ordering me here and there with the sharp iteration of a rattle

of musketry. At other times – when she decided we were off duty – she became amicable and often confidential. But she was never familiar. Her attitude was a masterly blend of friendliness and discipline. I was dear Mr Clive's daughter and was therefore entitled to affection; but I was by no means 'Miss Vandra Seymore' and must not be permitted to fancy myself anything of the sort. As I had not the least desire to do so, I bore Mrs Heaviside no grudge for keeping me reminded of my peculiar position; and for the sake of her gossip about old times and the stories she could tell of my father's boyhood, I would cheerfully have borne far harsher treatment.

When she was in the humour she loved to talk of Aughton; of Mr Clive's birth and of his mother's death after childbed; of poor Sir Everard's despairing grief; of the ailing babyhood of this only child and of the long fight put up by her and others to secure his slow growth to healthy, if delicate, boyhood.

She told me that his second name was Andrew, but that it had never to her knowledge been used. Instantly I seized on this as the name which I in my secret thoughts would call him. I had to have some name of my own for him – some name which, when I spoke it silently, would bring him before my mind's eye. Here was one which belonged to *him*, but had never belonged to that part of his life from which I must always be excluded. So I took 'Andrew' to my heart, and with it my own special Clive Seymore.

One afternoon, when he was not coming to see us and the housekeeper seemed in an approachable mood, I took my courage in both hands and asked a long-contemplated question.

'Nanny, why did Mr Clive marry?'

She looked sharply over her glasses.

'Why do most men marry, my dear? Because they want a wife and a home of their own of course.'

'No. I don't mean that. Why did he marry – as he did?'

'Her ladyship is the daughter of the Earl of Hillmorton' said Mrs Heaviside, with a sort of chilly formality.

For a moment I was tempted to do what she clearly wanted

me to do – drop the subject. But in a quiet way I am a persistent person, and I knew that if I yielded now I should never have the pluck to start again.

'But why is that a reason, Nanny? I thought a man married a girl because he loved her, not because she was —' Suddenly realizing where this remark was leading me, I stopped short, felt myself go hot all over, and sat there crimson with mortification and self-reproof. The old lady with true delicacy of feeling came to my rescue, and continued the conversation as though nothing had happened.

'So he does, Fanny, if he is free to do so. But sometimes he needs money for his career or to get into a different society or have someone to do his entertaining, which there's no denying her ladyship does to perfection. Mind you, I am not saying any of this applied to Mr Clive. It's no wonder if he fell in love with someone as pretty as her ladyship; beauty goes all the way with most men, as you'll likely find out, not having much of it.'

I smiled ruefully, and told myself I had already guessed something of the kind through being much with Lucy Beckett; but, having now recovered composure, I went doggedly on with my argument.

'Well, even if he *was* in love with her once, I don't believe he is now. Not one bit.'

'Hush, my dear! You mustn't say such things – particularly as you know nothing about it. Mr Clive and her ladyship get along very well together.'

'Yes!' I flashed 'by not being together any more than they can help!'

'Fanny! Control yourself! That was not a polite thing to say – not polite to me or to the master and mistress of the house we live in. You are much too young to understand these things – still less to lay down the law about them – and we will now talk about something else.'

'Oh, Nanny!' I cried 'I am so sorry! Please forgive me. It was very wrong of me to say that. Do be kind and tell me some more. I promise I won't interrupt.'

She looked at me sharply, and I suppose was convinced that I was really sorry, for, though her next words were tartly spoken, I could see that she was appeased:

'Tell you some more?' she said. 'I don't recall telling you anything so far.'

'You were going to explain to me about men needing money when they marry or to get into society or something.'

'I said *sometimes*.'

'Yes, Nanny dear; but you meant that Mr Seymore was one of the "sometimes", didn't you?'

'H'm! You're sharp, girl; I'll say that for you. And suppose I did?'

'What did he need?' I coaxed. 'Was it money or family connections?'

She rose beautifully to the bait, as befitted a true English-woman of the old school to whom most peerages were new-fangled rubbish.

'Money or family indeed! I should think not! Sir Everard is sounder and better gentry than a dozen flashy lords. "Money or family".' She snorted. 'Well, I never!' Then went on (for she was now wound up to talk) 'No – it was this way, if you must know. When Mr Clive had been what they call an attachy at several places abroad – he went without pay you see, to gain experience and so on – he decided he wanted to enter the Government service altogether. Sir Everard knew a man high up who said he could get Mr Clive a post, but he would find it a great help to have a smart clever wife and one who knew the kind of people the Seymores did not know – London people, you understand, for Sir Everard always lived quiet in the country and didn't care for London swells. Of course Sir Everard should have said nonsense, a Seymore is as good as the best; but he believed his grand friend and made inquiries and got particulars of likely young ladies....'

'How could he do that?'

'Bless you, child, it is not hard, if you ask in the right places, to get a list to choose from of young girls wanting husbands and offering rank or fortune in return.'

I was still so ignorant of life that the notion of girls being on record as available for marriage shocked me deeply.

'How horrible!' I cried so passionately that she stared at me in astonishment.

'Horrible? Goodness gracious, what's horrible about it? It's the usual thing.'

Her calm acceptance of an idea abominable to my unfledged romanticism seemed the final outrage, and I burst into tears. She made no attempt to console or check me; and when the storm had passed and I was blowing my nose and dabbing myself back to some sort of decency, I saw that she was still placidly knitting. She waited till I had finished sniffing and then smiled at me:

"Better now? I expect so. You must learn not to take on so, Fanny, over things you can neither end nor mend. It does your heart credit that you can believe in true love and all that, and Heaven grant you find it; but all sorts of things go on in the world that you will have to accept, and I daresay you will be busy enough keeping your own sheet clean without trying to improve those of other people.'

'I am sorry I was a fool' I said unsteadily. 'But I did not know about that sort of thing. It sounded more like a slave-market than ladies and gentlemen.'

'Call 'em slaves if you like, my dear' she said caustically. 'I call 'em something different. But that is Marriage as under-stood these days by the so-called "Quality"; and you may thank your stars you are just an ordinary girl like I was. You will have a *chance* to be happy or to make someone else happy – and that is what matters in life, more than anything else.'

For a moment I resented being labelled 'an ordinary girl' for, having determined not to be ashamed of my equivocal origin, I had persuaded myself to be proud of it. But absorbed interest in my father's past overcame any thought of self; and Mrs Heaviside's last sentence had moved me alike to pity and delight. He – who of all men ought to be happy – was not happy; who should comfort him but I? Eagerly I pressed for more information.

'How long have they been married?'

'Let me see now – it would be eight years or more. Mr Clive is over forty.'

'And Lady Alicia?'

'Ten years younger. More maybe.'

I brooded for a few moments over all that I had learnt, and once more the angry partisanship of youth came to surface.

'I hate her!' I said fiercely.

'Then you do wrongly' she replied 'and are behaving like a silly child. Her ladyship is an excellent woman who does her duty by her husband and home. I won't deny she has an uncertain temper, and blows hot and cold; also that she sometimes acts in ways which an old-fashioned person like me cannot approve – though that is no business of mine and does not matter. Eh, dear – it is a sad pity she has no children and therefore less time on her hands. But don't you go on getting into your head that Mr Clive is ill-used or whatever you like to call it, and rampage around with a grudge against the mistress. It's all nonsense, and you'll only make a fool of yourself.'

She glanced at the clock.

'Time's up, Hooper. Off you go. On your way take those new pillow-cases along to Peake and tell her to mark them. Also I want Gover to look out the dust-sheets for the summer-covering and see me tomorrow morning.'

'Yes, Mrs Heaviside' I said obediently, and bidding her goodnight returned to my work.

*   *   *

That evening, oddly enough, Lady Alicia was in her friendliest humour. I was laying out her things on the long ottoman in her bedroom, when she came in, humming gaily to herself.

'Evening, Only Hooper' she called (it was the first time she had used this nickname since I had offended her). 'It's the most perfect evening imaginable and I'm dancing at Ranelagh. They have marvellous luck with their weather, those Forsyths; every year the same.'

She was standing while I unhooked her gown, and chattered on as undressing proceeded. 'This afternoon I went to the Egyptian Hall – for the first time for years. It really is astonishing what they do at the Dark Séances – all the lights out, and voices seeming to come from every corner! You ought to go sometime, though it's rather ghosty. I must remember to send you one afternoon. But who with –' She was now in her shift only, and swung round to wag a finger at me. '*Who with*, child? We must be careful of our Only Hooper, seeing there isn't another, Carver perhaps.' With a tinkle of laughter she tripped across the room to where her bath stood ready with its cans of hot and cold water beside it. 'Pour me the water, there's a good girl. Not too much hot; I want it tepid.' She tested it with her toe, slipped out of her last garment and stepped into the few inches of water, where she stood half crouched with her hands pressed between her knees, in precisely the attitude later immortalized by Chabas in his famous picture *Crépuscule*. 'Now sponge me, please – the big sponge – over my shoulders – lovely! Go on till I say stop. I can feel the dust being all washed away.'

I held the large towel for her and she gathered it tightly round her body, holding it under her arms so that it trailed on the floor.

'Where were we? Oh, I know – Maskelyne and Cooks. Carver is to take Only Hooper. That ought to be safe enough, even though it *is* dark ... though as a matter of fact I believe ... Would *you* be afraid of being what they call 'molested' in the dark, Hooper?'

'I don't think so, ma'am.'

'I don't mean by Carver, silly; I mean if you went to the Dark Séance with – well, let us say one of the footmen.'

'I doubt if I should think about it, ma'am.'

'Sensible girl. But Carver would. Carver goes through life hoping to be molested – and because she isn't, complaining that other women are. There are lots like her. No, you shan't go with Carver; you shall go with anyone you like. When I'm dressed I'll look at my book and see when I shan't need you before dinner. Then you can ask your friend and I'll see you have tickets.'

'That's very kind of you, madam' I said without enthusiasm; and we began to get her ladyship dressed.

When I was brushing her hair, she asked suddenly:

'How long have you been here?'

'Three years, ma'am, and a bit.'

'How old? Sixteen?'

'Yes, ma'am, last April.'

'You look younger. And rather peaky. You must fill out and get some colour, you know. I daresay you need a holiday. Do the girls here get holidays?'

'They get a week, ma'am, after they have been here over a year.'

'And have you had a holiday the last two years?'

'Well, not exactly, though Mrs Heaviside lets me go to my friends for a day or two now and again. You see, ma'am, my home is so far away and if I cannot go out of London, I may as well stay here. While you and Mr Seymore are away in the summer there is so little to do that it *is* really a holiday.'

She nodded.

'All the same you ought to have a change. I will speak to Mrs Heaviside. I am going away early this year and taking Carver. There is no reason at all why you should not go to your home and even stay there a good long time. I daresay Mr Seymore will manage to get along without you.'

What did she mean by that? I kept a firm control over hands and face, in case I jerked the brush or she was watching me in the glass. What was I to say? I decided to behave as though I had not heard her last words. 'Thank you indeed, ma'am. I should like that very much.'

She said nothing more, but began humming under her breath again as she polished her nails with the long silver-mounted polisher.

*   *   *

Three weeks passed, and I had reached an agony of uncertainty as to whether Lady Alicia had ever intended her talk of

a holiday to be taken seriously. The visit to the Egyptian Hall
had been forgotten even while she was dressing. She had never
consulted her book or said another word on the subject. That
was of no consequence; but if the wonderful prospect of going
to Yorkshire and seeing my mother and walking in the lanes
where she and my father had walked was to be just a mirage, I
felt my heart would break. Surely a lady like her could not be
so thoughtless or so cruel as to set a poor girl hoping, and then
either forget or deliberately disappoint her? Yet even as I told
myself it was impossible, I remembered those curious words
of hers, and once again I was in torment.

But Lady Alicia had not forgotten and at last I was put out
of my misery. It was five o'clock and my father and I were
alone in the housekeeper's room. He sat in the armchair and I
on a stool at his feet, leaning against his knees. As the day was
warm, the window stood wide open and the chair had been
pulled round to face it. If I laid back my head on the arm of
the chair, I could look out at the cloudless sky and see the dust
dance in the rays of the sun, which had sunk just below the
house opposite and was throwing up golden beams from behind its parapet.

We had been sitting a few moments in silence. I could feel
his fingers moving slowly and tenderly over my hair in a sort
of rhythmic pattern. They slid from the centre parting along
my forehead to the tight plait over my left ear; then straight
up the parting to the crown of my head. A tiny pause and the
same thing all over again. It was lovely just to sit and be
conscious of the caress, to empty my mind of everything but
the touch of his hand and the pressure of his leg against my
side and the knowledge that he was there.

'Vannchen darling' he said suddenly (he liked this German
diminutive, which he had specially coined) 'I have some
news for you – real news. This house is soon to be more or
less shut up. I am going to Aughton and you are coming with
me.'

For a moment, I could neither speak nor move. The miracle
had happened after all and the joy of it overwhelmed me.

Then, forgetting with half my mind that I was not alone, I breathed: 'Oh Andrew, how wonderful! And I shall see mamma?'

'Certainly you will, and so shall I.'

I scrambled to my knees, turned towards him and threw myself into his arms, where I lay shaking with happiness, my head buried in his coat. The vehemence of emotion soon passed, and looking up into his face I began to laugh and talk at once. What was Aughton like? When were we going? For how long? He smiled back in his gentle indulgent way, and as well as he could kept pace with my torrent of questions. When he had answered most of them he said casually:

'What was that you called me, Vanny?'

'That I called you? When?' I had really forgotten those half-whispered words, spoken aloud yet meant only for myself. But even as I looked at him in bewilderment, I remembered and coloured with embarrassment and hung my head:

'Don't be afraid, darling. What was it?'

'I – I – called you Andrew' I murmured, and struggled on: 'It is a private name I use to myself. Please forgive me. I hardly knew I said it, I was so overcome. I won't do it any more.'

'But, my dearest child, you shall, and not only to yourself. It shall be your name for always, and I thank you for choosing it.'

His arm tightened about me and again we sat in silence.

VI

There have been happy times in my life, but with the exception of one period of mingled ecstasy, confidence and peace – a period which made my whole existence worth while – I doubt if any were so vividly happy as my first three weeks in the East Riding during the summer of 1873.

The intensity of my enjoyment was no doubt partly due to my youth, when few reservations or outside responsibilities distract the mind and a young heart is free to yield itself to the mere pleasure of being happy; partly also to the lovely feeling of release which came with sudden emancipation from the frustrations of my life hitherto. But a part arose also from my actual surroundings, human and material; for both at Aughton Hall and at Gowthorpe where my official grandfather lived, I was with people I loved and who loved me, had other cheerful, natural company, and dwelt in the midst of mellow beauty or of sturdy self-respect. I realize, however, that a protracted story of even three weeks of unalloyed contentment makes monotonous reading for those who have not shared it; and I shall therefore condense their happenings to within likely limits of a stranger's patience.

We – that is, Nanny and I, for Andrew was coming a week later – travelled to Yorkshire early in July. After York, as the branch-line train chuffed slowly on its way, I just gazed out of the window at the unimagined countryside – now in the rich panoply of high summer – and prayed that what I saw was true. At the wayside station a wagonette awaited us, with a red-faced groom on the box-seat, who greeted Mrs Heaviside as an old friend and squeezed my timid hand until the bones cracked. Twilight was falling as we trundled between flowery hedges and wide scented fields, in which the hay grew high and ripe or the grain was a gentle carpet of young green. That evening I saw little of my father's home save a dark mass of building and an open door from which a light shone brightly to welcome us. But as soon as I got inside I felt that this was a house of good-fellowship, where simplicity and courtesy and mutual affection ruled in harmony.

Next morning the crowing of cocks, the sound of someone chopping wood, voices and clanking of buckets, and the swish of water in the stableyard woke me a little after five. Hurrying on my clothes I crept downstairs and out into the pale promise of a day of sunshine. Alone with scents of grass and flowers, early morning songs of birds and an occasional sharp flutter of wings as a thrush or blackbird dived through the dense leaves of the horse-chestnuts, I started to explore a place whose name was already dear to me yet its every aspect strange.

Aughton Hall stood on the brow of a low but steepish hill, facing to south and west over a wide expanse of country, in a crease of which, about two miles away, lay the village of Aughton Seymore. From the front the Hall looked to be a large house, for its stone façade was long and of somewhat grandiose design, with a centre-block crowned with a pediment and two balustraded wings. Built in the early eighteenth century, the façade carried, on each of the three floors of the central block and on the two floors of the wings, tall narrow windows with rounded tops and keystones in relief. These windows, emphasised by the perpendicular lines of flat pilasters which rose at intervals from ground to roof, gave the house a startled expression – as though, with eyebrows raised in alarm, it were staring down the hill at some strange or fearsome sight. The buildings' look of dismay was intensified by the presence, at various points along the parapet which hid the actual roof, of huge stone birds with wings half-spread. These carved monsters were out of proportion to the rest of the house and, rising clear of the roof, made it look as though its hair were standing on end.

I imagine I took the more notice of this external effect of surprise and horror, because the interior of Aughton Hall, both in atmosphere and construction, presented so strong a contrast. To begin with, the impression of size given by the façade was a misleading one. The imposing stretch of stone work, with its columns and balustrading, had been overlaid by an ambitious early-Georgian Seymore on an old-fashioned Yorkshire manor house. Probably he planned to rebuild the whole, and gradually bring the rest of his home up to the scale of its new front; but his plan was never carried out, with the result that the only section of the house with any depth was the central block, the wings being only one room thick, and even at that never properly finished. Behind the central section of the façade – and practically unaltered – lay the original house. It was a spacious, homely rambling house, with no pretension to anything but roomy comfort. There had been a slight awkwardness in adjusting the tall front windows to rooms barely high

enough to accommodate them; but this surmounted, Aughton
lived on unchanged behind its pretentious mask.

Along the main front ran a broad gravel terrace, from which
a grass field, with cows grazing, ran down the hill to a country
road. There was no public access to this terrace, although it
had been intended as a main approach. But now shrubberies
closed one end and the gardens the other, so that it remained a
tranquil private walk, with a few trailing geraniums in pots
and a slope of pasture for a view. The gardens, simple enough
but full of flowers and fruit trees on old walls and casual strips
of lawn, lay to the south-east of the house. Behind, where the
original building could be clearly seen, were stables, outhouses
and a larged paved yard, on to which opened what was always
used as the main entrance to the house.

I returned in good time from my tour of inspection, and was
saved from having to hang awkwardly about in a strange
kitchen by the friendliness of a young maid, who was setting
the servants' breakfast and asked me to give her a hand. During breakfast, eaten in a comfortable servants' hall, I was made
to feel welcome by the senior members of the staff — Mrs
Dobson, the cook, and old Mr Tyas, the butler — who were
clearly delighted to see Mrs Heaviside and accepted me for
her sake. I noticed no grades of importance among the servants
were recognized — save those implicit in age and experience.
All sat down together, had the same fare and were equally free
to join in the conversation.

After we had cleared away and I had helped the kitchen-
maid with the washing-up, Mrs Heaviside told me to follow
her. I was to be presented to the master of Aughton. We went
along a flagged passage, through a swing-door of padded
leather studded with brass-headed nails and across a large
irregular hall to a room on the left of what should have been
the front-door. Seated at a table sipping coffee, with a newspaper propped on the coffee-pot in front of him, was the
cleanest-looking old gentleman I had ever seen. He had the
clear pink complexion of a child, a fringe of white hair round a
gleaming bald head and a long pure white moustache, which

curled down on either side of a pair of rosy lips and joined the white side-whiskers which edged his cheeks. When we entered the room, he got quickly to his feet and I saw that he was short in stature, and wore a black coat and trousers of black and white sponge-bag check, which almost gleamed, they were so trim and fresh. He had a black scarf tie with a pearl pin, and his starched collar and cuffs shone like snow.

'Well, Nanny!' he said cordially, holding out his hand. 'This *is* a pleasure! I hope you are well; though, even if you are not, our Yorkshire air will soon set you up. And —' turning on me a pair of bright and intensely blue eyes 'this, I suppose . . .'

'Yes, Sir Everard' she replied loudly, 'this is Fanny.

'Fanny, your duty to Sir Everard Seymore. . . . He is rather deaf' she added in an undertone.

I bobbed a curtsey, murmuring 'Good morning, sir'. But even while curtseying, and although I knew I was blushing, I could not help looking him in the face. Those blue, blue eyes were fixed unwaveringly on mine and would not let them go. He smiled kindly and took one of my hands, laying his other hand over it. His hands were cool and dry, with the pale wrinkled backs of age and nails spotless and beautifully shaped.

'I am happy to see you, my dear' he said 'and glad you have been able to come to Aughton. You look too much of a town-bird for a child of your age. We must get roses into her little cheeks, eh, Nanny?'

He dropped my hand and walked over to the window, where he stood looking out. Mrs Heaviside jerked her head toward the door and I understood she wished me to slip away. As I was closing the door behind me, I heard Sir Everard say:

'We shall have Mr Clive with us in less than a week. . . .'

I found my way through the walled garden and under a pergola loaded with roses, to a small swing-gate set in a low iron railing. It led into a spacious park of pale tussocky grass, with bright patches of green here and there and scattered trees. A rabbit got up almost under my feet, and went ricochetting away to safety. As I wandered on, passively surrendered to the

peace and beauty of the country, I asked myself how much Sir
Everard knew; then decided that it did not matter, for not
only was he clearly as kind as he was clean, but also – a fact I
did not seem to have earlier registered – he was my other
grandfather.

But almost immediately I was plunged from complacency
into gloom, for I learnt that I was to leave Aughton just before
Andrew arrived and go to grandfather Hooper's farm. The
news both hurt and frightened me. I felt I must revise my
judgement of Sir Everard, who was perhaps an ogre for all his
rosy affability. I even went to the length of wondering whether
the whole business of bringing me to Yorkshire were not a plot
to smuggle me out of London and away from my father, and
bury me for ever in some remote country place. I lay awake
most of the night, worrying miserably and imagining con-
spiracies each more fantastic than the last. In the morning I
must have looked worse than a fright, for Mrs Heaviside took
me to her room after breakfast and demanded bluntly what
was the matter. At first I refused to answer; but she insisted
and finally dragged from me a few disjointed sentences. Looking at me severely, she said:

'I am sorry after what has been done for you, you should
trust your friends so little. I also hoped you were too grown up
to frighten yourself with bogies. Oh, Fanny, Fanny, when will
you leave off being a fool? Please listen to me. Some visitors
arrive here shortly who will stay a couple of days after Mr
Clive comes and will expect him to entertain them. When they
have gone he will be here alone with Sir Everard for a bit, and
will be able to do as he likes – riding about the country perhaps and even spending some time with silly girls in neighbouring farms. Now do you understand?'

I nodded happily, too glad to be rid of my terrors even to
say I was sorry. Mrs Heaviside went on:

'In August a number of people will come to Aughton and
help will be needed in the house. You will then probably come
back again. And by the way – Sir Everard says you look an
intelligent girl and had better learn to ride while you are here-

abouts; so try to live up to his good opinion and run and tell
George in the stables that you'll have your first lesson in an
hour's time. Then come upstairs and try on those clothes there.
They belonged to a cousin of Mr Clive's who lived here at
one time, and should fit you well enough.'

*　　*　　*

So I came to Gowthorpe, five miles or so from Aughton.
The place was grim enough – a stark box of old red brick,
with no architectural ornament nor cared-for garden to soften
its bleakness. Yet it was wholly itself, and perfectly equipped
for the purpose it was designed to serve, standing in a cluster
of barns, rickyards and cow-byres, with a sombre group of
elms to northward and on every side the fertile arable and
pasturelands which make the Warp Land the richest agricultural district in the county of York. These surroundings –
the only convincing evidence of farming possibility and farming skill – were the core and justification of Gowthorpe. The
unbeautiful house was in fact subsidiary to what went on outside it, a necessary but minor appendage to the real business of
a farmer's life.

I confess that for a day or two I missed the comforts of
Aughton, and even of Upper Belgrave Street. Accustomed to
taps which brought hot water to the sink; to indoor lavatories;
to a wire-mattress; to meals on time for their own sake and not
dependent on the progress of work in the fields – I was ill at
ease with the primitive conditions in which Grandfather
Hooper, despite his prosperity, was content to live, and faintly
resented the assumption that a house must necessarily be
servant to a farm. But I soon outgrew this foolishness, and
with the adaptability of youth found a new level of expecta-
tion and therefore of content.

Of course the dominant delight was, for the first time for
three years, to feel my mother's arms about me and to hear her
voice. It was a joyous reunion. We had corresponded regularly,
though at longish intervals (I was not yet at an age when letter-
writing came easily, and she must inevitably have felt our loss

of common background); but the moment I saw and held her, the old trust and intimacy returned.

'Fanny, my little girl! Grown up nearly, but still the child I knew.'

'Oh mamma darling, how lovely to see you!'

We stood at arm's length, half-laughing, half-crying, as we looked one another up and down. She was very much as I remembered her – plump, rosy-faced and full of restless movement. Perhaps her skin had weathered; perhaps her hair, which had always been demurely neat, had been gathered into the bun of an early riser and thereafter left to shift for itself; certainly her clothes were different, for the rough serviceable garb of a working farmer's wife had replaced the quiet town-dwelling respectability of Mrs William Hopwood. But her eyes were the gay tender eyes I had known, and I felt that we were still the close friends we used to be.

I was soon assisting her in all her work. As we worked, and in the intervals of not working, we talked. How we talked! We re-lived the past in fond and foolish detail, recalling Panton Street and Chunks and Mrs Beckett; we laughed together over all but forgotten jokes. When we came to the time of our separation, and I begged her to tell me all that she had done since, she laughed and pointed to the pots we were scrubbing or the mending on the table or the jars of bottled fruit along the shelf.

'That and that, Fanny. All the time. Every month has its jobs. I have been happy enough, because I have been busy and can help your grandfather and uncles. But I have sadly missed my daughter. Has she missed me?'

I was slicing runners, and had to put the knife and basin down, in order to show her how much I had missed her.

'There, there, child' she protested. 'Whatever would anyone think? Now it's your turn. Tell me everything – and particularly about Clive.'

This started me off on a subject well nigh inexhaustible though not one free from pitfalls and compulsory evasions. Of Andrew I related every detail; and she nodded now and again and murmured 'So he wrote to me' or 'that was like him'. About Lucy I could be nearly as frank, for my mother's fondness for Mrs Beckett would make her sympathize with dissatisfaction under a new régime. My meeting with Chunks and our outing to Rosherville made good telling; but I felt uncertain how she would like my knowing about Hades and the final horror, so said nothing of them or of poor Hopwood. I was dealing one by one and volubly with the staff at Upper Belgrave Street, with Clara's relations and with dear Nanny, when mamma interrupted:

'You seem to have skipped Lady Alicia, Fanny.'

This was disconcerting. Rather clumsily I made out that I saw very little of her; that she was deliciously pretty and very smart; that she entertained a great deal or went out to parties; that – that – well, there was not much more I could tell.

She said nothing, but I heard her sigh. Then she left whatever she was doing and started towards the door. As she passed behind me, she kissed the back of my neck.

'I am sorry, darling' she whispered. 'I shouldn't have asked. But I just hoped I might have been wrong.'

*   *   *

Next day Andrew rode over to visit us. He walked into the dairy, where we were setting out the broad dishes for the standing milk, and greeted us with unaffected warmth:

'It is good to see you two together again, and here of all places. How are you, Mary? I hope they don't work you too hard, although you seem to thrive on it.' He took her hand and raised it to his lips. 'And my little Vanny – not such a stranger, except in these parts.'

Impulsively I threw my arms round his neck and kissed him; and even as I did so, I had an intuition that unwittingly I had made things awkward for my mother. Thinking it over afterwards, I began to understand – vaguely enough, I daresay, for I had not the experience to analyse the situation in detail – how odd and delicate was the relationship between the three of us. Any two had a formula in common; but the three

together (firm though they were in mutual affection) were out
of adjustment. Mr Clive Seymore could pay friendly visits to
Mrs Hopwood of Gowthorpe and, under the tolerant eye of
those who knew of their old intimacy, spend a pleasant hour in
local gossip and in doing her whatever kindnesses were in his
power. Mamma and I – or Andrew and I – could be perfectly
happy, standing on our respective common grounds and acting
as natural affection bade us act. But the trio was in different
shape. We represented three phases of a single human adventure, in no two of which the same pair of us had been involved.
Long ago she and he had been lovers; the contrast between
their ways of life and mental outlook had not mattered when it
was a question of a young girl responding to a man's passion
and of hot blood creating its own harmony. But now, over a
gulf of years, they faced one another in the presence of their
child, each having since – and in his own right – acquired a
new personality. There was Andrew – established Londoner,
temporarily released from the demands and luxuries of official
and fashionable life; there was mamma – the working mistress
of a farm, independent, within her sphere paramount, but
bound to feel circumscribed in contrast with him and therefore
ill at ease. And there was I – unable to help them, because
only an outcome of their love-story and not a part of it. In the
same way Andrew was excluded from the years during which
my mother cared for her little daughter, and mamma from
those which had brought father and child together.

Our meeting, in short, was incurably artificial. Underneath
was harmony, but we could not reach down to it. In consequence we had to let our longed-for encounter go by in a
mood of casual amiability. Admittedly Andrew's visit passed
off comfortably enough; but it fell far short of the carefree
happiness which my young enthusiasm had anticipated.
Mamma said nothing to suggest that she had been disappointed; but I knew that she had. I did all I could to comfort her, and I am sure that during the rest of my stay at Gowthorpe she was happy. In due course I was fetched back to
Aughton.

VII

The letter reached Mrs Heaviside on one of the first days of September. We were sewing together – doing some mending, I think, for the ladies then staying in the house – when she abruptly put down her work and, taking an envelope from her apron-pocket, handed it to me.

'Better read that' she said.

The envelope had a coronet embossed in black on the flap, and in the right-hand upper corner of the thick glazed note-paper was another one. Alongside it were the words:

Clipston Park,
Warwickshire.

Dear Mrs Heaviside.

Carver has been taken ill and goes into hospital in Coventry tomorrow. Most tiresome with all that is going on. I can't be without anybody, so please arrange for Hooper to come here at once. She will be better than nothing. Rugby station is probably the best for her to come to. Let me know day and train and she shall be met.

Yours truly,
Alicia Seymore.

My heart sank into my boots as I re-read this letter and realized what it meant. At last in a tiny and none too steady voice I managed to say:

'Does Mr Clive know, Nanny?'

'Yes, he knows. I talked to him just before luncheon.'

'What is Clipston Park?'

'Where Lord Hillmorton lives. Her ladyship is staying with her parents.'

'And must I go?'

She nodded sadly.

There seemed nothing more to be said. With my hands idle on my lap I sat and stared into space. I thought of the peaceful gaiety of life at Aughton; of the good fellowship of the servants' hall; the consideration and informality with which

Sir Everard, his son and his guests treated those who waited on them; of long days in the hayfield helping to turn and rake and load, and then, glowing with heat and health, drinking cold tea or nettle beer with the crowd of haymakers; of being allowed by the good-natured head-gardener to pick the last few bowls of raspberries and take them in to cook; of helping her to shell peas and slice runner-beans and top and tail gooseberries; of ranging over the fields on the chance of finding an early mushroom, and watching the blackberries ripen, and saying that in September here or here would be the best place to come with gloves and baskets. I thought of the cats and dogs and horses with whom I had made friends; and particularly of the little mare I had learnt to ride with confidence and ease, and how she whinnied when I came into her stable.

Now it was all to be taken from me – the daily greeting from my father and the frequent rambles in his company; the consoling presence of Nanny, always there to advise or reprove; the confidence which had come with feeling at home and that others were glad I was there; the plans for September; everything. What was I to be given in their place? I had no idea, beyond that I must face up alone to a strange house in which the only human being not a stranger to me was an incalculable imperious woman, of whose very amiability I was vaguely afraid and whose anger I dreaded.

The feeling that there was no escape beat me down into a misery too hopeless for tears. I just sat dry-eyed and wished that I were dead. I was conscious of Mrs Heaviside getting out of her chair and, as she walked to the door, patting me gently on the shoulder. Then she left me alone.

Minutes passed and I remained in a sort of coma. I did not even hear the door open; but I felt a hand on my hair – a hand whose touch I knew.

'My darling' he said softly. 'I am so dreadfully sorry. It is cruelly bad luck. We were so happy here.'

He laid his other hand on my shoulder, and I took it in mine and pressed it hard against me.

'Must I, Andrew?' I whispered.

'Please, dearest Vanny – for my sake. I know too well that you will not enjoy it. It is a gloomy unfriendly house, full of noisy unfriendly people. But it will not be for very long, and not to go would raise all manner of questions.'

'Will you be coming there later?'

He had moved round in front of me, and was now holding my hands in his.

'No, darling. I hate that place, and it hates me. Even if I were invited ... but I am not, nor likely to be. That is what hurts me, that you should have to go and face it alone. Can you, Vannchen?'

'If you say so, I can. If it helps you ...'

He raised my hands to his lips, kissed them (it sounds silly to say 'with ceremony' – but he was much moved) and went quickly away.

*   *   *

It was a long and tiring journey; but by starting very early I was at Rugby station at four o'clock, so had the first sight of my new home by daylight.

After passing a lodge much too rustic to be true and driving for half a mile along a yellow gritty road, I saw what looked like a mammoth vicarage erected in the middle of a polo-ground. Built in the bastard Gothic of the eighteen-forties, the house was a confused mass of gables, battlements, chimneys, balconies, porches, conservatories and outhouses. The principal rooms had elongated mullioned windows which used a maximum of imitation stone-work to admit a minimum of light, while the minor rooms (those which did not show) had not even the stone-work. The innumerable gables were edged with elaborate barge-boards, pierced and carved in flamboyant Gothic. The steep-pitched roofs oversloped the walls so deeply that the bedroom windows cut right back into them, and had little dormer-roofs of their own, with cusps and crockets clustering in the angles. The walls were a mixture of brick and imitation stone – brick interstices with exaggerated coigns, skirtings and mullions in whitey-grey. The woodwork (when originally painted) had been brick-red, but was now a sort of muddy ochre.

On every side of this bristle of misguided ornament stretched grass – grass unadorned by flowers or even shrubs, grass which came right up under the windows save where a barren stretch of gravel drive cut it off. Here and there in the middle distance was a tree, or a clump of trees railed round with iron railings; but, these apart, nothing broke the monotony of dull flat grass or helped to cheer or hide the contortions of the house itself. Clipston Park, in short, was a dreary pretentious sort of place to look at – and, as I soon found out, the same to live in.

After I had been there a few days I decided that the only part of the establishment which seemed to have any inherent vitality was the stables. These stood some little distance from the house and were also of Gothic design. They were of great extent, accommodating numerous grooms and stable-boys, as well as hunters and carriage-horses and a string of polo ponies, which last were one of the two dominant interests in the life of Lord Hillmorton, Lady Alicia's father. The other was the local Volunteer Corps.

The owner of Clipston was the second Earl of Hillmorton. His father, the first Earl, who had died twenty years previously at the age of ninety-two, had not only been the founder of the family fortunes but had also done his best to be their destroyer. Of quite humble origin, he had catered to the 'sporting' tastes of the Prince Regent, becoming a kind of impresario in all matters pertaining to horseflesh, boxing, cock-fighting and the rest, and was without scruple in exploiting their financial possibilities. A genuine expert on these subjects, he won the complete confidence of his royal patron, both as an organizer of sporting events, and as a tipster who only left the winning of a wager to chance when he could not make a more reliable arrangement. Certainly he himself became a rich man; and spiteful people said that in his time he had made still more money for his master by means which he threatened to reveal, unless the King pushed him some rungs higher on the ladder of honour than even a careless cynic like George IV would ever have thought to do. However that may be, he was given an earldom late in the eighteen-twenties.

After 1830 the new Earl found himself an uneasy relic of a vanished epoch. For a while, he tried to keep his place in such raffish society as still contrived to cling about the Court; but he found that one by one his former friends were hastening to change their coats, while he had no other garment than the gaudy patchwork of his own making. Resentful yet defiant, he withdrew to the bleak estate near Rugby which he had bought in justification of his title, and there built himself a house – at enormous expense and in what he was told was the most elegant taste of the day. When it was finished, he characteristically gave it his family name, and falling back on his old fondness for horses about which he still believed himself infallible, became a mixture of horse-coper, racing man and sporting squire. But he was now eighty years old, and though his body was remarkably active for his age, his mind, though he did not know it, was in decay. He lived with crazy extravagance, was cheated right and left, and, no longer able to make new money by the ingenuities of his youth, plunged heavily and disastrously into the quicksands of the railway boom.

Long before this his wife had died in bewilderment and neglect. She had never been well treated, but the moment her husband became a Lord she had been shut away entirely, for she reminded him too vividly of a past he was determined to forget. Her place had been taken by a succession of complacent beauties, who endured the grossness and vanity of the new peer for the sake of his guineas and the jewels he hung about their necks.

There was one son of the Clipston marriage, born in the year the Prince of Wales became Regent. A forlorn boyhood of lonely expensive schooling and of holidays spent with his mother while she lived and thereafter with miscellaneous relations, was followed by three years at University, where he was conscious that his huge allowance and brand new courtesy title brought him more sneers than friendship. In the early 'thirties the young man joined his father, whose footing in society was already insecure and his temper the shorter for it. The two quarrelled bitterly, but at last agreed on this – that the son be bought a commission in the army and spend his life as far from his parent as possible. Throughout, therefore, the last spendthrift decade of his life, the old man was quite alone. Unable to understand that his fortune was dwindling, ignorant of the ways by which a house can be made comfortable and cheered with flowers, or land improved by tillage and afforestation, he sank into squalid senility, surrounded by the naked acres of his park, while on his Gothic mansion the paint-work blistered and the plaster crumbled and the cold damp of the Warwickshire uplands seeped into the walls.

Meantime his son in India had found contentment and a certain amount of self-respect. He was an efficient officer and was well enough liked. He married a dashing young beauty in Calcutta, who had a little money, and, as he had some also (for he had been shrewd enough to extract a portion of his birth-right from his father before they parted company), they could live the sort of life they liked. When tidings of the old man's death reached India, the new Earl had no inclination to return home. He was quite happy in his pleasure-full existence in Calcutta and in the Hills, and, being now deservedly a Colonel, felt that he was someone in his own right and not merely the gilded offspring of a *parvenu*. He instructed the lawyers at home to clear up the dead man's estate, put caretakers into Clipston Park and let him have a report on the general state of affairs. This, when it arrived, gave him a considerable shock. The late Earl, when all debts had been paid, was worth twenty-five thousand pounds and the house and grounds near Rugby. That was all.

Leaving his wife and three daughters in India, Lord Hill-morton sailed for England to take stock of his prospects. He was advised that Clipston Park was unsaleable, being not only quite out of the fashion, but in bad repair and without the graciousness of gardens and rural surroundings which the buyer of such a house would require. If, however, he was content to live in it himself, the cost of putting it into habitable shape would not be prohibitive, and with his own money and his wife's he could make ends meet with something to spare. This, very reluctantly, he decided to do, and in due course established himself and his family in a home they all disliked.

The second Earl of Hillmorton was not a vulgarian like the first. A brisk, rotund, rather flashy little man, he could adapt himself to people of all kinds, was quite without arrogance, and, having inherited his father's talent for horses, soon made himself popular in hunting circles in the neighbourhood. When, after 1870, polo clubs began to be formed all over England, the one at Clipston was among those earliest established and most energetically conducted. By this means, also, the wide spaces of the park were transformed from a liability into an asset, for they were polo-grounds almost ready-made and were soon in active use.

In another respect also the Earl's unwilling return to the home of his only ancestor proved more congenial than was expected. He had not been at Clipston above a twelve-month when, under an apparent threat of invasion, the Volunteers made their sensational début. Lord Hillmorton, who sorely missed the military duties he had performed so well, threw himself with enthusiasm into a movement at which the vast majority of his contemporaries sneered. He was immediately and amazingly justified; and as gradually what had been shrugged aside as an army of opera-bouffe became almost a nation in arms, he, as one of the first of the local gentry to give time and labour to the cause, gained greatly in prestige. From then onward he continued to work hard at a job he really enjoyed, and in 1872 had the satisfaction of commanding his battalion on Salisbury Plain, when for the first time the Volunteers were put in brigade with regular troops at large-scale manoeuvres.

*   *   *

No doubt Lord Hillmorton was lucky in that, during his residence at Clipston, his only two specialities happened to

chime with the uprush of corresponding enthusiasms among
men of the English upper and middle classes. But he must be
given credit for turning his good fortune to practical account.

Financially, thanks to a period of general prosperity, he
found himself better off than might have been expected. By
exercising economy in Warwickshire he could afford a tolerably furnished house for the London season; and his wife and
daughters soon made for themselves a large and strenuous
circle of smart acquaintances, of the kind to be influential on
the fringe of government, Society and the City, yet still
susceptible to the lure of titled friends.

At the time, therefore, that I was summoned to Clipston,
the family had found its level both in town and country, and
its members enjoyed themselves according to their lights.

Unhappily for me their lights were not those of Aughton,
nor of that type of mentality which I had inherited from
Andrew. Although the Earl was personally an easy-going
unpretending kind of man, his wife was highly conscious of her
rank and continually uneasy lest lack of means disgrace it. A
withered-looking woman, still showing traces of a conventional
beauty but dried by the sun of India into wrinkled sharpness,
her face was always heavily powdered and her wasted hands
loaded with rings. She had a loud imperious voice and her
movements were carefully majestic. Like others of her kind,
she believed that self-assertion spelt authority and pomposity
distinction.

In order, I suppose, to underprop her sense of aristocracy,
she organized her household on extreme hierarchical lines. But
as (if there were to be money to spare for London) she could
not afford sufficient servants at Clipston to fill every rank and
as even those she could afford were of mediocre quality, life in
the staff quarters was at once ostentatious and threadbare. For
example, there was a gloomy cavern known as the 'Steward's
Room'. But as there was no steward to occupy it, it was used,
at great inconvenience, for the meals served to the butler, to
Lord Hillmorton's valet and to the Countess' lady's-maid. Nor
was there a housekeeper, the duties of that office being in fact

performed by her ladyship and her two unmarried daughters. But great care was taken to pretend that this was not the case, orders being given and control exercised through the head-housemaid, who, poor soul, was badly driven, having to do all her own work as well as act as cover for a non-existent superior.

Kitchen-meals were a noisy scramble of bad food and bad manners. Lady Hillmorton had learnt that in very large households the females sat on one side of the table and the males on the other. Orders had accordingly been given that this arrangement should be observed at Clipston. The servants being a second-rate lot in themselves and, with reason, dissatisfied with the quality of their board and lodging, found in this absurd formality continual opportunity for horseplay. The men and girls threw bread at one another, wrestled with their legs under the table, fought across it for the potatoes or the beer, and so made of every meal an uneasy turmoil. Another snobbery of Lady Hillmorton's was to insist (again in imitation of the great houses of the time) that her maid – a raddled Frenchwoman with a bad temper and a corrupt mind – should take her breakfast, tea and supper in the Steward's Room, but the meat-course of her midday meal in the servants' hall. When that course was finished, she was to retire to the Steward's Room for her sweet. Her presence among the lesser servants for the first half of dinner-time meant sullen silence, broken by nudges, whispers and giggles; everyone was frightened of Mademoiselle, who had the ear of the ladies and an evil tongue. But the moment she left the room pandemonium broke out, as though these adult men and women were a gang of slum children released from discipline. The principal meal of the day, therefore, was an exaggeration of two opposites and an occasion to be dreaded.

VIII

I do not care to dwell in detail on my experiences at Clipston. They were hateful in themselves and worse than hateful in what they presaged; but I cannot avoid telling of certain incidents, because of what came after.

Lady Alicia received me amiably enough, but casually remarked that she supposed I was prepared to lady's-maid her sisters also, as they were temporarily without their personal helps. She added with characteristic flippancy:

'That's not really true, you know, Hooper. They never have maids of their own. But the Countess likes to pretend they have, and so I put it that way. You'll have your hands full for once; but that won't hurt you, even if it did finish Carver.'

Next morning, when I called her and asked for the day's instructions, she suddenly said:

'How was Aughton?'

'Very nice, ma'am, and the country looked lovely.'

'And that baby-faced old skinflint of a father-in-law of mine – did you see much of him?'

Her words shocked me, but the venom with which they were spoken shocked me more. Fortunately I had the presence of mind to conceal my anger, though in that moment I could have struck her. All I said was:

'Very little, ma'am.'

She sat up in bed and stretched.

'What's the day like?'

'Close and cloudy. It feels like thunder.'

'Damnation! It will probably pour all this afternoon. I'm riding at eleven and shan't change for luncheon as it's at half past twelve. The second round for the Clipston Cup is at two o'clock. I shall want you to help me dress. And people for dinner and the night. Have the letters come yet?'

'No, ma'am. Not yet.'

*   *   *

Lady Alicia spoke the truth when she prophesied that I should be kept busy. I soon suspected that the Ladies Edina and Petronella saved up all possible pieces of mending for the annual visit of their sister's maid. Presumably Miss Carver had made a start on the accumulation of garments which were piled in the room allotted to me; but enough remained to fill me with despair. I must do the young ladies this justice – that they did not demand from me much personal attendance. Perhaps Lady Alicia had made it clear that, although her maid was at their disposal, she had first call and must be served when she wanted. But I had to see their baths were got ready on time and dress their hair in the evening, as well as do my best to keep their clothes in some sort of order. They were younger than Lady Alicia and quite unlike her in appearance. They took after their mother in stature and large-featured good looks, while their elder sister was small like the father, and showed his bird-like alacrity refined and feminised into an exquisite gaminerie. In character the three sisters were more similar – as might be expected in products of the same up-bringing. But whereas the eldest expressed a natural irreverence and flippant cynicism in witty unguarded speech, and her personal vanity in being chic to the smallest detail in dress and deportment, the two younger girls – equally unabashed and impudent, but taking their attractions at face-value and lacking Alicia's wealth and her quick mordant tongue – were tomboys, careless over their clothes, noisy and sometimes ribald.

Nevertheless on the whole I preferred them to their far cleverer sister. They were not dangerous; merely rackety and a little uncouth. It never occurred to them to treat me with sudden and disconcerting familiarity or, as Lady Alicia would sometimes do, to make some outrageous remark and watch me maliciously to see how I took it. On the contrary they completely ignored me, except when they wished something done or found. Then they demanded it rudely enough; and, bad-mannered though they were, I disliked their blunt uncivility less than a spasmodic intimacy which I did not trust.

One evening before dinner I was doing the Lady Edina's hair. Her younger sister sprawled on an ottoman and the two talked as though they were quite alone. There were several officers staying in the house for a polo tournament, and the girls' conversation was mainly – and rather crudely – concerned with these visitors.

'I hope we dance after dinner' said Edina. 'Mr Foulsham looks as though he would valse beautifully.'

The other gave a snort of laughter.

'Hypocrite, Edie; that's what you are. Why not say straight out you want to be in his arms? As for dancing, I don't believe my shoes will stand another evening. They are just awful, and I haven't a shilling to buy a hair-ribbon with, much less a pair of shoes.'

'Why don't you ask Alice?'

'I have done. I asked her to lend me five pounds only this morning, and she said she couldn't spare it because Seymore hadn't sent her the money he had promised.'

'Good heavens, how abominable! If that man is going to keep her short of money as well, I don't see what is the use of him.'

At this remark both young ladies exploded into noisy gaiety. Edina went on:

'He's a prig, that we always knew; he's no stayer as a husband, that we have found out; and now he's mean into the bargain! Ugh, I hate him!'

'Oh come now, Edie. He's not so bad as all that. He's really very good-looking, you know, in a solemn sort of way and very gentlemanly and awfully clever.'

'I don't care. When I have a husband, he's either got to be very rich and free with his money, or passionately in love with me and free with his —'

'Ssh!' cried Petronella, stifling another burst of mirth. 'Not with the maid here. Anyway, you needn't pity Alice on that score. Charlie Tennant will look after her all right.'

At this juncture, and deliberately, I gave Edina's hair a vicious tug, which caught her in that sensitive spot just above the ear.

'Ow!' she shrieked. 'You little fool, Hooper; what the devil do you think you are doing?'

'I beg your pardon, me lady' I said indifferently. 'My hand slipped.' And I added to myself 'If you would prefer my fingernails in your throat, as they very nearly were, you've only got to say so.'

'You hurt me, you clumsy idiot. Aren't you finished yet?'

'Almost, me lady.'

I had reached the hair-pin stage, and wondered whether, with a nice sharp one, to give her a good jab in the skull. 'Better not' I told myself.

So she escaped that time; and I went quickly away to ponder what I had heard.

Oddly enough, the gossip was amplified during the evening by the Countess' mademoiselle. I had avoided this disagreeable woman as much as possible and with considerable success. But tonight she came in search of me while I was laying out Lady Alicia's night-things, and cornered me in my mistress' room. The bedroom floor was silent and deserted, for the company were all downstairs and the housemaids had finished their work and gone to bed. There was, therefore, no likelihood of her being found there or good excuse for me to escape.

'Ah, Miss Hooper' she began (she spoke remarkably good English, with only a slight thickness of accent and jerkiness of intonation to betray the foreigner) 'I must beg you to lend me some white silk, if you will be so kind. But what a charming nightgown! Please permit me.' She took it up from the bed where I had just laid it and held it in front of her by the shoulder-straps. Then she cocked her head at me and looked roguish: 'Article de Paris, as anyone can see. Does the Lady Alicia always wear such ... such ... revealing night-clothes?'

I ought to have checked her impertinence by some non-committal reply; but I was fidgety in her presence and, trying to conquer my nervousness, became too informative:

'Well, no; not always. As a matter of fact she has not worn this before. It is quite new. She told me she had bought it in London before coming here, had forgotten it and would wear it tonight.' I was going on to comment on the garment's texture and embroidery, when I saw that Mademoiselle was not listening to me. She was nodding her head in a leery manner, and so obviously that I was clearly expected to take note of it. Seeing that I was now paying attention, she half-closed her eyes and twisted her long thin lips into a smirk.

'Ver-rry interesting, Miss Hooper, is it not? Bought in London: brought to Clipston: forgotten, but remembered – oh so fortunately remembered – tonight of all nights.'

As she spoke she kept blinking her eyes and twisting up her mouth, with such remarkable results that I stared at her, wondering if she were a little queer in the head.

'I don't understand.... Why "of all nights"?'

'*Par-ce-que*' – she began, broke off and with a poor assumption of indifference said in English 'Nothing, my dear, I meant nothing.' She took a few dancing steps across the room and back again, stood by the bed and gently fingered the night-gown as it lay across the sheet. She was humming softly to herself. Suddenly she gave a nasty little laugh and exclaimed: '*Oh, le beau Tennant! Qu'il a de la chance!*'

I did not understand her actual words, but I heard the surname (which she pronounced in the English manner) and her tone made her meaning obvious. While I hesitated as to what to do or say, she cried:

'Heavens, it is getting late! I must not dawdle here. Do please be kind and let me have that silk. I need it tonight.'

I followed her to my room, found her what she wanted and then sat down to think.

Perhaps 'think' is the wrong word, for my mind was in too much of a turmoil to work coherently. I was furiously angry; I was miserably suspicious; I was frightened; and I felt that I ought to do *something*, but had no idea what. I told myself that the loose chatter of two hoydens and the hints of a spiteful woman were no evidence of anything save the nasty minds of their originators. All the same, the incident of the nightgown *could* be interpreted as Mademoiselle had interpreted it, and I further recollected that Lady Alicia had told me while she was dressing that she would not need me again this evening and that, after putting out her things, I could go to bed. This was unusual, for she was not considerate in matters of the kind and I had often sat up until after midnight and then been told I was not wanted. And why should that coltish Edina have said what she did, unless there were something in it? She was much too stupid to invent scandal on the spur of the moment, and it had been obvious that the mention of Charlie Tennant was no surprise to her sister.

I felt an urgent desire to see this man, whose name I had never heard until a few hours ago, yet now was the only name in my head. Tiptoeing down the back stairs I listened for sounds to tell me where the company were. There were still lights in the back premises and I could hear noises in the scullery; but I had stopped at the turn of the stairs and no one saw me. Then I heard a piano strike up and I knew that they were dancing in the Saloon and that luck was with me.

The main drawing-room at Clipston Park (called the Saloon) was suitably ecclesiastical. Indeed it might have been a church, save that it lacked east window, altar, pulpit, font and pews. It had an open roof and, high at one end, a gallery, which corresponded to an organ-loft and opened on to a narrow passage on the first floor. I slipped through to the front part of the house, and managed to open the gallery-door without more noise than its horrid drop-ring handle and heavy iron latch made inevitable. Keeping carefully in shadow I peeped down into the Saloon. They had rolled back the carpet at one end, and three or four couples were dancing. His lordship was skipping industriously round with the insignificant wife of a successful novelist who had been staying in the house for the last day or two. The novelist was at this moment playing a valse with skill and steadiness. I could see Edina dancing with a tall, droopy youth who might, I supposed, be Foulsham. Petronella and two other girls were also dancing with miscellaneous men. Alicia was sitting on a sofa in that part of the room which had not been cleared, talking vivaciously to two men standing in front of her. One was a red-faced jolly-looking man, with sweeping moustaches and a massive body which shook as he laughed. The other was small, wiry and very dark. He had a large rather ugly mouth, with prominent teeth which flashed under his small black moustache as he threw back his

head in enjoyment of one of the lady's witticisms. I watched
them for a few moments, hating them for their enjoyment, and
was working myself up into a general rage against my mistress
and her family, when it occurred to me to ask myself what
particular good I thought I was doing. This brought me down
to earth and I had to admit that my spying escapade had had
no real purpose. I had no means of knowing one man of the
party from another now that I *had* seen them, and, by creeping
about the house and peeping round corners, was risking looking a fool to some fellow-servant or something worse to my
employers. So I withdrew as quietly as I had come, hurried
upstairs and locked myself into my dingy little bedroom, feeling a good deal ashamed of my foolish impulse.

Lying in bed I tried to recapture some of the fierce emotions
which had possessed me after the talk with Mademoiselle; but
to my further mortification found it impossible. I seemed to
have flopped into an empty exhaustion, and just lay there,
unhappy and vaguely distraught until I fell asleep. I woke
early, and must, while sleeping, have been straightening up the
muddle of my mind, for a definite if inconclusive sequence of
ideas immediately took shape. Lady Alicia had married
Andrew for his money, not for himself. That being so, she
might, without violation of her own feelings, be tempted to
amuse herself with another man. But she must not be found
out or her money would be cut off. Why had Andrew married
her? Mrs Heaviside had talked of social influences; but surely,
I asked myself (at that time unaware that smart second-raters
often make better careerists, both for themselves and their
friends, than persons of better quality), the Seymores were
more genuine gentlefolk than this Hillmorton lot, for all their
titles? Had he then fallen in love with her? The idea was
distasteful, and I told myself it was ridiculous because she
wasn't the kind of woman he could fall in love with. But,
though I tried to reject the possibility of Andrew having ever
loved his wife, there seemed no other explanation of his having
married her, and undeniably she could fascinate when she
chose and was always charming to look at. Perhaps then he

was still in love with her? If he was, the knowledge that she was carrying on with someone else would hurt him grievously; if he was not, would he care?

At this point my alarm clock went off. Seven o'clock. In two hours' time I should have to go into Lady Alicia's bedroom and call her. I dressed and went downstairs for a cup of tea. Mademoiselle wished me good morning, and with a sly smile suggested that I keep my eyes open for anything out of the ordinary. I merely returned her greeting and went upstairs again to do the various small jobs which preceded my mistress' waking. At nine o'clock I was outside her door. There was no answer to my knock, so I went into the room and half-drew one of the curtains. She was fast asleep, lying diagonally across the bed with her arms loosely spread and her face buried in the pillows. The bedclothes were thrown back to her waist and I became suddenly and vividly aware that she had nothing on. Then I saw the nightgown lying in a small crumpled heap near the foot of the bed. Very quietly I redrew the curtain, crept from the room and left her sleeping.

Nearly an hour later a breathless maid came to my workroom, to say Lady Alicia had rung downstairs and said no one had called her and I was to go to her at once. I was in a jumble of agitation and self-questioning. What ought I to do? I had no idea. What *could* I do? I could write to Andrew. What about? I imagined him receiving a letter saying his sister-in-law had said this, his mother-in-law's maid had said that, and his wife was not wearing a nightgown at nine o'clock in the morning. He would think I had taken leave of my senses, and be angry with me into the bargain. And what else could I tell him? Nothing.

In a mood of confused unhappiness I returned to Lady Alicia's room. She was sitting up in bed wearing a dressing-jacket, and her eyes were hot and hard. The nightgown was no longer on the floor.

'Perhaps I may be informed why I was not called this morning?'

I longed to answer in such a way as would break off

relations for ever – to say, for example: 'You may – but you won't like it.' Instead I merely replied:

'I am very sorry, ma'am.'

'Sorry! That is charming. You neglect your first important duty of the day and are "very sorry, ma'am". Not a word of explanation. *Why* was I not called?'

I felt tongue-tied, and stood stupidly with my eyes downcast.

Fortunately, in her anxiety to show quickness of memory, she did not wait so as to force me to speak, but burst out again:

'Seeing that last night I particularly told you to go to bed in good time and excused you from waiting on me, you can hardly expect me to believe that you slept two hours longer than usual this morning.'

'Oh' I thought to myself, 'so last night's generosity was special enough to be remembered?' And I decided to frighten her.

'Yes, ma'am: it was a kind thought on your part. I – I – did – come in to call you – as usual – but you were – well, I didn't like to wake you. . . .'

For a moment my wits deserted me. I felt that she was suddenly alert and waiting for my next words. I had no next words. Then inspiration came: 'As I had some mending to do for Lady Petronella, I thought, perhaps — '

She looked at me searchingly, and I could feel her eyes trying to pierce the shield of demure humility which I held between her and my secret knowledge. She was afraid; of that I was sure. For a moment she did not speak; when she did, it was with the condescension of patient teacher to erring pupil.

'Very well, Hooper; we will overlook it this time. You are a good girl on the whole and I don't want to be unreasonable. But do not let it occur again, please; and if you have too much to do helping my sisters, you should tell me. Your first duty is to me. If we were remaining here, I should put a stop to your working for them at all; but we are leaving tomorrow to stay with some friends of mine near Northampton.'

She was more at her ease every moment, and went on in her usual faintly ironical manner:

'It will be an early start, so you'll have more or less to finish the packing today. Now help me to dress; and then you can begin getting my things together. Goodness knows where Carver has put them all or how many are mixed up with my sisters'. But those are your problems, not mine.'

As she talked, the tension of my mind relaxed. Indeed I felt almost kindly toward her for sparing me what I most dreaded – another fortnight in this detestable house. I had already had my fill of the showy discomfort above stairs and of the racket and boorishness of the servants' quarters. With the added torment of wondering what game she was playing and whether I were called on to take part or should remain an onlooker, I doubt if I could have borne even a further week of it. Now, however, we were moving on; and decisions of any kind could wait.

Our Northampton visit was pleasant enough. The house was agreeable, and the persons with whom I was thrown hospitable and polite. Only one incident of any importance occurred while we were there. I was taking a walk with the talkative lady's-maid of the mistress of the house, and we passed a property which was immediately noticeable for its spruceness and new paint. The house was long, low and white, with green shutters to every window and even the chimney-pots clean and red. A well-clipped privet-hedge, white posts and chains and a margin of mown grass bordered the road.

'That's pretty' I said 'and so spick and span. Who does it belong to?'

'A Mr Tennant' she replied. 'He made his money in cotton and has now retired here.'

'An old gentleman?' I inquired casually.

'Oh yes. Middle-aged and a bit more. Very good to their people, they say; generous and so on, which is not always the case with money-out-of-trade. The son is a military officer and the daughter is married, so the old people are mostly alone.

But Captain Tennant has just come home for a short visit, which will be a pleasure to his mother, won't it?'

'I'm sure it will' I said. 'Does your lady know Mrs Tennant?'

'Yes, indeed; though of course, we are proper gentry and have lived here since the time of the General's grandfather. Still, my lady finds Mrs T a very worthy body and a help with the church-bazaar and that, and we ask them to dine two or three times a year and sometimes go there in return.'

We were now following a field-path which would take us round through a wood and so back to our own house. As we entered the wood, I saw some little distance away a man and a woman walking their horses down a ride which struck away to the left. They were going away from us, but as soon as she caught sight of them my companion cried:

'Why, there *is* the Captain – and with a lady too! He's a one for the women, they say, and why not? A man's only young once. I wonder what lady he has got hold of now?'

'I think' I said 'that the lady he has got hold of now is mine.'

IX

We were back in Upper Belgrave Street early in October. Andrew and Nanny had returned a few days earlier; and it was so lovely to see them again and to feel that there was once more solid ground of affection beneath my feet, that the trials and tribulations of recent weeks faded into insignificant memories. I was equally glad to be back in my room with Clara, to talk to her of my doings and hear such news as she had to tell. The others also – from Mr Croggon downwards – seemed like old friends if only because they were familiar faces, and they for their part expressed themselves pleased to see me. The whole house, indeed, was warm with the spontaneous if transient cordiality of reunion; and one could feel it settling down to enjoy the cheerful informality of the little season.

Miss Carver was not due back for another month at least. She was still in hospital, and, although she was making good progress, would not be fit for work until after three or four weeks at home. So I continued to work as understudy.

Lady Alicia had entered on a most unusual period of even, almost nonchalant, temper. She seemed in less of a scurry than usual, neither stormed nor teased, and treated me as a lady's-maid likes to be treated – with civility and practical good sense but with level aloofness. At first I felt only relief and surprise at her mood of reasonableness; but as the days went by, I began to wonder whether she had not indeed changed. She had always been deliciously pretty, but a light tartness of expression and an edge of appetite on the fringe of her dazzling smile had, to those who saw her often, tended to mar her charm. The tartness and the hint of hunger were now imperceptible; the eyes were calmer and more detached; and in the place of her former needle-sharpness – as of one who lived perpetually in the present and must not miss a moment of it – was an indifference to what was going on around her, or at any rate a willingness to accept it without concern.

Andrew said to me one day:

'What have you been doing to Lady Alicia, Vanny? She looks much better than when she went away – less nervous and less inclined to overdo things.'

'I'm afraid it's not me. Probably the country air and quiet were what she needed.'

'Then Clipston was not so bad after all? I wondered when I got your very occasional letters – *very* occasional, you naughty girl – whether you were putting a brave face on it; for, as I recall the place, it is not particularly beautiful or restful.'

Here was an opportunity to remove a small but lingering embarrassment which clung to me. My letters *had* been very rare; and I had purposely assumed a cheerfulness I did not feel, for I knew he could do nothing to alter things and did not wish to worry him to no purpose. I had, however, an uneasy feeling that, when we met, he might challenge me; and, though I had tried for his own sake to deceive him on paper, I knew I should never be able to do so to his face. Now, by a fortunate coincidence, he was willing to believe that I had really meant what I said; and I took the chance of convincing him, by what I hope was no more than half a lie.

'Clipston wasn't at all bad, Andrew. It's not so pretty as Aughton of course, but the weather was fine and her ladyship enjoyed the polo and the coming and going. And that is a very nice house near Northampton – General Walker's you know – and there she rested and the garden is beautiful. . . .'

'Yes, yes; the Walkers are pleasant people. Well, whatever the cause of it, the improvement is there, and I shall continue to believe that you had something to do with it. Carver never brought her back so tranquil and blooming.'

There flashed before my eyes a vision of Lady Alicia sprawled asleep across the disordered bed; then another of her sitting up and glaring furiously at me for neglect of duty. 'Tranquil and blooming!' Another few moments play-acting, and we were safe.

'Silly old dear' I said, with a cheerful laugh. 'What could I have to do with it? I won't be praised at poor Miss Carver's expense, who I am sure looked after her ladyship much better than I knew how to do. Though I'm learning' I went on quickly 'really I am; and now that we are home again with everything to hand, I believe I will become quite a skilled lady's-maid. Then perhaps I'll turn into a valet, and come and look after you. How would you like that?'

'Much better than poor Olley would' he replied, smiling and putting an arm round my shoulders. 'You are a sweet child, Vanny, and kinder to me than I deserve.'

*   *   *

One morning Lady Alicia rang for me to her boudoir. I found her seated near the window with some papers on her knees.

'Come over here, Hooper, and look at this ball-dress. Don't you think it's pretty and would suit me?'

I looked over her shoulder and saw that she was holding a

pen and ink sketch, drawn with great spirit and coloured in
with water-colour, of a striking though simple evening gown.
Behind the drawing, and held in the same hand, was a sheet of
letter-paper of slightly larger size, the top of which projected
above the sketch. I saw elegantly engraved across the top of
this paper the words: NELDÉ, BROOK STREET, LONDON, W.

Hastily fixing my eyes on the dress design, I said:

'Yes, it looks very pretty, ma'am.'

'Then we will go and see it this afternoon.'

'Very good, ma'am. You said "we": do you wish me to go
with you?'

'Yes, I do. I want you to help me get it on and off and, if I
like it, see how it should be adjusted.'

In the brougham on the way to Brook Street she was
animated and talkative. I supposed that the prospect of a new
gown excited her.

'I've never been to Neldé before' she said 'though several
people have told me of her. I believe she was thought to be
rather – well, not altogether "the thing" – when she started. I
know Carver was very shocked, when a few months ago I
admired a negligée in an advertisement. But she is certainly
original and inventive, and her things do look smart. You
know, Hooper, even today I should not have dared to go, if
Carver had been here. But you're such a meek little thing, and
wouldn't say boo to a goose, let alone the goose who pays your
wages. So here we are.'

I was only half-listening to her, for my mind was full of the
curious freak of chance which was taking Lady Alicia to the
very place to which Lucy had begged me to bring her. I wondered if I should see Lucy and, if so, whether I ought to
recognize her; also how she would contrive to claim credit for
introducing this new and valuable customer, seeing that
neither she nor I was in the least responsible for her coming. It
was a queer affair altogether, and I was eager to see what
would happen.

The dressmaking establishment looked like a large private
house. Double-fronted, it had no show-window and no name-

board; only a neat little brass plate, like a doctor's, in the centre of the front door, with engraved on it, in the same simple and unusual lettering as appeared on the notepaper: NELDÉ . MODES. The door and area-railings were painted black and highly glazed; the porch, window-frames and reveres were a dusky cream. Apparently the whole building was given up to the business, for the windows of each floor were uniformly and impenetrably curtained with closed puckered cream muslin.

The front door was closed, and, after glancing about her for a moment, Lady Alicia said:

'I suppose you had better ring, Hooper. It all looks very private and dignified, doesn't it? I wonder if I shall be expected to leave cards?' She giggled, and for the first time it dawned on me that she was nervous, and not merely exhilarated at the thought of her new gown.

I did as instructed and rang the plain circular brass bell labelled 'Visitors'. After a short pause the door was opened by a sober-looking maid, wearing regulation black, but with a darkish cream silk apron and a muslin mob-cap of the same colour. She stepped civilly back to admit us, but immediately after closing the front door asked Lady Alicia her name. She then consulted a piece of paper which she took from her pocket and with: 'Will you please come this way' preceded us down the hall. The house was of the type in which the stair-well is set back from the façade, so that a broad hall-way, thickly carpeted, led from the front door to where the staircase started. I noticed that there were two or three doors in each wall of the hall-way (surely an unusually large number?) and also that the staircase, instead of rising in the open and being visible as it mounted from floor to floor, was walled-in and heavily curtained, so that not even its first flight could be seen from below. We followed the maid past the foot of the stairs and were ushered into a doorway in the left-hand wall. 'If you will kindly take a seat, Madame Céleste will be down in a moment' she said, and silently withdrew.

We were in a small dimly-lighted sitting-room furnished

and decorated entirely in brownish-grey. The walls and the inside of the door also were what the French call *tendus* – covered with a smooth grey cloth, quilted and buttoned; long grey curtains hung in front of the window, just parted in the centre and showing an all-over cream muslin casement curtain, identical with those I had seen in the front. The carpet was grey and very soft; the few chairs were upholstered like the walls.

'Well, I declare' said Lady Alicia a little breathlessly, 'this is the queerest dressmaker's I've ever been to. It's more like a fortune-teller's parlour – all these curtains and a half-light. And so quiet too. . . .'

I noticed that the place was indeed strangely silent. Neither voice nor footfall sounded anywhere. My curiosity grew keener. I was thoroughly enjoying myself.

Then, without even a click, the door opened and a woman came into the room. She was middle-aged, with a smooth melancholy face, and wore black satin with cream lace at the neck.

'It is a great privilege to welcome you to Neldé's, my lady' she said in a low educated voice. 'I have your gown all ready upstairs for you to try on. Will you be so good as to come with me?'

Lady Alicia, feeling herself in the familiar position of buyer to seller, regained her normal assurance.

'You understand, of course, that I am only looking at this dress to see whether I like it?'

'Of course, my lady. You are perfectly at liberty to buy it or not, as you wish. It has been designed especially to suit your type of beauty; but we are already repaid by the inspiration you have given to our artists, and it is for you alone to decide whether you share their taste.'

Lady Alicia was gratified by this handsome speech, and with a quick: 'Come along, Hooper' moved toward the door. I started to follow her; but to my astonishment the woman stood in my way. To my mistress, with respect but firmly, she said:

'I beg your pardon, my lady, but we have a rule that our

clients, while on the premises, are attended only by our own
staff. I am sure you will understand that, living as we do by
the creations of our designers, we dare not admit skilled eyes
to the secrets of our craft.'

Lady Alicia looked at the woman, and I could almost see
her new-found courage ebbing. Madame Céleste stood there,
correct but indomitable, and I certainly would not have dared
to challenge her.

'Very well' said my mistress at last, with a jauntiness which
I knew for Dutch courage: 'That dangerous informer, Only
Hooper, must stay here. But if I *do* buy the gown, she must
have it explained to her by someone.'

'Naturally, my lady. Once a client has favoured us with an
order, the dress is hers, and her maid is gladly given every hint
and assistance in our power.'

They passed out of the room and shut the door behind them.

Five minutes later it opened again; and a pretty young
woman slipped into the room. She also was a study in black
and cream, but her costume was so designed as to be less of a
uniform than that of the maidservant, but not so managerial as
the gown worn by Madame Céleste. Clearly every detail was
'considered' at Neldé's, and black and shadowy cream the
stable's racing colours.

'You are maid to Lady Alicia Seymore?' she asked,
pleasantly.

'I am' I said.

'Would you mind telling me your name?'

Rather surprised, I told her.

'Madame Neldé has instructed me to give you this, Miss
Hooper' (handing me an envelope) – 'and to say that she
greatly appreciates your having introduced the Lady Alicia to
her Salons.'

Not knowing what to say, I opened the envelope. It contained two five-pound notes.

'But, please . . .' I began. 'There must be some mistake. I
have not introduced —'

She interrupted me.

'Come, come, Miss Hooper. Why look a gift-horse in the mouth? Miss Beckett guessed you would be over-modest —'

It was my turn to interrupt.

'You know Lucy Beckett? She *is* here, then? Oh, I do so want to see her! May I?'

She laughed indulgently, as at an excited child:

'Yes, indeed she is here, and I know her well. She works under me. But I am afraid you cannot see her just now. She is "showing" upstairs. Besides Lady Alicia Seymore will probably want you very soon, as she will certainly buy that gown the moment she has it on. But you *shall* see Lucy and I'll tell you when is the best time. Let me think.... You are free in the afternoons sometimes?' I nodded. 'Well, on Fridays we do not "show", and a girl can get off if she wishes about four o'clock. Could you call at the staff entrance (that's at the side in Avery Row) just after four on Friday?'

'I'll try' I said. 'Does Lucy live here?'

'Oh, no' she smiled 'she only comes here to work. We all only come here to work. Goodbye, Miss Hooper. I hope we meet again.'

Before I quite realized it, she had vanished, leaving me with the two bank-notes in my hand. I pushed them into my reticule, determining to have it out with Lucy when we met and make her return them to her employer.

It was a quarter of an hour before my mistress reappeared, and to my surprise she came into the room wearing the evening dress of which I had seen the drawing. It was a miracle of tact and impudence – well-bred, harmonious, yet at the same time subtly outrageous. Madame Céleste and a younger woman followed her, the latter carrying a bundle of clothes over her arm, and in her hand Lady Alicia's walking boots. Céleste went to the wall opposite the door and released a spring; a panel swung back revealing a long mirror on its inner side, and behind it an alcove with a shelf bearing various toilet requisites.

Her ladyship pirouetted in front of the mirror, smoothing the dress over her hips, fingering the décolletage, wriggling her little body into the clinging embrace of the lovely silk.

'There now Hooper! Isn't it divine? Neldé must be a genius. You will now take it off under this lady's instructions, and help me to get dressed again while it is being packed.'

As we got back into the brougham, a long box of black cardboard was laid on the narrow seat opposite. No name of the establishment or address appeared anywhere; but in one corner of the lid, embossed in cream, was a capital N between wreaths – an adaptation, if not a copy, of the Napoleonic cipher.

*　　　*　　　*

That very evening Andrew told me that he was being sent on urgent official business to Washington and must sail immediately. He hoped to be back before Christmas, but could not say for certain until he saw how his mission prospered. I must promise to write to him once a week, and he would find time to enclose a letter for me in one to Nanny. I was sad to think I should not see him for so long; but I am afraid that the prospect of seeing Lucy on Friday, and anxiety as to whether I should be set free for long enough, so filled my mind that I was not so wholly taken up with his news as I might have been. He went off on the Thursday, looking very important and luggage-ridden and wearing an enormous ulster.

On Friday morning I called my mistress, setting her things to rights and ringing for her bath to be brought, while she glanced over her letters. When the housemaid had retired, she said:

'I shall not need you this afternoon or evening, Hooper, if you want to go out anywhere. I shall be out myself till after ten o'clock. So long as you are in before then it will be all right.'

I thanked her with real sincerity. This was luck indeed.

*　　　*　　　*

I approached Brook Street from the south, having cut the corner of Hyde Park, gone along Mount Street and up Davies Street to the western end of the mews. As I had a few minutes in hand, I thought I would walk through the mews to Avery

Row and see what Neldé's looked like from the back. It was the last house on my left and I immediately recognized its impenetrable muslin and the careful external symphony of black and cream. A curious feature of the building was a covered stairway, which mounted from the paving of the mews to the second floor of the house. This stairway was walled and roofed in solid wood, was windowless save for an occasional skylight, and was painted black. Idly I wondered whether it were a fire escape. Turning into Avery Row, I saw the staff entrance, down a few steps to the left. A projecting porch threw the door into deep shadow, for it was two-thirds below road level and the light was already fading.

I had been told to call for Lucy, but there was no sign of her. The door was shut, and groping around I could find neither bell nor knocker. A little intimidated by my adventure and by the memory of the muffled grandeur of Neldé's interior, I stood a few moments wondering what to do. I was in the embrasure of the doorway and well under the porch, so would hardly have been visible to a passer-by. I heard steps turn into Avery Row from Brook Street and cross the road toward where I stood. I drew still further into shadow, and in idle curiosity peeped upward to see who was coming.

Two men were just stopping at the kerb nearest to me. As they passed, I recognized one of them as the dark young man with the ugly mouth who had been laughing with Lady Alicia at Clipston. They were taking leave of one another:

'Good luck, then, Charlie' the other man said, winking and digging his friend in the ribs. 'If she's all you say, you'll not be in circulation again before luncheon tomorrow. I'll have a gin and bitters ready for you at the Club at twelve-thirty.'

'Thanks, old fellow. I'll accept with pleasure, though I shan't need it, I can assure you! I'm the luckiest beggar alive and feel like a lion. Goodbye for the present.'

They shook hands, and the man I had not seen before swung round on his heel and strode away northwards. 'Charlie' stood a few seconds, flicking dust off his hat with his gloves, straightening his tie. Then he began to move slowly in the other direction. I don't know why at that moment I became suddenly inquisitive, but I had an impulse to see where he was going. I slipped up the steps and reached the pavement as he turned into the mews. He went straight to the foot of the queer covered stairway, opened the door, went in and closed the door behind him.

Completely puzzled I returned to the staff entrance, to find Lucy waiting for me.

'Where do we go?' I asked, as after affectionate greetings we moved arm in arm in the direction of Bond Street.

'Back to my place to make some tea.'

'Your place?'

'Yes, my dear – lodgings in Castle Street – just over Oxford Street. Not far.'

We crossed Oxford Street, passed through a small square littered with market refuse, and came to a narrow, rather gloomy house in a street running parallel to the main thoroughfare. The passage smelt musty and the stairs were none too clean. The paint-work was scratched and the treads were covered with worn drugget. But Lucy's sitting-room was cosy enough, with drawn curtains and a cheerful fire.

'Oh, how nice!' I said, anxious to please her and seem pleased myself.

She stood and looked about, and in the fire-light I could see her little pout of discontent.

'It's all right' she said 'for the present. But I'd like to live in one of the little houses near Lord's Cricket Ground, with a garden and a balcony —'

'Perhaps you will some time' I soothed her. 'When you are a famous dressmaker.'

'Thank you, my dear; but I'll find someone to pay rent for me long before that!'

I laughed, instinct telling me she was being humorous – in which (as sometimes happens) instinct was wrong.

When the lamp was lit I had the first opportunity of looking properly at my friend, whom I had not seen in recent months. She seemed to me more beautiful than ever, slim and flower-like, with her pale gleaming hair bound smoothly round her head and a slow grace of movement which it was a delight to watch.

I noticed that she was very well dressed. Although her gown was black and deceptively simple, I knew enough about clothes by now to recognize expensive plainness when I saw it. Presumably Neldé's employees were clothed on the premises, and at special rates; but even so I remember thinking that she must be better paid than one would have expected. It was clear that she took as much delight as before in her own beauty. After taking off her jacket, and before in any way doing the honours of her home, she studied herself in a long wall mirror, turning this way and that and smiling contentedly. Then she remembered me, fussed me into a chair and ran out to fill the kettle and get the tea-things.

While we waited for the kettle to boil, she chattered about her work at Neldé's. She had made good progress since I saw her last, and was now of full mannequin rank. She rattled on about the smart women who came to the place, and the grand 'displays' at which several gentlemen, as well as a crowd of ladies, were usually present. It sounded to me an embarrassing, fidgety sort of life, always posing about and being stared at and putting things on and taking them off, and for ever and ever tidying up. But she seemed to like it.

Almost in the middle of one sentence she broke off and, after staring at me, said:

'You know, Fanny, you are getting to be a pretty girl – the brown, twinkling type that lots of men go mad about. How you *endure* service – being at someone's beck and call all day, and not even your evenings your own, I can't imagine. Let alone always wearing the same dull dark clothes. I know I couldn't.'

That this girl, only a few months my senior, should adopt an air of critical superiority neither surprised nor annoyed me. I was still prepared to accept Lucy as more grown-up and proficient in worldly matters than myself, and found compensation in keeping secret from her my relationship to Mr Seymore and the reasons why I was in Upper Belgrave Street.

'Oh, well' I said mildly 'I daresay I shall have had enough of it sometime, but I'm quite happy at present and had a lovely time in Yorkshire.'

While we were having tea I suddenly recollected the five-pound notes, which were carefully folded in my pocket. I flung them across the table so that they fell in her lap.

'And now, Miss Lucy, please explain those.'

She coloured a little and laughed.

'Explain them! Ten pounds of one's own need less explanation than most things, I should have thought. What's the matter? Aren't they enough?'

'Don't be an idiot and don't pretend. Even if *you* knew Lady Alicia was going to Neldé's, I didn't; and I've never even mentioned it to her.'

She made the notes crackle between her fingers, and sat with downcast eyes, a tiny smile twitching at her lips.

'No' she said at last 'I know you didn't. But I saw no reason why we should not both be a little richer for her coming. The money is nothing to Madam, and she likes to be on good terms with her clients' maids – particularly if they are also attractive girls.'

She was silent again, and still the enigmatic smile came and went.

'Oh for goodness sake, Lucy, stop being mysterious. *What happened?*"

'All right. I'll tell you. But you must not breathe a word. Promise? Well, one morning last week the four of us who made up one of the shifts of parade-girls were getting the things ready, when our head girl Madeleine – that's the tall fair one you saw – said the workshop was in a fluster over a gown being specially made for Lady Alicia Seymore. You can imagine that I pricked up my ears! I ran about making a few inquiries, found it was quite true about the gown and plumped straight in on the superintendent. I said I was responsible for getting the lady as a client. She looked at me without a word, began turning over a pile of letters at her elbow, picked one out, read it and then threw it back on the table. "No, you aren't" she said.

'That was a facer; but I stuck to my guns.

'"I am really, madam" I declared "—indirectly at any rate. Lady Alicia's maid is my oldest friend and I specially spoke to her about her mistress coming here!"'

'She stared at me thoughtfully. "So you know her maid, do you? That is interesting. Wait here a moment." As soon as she was out of the room, I darted for that letter and – my word! – I saw it all then. Back she came, to find me sitting quiet as quiet. "Miss Beckett" she said smooth and pompous as never was, "Madame Neldé appreciates the loyalty you have shown, and is also grateful to your friend for helping to get a new client. She wishes me to say that you will receive her thanks next pay-day and that Lady Alicia's maid will be similarly rewarded when she comes with her mistress on Monday." And sure enough, on Saturday there were two fivers for me and on Monday two for you! There – isn't that a triumph? Now say: thank you Lucy, and take your chinkers and be grateful.'

She threw herself back, clapping her hands and laughing. She was so pleased with her shameless achievement that I could not help smiling with her, although inside I was startled and mystified.

'You *are* a wicked girl!' I said.

'Why wicked? We get money; Neldé sells a gown, and our little Fanny's mistress becomes someone else's as well. So everyone is happy. You know, I suppose' she added quickly and casually, 'that she is there this afternoon?'

'Who? Where?'

'*Lady A. is at Neldé's.* Bless the child, I'll have to spell the words next!'

'Lucy, what *are* you talking about? Why should she be there?'

'To meet her friend, of course.'

'What friend?'

'The one who wrote the letter I saw on old Doughface's desk.'

I felt more and more bewildered.

'I'm sorry' I said humbly. 'I just don't understand what all this means.'

She gazed at me seriously, took two turns up and down the room, tightened her lips and said:

'Here goes, then. I see I must begin at the beginning and go on to the end. Don't blame me if it shocks you.'

This, in summary, is what she told me.

'Madame Neldé' was in fact a man, a Viennese Jew called Kramer. He had been dress-designer to a fashionable house in Vienna; but, seeing that his genius only went to enrich his employers and that he had no prospect of being invited to join them, he evolved a daring plan, in conjunction with an English actress who was at that time his mistress. This woman had connections with two or three wealthy men in England and, returning home, interested them in Kramer's project – which was nothing less than to establish in London an ultra-smart dressmaking business which should also serve as a house of accommodation. The surface-puritanism of the English had created a state of affairs in which would-be lovers had nowhere to go – nowhere, that is to say, either civilized or discreet. At the same time English wealth and English snobbery could be trusted to follow a continental chic. It should not, therefore, be difficult to collect a rich clientèle willing to pay high prices for smart gowns, or luxurious privacy, or both.

The necessary money was raised and, regardless of expense, Neldé's was planned and decorated. Kramer had faultless taste, and insisted that to the smallest detail the décor should be restrained, effective and unmistakably special to the establishment. It was also essential that the dressmaking side of the business be given a Parisian colouring and its products be absolutely first-class. Its designs would purposely be more provocative than those of its competitors, and at first it was to be expected that the clients would be aristocrats of the half-world rather than of the whole. But Kramer was confident that he would draw Society in time, for many English ladies are smart dressers, and quite a few less virtuous than they have to pretend. So artists and craftswomen of the highest quality were engaged, the subtlest of clothes were imagined and produced and, though prices were exorbitant, the goods supplied were beyond criticism.

Kramer apart, the entire building (with the exception of two or three draughtsmen, an expert tailor and some embroidery girls) was staffed with people from the British Isles. Most of them were given French names; but that was all in the way of business.

The lay-out of the building was as careful as its embellishment. No one was seen except by invitation or appointment. The ground floor was divided into a number of small reception rooms, to which clients were conducted on arrival and in which any strangers who might accompany them could, if desired, be detained on one excuse or another. On the first floor was the large saloon used for mannequin-parades, and several fitting-rooms. The second floor was chiefly occupied with offices, workrooms and studios; but from it started a private staircase which led up to four self-contained suites, representing the secret element in the Neldé business. To this third floor also led the outside stairway from the Mews – a stairway reserved for gentlemen visiting their lady-friends. The door at the bottom was kept on the latch, but only gave on to a small lobby, shut off from the actual stairs by a second door. This was always locked and the caller had to ring for admittance; but while waiting he was in privacy and could be seen by no one. On the fourth and fifth floors of the building were more work and store-rooms, and the apartment of Kramer himself.

Stringent care was taken that the establishment should not in any sense rank as a brothel. No employee of the dressmaking business was permitted on the third floor or had access to it. The suites were available only to clients and their friends, and were waited on by a special staff. Finally, as the cost of accommodation was merely added to the dress-accounts, there was no documentary evidence that such suites even existed.

Of course every member of the staff knew what went on. But they kept their mouths shut, and for good reasons. Not only did Kramer pay generously and give better conditions to employees than most of his competitors; he also conducted a bureau of external prostitution – that is to say, he supplied girls to hotels or private houses at the request of persons he knew. Suppose you fancied a mannequin at a dress-parade. You passed an inquiry through a sympathetic overseer, and next day (provided your references were satisfactory) you received a quotation – at your house or hotel. You posted (or handed in) the money; and you could rely on the arrival of the girl you wanted at the specified hour and place. Thus you were spared an embarrassing settlement after the party was over. This system, as efficient and reliable as Kramer's other activities, naturally proved of great advantage to girls in his employ. They had a half share of their casual earnings: they stood a good chance of meeting a more permanent lover, and one or two had actually found husbands. It was hardly likely, therefore, that they would take exception to the purpose of Kramer's third floor or betray its secrets by random talk outside.

*   *   *

When Lucy had finished her recital, I sat for several minutes, wondering what I thought about it all. Now, years after the event, my chief feeling is one of admiration for Kramer's brilliant reading of English social hypocrisy and his skilful energy in exploiting it to his own advantage. He supplied exactly what the rich wanted; but in such a way that they did not feel guilty or unworthy of their traditions. At the time, however, my reaction was not general but highly personal. I remembered that Lucy – the very girl who had just told me this extraordinary story, the girl who was sitting just across the hearth-rug, the girl whom I had known all my life – was herself at Neldé's. I was very literal; indeed I was unnecessarily blunt:

'Will you get sent here and there, also, Lucy?'

'Of course I shall. Why not? Indeed I have begun to be.

Actually I have to be at "Jimmy's" in Piccadilly tonight at eight o'clock, and ought to start getting dressed.'

'Oh dear' I said, genuinely concerned. 'I mustn't keep you!'

She laughed, a little too heartily.

'You couldn't afford it, darling, even if you wanted to.'

*   *   *

As I walked home, the other and more serious implications of this extraordinary afternoon crowded Lucy from my mind.

What was I to do?

RIVER ROW

I

I WAS home by eight o'clock and crept upstairs to my room. Clara was downstairs at supper, and for an hour or more I should have the place to myself. I sat in the dark, and wondered what I ought to do. I was obsessed with the idea of Lady Alicia at Neldé's – probably *still* at Neldé's; of the man with the big mouth; of Andrew in America. Compared with these individual complicities, Lucy's description of the dress-shop and the activities for which it served as mask seemed unimportant. The revelations neither revolted nor excited me, except in so far as they posed a personal problem.

What ought I to do? What *could* I do? I could confront Lady Alicia with my knowledge. I could tell Mrs Heaviside. I could write to Andrew. If I did the first, I should be dismissed on the spot or maybe accused of attempted blackmail, with all appearances against me seeing that I could not prove what I said. If I did the second, I should be disbelieved and, suppose I insisted, risk provoking inquiries and gossip which would mainly serve to make public what, for Andrew's sake, should remain private. If I did the third, I should only distress or worry the man I wanted to serve, and at a time when he could do nothing in the matter; also I might myself appear in the unattractive role of mischief-maker, tell-tale or, worst of all, spy. Finally, if I did any one of the three, I should be giving Lucy away; for I could not make even the beginning of a case in my own support without admitting to inside information, and it would not take long to identify my informant.

I had reached this deadlock when I heard Clara's footsteps, and had to bustle about and put clothes away and pretend I had only returned a few minutes earlier. Then I went downstairs to prepare for my mistress' return. She came in at ten o'clock. Attending on her was a queer experience, knowing what I now knew of her, yet going through the habitual routine of helping a familiar woman with her every-night toilet. She asked me no questions and made none of her habitual little quips about her own movements and encounters. Indeed she hardly spoke to me; but, when she did, it was mildly and pleasantly. I left her before eleven.

As, while with her, I had not consciously thought further of my next move, it surprised me to find that, even before I got to bed, I had decided what to do. I must run away – just disappear from Upper Belgrave Street, taking my secret with me. Whether later on I wrote to Andrew or made contact with him, must depend on circumstances; the immediate thing was to leave this house, and get away from the woman for whom at one moment I felt a murderous loathing and the next a sort of bitter gratitude. I could strangle her for cheating someone I loved; but I could almost thank her for making possible his release, if release he wanted.

Lying wakeful in the dark, I thought of places to run to and when. There were only three possibles – apart from a solitary refuge in strange lodgings, for which I had neither courage nor means – only three places where I could reasonably hope to be cut off from the Seymore household; and two of these were none too certain.

Lady Alicia knew the Becketts' address – or had known it; and, as Mrs Heaviside had said, she never forgot what one wished her to forget. If she recalled it, she would certainly send there to inquire; and I could hardly ask Mr Beckett to perjure himself to help a refugee from nothing in particular. Also Aunt Mattie was far from reliable, her continual curiosity as to smart gatherings in Upper Belgrave Street and her relish for details of luxury and expenditure had long ago shown me that she was a flunkey at heart. To gain the favour of Lady Alicia she might well betray a dozen humble fugitives.

Lucy's lodgings were little safer from discovery and had serious drawbacks of their own. The trail lay straight to her from Chandos Street; so much for being traced. This apart, I felt fairly sure she would not want me. She would warmly sympathise with my adventure and never give me away; the whole affair would strongly appeal to her love of intrigue and delight in undercover escapade. But sympathy, I suspected, would not extend to an offer of semi-permanent hospitality, it being evident that Lucy was now going her own way and wished to be free of past associations. Also she shared her place with someone I did not know, who would have to be consulted. Lastly there was probably no room to spare.

Chunks remained – Chunks and his Jolly Bargee – and it was overwhelmingly plain that there was the solution. He had offered me help any time I needed it, and had meant what he said. He was completely unknown to everyone at Upper Belgrave Street. His inn was the other side of London and, being an inn, would surely have some sort of unoccupied corner where I could hide until I had found a new job. To Chunks, therefore, I would go.

As for when, the sooner the better. The next day was Saturday when work was relaxed and hours easy, and I hoped to be able to pack a small hold-all and slip from the house in the early afternoon. My trunk and most of my clothes must be left behind, but this was the price of escape. Unluckily everything combined to delay me. Her ladyship had friends to luncheon, and kept me upstairs till nearly four o'clock dancing attendance on her and two other ladies who were discussing clothes and experimenting with feathers and laces. When at last I was free, I found Clara waiting for me in our room, saying she had leave from Mrs Heaviside for us both to go to tea in Pimlico. I had neither heart nor excuse to refuse an outing which the poor girl was so proud of having arranged. Off we went, and only came back just in time for staff supper. Knowing that Lady Alicia would want me in half an hour's time, I faced up to the fact that it was now or never. Food didn't matter. I must get Clara down to the kitchen and be off. Besides Neldé's two notes, which I regarded with some uneasiness, I had three pounds and some odd change. This money, my precious brooch and such essential clothes as could be crammed into the hold-all, I feverishly put together. At half past seven I was out in the dark street, walking quickly northward. I was lucky enough to find a growler on the cab-rank at the top of Sloane Street, and told the driver to go to the Angel. It took him over an hour, and he charged me 3s. 6d. and 1s. extra for being more than some distance or other from Charing Cross. I think he cheated me.

When I found myself standing on the pavement outside the Angel, the qualms I had firmly kept at bay rushed at me. Till now the need for haste and a determination not to anticipate trouble had sustained me; but I felt far from heroic, alone and clutching my hold-all, in the strident turmoil of an Islington Saturday night. It was nearly nine o'clock on a grim November evening, and the gas flared in the public-houses and yellow lamp-light quavered in one after another of the sordid little shops. I remembered Chunks' address, and that it was just to the right at the beginning of Lower Street. Pardonably, in one ignorant of London and its bland illogicality, I assumed that Lower Street would be below – i.e. to the south of – Upper Street and, knowing that Islington began at the Angel, expected to find myself almost opposite the mouth of River Row. But having crossed the big road and started to walk north, I could see no sign of my wanted turning, or indeed of any turning at all, save an occasional tunnel-entry which seemed to lead to a court behind the houses and frankly frightened me.

The pavement and roadway swarmed with people, and a rough lot they looked. Two louts barred my way at one point. After inviting me to take some refreshment in a manner which they imagined was a caricature of a West-end swell (and seeing that I was part disgusted and part scared), they suddenly relapsed into their natural animality and made a grab at me. I did the only thing possible – darted sideways into the nearest doorway, which was a small shop selling stationery, string, cheap magazines and so forth. The louts did not attempt to follow, and as the door closed behind me with a second tinkle of its bell, I felt momentarily safe.

Behind the counter was an emaciated woman, wearing wire spectacles and with hair brushed tightly back to a small bun behind her head. I was too flustered to pretend I had come to buy.

'Please excuse me' I said breathlessly. 'Two men frightened me. I am trying to find River Row, and if you could direct me—'

'River Row?' she repeated, and through her glasses hard brown eyes surveyed all she could see of me. 'River Row? That's a queer kinder place for a young gal to ask for. And what might yer need with River Row?'

I wanted to tell her to mind her business; but she was my hope as well as my refuge, and I swallowed my temper.

'An old friend of mine keeps an inn there – Mr Box his name is – and I am going to visit him.'

'Never eard of im' snapped the woman, 'nor anyone er the name either. Not but what there's publics and to spare in them streets by the water and no place for gals though welcome enough I've no doubt.'

Again she stared at me.

'Is this ere Box expectin yer?'

'Of course he is' I lied sharply, and the touch of temper seemed to shake her a little.

'Satdy night and a dark one too' she said doubtfully. 'Not a time for a chit like you ter go pokin round the canal. Ere, I tell ye wot; wait a jiffy while I shut the shop and I'll put yer on yer way.'

I thanked her, and to pass the time looked over a number of *The London Clipper* which lay among other luridly illus-trated weeklies at one end of the counter. Arthur Sketchley's at-that-time famous 'Mrs Brown' was discoursing on the School Board, and I was enjoying her cockney volubility and thinking how similarly the proprietress of this shop would ex-press herself on the same theme, when the woman returned from the back room wearing cloak and hat, and announced herself as ready. She put out the light in the shop, locked the door from the outside, and turned to the right. The street seemed a solid mass of people. There was hardly any wheeled traffic, though an occasional dray loaded with barrels whip-

cracked and swore its way along, and two costers pushing a
loaded barrow caused shouting and confusion by cutting at a
run into a narrow entry. Islington Green was a flare of torch-
light from stalls selling everything edible from boiled sweets to
very fishy fish, and everything wearable from petticoats to the
slouch hats worn by dustmen. Facing us from beyond the
Green was Sam Collins' Music Hall. The façade of the house
was picked out with gas-jets, and their yellow glare, together
with the wild flicker which the torches of the street-market
threw upward, showed the name of 'The Great Vance' plastered across the front, in letters large enough to proclaim
Islington's pride in having secured (at enormous expense for
one week only) this Lion of Variety.

We had hardly passed the Green when my companion
turned to the right, into a dark and narrow street which slanted
sharply back the way we had come.

'River Row' she said, with an acid triumph I did not like.
'Dye fancy it? And now where dwe find Mister Box?'

At this point I wanted above all things to shake her off. I
felt that alone I could face the ordeal of walking down the
sinister street, finding and entering the Jolly Bargee and asking
for Chunks. But with this vinegar body at my side (her pretence of helpfulness no longer disguised her impertinent
curiosity and sour mistrust) I dreaded the moment when I
must without warning confront my poor old friend and be
given the lie by his astonishment.

'I am most grateful' I said. 'I would not think of troubling
you further. Thank you—'

'Young woman' she interrupted, and her very unction was
acid, 'Emily Pott never sets her hand to the plough but she –
she – well, in other words, I'm going to see you to your
journey's end.'

There was nothing to be done. I followed her into the
menacing shadows of River Row. Low houses, so lifeless and
shuttered that they might have been abandoned, edged the
street. One lamp, set in a projecting bracket, shone feebly in
the distance. Beyond it there seemed to be a faint glow, but

why or whence there was no knowing. River Row had no pavements; uneven setts sloped slightly toward the centre, so as to make a central drain, in which rubbish, liquid and otherwise, lay stagnant. I hardly knew whether to keep under the lee of the black house-fronts or brave the horrid jetsam of the street's middle. My heart sank lower with each fumbling step. We seemed to be penetrating into a noisome slum, the last place likely to contain such a tavern as Chunks would care to own. But when at last we reached the projecting lamp, I saw that it was fixed in a wall at the extreme end of River Row, which here debouched into a small open space, with houses on three sides, and on the fourth (that opposite to us) a low parapet. I could see these details in the light which streamed from broad windows to the left. I also saw a nameboard: THE JOLLY BARGEE: CRABWORTHY'S ENTIRE, and knew that I had arrived.

I was about to make a final effort to rid myself of the persistent Pott, when from behind the lighted windows came a sudden burst of singing – or rather of what a number of loud-voiced and convivial watermen would regard as singing. They began a little raggedly, but soon settled down to a steady and more or less rhythmic roar, beating pewters on wood to mark the time:

> *Tommy make room for your Un-cle,*
> *There's a little dear:*
> *Tommy make room for your Un-cle,*
> *I want him to sit ere.*

We had that twice through, and then crashed into:

> *Slap! bang! ere we are again,*
> *ere we are again,*
> *ere we are again*
> *Slap! bang! ere we are again.*
> *What jol-ly dogs we are!*

The second rendering of this irresistible polka must have set some of the company dancing. There was a roar of laughter, and heavy boots began stamping on the floor. Then came the sound of breaking glass, more shouts and laughter, and the swing-doors of the tavern crashed open, as two men, hugging one another like bears, came dancing into the road. They were followed by a small group, now all singing at the tops of their voices, and soon the lot of them were jigging up and down, in pairs or singly, reeling and stumbling but thoroughly enjoying themselves.

I had crouched back into the shadows at the entrance of River Row and was watching with a mixture of alarm and amusement this grotesque saraband of jumping bargees, when the oily cockney of my companion oozed into my ear:

'Are yer still visitin at Mr Box's public, Miss? If so, I wish ye a very good night though not a quiet one. If not, where do ee go next – back to the Aymarket, I ope. I'm a respectable woman I am, but I know your sort, with yer baby-ways and sham innercence. "Expected" eh? And not only by her old friend, I'll be bound. *Good* night to ee, and if any *more* men frighten ee don't come snivellin to Emily Pott.'

With a rustle and a sniff she hurried away toward Lower Street.

It was at this juncture that one of the merry-makers, who had wandered away from the rest and with the solemn idiocy of a simple drunk was hop-skip-and-jumping to a tune of his own, caught sight of me. For a moment he stared open-mouthed at what must have been merely a piece of darker darkness; we were out of the light radius of the tavern-windows and almost behind them. Then he peered a little closer and yelled out:

'Gaw A-mighty, it's a gel! Hi, boys, eres a lydy come to join the dance. Come on, lovey, dance with pore Claringce!'

He seized me in his arms and began clumping me round, gradually circling towards his friends. I could only grip my bag and pray he would not crush my feet under his huge boots. I was too breathless to cry out and too frightened to think. As soon as the others saw us, they crowded round with whistles and tally-ho's, leaving a circle in the centre, in which for a few minutes more Claringce and I jigged solemnly up and down. Then my partner abruptly left hold of me, staggered two steps

and, subsiding gently on to the ground, sat there grinning foolishly.

The crowd had stopped their singing and, after a few
guffaws at their comrade's collapse, were eyeing me silently.
From the open door behind them came a voice – recognizable
and familiar, but speaking with a strident accent I had not
heard before:

'Ullo, gents, why so quiet all of a sudden? Fill up, you
buggers, and we'll ave some more music. Why, what's the
matter with ee? Playing kiss-in-the-ring or what?'

Elbowing his way through the group, Chunks stopped short
at the sight of me.

'Ere, what's this? Where's the piece from? I won't ave yer
coming ere for yer greens as you well know —'

'Chunks!' I cried feebly. 'Chunks, it's me!'

And I lifted my face full into the shaft of light and took a
step toward him.

'Fanny!' His voice cracked, and the noise was a stuffless
wheeze. 'Fanny, by all that's oly!'

He pulled himself together, and turning to the staring group
addressed them with brusque authority.

'See ere, pals. This young lady's a friend o' mine and if
you'll all go back in and get Polly to serve you another round –
on the ouse, too – I'll ave a word with her and then perhaps
we'll join ye. See? All right, then; off with yer!'

They obeyed readily, hauling the still-seated Claringce to
his feet and dragging him with them.

'And now, me dear' said Chunks quietly, and in the
moderate cockney I was accustomed to: 'What's up?'

'I've run away, Chunks. You must trust me for the reason
till there's a chance to tell you quietly. But it's a good one.
And I want you to let me be here with you – just a little while
till I find another job. I don't wish anyone to know where I've
gone. Oh, don't turn me away, Chunks – please!'

He patted my hand comfortingly.

'There, there, don't take on so. So you've run away? Good
for Fannikins! And o' course yer shall stay as long as yer like.

They'll not find you ere, never fear.' A burst of laughter from the inn reminded him of his customers. He asked almost sharply: 'Them chaps didn't annoy yer, did they? They're good chaps enough, but they've got a drop inside em, and pretty gels is scarce after dark in these parts. Still, if any of em—'

'Oh, no, Chunks. They were only jolly. You *are* a dear soul. I'll try not to be in the way and I can help, if you'll let me'.

'Come on in. I'll show you the place and then introdooce yer. As for elpin, that depends. I dessay Polly'll be glad of a and now and again, and' – he broke off, adding with a sort of embarrassment: 'Harkye, Fanny. I forgot. I live alone, ye know. No woman in the place nights. Maybe you'd not fancy—'

'But, Chunks' I cried, 'who does for you?'

'No one. I does fer meself.'

'Then, you old stupid, you'll not do for yourself a day longer. I'll look after you.'

He took me in by a side door, showed me the 'cosy' behind the bar, and the kitchen and the rooms upstairs. There were two bedrooms besides his own, small but adequate. The place was only surface clean.

'Now' I said. 'Tell me where the sheets and blankets are and I'll fix myself up. Tomorrow I'll get busy with a pail and brush.'

'I don't arf like makin a servant of ye, Fannikins—' he began.

'That's the only thing I know how to be' I replied 'and anyway *you* aren't making me. I am. But you can call me 'housekeeper' if it's any easier. Now run along to the bar and let me make up a bed.'

'Ave you ad any supper?' he asked.

I shook my head.

'It doesn't matter, Chunks. I'm not hungry.'

'Stuff and nonsense! Supper ye *must* ave. I'll show you wot we've got and you can please yerself.'

We inspected the larder and collected two sausages.

'There's bread and cheese in the cupboard' said Chunks,

'and you shall take a half-pint of what yer fancy from the bar.
Before fryin them sausages you come along o me and meet
Polly and the boys. Polly is barmaid, and a jollier better-
natured female don't exist. As for the boys – these are me
Sat'dy night reglars, all work on the canel-barges, and though
rough to the eye are warm to the eart.'

As we entered the bar-room from the back a silence fell.
Chunks, with his thumbs in the arm-holes of his waistcoat,
cleared his throat noisily:

'Lady *and* gents! It gives me much pleasure to interdooce
to you, Polly, and to you, mates – the haristocrats of the City
Basin – Miss Fanny Ooper, oo I've known since she was a
babby and is now come to live at the Bargee with old Joe Box.
Fanny, me dear – Miss Polly Crowe, the best barmaid in
Islington.'

Polly simpered and said she was pleased to know me she
was sure. The clients touched forelocks or grinned sheepishly.
I was given a stool in the corner. A slight constraint hung over
the company, until Chunks called for another song:

'You, Arry, give us the one Vance is singin at Sam Collins'
this very week.'

A short squat man, sitting bolt upright on a bench near the
door and wearing his hat, began to sing, very loudly and with
the mechanical rigidity of the ventriloquist's dummy. He moved
nothing but his lower jaw until he came to the chorus, when
he solemnly wagged a clay-pipe in time with the tune:

> *The Stilton, sir, the cheese, the OK thing to do*
> *On Sunday afternoon, is to toddle to the Zoo*
> *Week Days may do for Cads, but not for me and you;*
> *So dressed right down the road, we show em*
>   *oo is oo —*

The pipe was raised in the air like a conductor's baton.
Down it came as he bellowed:

> *The walkin in the Zoo*
> *The walkin in the Zoo*
> *The OK thing on Sunday is the walkin in the Zoo!*

There were three verses, and by the time the encore was over, I felt I had earned my sausages. I whispered to Polly that I was going to have some supper. As I went out of the door behind the bar, they were warming up to another of Vance's favourites – the best of his haw-haw songs, whose refrain ended ideally for singers addicted to emphatic noise:

> *But we've nothing of that sort he – ah!*
> *Certainly* NOT!! *Certainly* NOT!!

II

I stayed three months at the Jolly Bargee; and although when the time came I was ready for a change, they were pleasant months enough and taught me many things.

The little inn stood at the head of a small basin – an artificial branch of the New River which at that time flowed down the centre of Colebrooke Row. This basin was filled in when, later, the River was tunnelled over. The three-sided square marked the end of the basin, whose water lay stagnant and rubbish-choked just over the low parapet which I had seen on the night of my arrival. I have no doubt the place was very unhealthy, especially in hot weather; and even during my short winter sojourn the smells and sights were often disagreeable. But Chunks, his neighbours and his customers seemed to notice nothing amiss or be the worse for their surroundings, so I suppose that in time one became acclimatized.

The neighbourhood, especially to the north and east, was a bad one. Immediately off Lower Street was a patch of old and neglected houses, huddled in a tangle of narrow streets and courts; here in miserable poverty lived hundreds of London's most pitiable citizens. Further to the east was a more sinister district. Some twenty-five years earlier, an ambitious speculator had planned to lay out a few acres with showy, though shoddy, houses. He had suddenly gone bankrupt, leaving his plan unfinished. The jerry-built terraces were sold for what they would fetch, and within a very few years had become a still pretentious but rapidly crumbling rookery, in which congregated as dubious a population as one could hope to avoid. Chunks had no illusions about this area.

'Keep out of it, Fannikins' he said. 'Never strike Kingsland way from ere without you go by Lower Street. River Row is dingy enough; but then it's what they call condemned and mostly empty and comin down and, being straight, can be watched from either end. But them arf-finished crescents and archways and steps up and down and dead ends are nobody's business.'

I asked him how, with a bad crowd so nearabouts, he kept the Bargee free of them.

'I ad a job doin it when I first came' he replied. 'But I took a tip from the old guvnor and started by refusin admittance to women. Women in pubs is arf the trouble, with their filthy minds and mean tricks – the sort o women I'd get ere I mean. Then I ad a dust-up or two and showed them fancy-boys I could chuck em into the water when so inclined. So bit by bit I got the ouse kind of special for the watermen. They drink eavy and make noise fit to wake the dead; but they're honest workin chaps, not like them rats yonder. Ye see, before I came ere this pub was nothin better than a lush crib for duffers and kiddies, and decent bargees kept away. But it's a tidy step down to the ouses serving Wenlock and City basins, and they were glad enough to use the old Bargee once it was cleaned up.'

From Polly I learnt enough about a barmaid's life to turn my ambitions elsewhere. She was now settled and content; but had had a grim enough time to embitter anyone less incurably good-humoured. Well on in her thirties, she was a massive piece of peroxide joviality, designed and decorated on traditional barmaid lines, and with a splendid bust which had at one time actually provoked the lily-of-the-valley joke – at least so she assured me, though I have always thought the preliminaries too coincidental to be relied upon.

Polly had been behind a bar since she was twenty. A parentless domestic drudge in a provincial town, she had answered an alluring advertisement in some London paper, offering good wages and a life of variety and fun to young girls of address and sound physique. The advertiser was a publican and he engaged her on the strength of a half-length photograph which she sent with her application. This first employer had been no slave-driver. He paid her well; he gave her a chair on which to rest at odd hours; he let her off regularly for an hour in the afternoon and at three o'clock on Sundays; he protected her from insolence while he was in the bar, and he did not expect the impossible in the way of dusting and glass-washing when business was heavy. But he wanted his quid pro quo; and after she had been there a week, made it clear that on Wednesday and Saturdays nights she shared his bed. He was a methodical man.

She would probably have stayed there indefinitely ('I didn't mind im avin me' she said. 'You get used to it, you know, and e seemed to enjoy it and was a decent old sort') if the publican's sister had not suddenly decided to come and live with him. The poor man struggled to avoid this unwelcome favour: but the lady arrived, and soon set about dislodging the attractive barmaid, whose relations with her brother she immediately guessed, and disapproved as leading to over-indulgent treatment of an employee and to waste of money. One evening Polly bought something she wanted over the bar from a pedlar. She had only two half-sovereigns, so she took ten shillings worth of change out of the till, replaced it with a half sovereign, paid for the small purchase and slipped the rest of the money into her apron pocket. An hour later she was called to the back parlour, where she found her new mistress and a policeman. Ordered to turn out her pockets, she was accused of robbing the till which, the lady declared, had been full of silver a short while ago but now was ten shillings short. Polly told the exact truth, wept and entreated, but the woman denied that an extra half sovereign was in the till and gave her in charge. Next morning the magistrate ruled that she repay the ten shillings, fined her as much again, and put her on the streets with a few coppers in her pocket.

There now followed weeks of desperate hardship. She did not know how to start looking for work, and was too confiding

and inexperienced to hold her own with the waifs and outcasts
to whose level she now sank. They planned to use her as a
decoy; but, in order to have a hold on her, forced her to
experiment in petty crime. She was set to picking pockets outside the London Pavilion at midnight, but was so clumsy that
the first man she tackled caught her red-handed. He looked her
over, and offered to let her go if she went to a hotel with him.
Lying in bed, he asked her questions and, when he had heard
her story, advised her against picking pockets without
adequate training. Before they parted in the morning he
offered her a job as barmaid in his City winehouse. 'But no
thieving, me dear' he said. 'It's a select little place, very
select.' 'Oh no, Sir' said Polly.

She soon found that her new place of business was a girlery
as well as a wine-bar. The single bar-room was cosy and discreet, and throughout the afternoon and evening men came in
and out. Sometimes they just took their wine in the comfortable little saloon, inviting one of the barmaids to join them and
fondling her according to their taste. Sometimes they asked for
a private room, of which there were two upstairs. It was then
the girl's duty to take champagne or claret up to the customer
and stay with him till he was ready to leave. There were three
girls on the staff, and for a while Polly (whose temperament
was equable, and as little affected by yielding a man her body
as her lips) was well content with life. The clients were mostly
good-class men who treated the girls civilly and generously,
and she saved quite a bit of money. Then she had a quarrel
with one of her colleagues. They were both in drink (for life in
a wine-bar taught girls to drink, if it taught them nothing else)
and the dispute flared into savage fury. What it was about, she
could not remember. 'Something silly enough, I daresay. But I
was screamin mad and we near scratched one another to
pieces. In comes the boss in the middle and seein as ow she ad
been there longer than me, out I went.'

Her next place was a bad one. The guvnor was a close-fisted
brute and his wife drank. The barmaid and the potman were
sometimes at work from five in the morning until twelve at

night. They had to wash the glasses, polish the metal-work and mahogany, dust the shelves, swab the floors of the bars, clean the windows and have everything shipshape by opening time. During the day and evening they were on their feet for hours at a time, and in among they had to cook for their employers, do the housework and submit to any incidental drudgery which might be put on them. The mistress, who slept apart from her husband, used to bribe Polly to smuggle a bottle of brandy upstairs and hide it under the pillow when she made the bed. More than once, having gone to bed already stewed, the woman started in on the brandy, got shouting drunk in the middle of the night, and finally crashed out of bed on to the floor. The boss, hearing the noise, did not go near his wife, but knocked Polly up in the middle of her few hours of sleep and told her to get the missus in order again and stay with her till morning. He himself went back to bed.

She could not stand this for long, and moved to a large basement tavern near Holborn Viaduct station. Here the trouble was the customers. Apart from casual in-and-out traffic, there was a gang of low-class tarts whose language and behaviour was disgusting even to Polly's uncensorious mind, and a crowd of elderly lechers who haunted the bar and forced suggestive conversation on the girls behind it. Being out for fun on the cheap, they took no notice of the public girls on their own side of the bar, for these had to be paid. They never gave a barmaid a present, and would hang about for an hour on one sandwich and a gin-and-water.

What satisfaction they got out of leering at a barmaid, patting her hand and asking her if she'd heard the one about the stockbroker and the Thames Tunnel, Polly could never understand. But they persisted day after day until she felt she should go mad.

Then came a stroke of luck – or what seemed like it. A quiet genteel sort of man began coming in to the place, who usually contrived to be served by Polly when she was on duty. From an exchange of 'good-days' they progressed to casual conversation, and in time she looked forward to his coming, for he

never talked silly like some of them, still less did he embarrass
her by extravagant behaviour or unmannerly remarks. He told
her he was travelling agent for one of the big Fire Offices and
lived in comfortable lodgings in Manchester, from where he
toured his exclusive territory of Lancashire, Cumberland and
Westmorland. He was at present in London for some months,
taking the place at Head Office of a man who was ill.

These and other details of himself were not given all at
once, for, unlike most men, he showed interest in Polly's life
as well as his own. But as day succeeded day, the conversations over the bar covered plenty of ground; and when at last
they reached the point of an occasional outing on a Saturday or
a Sunday afternoon, not much remained untold that either
wished to tell. Among other things Polly, in her communica-
tive way, confided to him that she had a matter of eighty
pounds put away, and not in one of them banks either, but
where she could lay her hand on it any time. She did not admit
to it having been earned. She said it was a legacy from her
grandmother.

At last her beau (as he was now generally considered by the
barmaids and barmen in the tavern and by Polly herself) made
her the expected proposal of marriage. She accepted; and after
a visit to a registry office the couple left for Manchester. He
had delayed his offer until his time in London was over, feeling
that his bride deserved all the comfort he could give her; also
that, as their home must be in the North, the sooner after
marriage they began their search for a little house, the better.
The lodgings on the outskirts of Manchester were warm and
agreeable, and Polly soon convinced herself that her troubles
were over. Her husband resumed his journeys, but at present
undertook only the shorter ones, so that at night, or every other
night, or at least for weekends, he could rejoin his wife. Meantime she went into the city and bought furniture and so on,
hunted houses far and wide, and, when he had time to spare,
took him to see her bargains and the most likely of her house
discoveries. Eventually, one Saturday, they found a place to
his taste. He was off on the Monday for a trip of two weeks,

and decided that the most considerate thing he could do for his
wife would be to see the agent in the town on the Monday
morning, pay the deposit and close the deal. He would also
have time to settle the various accounts for household stuff
which was being held by the sellers pending full payment and
delivery instructions. Then she could move in at once, and be
happily occupied during his absence in getting the house to
rights.

He was very sweet about all this, and his anxiety to save
her trouble and hasten the building of their home touched her
greatly. When, therefore, he explained apologetically (she
found even his embarrassment engaging, so strong was his
appeal to her natural generosity) that his quarterly commission
cheque was not due from London for a few days, that he was a
bit short, and might he borrow her nest-egg, she joyfully
agreed. He left her on the Monday morning, with seventy
pounds of her money in cash, and she never saw him again.

'Quite like one of them cautionary tales for girls, wasn't it?
But then they are always mixed up with morals and keepin
pure and that, and never havin been much of a one for purity I
didn't believe em. Serve me right I suppose; but I thought
then and I think still that a damn lot of things are more important to a girl than keepin pure, whatever the reverends say.
Let em try bein cold and ungry and lonely and then think
again!'

She tossed her head and laughed her little tittering laugh –
the queerest laugh to come from a downright, deep-breasted
incorrigible like Polly Crowe and, I can only suppose, her one
attempt at refinement – before rattling off again:

'Anyway I was in a nice pickle up there, with a few odd
quid in me purse and one somewhere else and all them bills to
pay, let alone the diggins which is lordship ad forgotten to
settle for two weeks.'

'But what *did* you do, Polly?'

'Well, I couldn't bury the landlady, so I paid er. Then I
vamoosed to Liverpool, and left the others to put their stuff
back into stock.'

'And in Liverpool?'

'On the game, ducky, for a bit, till I found a job in me real line. That was a bad time, that was. Yer meet up with orrors in them sea-port towns, and I was clean broke when me luck turned and I was taken on temporary at a pub in Aintree. The boss was pleased with me and kept me on, and I've not bin out of a job for more than a week on end since – and got about the country too.'

She certainly had. From Liverpool to Belfast, to Glasgow, to Leeds, she moved from pub to pub. She was just the type to make a popular and efficient barmaid, ready with laughter and back answer, always willing to take a drink, kindly to the timid and fully equal to the fresh. Experience had taught her how to keep strangers at a distance without seeming to do so; and even those employers who regularly bullied their barmaids for standing up to offensive clients, never tried it twice with Polly.

In due course she arrived at Newmarket, and there she met Chunks. He was in some obscure way connected with a boxing-club to which many of the stable boys and jockeys belonged, and seemed to be a combination of trainer, sparring partner and impresario to his very various material. At the same time he was well up in racing gossip, and in great demand as adviser and organiser of precautions, when foul play was expected or some important stable secret had to be kept. He used to frequent the hotel-bar at which Polly was engaged – usually with a crowd of admiring juniors – and she noticed from the first his lack of swagger and his simple acceptance of the homage paid to his knowledge of the ring and the racecourse. Among the occasional visitors to the bar was a wealthy but boorish baronet – an owner of doubtful reputation, but for his money's sake ranked among the élite of the place. This man would boast that he had a taste for low company, by which he meant the jockeys, ostlers and bookmakers' touts on whom he depended for his racing triumphs. He therefore made a practice of visiting the public bars of the principal hotels, and there divided his time between patronage of the more or less humble clients and offensive familiarity toward the girls behind the

counter. One evening he made a set at Polly, and after leering
at her, while making a number of semi-salacious asides to a
little group of hangers-on, suddenly reached across the bar and
pawed her bosom. To his astonishment she gave him a stinging
smack across the cheek and, picking up his glass of rum and
water which he had set down on the bar to free his hands,
threw it full in his face. When he emerged from the sputtering
confusion of this surprise attack, he found Chunks at his
elbow.

'Not a word, Sir Welby, not a word, if I may make so bold.
Out we go, nice and quiet, and forget all about it, or we find
Sunspot unplaced this very Thursday.'

The bully looked round for his toadies, but they had disappeared. With an ill-grace and muttering to himself he
lurched out of the saloon. Chunks came to the bar. 'Pluck, me
dear' he said to Polly 'is always pluck, and twice so in a
woman. Let me shake ye by the and for putting a hardneck in
is place.'

From that moment their friendship began; and when a year
or two later Chunks decided to leave Newmarket and become
the landlord of a disreputable public east of Lower Street, he
invited Polly to come with him. She had set up house in Newmarket with a feckless but amiable creature, who wrote light
music and lyrics for minor music-hall singers and appealed to
her maternal instinct. Chunks found the pair of them decent
lodgings in Pentonville, paid her good wages, and here she had
been for the last four years.

*   *   *

I did my best to repay Chunks' hospitality. The house was
kept really clean, I took every pains over my shopping, and he
often declared he had never fed better in his life. Polly also
was good enough to approve of my cooking, when she took
meals on the spot. My spare time was mostly spent in sewing
or talking to Polly. Occasionally during quiet times I would
take her place behind the bar, to set her free for shopping or a
breath of air. I soon got to know the familiars among the

customers, and was on excellent terms with them. They were noisy and foul-mouthed, and had no more polish than pieces of sandpaper; but I came to enjoy seeing men enjoying themselves and they never treated me with rudeness, so both sides were soon at ease. I suppose that I heard nearly all the bad language there was, and each man had his regular nights for getting very drunk. But they were simple-minded creatures, and their oaths and jokes and horseplay were natural and spontaneous.

This experience of males in the rough taught me an invaluable lesson, thanks to which I have always been able to make friends with any man I have wanted to be friends with. It taught me never to disapprove *on principle*, and to prefer a man to behave in my presence as he naturally behaves when he is happy. If that involves swearing and getting drunk, then let him swear and drink. You can always tell when a man is talking dirt and drinking too much in order to show off, or to nerve himself for something, or because he despises you and is purposely bad-mannered in order to underline his contempt. I have known that sort of thing only too often, and very disagreeable it is. But most men have some genuine and individual line of relaxation, and a woman, if she likes a man well enough, does well to let him follow it.

*   *   *

Christmas went by with suitable jollity. We had an immense Turkey-and-Plum-Pudding-Dinner, attended by Polly and her friend (an infinitely nondescript man, with drooping moustaches and watery eyes), and by two of Chunks' best pals among the bargees with their wives or equivalents. The Bargee corps of regulars had a more than usually glorious drunk; one of them was with difficulty restrained from stripping to the skin and diving into the basin from the nearest parapet; and Claringce and I, by special request, did our dance-act, which ended in his sitting in a puddle and singing 'Christians Awake'. One evening Chunks took me to the pantomime, another to Collins' Music Hall; and on New Year's Eve to see the amazing and terrifying sight of the yelling crowd at the Angel greeting the coming of 1875.

Then January, cold and grim and (as always) flat after the festivities, began its dreary course.

One day I said to Chunks that I must find some work to do, and had written to a friend for her advice. He protested that I could stay where I was for ever and who was the friend. I told him I couldn't and what did it matter who she was? He looked glum for a moment; but then, like the generous soul he was, begged pardon for poke-nosing and agreed that I could not lie up in the Bargee all my life.

I wrote a cautious letter to Lucy, saying I had left the Seymores and would like to see her. Should I come over to Castle Street or would she come to Islington? She chose the latter.

Two or three days before she was due to come, Chunks said he was walking up to see a man on business in Balls Pond Road, and as it was a dry morning would I care to go with him and see the bad patch he had warned me to avoid.

We set out, I with a slight sense of adventure and thankful for my massive escort, he in his workaday clothes and carrying a heavy stick.

'Between you an me, Fannikins' he said 'I run across some funny monkeys in Newmarket. One or two of em did me down before I was fly, and pals of mine too, and I was partly drawn to the Bargee because I thought I'd be well placed for keeping an eye on em and maybe paying em back. It's a basket of bad eggs, this part we're just comin to, and sooner or later every cross-cove and faker in the country goes to ground ere. So I planted meself on their doorstep, and take a stroll around now and again to see oo's to be seen.'

We were walking along a street of mean houses, over the tops of which I saw a sudden outcrop of taller buildings. But before we reached them our street terminated in another, running to left and right crescent-wise, and the entire house-scape changed. Instead of dun, flat dwellings edging the pavement, there were florid villas, set back behind railings and separated from the road by a few yards of trodden earth, in which scraggy shrubs made pretence of growth amid a litter of broken shards, old boots and other rubbish.

'Eres the frontier' said Chunks, and turned to the right.

The houses were in an indescribable state of premature decay. Balconies sagged or in places had been roughly broken away; the railings along the road, supposedly set in a low plastered wall, were bent this way and that or were torn into gaps, or even here and there lay in twisted foot-traps on the side-walk. Many of the windows were broken and stuffed with rags, others were shuttered; but as half the shutters hung by one hinge, there was usually a black space of window, like a leering eye, peering over the top or round the side of the blistered and rotting woodwork.

Not a soul was to be seen. There were no carts or barrows in the street, and almost no sound save of the wind rustling the bare twigs of the shrubs or clap-clapping a loose board or a faulty end of guttering.

Nevertheless smoke rose from several of the chimneys – ornate brickwork affairs, coarse imitations of Tudor elegance, and as often lopsided or missing a brick or two as tolerably complete – and one had the uneasy feeling of walking a no-man's-land between two rows of secret lives.

Chunks crossed the road and took a diagonal street to the left. It ran straight and slightly up hill, and at the far end passed beneath a high archway which joined two blocks of lofty houses. These houses – the ones I had already seen in the distance – had their backs to us, were built on a curve and must face on to a circular space which lay beyond the arch. The houses lining the road up which we were walking were no less exaggerated in design or stained and cracked than those in the first crescent; but they seemed in better repair, so far at any rate as concerned their doors and windows. They were perhaps on that account even more sinister, suggesting occupants barricaded as well as furtive.

We reached the archway, and I was noticing that two heavy lamps were bracketed with elaborate iron scroll-work to the walls on either side of the entrance, when a man sidled out of the short tunnel ahead of us and stood markedly on one side to let us pass. I felt his eyes raking the two of us, and with a sudden twinge of fear took firmly hold of Chunks' left arm. We were just inside the archway when he called to us:

'Beg y' parding, guvnor, will yer be wantin anyone partickler?'

Chunks threw back over his shoulder a sentence which to me was gibberish, but evidently met the case. The man muttered something and lounged away, and we passed through the archway into a round area of uneven pebble-strewn earth, surrounded by tall houses and centred by a single plane-tree.

'This ere is Larne Circle' said Chunks in an undertone, 'and the middle point of what they call Ganderton's Folly, that bein the bloke as built this loony set-out. Eres where the big pots ang out.'

As we crossed the open space, I took in the main features of one of the queerest spots I have ever seen. Clearly the hapless Ganderton, when he started his hopeful operations, had a boldness of fancy and some generosity of vision. Larne Circle was façaded on a continuous curve, pierced by entries at four opposite points, each of which passed under a shallow tunnel or deep archway like the one by which we had entered. Between these entries the buildings rose sheer – three houses to each segment of the circle – and showed an ornate but enterprising sense of the decorative possibility of ironwork, moulding and occasional bas-relief. The name 'Larne Circle' was displayed in large raised capitals on the panels sunk in the architrave of each segment. The plaster house-fronts were paintless and blotched with damp; the flat pillars of the doors were chipped and kicked and greasy at shoulder-height with the rubbing of dirty coats; in places near the ground the plaster had crumbled away entirely, showing brickwork beneath. But the windows were sound, and I observed that one house had them closely barred. On the other hand, the main doors – except that of the house with the barred windows – stood wide open, showing a filthy hall-way and the lower treads of stairs. I must have been so occupied in absorbing all that I could of this extraordinary place, that I neither saw nor heard anyone approaching. But one moment Chunks stopped dead and the next I heard a strange voice:

'Why, strike me pink, if it isn't Mister Box! Well, this *is* a pleasure to be sure, and out with his young lady too! Good morning, ma'am.'

With my first startled glance I saw a tall man, who bowed with a flourish holding a billycock hat in his hand. Chunks returned the greeting, as though he too were surprised.

'Mr Slode, I declare. It's quite a while since we met. You livin around ere now?'

'I am. My father has lived here some years. The neighbourhood has sadly deteriorated; not at all what it used to be. But you know how elderly people are – they get set in one place – and my father prefers to remain. So I have decided to keep him company.'

He spoke in an educated voice, but with a suavity I distrusted. He had a plump round face, bold black eyes and, under a divided moustache which swept to right and left, a pair of glistening crimson lips. He was neatly dressed in short-tailed coat and dark trousers, a light-coloured waistcoat cut very low, and a turned-down collar with a black bow tucked under the corners.

Chunks, in reply to a question, told Mr Slode that he owned the Jolly Bargee and that we were now on our way to Kingsland, it being a nice morning for a walk.

'Then I will not detain you' the other answered. 'We must not let this charming young lady take cold. Perhaps I may call in one day, now that we are neighbours? I seem to remember that the Bargee was something of a – well, had no very good reputation at one time. But I daresay that is all different now?'

'It is' said Chunks stolidly. 'Quite different. As you'll see if ye onner us with a visit. Good day to ee, Mr Slode.'

When we were clear of Ganderton's Folly (there was a corresponding area of once tawdry desolation beyond the northern curve of Larne Circle) I drew a deep breath.

'I'm glad to be out of that' I said. 'And who is Mr Slode?'

'Evan Slode, me dear, is the worst scoundrel I know except one (and I know a few), and the worst is is precious old guv'nor. I'm arf glad Evan's ereabouts and arf sorry. E'll be round before long, mark my words: and sad though I'll be to lose me little Fanny, she's better away when them sort is about.'

'But you asked him to come, Chunks?'

'Ay, I know. No use trying to stall Evan Slode. Ye got to give im jolly-dog as fake as is own. But e'll go careful with me, never fear. E's tried the other way and it didn't work.'

On Sunday Lucy came. I had arranged to meet her at the Angel, she to take an omnibus to that point, arriving as nearly as possible at noon. It was an unkind, blustery day, and I was glad not to have to wait above ten minutes before she emerged from the inside of a Marble Arch-to-Islington. She was very smart in a tight little frogged jacket edged with fur, a frilled and scalloped skirt, and an apology for a bonnet, which was little more than a bandeau of fur and velvet tied round her high, tilted chignon. She carried a muff and round her neck was a brightly striped woollen scarf, with tassels at the ends which blew out behind her in the wind.

I had my story ready; and, as we went along Upper Street, told her that Lady Alicia had suddenly become very unkind to me, that Carver had been about to return, and that I saw no prospect in Upper Belgrave Street save being degraded to my former position and dragging along unhappily for ever. So, knowing that Chunks would take me in, I had decided to run away and, rather than involve Mr Beckett in tiresome inquiries, to keep my whereabouts absolutely secret.

She asked very few questions and seemed to accept my explanation as adequate. She did not even, as I expected, make fun of my living in a back-street public with 'that fat old man' Chunks. Indeed she seemed strangely interested in Islington and looked about her eagerly, asking questions. At one moment she remarked that Lady Alicia had been a regular visitor to Neldé's, 'both up and downstairs'. I longed to inquire whether Andrew had returned to England but did not know how. Luckily she answered the question without my asking it.

'Her lord and master should be home about now' she said, 'but I don't suppose that will choke her off. She seems in full swing with her Captain T.'

'How do you know about Mr Seymore?'

'Oh, Miss Carver told Madeleine in December he was due back early in the year. She's a chatter-box, that woman; Mad says you can get anything out of her if you handle her right. By the way, Mad was disappointed you didn't come again; she liked you, and even wondered if sometime —'

' — if I'd join the staff?' I laughed. 'No, I don't think it's my line, swaying about in tippies. Pity, because I want a job and want you to help me find one.'

Lucy said quickly:

'As a matter of fact I shan't be there myself much longer.'

Glancing at her, I saw she had coloured slightly.

'A friend of mine' she went on, too casually 'has got me an opening on the stage. It will be much more free and gay not being cooped up from nine in the morning till six or even later.'

'Lucy! How exciting! I must come and see you. Will you have a speaking part?'

'Not at first, but they say I ought soon to be front-row chorus.'

'Oh, chorus – but then what about money? You won't be paid as well as now.'

'The money will be all right' she replied.

*   *   *

Over dinner at the Bargee Lucy made herself extremely pleasant to Chunks, who could hardly take his eyes off her, so glowing and vital was she. The meal done he went upstairs for his nap, and she and I settled by the bright fire in the parlour.

'What sort of job do you want, Fanny?' she asked suddenly.

'I suppose a lady's-maid of some kind. It's the only thing I can do.'

'And are you high-flying about the style of place – I mean, must they be lords and ladies or some kind of Society swells?'

'Not for my part, but I suppose anyone who wants a maid is more or less of a swell, isn't she?'

She did not answer, but sat looking into the fire, pinching her lower lip between thumb and finger. I remembered she had sat just so that evening in Castle Street, before she told me the true story of Neldé's. I wondered what was coming now.

'Well, look here; don't fly out at me, no offence meant, but I do happen to have heard of someone who wants a sort of assistant in running – well . . . a kind of hotel, you might say . . . someone practical and energetic and – like you, in fact . . . But, you see, I don't know how you feel about . . . about things that go on and all that. For instance I suppose you are still – still a —'

She petered out altogether, and I, who had been enjoying her stammering circumspection, decided that a little surprise would be good for her and silently gave thanks to Polly for enabling me to give one. I said calmly:

'I suppose you mean, have I sprained my ankle yet?'

She jumped round in her chair and stared at me in astonishment.

'Fanny!' she gasped. 'Where on earth did you learn that kind of talk?'

'But *don't* you?' I insisted.

'Well, yes . . . I suppose I do. . . .'

She was still disconcerted and I relished my moment of triumph.

'Then I haven't; but I've no objection in life to doing so, at the right time. Now tell me why your job hangs on so queer a thread.'

She looked at me uncertainly for some moments, twisting a handkerchief between her fingers. There was a new look in her eyes, almost a look of respect, in the place of the friendly patronage to which I was accustomed. Then the real Lucy – the candid, unaffected Lucy whom I had always known survived under the airs and graces of recent months – asserted herself.

'I'm very, very sorry, Fanny dear. I have been a stuckup stupid thing to you lately, and all the time you are wiser than I; you always have been. I'll never come it with you any more. I promise. Please forgive me.'

I went across and kissed her.

'Nothing to forgive. I don't mind a bit. We're friends and that's all I care about.'

She squeezed my hand and smiled upward with tears in her eyes. Anything lovelier I never saw.

'The job, please' I prompted.

'Have you ever heard of Kitty Cairns?' she began.

I shook my head.

'Well, she has been a customer of Neldé's almost since the start and a very good one too. She dresses quietly, but in perfect taste and wears her clothes beautifully. She runs about the swellest gay-house in town, just by Regent's Park, and needs – as I said – an assistant.'

'Meaning?' I asked.

'Oh no, not that – unless of course you want to. No; on the management side. Miss Cairns was quite definite on the point, so our overseer said when she was telling us about it afterwards. It's a mixture of secretary and personal attendant, I suppose.'

'Good money?'

'M'm. I don't know exactly how much, but good.'

'I'll have a try for it' I said. 'I've been here long enough, and I'd like to see another kind of life. What do I do next? Probably the lady has got someone by now.'

'I doubt it. It was only a couple of days ago she spoke of it. Look, I'll ask Corinne – that's the overseer – first thing to-morrow and write to you. Shall I? Are you sure you want me to?'

'Quite sure, angel; and you are a dear little brick to help me.'

*   *   *

In the afternoon of the next day I was sitting alone behind
the bar of the Jolly Bargee, doing a piece of crochet and thinking over my conversation with Lucy. I felt a growing curiosity
about the possible post with Kitty Cairns and knew that I
should be deeply disappointed if it were denied me. I had been
happy and safe at the Bargee; Chunks was a darling, and
everyone had been as nice to me as they knew how. But I
wanted to get back into the world, to some place where I could
hear what was going on, find out whether Andrew was home,
meet fresh people, earn some money. Polly had gone down to
the market to buy some stockings, and Chunks was out on one
of his mysterious business jaunts. The house was therefore
empty, except for the young boy who did the rough cleaning,
and he was clanking buckets somewhere in the back. All at
once I became aware of a figure standing on the outside of the
glass-panelled doors. Next moment one of them was pushed
cautiously open, and the head of Mr Evan Slode poked round
the edge. The head was followed by the rest of him, still
moving warily, nor did he take any notice of me until the door
had swung to behind him. It was almost as though he had not
seen me, tucked away behind the high barrier of the bar. With
an effort I remained quietly seated on my stool and went on
with my crochet.

He had seen me, however, for with a sweeping bow he bade
me good afternoon.

'I had, I believe, the privilege the other morning Miss – er –
Miss – do you know, our excellent Mister Box omitted to
introduce us! My name is Slode. May I be permitted to know
yours?'

'Mine is Hooper' I said composedly. 'Can I serve you with
anything, Mr Slode?'

'This is very civil of you, Miss Hooper; very civil indeed.
Yes, I think I *will* take a drop of Old Tom. You will join me,
I hope? No? Something more suited to a lady's taste, per-
haps? A glass of champagne, now; just a taste of champ?'

'Thank you' I said. 'I don't like anything but tea in the
afternoon.'

I served him his gin. He perched on a stool and leant his elbow on the bar.

'Mister Box not at home?'

'He'll be in any minute' I replied. 'Do you want to see him?'

He pouted his fat red lips, and winked invitingly.

'I'd rather see *you*, my dear; and also, if she is anywhere about, that divine creature who was with you yesterday.'

This alarmed me. If he had been spying on us, his visit at this hour was calculated. What was he up to? I rallied my courage.

'My friend is not here, I am afraid. When did you see her?'

'I never miss a pretty girl' he grinned, 'and two neverer still! Happy chance put me in the wake of a couple of the dinkiest little ladies that ever tripped along Lower Street and – the old Adam did the rest. I followed em up, marked em down, and here I am. Come on now, ducky, give poor Evan a kiss.'

He hoisted himself on to the bar, and sliding along its polished top leant over to where I sat. Remembering Chunks' warning, I made a final effort and pleaded with coy confusion:

'Not in here, Mr Slode, please! Mr Box wouldn't like it. Some other time – if *you* have the time. . . .'

He looked at me, weighing his chances.

'Some other time, eh? Can the little girl slip up one evening to the Circle to see her lovelorn swain? All cosy and cuddle-me-ree?'

My quick ears caught a familiar step.

'Look out! Here's Mr Box. I'll try. Call for a letter at Pott's the stationers in Upper Street. In a few days.'

He nodded, was off the bar and decorously finishing his gin, when Chunks walked through from the back.

I said demurely 'Here is Mr Slode, waiting to see you.'

And I collected my crochet and slipped away, unreasonably delighted to have involved the hateful Miss Pott with this very nasty man.

PART TWO

Told by Harry Somerford

'FLORIZEL THIRTEEN'

I

THE FIRST I heard of Clive Seymore's trouble was at the Chatham Club in the autumn of 1875. I came into the smoking-room in the late afternoon and found a group of men round the fire, several of whom I knew.

'Hullo! There's Somerford!' cried one of them. 'Come here, Somerford, and tell us about poor Seymore.'

'I don't know anything about him to justify "poor Seymore"' I replied, ringing for a drink. 'What's the trouble?'

'The innocence of the Civil Service!' another laughed. 'They never know anything. It's what they're paid for.'

'See here, you chaps' I said. 'If it's a riddle, I give it up. If you want me to say you're all up to snuff and I'm yesterday's dream, I'll say it. But what in Heaven's name are you talking about?'

They looked at me and at one another, and their silly chuckles died away. They began to look uncomfortable.

'Sorry, old man' said one. 'Thought you'd be sure to have heard. Seymore's in Queer Street and there's talk of a divorce into the bargain.'

I gaped at them, while the shocking news sank into my mind. 'I had heard nothing' I said at last. 'I am very sorry. "Poor Seymore", indeed – and such an A1 fellow.'

After a short talk on other things I hurried home. Better get the facts from a source more certain than club-chatter.

*　　*　　*

Clive Seymore was an important person in the department

in which I worked, and marked down for a Permanent Secretaryship if ever a man was. Ten years my senior he was twice that ahead of me in capacity and prospects. The only son of a wealthy Yorkshire squire, whose money came partly from coal, but mainly from the wonderful agricultural land in the East Riding, thousands of acres of which belonged to him, Seymore had married the daughter of some fairly recent peer – a smart, pretty, clever girl who did the social end of his existence to perfection. I had always imagined him lucky in his wife; for dinners and soirées were not in his line at all and, left to himself, he would never have gone near them – which may be good sense but is bad careerism. Some of the men in the office pretended to think him stand-offish and conceited; but he was only shy – that, and a little better quality than most of us. The previous autumn he had been sent to Washington on a very special mission, which had kept him out of England far longer than was expected. Indeed he had not got back till the early summer. And this is what he had come back to find! I could not believe it. He seemed the most established person in the world, and as for divorce – one could hardly imagine him even aware of such a thing.

Next day I sought out my opposite number in the department over which Seymore ruled (I was myself in the Legal Section, and some way from the top of it) and made discreet inquiries. The story was perfectly true. I knew of course that during the year there had been a serious general slump; that the Stock Exchange was wearing black and world prices were in the depths. But I had not known how serious was the crisis in agriculture. Seymore's father, with thousands out on mortgage and extensive commitments to his tenants (which – being a model landlord – he was too proud to repudiate), found himself almost on the rocks and at a few months' notice. The money which had made Seymore's own existence possible suddenly dried up – and at that moment of crisis his wife had turned on him.

A week or two later I heard that he had resigned.

In the ordinary course of affairs I was acquainted with many members of the legal profession; and it happened that one of my special friends was a junior partner in the firm which did the Seymore family business. I invited him to dine with me one night, and took him off for coffee and cigars into a retired corner of an almost empty writing-room.

'George' I said. 'I'm going to ask an indiscreet question, though with no indiscreet motive. If you want to, you can shut me up.'

He winked at me over the top of his coffee-cup.

'Go ahead' he said.

'How serious is Clive Seymore's affair? Has it broken his back?'

George gave me a quick look, and then sat pulling at his cheroot, staring in front of him.

'Why do you want to know?'

'Because I admire the fellow and, so far as a younger man can be, who does not know him well, I am very fond of him. I ask only for myself and you can trust me not to repeat a word you say – if you decide to say one.'

'All serene, Harry. You're on old friend and we're out of harness. But for God's sake don't give me away. Very well then: "How serious?" ... It's early days to say definitely, but the financial position is pretty bad. Anyway it will kill poor old Sir Everard. I hear the old man is breaking up and can't last long. As for actual facts, the greater part of the farms will have to be sold, though Heaven knows who'll want them except at knock-out prices, while things are so bad. One or two of the tenants may have the cash to buy their own places; but they have lived in clover up there for so long that they have lost the habit of thrift. Those farmers have made money and made money, with so little idea of what to do with it that they would drink champagne regularly with their old-style country meals. That's true, Harry, literally true. And the poor souls went on living in acute discomfort because they just didn't know how to spend money on making their homes nice. Their only idea was to chuck it about right and left on junketings and filling their bellies. Then old Sir Everard – the dearest old tenderfoot you can imagine – never refused a tenant anything; never conceived anyone would cheat him, just built and repaired and gave yearlong credits and underwrote loans, and would have gone on doing so until the cows came home. And all the time he was lavishing money on your Mr Clive – or rather on your Mr Clive's missus, who knows a thing or two, and among them how to make the thick-uns fly. Mr Seymore may be a stunner; but I think he should have started in and driven my lady on a curb from the beginning. Anyway she's bolted for good now, and he won't be troubled with her much longer – though at a price. So perhaps it's an ill-wind. . . .'

I prompted him:

'In what sense "bolted"?'

'Oh, not "run away". Dear me no; the mare is too fly for that! Merely smashed the cart to bits and thrown the driver, and then told him to foot the damage. You see, while Mr Seymore was in America, the lady consoled herself with somebody else and liked it so much that it became a habit. I daresay her husband would never have found out – or not for a long time – for he's probably as unsuspicious as his father. But when the crash came and madam saw the money running out, she had no further use for him, so she told him they were splitting out and that he was to be the guilty party.'

'But, George, that's all bunkum! Couldn't he tell her to go to Hades?'

'You'd think so. But I gather (I've never spoken to him personally, you understand; but Biddulph, who dealt with all this, told me what happened) that he is not the sort of man who would do that willingly or well. Besides – to make matters worse – she had something up her sleeve. It appears – or so she alleges – that he introduced a by-blow of his own into the house, as a sewing maid or something, and set the girl to spy on her. The lady threatened to make this public unless he gave her grounds for divorce. I suppose there must have been *some* truth in it, for he consented to do so. The case will come on some time next term and will go through undefended. So you see the poor chap is fairly sunk, for he'll be made to stump up some part of what's left for the benefit of the injured wife – who, I suspect, is an outsize bitch.'

As I brooded over this sickening story (for sickening it was to anyone who knew Seymore) I felt more and more depressed. So far as public life was concerned, the unhappy man was certainly done for. No wonder he had resigned.

'Thank you, George' I said at last. 'I am most grateful to you, and mum's the word until it's all public property. What a horrid mess! I'm on his side from A to Z, though damned little good that can do him. And the Service has lost a top-notcher.'

II

I think it was partly due to delayed action by George's story that a week or two later I went to call on Kitty Cairns. I used to go to her place at fairly regular intervals, because I liked talking to Kitty and because now and again I liked having a nice girl. But this particular visit had an impulse of its own. In a confused sort of way I was indignant with so-called respectable society, which made it easy for a spiteful woman like Lady Alicia Seymore to wreck the career of a fine public servant. Evidently there were faults on both sides but his flutter outside the blanket was oldish history, whilst her adultery was not, and in my case which of the two was the greater asset to his country? Resentful against respectability, I turned instinctively to women who neither pretended nor wanted to be respectable, but at least were honest.

Kitty Cairns and her house were both unique, not only in their own time but (I'd be prepared to wager) in any other also. Kitty was hard – hard and completely cynical; but she had some breeding and considerable imagination, and conducted business with a mixture of style and humour which must be so rare in her trade as to be practically non-existent.

She was (so she told me, and I am sure she spoke the truth) in actual fact a clergyman's daughter. Her father got into bad trouble in his north-country parish, had to resign his Orders

and, sinking slowly into destitution, died three years later in
the slums of Newcastle. The mother had succumbed – dying,
as they say, of a broken heart – very soon after the catastrophe; and with her father gone, Kitty found herself with no
alternative to making her own way in the world save living on
the meagre charity of two grudging aunts. She was about
twenty years of age.

There must have been a strain of rebellious humour in her
nature, on which her father's downfall worked in a curious
way. Despite his transgressions she loved him, and it hurt her
bitterly to witness the hypocrisy of some of those who drove
him into the wilderness. He had been a hard-working sincere
priest, who had given the best half of his life to the service of
his flock; yet one moment of madness was allowed to obliterate
from the minds of certain of his leading parishioners all
memory of his years of sanity and self-forgetfulness. Kitty felt
no resentment against the Bishop and the Ecclesiastical authorities for taking action; manifestly such a scandal could not be
condoned. But it seemed to her unforgivable that the Squire's
family, and the two rich old ladies who lived in the big house
next the church and had a finger in every parish pie, should
not only have deserted their incumbent after twenty years of
apparent friendliness, but also have visited their spite on the
sinner's innocent wife and daughter. During the months she
spent watching, first her mother, and then her father die, this
grievance against certain individuals hardened into a general-
ized and wholly unreasonable resentment against well-to-do,
established households – and especially against their female
members. Female society, she told herself, had driven her
mother to her death, and on female society she would be
revenged.

But revenge needed money, and at present she was a penni-
less outcast. Her first step was to travel to London, take a new
name and, as Kitty Cairns, earn at least board and lodging
while making her plans. Her experiences as a governess did
nothing to soften her hostility toward the enemy, although the
behaviour of her employers' husbands and sons gave her un-

mistakable hints as to the most promising line of attack. When in her fourth or fifth job the son of the house made really desperate love to her, she led him on, blackmailed him to the tune of fifty pounds, and then complained of him to his mother. She was, of course, dismissed; but the sovereigns were in her purse, and she had had the satisfaction of seeing the woman's face a battlefield in which fright, mortification and anger struggled for victory.

Kitty decided that she must now give attention to the converse of her problem.

It was clear that the weakest point in the citadel of female respectability was male incontinence; and in order to study that phenomenon she went no more to registry offices, but began instead to frequent the girl-markets of the metropolis. For some miserable months, wearing her cold ironical smile, she sold herself to any who paid her price. Her little store of money was growing, but very slowly; and she was beginning to wonder what should be her next move, when she had a stroke of luck. She fell in with a Nepaulese Rajah – a man of fabulous wealth and sadistic tastes – who took her to Mother Stewart's School of Flagellation, just off Wardour Street. The receiving and giving of pain, as a means to more money, fed Kitty's phobia. She had courage, self-control and a remarkable capacity for detaching her inner self from what her outer self was doing and suffering. The Rajah was delighted with her; Mother Stewart, who had a more select private academy near Cremorne, transferred thither this exceptional recruit, and soon put her more or less in charge. For a couple of years she worked in this academy, showing an inventiveness and a talent for management as striking as her personal skill in satisfying clients. Then the Rajah paid a second visit to London, sought her out and begged her to return to India with him. But she contrived to refuse with such diplomacy that they parted on the friendliest terms, and Kitty the richer by a thousand pounds and a string of flawless pearls. She was now virtually a partner of Mother Stewart's, and made the acquaintance of many prominent men – peers, cabinet ministers and financial magnates. Her fortune grew rapidly, for she was a careful spender and coldly proof against the follies and temptations which beset women of her kind and lead them to squander their savings.

Then, when she was over thirty years old, she fell head over ears in love. Such a thing had never happened to her before; and the discovery that she was capable of forgetting herself in devotion to another completely transformed her. The man was a successful architect, whom she met at a very mixed and very rowdy party held in a private room at the Star and Garter. His fastidious disapproval of the talk and ragging which developed as the wine circulated piqued her curiosity. With her usual cynicism – and to see what would come of it – she played up to him, and they left the other revellers to their dissipation. Outside the hotel was her companion's brougham, and he suggested that they take a drive. When they had started, he explained that he slept badly and often drove around half the night, keeping a special night-coachman on duty in case of need. That night they drove for three or four hours. Where they went to, Kitty had no idea; for the man began to talk and she sat back in her corner and listened spellbound. He talked of the pleasures of love, of how they were (and always must be) pagan pleasures, with which sacraments and polite conventions had no concern beyond a certain degree of social convenience. He stressed the absolute necessity of both parties finding equal joy in their association, and denounced at length and with eloquence those men who made cruelty an element in their passions and those women who catered to their bestiality.

Kitty hardly said a word. When he left her at her private lodgings, having arranged to meet her for dinner three days hence, she felt bruised and shaken. Next day she did not go to the academy, nor the next, nor the next. She saw her new friend with increasing frequency, and told herself with characteristic candour that she was his slave. Shortly afterwards he proposed that they form an association, and she felt that heaven had opened. He installed her in a small house near Brompton Road, and spent there all the time he could spare.

For five years Kitty was blissfully happy. Her lover was a married man (but rather formally so, even before he met her) and had been accustomed to work at all hours in his office rather than at home. He was able, therefore, by transferring his personal drawing-desk, reference-books and instruments to Brompton, to pass his creative hours as well as his oddments of leisure in the company of his mistress. She proved an intelligent and sympathetic helper, who took the keenest interest in his work, learnt from him all he knew of styles, decoration and the irrational changes of popular taste, and by her feminine approach to the problems they involved was often of real assistance to him. They went on holidays together, spending some weeks in Paris and Vienna; and these shared experiences helped to make their partnership even more harmonious and complete. The heaviest penalty usually paid by a woman in Kitty Cairns' position is an inevitable isolation, often leading to dangerous boredom. But isolation, thanks to a natural self-sufficiency, to delight in caring for her charming little house and to the part she was able to play in her lover's career, Kitty actually welcomed. She had always played a lone hand when things were bad, and now that they were good needed no allies save him who made them so.

It might well have been that a woman less level-headed than Kitty should have come to think herself a paragon of feminine accomplishment and discretion, so comprehensively successful was her experiment in *collage*. But she believed in self-discipline; and whenever she felt in danger of complacency, forced herself to take a dose of humiliating memories, which checked any hasty impulse to regard herself as more than temporarily Mistress of the Event.

A day came when these periodical bouts of mortification stood her in good stead. Her lover was directing the work on a large block of new buildings in Westminster, when, owing to a careless manipulation of a crane, a mass of masonry fell from a height and killed him on the spot. Not being officially part of his life, notification of the accident was not sent to Kitty, who learnt of the disaster from next morning's paper, after a night of miserable anxiety due to his non-arrival at her house. For twenty-four hours she was prostrated by the shock; but thanks to having trained herself to expect no permanence even from happiness, she was not wholly crushed. Then, to reinforce recovery, there came a return of her old grievance against established society. At the funeral among the crowd of mourners would be his wife, his sisters, other women with conventional claims to weep for him; yet not one of them would have a fraction of *her* claim, who had done everything for him and been everything to him. And she would be shut out. She would not even be told where the funeral was, or when. Her friend and her lover were both dead; yet she alone might not pay a last tribute to their cherished memory. She set her lips in a hard line, choked down her desolation, and coerced herself into some sort of normal life. Some weeks later she was notified by a firm of lawyers that their late client had left her the lease of her house, its contents, and the sum of ten thousand pounds. They enclosed a letter, bearing her name, which had been confidentially entrusted to them by their client, with instructions to deliver it in the event of his pre-deceasing the lady to whom it was addressed. That letter became Kitty Cairns' most sacred possession – indeed her only one. She would talk freely of her good and evil fortune, of her material treasures, of her speculations, wise and otherwise. But no eyes save her own had ever read what the dead man wrote to his mistress; and the few who knew that his letter existed were merely told it was a letter so beautiful that only he could have written it.

When, in course of time, the agony of her loss had become a dull ache, Kitty considered her lonely future. She was now in her late thirties, a cultivated well-to-do woman but without an intimate friend of any sort. To the circles in which (but for her prejudice against women within the pale) she would have been at ease and interested, she had no access. Those to which she could easily have returned – and been received almost like Royalty – would have bored and disgusted her. So she conceived the idea which ultimately came to birth as Florizel Thirteen. By conducting with propriety an improper house; by choosing for its inmates only girls who from poverty or ignorant indiscretions had become outcasts from their kind; by securing for these joy-girls some of the joy they were expected to give; and by offering gentlemen temptations to which they could yield without being jarred into embarrassment or apologetics by unsympathetic company or sordid surroundings, she decided that she could at once do grievous damage to her enemies and help a few unfortunate young women who suffered, as she had suffered, from the obtuseness or cruelty of the righteous.

When I first met her, Kitty Cairns was a dignified cold-eyed woman, with greying hair swept plainly from a side parting across a calm unwrinkled forehead. She always wore black, touched – but only touched – with white, and I sometimes wondered where she found a dressmaker with a severity of taste and a love of rich materials equal to her own. I never saw her wear any jewels save her single rope of magnificent pearls. She was, I suppose, not far from fifty years of age, and had ruled Florizel Thirteen for a decade.

She was very proud of her establishment; and no wonder, for it was a masterpiece of suave illegality, and in location and planning beyond criticism.

When the Regent's Park was laid out, with the Canal sweeping in a great loop round its northern boundary and throwing off a branch south-eastward to the basin behind Cumberland Market, there was left, between the Barracks and the bridge leading to Camden Town, a triangular space of land. On this, with deliberate irregularity, were built a number of charming houses, served from Albany Street by a road all twists and angles, and achieving the sophisticated rusticity at which their designers aimed. When they were new, it was fashionable to assume (with what justice I do not know) that these houses were mainly occupied by lovely ladies in whom the Regent and his cronies were interested. Hence it arose that among the *ton* the area was nicknamed 'Florizel' – this being one of the soubriquets bestowed on the Prince Regent by writers of satire. Although the name was unrecognized by cartographers, post-office officials or any reputable authority, it continued to be current among men about town; and no clubman even of my recent generation would have dreamt of referring to the settlement as 'Haliburton Road' (or whatever it was officially called). They spoke of it and knew it as Florizel.

It was wholly characteristic of Kitty Cairns' virtuosity (and showed to what good use she had put her years in Brompton) that she realized the value to such an undertaking as hers of the style and record of this forgotten corner of London. Consequently, when she decided to establish an academy on the lines which appealed to her, she awaited an opportunity of acquiring a house in Florizel. The first one to fall vacant (probably for that reason) was numbered thirteen. Kitty was delighted, displaying once more the subtlety of her finesse. 'Within the pale' she said '13 is unlucky; outside it everything is topsy-turvy and I shall make 13 lucky.'

Having secured the house she wanted, she took precautions, before opening up, to secure her retreat. The canal flowed in a deep cutting along the east of her little garden, and across the canal were the back gardens of houses in a road which ran parallel with the canal and between it and the tracks of the London and North Western Railway. Through an intermediary she set about buying the house in this road whose garden, backing on to the water, was opposite to hers. She had to pay very heavily, she told me, because the owner, although he had not the smallest idea of their origin, recognized the urgency of the overtures made and held out for a fancy price. But she got what she wanted in the end; and by means of two water-gates and a small boat, ingeniously housed in the wall of the cutting, provided herself and her clients with an emergency exit.

This exit was the most effective imaginable. It debouched, not only into another street, but to all intents and purposes into another part of London, so totally different in atmosphere and population was Regent's Park with its fine terraces and villas from the humbler workaday region just over the water to the east.

In the actual house across the canal lived the male staff of the establishment – the chef, the butler, the footmen, the

gardeners, the ferry-men and the powerful watchdogs whose
services might be needed in a sudden crisis. By this arrangement Kitty kept 'Florizel Thirteen' (by which name it was
generally known to the cognoscenti) quiet, dainty and (in
appearance) exclusively feminine; and although during business hours there were always men about the place, they were –
except for those serving – unseen and unsuspected. As for the
subsidiary house, it had no official existence; it was a 'way
out' only. The sole entrance to Kitty's domain was from the
crooked road off Albany Street.

A woman shrewd enough to appreciate the recommendation-
value of her house's striking nom-de-plume was not likely to
overlook its utility in the concealed advertising which was the
only publicity possible to her. Yet it was in exploiting that
utility that Kitty Cairns showed what can only be termed her
genius. In the small square hall of her house hung a little card,
beautifully mounted and plainly framed in gold. The only object hanging on the walls, and therefore certain to be noticed,
it was a genuine trade-card, of a kind handed by brothel-
keepers' touts to the British officers who flocked to Paris after
Waterloo. At once a battle-cry, a mascot and a delicious piece
of impudence, its very survival was a miracle, and that Kitty
had the intelligent audacity to hang it in her entrance-hall
completed its perfection.

Here it is:

ADVERTISSEMENT

There is amusabel Bedds, Sir English Millitarys, upon
the No. 176, Rue Vieux Cocq, in koming your Ladys to
that Cohabitation. The constant money for all Triks, and
Sope, is indeterminabel to 5 fr.: when the deversion take
not for all Nite. If the wishes is to tomoro for indulgency
by the said amusabel Bedds, the constant money is for 8
fr.: into your humbel Servant. The customabel prise at
the Ladys, to be paid in your conveniency.

From this precious absurdity Kitty took two words which,
in conjunction with her disguised address, constituted the only

advertisements she sent out. Regularly in good class papers of the raffish and sporting kind, and once or twice (until they found out) in the agony columns of the most sedate and ponderous news-sheets, appeared the words: FLORIZEL THIRTEEN: AMUSABEL BEDDS. Just that. It was superb publicity, for it delighted those who remembered, reminded those who had forgotten and set the rest wondering.

The organization of the academy was rigorous. Though there were as a rule half a dozen girls in residence, casual dropping-in was not tolerated. Everything had to be done by appointment. When writing ahead, a habitué would ask for the girl he liked best and, if possible, she was booked for him. A new-comer (and to qualify required unchallengeable references) was first invited to an informal soirée, at which the young ladies, Kitty herself and one or two of her men-friends met and talked and listened to music and took light refreshments. It was all very correct and conventional and (suitably) rather dull. The candidate was charged nothing for this entertainment; went home after it was over, and was expected, when writing for a proper appointment, to indicate his preference.

Once a month Kitty gave a dinner-party, attended by her pensionnaires and any men she wished to ask. It was a great honour to be on Kitty's dinner-list; but, as the evening developed into more or less of an orgy, it was a privilege requiring a full purse and considerable staying-power.

The only kind of visit which could be made to Florizel Thirteen without invitation, appointment or expense, was a personal call on Kitty Cairns for the purpose of a friendly chat. This could be made any Thursday between the hours of three and five. From Monday to Friday the entire establishment was closed between noon and five pm. On Saturday it did not re-open until eleven pm. On Sunday it closed at nine am and opened again at three pm. The young ladies were sent out walking or riding every week-day afternoon; but Kitty stayed indoors on Thursdays and welcomed anyone who cared to pay her his respects.

At the time of which I am writing, I had graduated to the

extent of being an occasional Thursday caller and (as I have said) an accepted client when I cared to find the money. I had, however, not yet attained the dinner-list; nor was I anxious to, because I could not hope to stand the pace unless some nice fat legacies came my way, of which there was no prospect.

*   *   *

The afternoon on which I decided to pay my call was November at its worst – dark, raw and wet. I took a hansom to Gloucester Gate, and scurried through the rain to the porch of Florizel Thirteen. The man-servant recognized me and greeted me by name – a trifling circumstance which restored my self-confidence out of all proportion to its significance. I felt better still when, on entering the drawing-room, I found only Kitty and another woman. The curtains were undrawn and the day-light dim; but Kitty – with her genius for recognizing every-one – rose from her chair and came graciously toward me:

'Harry! How nice of you, my dear – on this horrible after-noon! Come and dry and warm. Oh, I beg your pardon, let me introduce Miss Hooper. Fanny, this is Harry Somerford. I am so sorry. I forgot you had not met. It is so long since you came, you naughty man, that I thought you had forsaken me!'

We talked weather and theatres for ten minutes until Kitty suddenly realized it was almost dark. She rang for the curtains to be drawn and the gas lit. For the first time I was able to see clearly my hostess and her companion.

There was nothing new about Kitty, except the perpetual novelty of her ironical serenity and unchanging elegance. But Miss Hooper was at once a novelty and a conundrum. At first glance she was just a small brown girl, with a lively high-cheeked-boned little face, a long merry mouth and two very dark eyes, which made holes in her face, and shone as velvet would shine if it had a gleam in it. The next time I looked at her she was laughing at a remark of Kitty's, and had become more like a happy elf than a young girl of flesh and blood. The third time she was emphasizing some argument of her own with quick eager gestures, and it seemed that her whole body was fluid with movement. I came to know well that not the least of Fanny Hooper's fascinations was her outward changeability. At one moment she would be all velvet eyes; at another all smiling mouth and white even teeth; at another all flickering hands. I have often been glad to think that at my very first sight of her I took notice of this delicious characteristic – and of another one also, no less precious and no less her own. That was her voice – a low-pitched, slightly husky voice which, like her eyes, had something of the quality of velvet and was strangely exciting.

But who was Miss Hooper and what was she doing in the drawing-room at Florizel Thirteen? All the time we were having tea I was trying to make her out. She was certainly not one of Kitty's girls. They were delightful girls; but there was a something about them when men were present which betrayed their profession – a mixture of a desire to please and a rather pathetic pretence of being coquettish and difficult. Miss Hooper had none of this. She was retiring in manner, but perfectly natural and at ease, and took no more notice of me than would any well-mannered girl meeting a strange man in a friend's house.

Kitty was jokingly giving me a character, and on the whole a good one:

'Mr Somerford is a nice man when you know him' she said, adding: 'I think you'll like him in time, Fanny, though he does seem a bit intimidating at first.'

While I was muttering disclaimers I was saying to myself that apparently I should see Miss Hooper again, and was surprised at my own pleasure.

'But you must be careful' went on Kitty. 'He's very handy with his fists – would have been the Tom Cribb of his day if he'd taken it up professionally. Not that I've ever heard of him lifting his hand to a woman. But you never know with these fire-eaters; one moment they're all sugar and spice, the next they fetch you a slog-dollager —'

'Kitty!' I broke in. 'I won't have you setting Miss Hooper against me with all this nonsense! She'll think I'm a sort of

Bashi-Bazouk, instead of an inoffensive fellow who is rash enough to come here and be made a fool of.'

Miss Hooper got up and smiled her wide engaging smile.

'Never mind, Mr Somerford. I won't think worse of you than I can help – and that won't be very badly I assure you.' She turned to Kitty: 'I must be off, Miss Cairns, if you are sure you won't need me.'

'Oh, Fanny, I am so sorry! I quite forgot. Run along and get your things on and come and say goodnight.'

When the girl had left the room, I made the most of my time.

'Who is she, Kitty, and what is she doing here?'

'She's – well, I suppose she's my secretary or – assistant. I don't know what you'd call her.'

'Not the sous-maîtresse?' I interrupted.

Kitty raised her eyebrows.

'Tck – tck! Aren't we interested and ready to be indignant! Dear Harry; you are so sweet and transparent. So you like my little Fanny?'

'I did not say so' I answered, rather surly.

'Of course you didn't. How stupid of me! Would you be very kind and see her home? She lives in rooms in Marylebone Road, and it's a horrid evening.'

I looked at her severely.

'See here,' I said. 'If it's transparency you are after, look nearer home. I never saw a more brazen attempt to —'

'To what?' she asked sweetly.

'Oh, dash it; to nothing, then.' There was a moment's pause; but I could not afford to lose time, even over dignity, and asked hastily: 'Does she come here every day?'

Kitty nodded.

'And – and – realizes . . . ?'

'Oh! aren't men comical? Of *course* she realizes. She'd have no work to do, if she didn't. Any more than I should if I didn't. And women *can* mind their own business, you know.'

I saw that in my stupid, conventional way I had got myself

into an awkward corner, and there had been more than a hint of a snub in Kitty's last words.

I liked Kitty Cairns, and was here for that reason. Yet I had blurted out a most uncivil discrimination between a 'nice' girl and members of the half-world. I opened my mouth, probably to say something idiotic, but she mercifully forestalled me.

'Not now, Harry. Some time I shall try to put a little sense into that handsome head of yours; but now there is no time – for I shall shock you, and you will shout at me, and all that drags on. But I will say just two things. The little Hooper is an unusually open-minded unspoilt person. Her bringing-up has not filled her head with all manner of lady-like hokey-pokey, nor is she one to want to set the world to rights. She needed a job and I needed a secretary. It was for me to ask the questions and she had the sense to know it.

'The second thing is this – do not make the mistake of rating the work done by my girls here (and by me, if it comes to that) in terms of ordinary sex-relationship. A woman in business is one thing and a woman in love is another. The two are utterly different, though they may well be combined in a single living person. It may surprise you, but it's a fact that any one of these girls is capable of acting with almost maidenly modesty toward a man she has met away from business and has begun to like. The better she likes him, the less "easy" she will try to appear. She knows instinctively there is more to it than just coupling, so she holds back. That is, of course, true of all girls, though the contrast is less startling and the blacks and whites less definite with those not making a living. But watch out and you'll find I'm right. Ssh! here is your little friend come for her escort. . . .'

The door opened, and Miss Hooper in hat and jacket peeped into the room.

'Just come to say goodnight' she said.

'Wait a moment, my dear. Mr Somerford has kindly said he will see you home; it is such a wretched evening.'

The girl began to expostulate; but I was on my feet, assuring her it would only be a pleasure. I turned at the door to wave goodbye to Kitty. She blew me a kiss, and came nearer than I could have imagined possible to a vulgar wink.

III

Kitty's lecture on female psychology lingered in my mind. She put things crudely; but she lived in an atmosphere of 'whole measures' and talked primary colours rather than pastel shades. It was only necessary to modify her terms; the basic argument remained. The statement which intrigued me most was that the more a girl liked a man, the less accessible she seemed.

At first I amused myself by applying what I called 'the Cairns test' to casual acquaintances. I tried to judge from the apparent accessibility or otherwise of the young women I saw in company with men, whether they were out for a marriage settlement (business, in fact) or becoming emotionally involved. But I rapidly lost interest in other people's concerns, as I became aware of my growing preoccupation with Miss Hooper of Florizel Thirteen.

Ever since I had walked across the park with her on the evening of our first encounter, I had not been able to get her out of my head; and each additional meeting made matters worse.

The problem of seeing her at all was not an easy one. I lived in Kensington with my mother and sister. We were a tolerably harmonious family, though I considered my sister Kate a good deal of a prig, and often teased her so brutally about her readiness to show moral disapproval that she got cross and flounced out of the room.

These tiffs apart, we rubbed along happily enough – the ladies respecting my reasonable liberties, I playing their social game when I saw they really needed me. But although they observed custom and left a man to pursue his business and his pleasure without attempting to accompany or to question him, both my mother and Kate were equally conventional in regarding certain departments of my life as their concern. Among these was the department labelled 'Settling Down', which included the important sub-section 'Meeting Nice Girls'. This department had been working overtime for quite two years before the night when I first set eyes on Fanny Hooper, and a series of Nice Girls (each to my mind sillier or more boring than the last) had been pressed into the service. I don't know whether my poor mother wondered if I were a confirmed misogynist or (Kate would not have allowed herself to contemplate anything so degrading) found outlets elsewhere for a man's natural instincts. If she suspected the latter, she may have sighed; but she would have said nothing, it being part of the creed of a respectable matron that 'gentlemen are different'. If, however, it had even occurred to her that I might, having strayed over the border into the wicked world to which men had access but of the very existence of which their women-folk pretended to be unaware, there come across a girl whom I could conceivably regard as a possible factor in Settling Down, she would have been appalled. Yet precisely this (though I did not immediately realize it) had come to pass.

It would hardly be fair to say that my mother would have preferred me to pass my time in riotous living rather than in genuinely falling in love with the wrong sort of girl; but she would certainly have felt that the former was at least no infringement of her prerogative, while the latter was not only that, but a folly deliberately provoked by some designing minx. Of this I was obscurely aware: and I felt myself bound to spend in her company, or within the purlieus of her set, what had become by custom the 'family' share of my time. This left available for improving my acquaintance with the 'little brown girl' only the hours of liberty which were regarded as my own. I was, therefore, in the highly delicate position of having to elude my fellow-men at times when I had formerly been in their company, yet of continuing to waste precious hours at tedious social gatherings, making polite conversation to people I never wanted to see again.

Further complications lay in Miss Hooper's place of business, working hours and willingness to be seen. I could not visit her at Florizel Thirteen; for although, in one sense, 'followers' constituted the establishment's livelihood, in the other – which was *my* sense – they were impossible. She was normally at work from eleven am till seven; and if from the latter hour onward I was continually missing from the club or from home, someone was bound to start asking awkward questions. Finally, I had to be very careful how I handled the young lady herself. Working as she did in the most equivocal surroundings possible, any undue persistence would look like trying to take advantage, like arguing from the general to the particular. Instinct told me that it was of the utmost importance to avoid the slightest hint of such presumption, and in truth nothing was further from my mind. I was not interested (at this stage) in possessing Miss Hooper; I wanted to get to know her.

But did she want to get to know me? At first it seemed 'yes'. When we parted at the door of her lodgings, I asked when I might see her again. She suggested I call on Kitty Cairns next Thursday, and we could repeat our walk. But the thought of that shrewd observer's muted smile frightened me; and I began making excuses. I might be kept late at the office; there might be other callers beside myself; half a dozen 'mights'. Could we not meet on the Avenue Bridge – how early could it be? With the frankness of a child she agreed. At half past six. She was always early on Thursdays, though not so early as tonight, when she had to meet a friend and Miss Cairns had most kindly ... I did not like that friend; even at this early stage the words made me uneasy. But I had secured my rendezvous; and that was enough. Next week she was there – cordial and friendly. Without demur she came with me to a respectable Private Bar in Park Street, and we talked for an hour over sherry and water.

She told me something about herself, though less (when I came to think it over) than I had thought at the time. Indeed it boiled down to this. She came of a north-country farming family, had been born in London, went into service as a child of thirteen and ran away four years later because her mistress was unkind to her. She had then lived with an old acquaintance in another part of London until a girl-friend of hers told her of an opening with Kitty Cairns. She had been secretary, sub-housekeeper and general factotum at Florizel Thirteen since the early part of the year. She was now eighteen and a half years of age.

I wanted to ask a lot of questions. Manifestly her childhood and upbringing had not been the usual preliminaries to a career as a servant; she must have had something other than an elementary education, for she spoke well, and I doubted whether, even on a prosperous farm, a girl-child would acquire the self-possession and good manners which seemed natural to her. But I did not wish to be intrusive, especially as certain gaps in her story suggested misfortunes or dislocations of which she did not wish to speak. So I concentrated on the only subject which (so far) we had in common, and asked about her work with Kitty. She replied so freely and with such a complete lack of embarrassment that it was obvious Kitty had defined her assistant's attitude with perfect accuracy. It was clear, Miss Hooper said, that the running of such a place as Florizel Thirteen involved much correspondence; careful accounts; continual supervision of furniture, plate, linen, crockery, curtains, carpets and so forth; a watch on tradesmen's books; a check on the butler's reports as to wine in the cellar and cigars in the cabinet – not to mention the adjustment of disputes which occasionally broke out among the young ladies, although on the whole they were an amicable lot. Miss Cairns was ideal to work for – clear-cut, strict, but fair-minded and generous. 'I took to her at once' said Miss Hooper 'because there is no nonsense about her and I'm that way myself.'

I walked her back to her lodgings, and ventured to suggest that next Thursday she take supper with me. She agreed without hesitation or coyness, bade me a cheerful goodnight and went into the house. I listened for the door to shut behind her, and strolled slowly towards the Yorkshire Stingo, feeling a little breathless, and wondering why.

While the winter lasted, with its early dark and frost and

rain and fog, I managed to maintain our Thursday meetings with fair regularity. At my end I made ingenious use of the Working Men's College in Great Ormond Street, whose Principal, Thomas Hughes, had invited me to teach boxing one or two nights a week. This invitation got me Thursday evenings safely in hand. At her end, however, there were occasional disappointments; and as time went on I began to notice that these were becoming more frequent. Also when she was with me, though never anything but sweet and kindly, she seemed at times to withdraw into a gentle privacy whither I might not follow her. These developments worried me increasingly. I had now no illusions about my state of mind. I was in love with Fanny Hooper – completely and deliciously in love with her. To sit and look at her was sheer happiness – watching her eager little face fall suddenly serious, waiting for the long dark lashes to flick upward from her high-boned ivory cheeks and unveil those sombre but brilliant eyes, guessing whether her lips would lengthen into a smile and dimple the corners of her mouth or be pursed into the conglomerate of rosy wrinkles which marked her moments of sudden thoughtfulness. Often, I fear, I just stared at her in silence, and she would glance up and catch me staring, and bite her lower lip and flush a faint ivory-pink under her lovely dusky skin. It seemed to me that her skin and her voice were perfectly matched, each a few tones lower than the normal in the respective scales of tint and sound. Thanks largely to this quality of contralto in colour and voice, she seemed wrapped in warm shadows; and her shadowiness, combined with the vitality and humour which shone in her eyes and smile and guided the movements of her expressive hands, gave to the whole of her a remarkable effect of depth and richness. I felt that behind her simple acceptance of what life brought to her were reserves of power and patience, as well as an innate humility which touched me to the heart. She was so pitifully alone; and her uncomplaining courage made me, each time I saw her, the more ambitious to fight her battles – not for her, for that she would never permit, but at her side.

Yet the deeper I fell into love for her, the more elusive she became. Kitty's worldly wisdom – so amusing and so apt when applied to others – was no comfort in my own distraction. For three Thursdays running Fanny evaded a meeting, half-promising to come on the fourth. I waited on the bridge, but she never came. Next week in despair I made an afternoon call at Florizel Thirteen. It was early April and the park smelt of spring. There were several other visitors, but no sign of Fanny Hooper. After chafing through an hour of ribald gaiety, I cornered Kitty in a way which must have been only too conspicuous. She looked at me under her eyelids:

'What is it, Harry?' she said quietly.

I felt suddenly tongue-tied, and my restless irritation sank into confused timidity.

'I wanted to say goodbye,' I said sullenly. 'I'm am afraid I must be going.'

She raised her eyebrows and smiled with her lips only.

'Goodbye then. It was nice of you to come.'

I hesitated a moment and she watched me sardonically. I had turned to go, when I felt her hand on my arm.

'I should write, if I were you' she said.

Before I could reply she had moved away and was talking to someone else.

I took her advice. To Fanny at her lodgings I wrote a letter which I tried to keep as much under control as possible, though it is hard to plead desperately that a girl should see you, without expressing yourself with greater urgency than is usual in polite correspondence. In reply I got a few lines, in a firm but very youthful handwriting, which seemed at once plucky and defenceless and brought a lump to my throat.

Dear Mr Somerford,

Thank you for your letter. I should like your advice and will be at Avenue Bridge next Thursday at six o'clock. I hope this will not be too early to be convenient, but I have someone coming to see me at seven.

Yours truly,
Fanny Hooper.

I found this a perplexing, rather disquieting note. She wanted advice; and for that reason she would come. No reference to our earlier meetings at the very place now suggested. Finally a time-limit – and a narrow one at that. I worried through the intervening days and arrived at the bridge in a state of acute but diffident apprehension. She was already there; and, after greeting me with a pleasant smile, asked whether we could go to the quiet bar in Park Street.

As we walked along I purposely said nothing. I had the impression when I met her that she was troubled in spirit, and this was quickly confirmed when I saw her in the gaslight of the almost empty saloon. She looked wan and tired, and all manner of forebodings began to jostle one another in my mind. Perhaps she really needed me – and the thought dispelled my nervousness and provoked me at once to force the issue.

'Fanny' I said 'you want more than advice. You want help. Now tell me what I'm to do and I'll do it. Anything in the world. I cannot bear to see you like this — '

I had never dared to speak so warmly to her before; and it thrilled me, despite my anxious sympathy, to see that my vehemence brought a little colour into her pale cheeks. When she replied, her voice was low but steady.

'I wanted to ask you something which, being a lawyer, you will be able to tell me. How can one find out when a divorce case is to be tried?'

I felt a mixture of disappointment and bewilderment. Was that all? And what an extraordinary question!

'A *divorce* case? Quite easily. They are set down for hearing some while ahead and any solicitor can find out.... Is it some special case you are interested in?'

She nodded, and sat pulling nervously at the gloves which lay on her lap.

My forebodings returned. Was she herself involved in some scandal? With an effort I kept my manner cool and casual.

'If you will tell me the name, I will find out for you and let you know.'

She swallowed hard and was evidently near tears.

'The name is Seymore.'

'Seymore!'

I stared at her in blank astonishment, then pulled myself together.

'What is the other name?' I asked.

'Clive Seymore' she whispered.

This was staggering.

'But ... but – why – what have you to do with Clive Seymore's divorce case?'

'Nothing – really —' she stammered 'but I – was in service – in – his house.'

For ten seconds I sat, trying to bring order out of the chaos of speculation and amazement which choked my mind. Then in a flash I saw it all.

'So *you* ...' I cried; but broke off, realizing that I must handle this extraordinary situation with the greatest delicacy. An ill-judged remark might finish me for ever; if on the other hand I were skilful and considerate, I might ... I might ...

After a moment's pause, I laid a hand on Fanny's arm:

'Is it imperative that you get in by seven o'clock?'

She gave me a startled glance.

'Ye-es ... at least I promised to.'

'Whom did you promise?'

'My friend Lucy, who is coming to see me.'

'Is Lucy anything to do with this divorce case?'

'She told me it was to happen.'

'Until then you knew nothing of it?'

She shook her head.

I weighed my next words carefully.

'It is a very strange thing, Fanny, that you decided to ask me about this case. Clive Seymore was a superior officer of mine. I knew him as well as a junior can know a senior in a big government office, and respected him as much as one man can respect another. I am every bit as interested in what befalls him as you can be, and you may be sure that I will find out all details and let you know them. I don't want to pry into your affairs; and I daresay your Miss Lucy is the first person you want to tell that the needed information can be got. In that case, we will start back now and you will be in plenty of time.'

To my surprise she showed signs of agitation toward the end of my embarrassed and rather stilted speech, and when I stopped talking, clasped her hands together and beat them several times against her knee.

'Oh no, no!' she cried. 'Lucy knows nothing, nothing! Only that there was to be a divorce. I couldn't possibly ask her for more particulars and there was no one else – no one but you. But I wanted to know so much – for myself – only for myself—'

She covered her face with her hands, and I could see her body racked with stifled sobbing. The sight was too grievous to be borne, and I burst out:

'Fanny, my poor unhappy little girl, don't cry! Please trust me! Tell me what is the matter and let me help you. You *must* let me help you, Fanny – if only because I love you.'

It suddenly occurred to me that we were in a public bar and someone might be watching my darling's tears. Ready to deal faithfully with even the smallest impudence, I looked round. There was no one. The place was deserted; but beyond the partition I could hear the barmaid talking to a man whose voice I recognized. Five minutes ago he had been propped in semi-intoxication on that stool yonder; now he and she had moved – to leave us alone. I had often talked loosely of the innate tact of the Londoner and his sympathy with love and sorrow; but this was my first actual experience of it. Blessings on them both – barmaid and toper; may their shadows never grow less!

Turning back to Fanny, I found that she had dropped her hands and was gazing at me with tears shining in her eyes.

'Do you know what you said?' she whispered.

'Yes, precious, I know. And I say it again. I love you, Fanny. I have loved you for a long time, only I have not dared to say so. The sight of you crying gave me courage.'

She just looked at me; then groped with her hand for mine. 'Is it true?' she said, with such urgency that her voice almost broke.

I lifted her hand to my lips.

'On this hand – which like its owner is sacred to me – I swear it is true. When can I see you for long enough to tell you all about it?'

She gave a low cry but said nothing; only sat, kneading my hand between both of hers and crooning a queer little tune to herself. A few moments later she threw back her head and I felt a quiver run right down her body, as though she were an animal shaking water from her fur. Then she spoke; and her voice was clear and strong:

'I want to go now, Harry. I want to repeat to myself again and again what you have said. But next Tuesday is my birth-day and I will ask Miss Cairns to let me off the afternoon if I stay late on Monday night. Can we go somewhere? And then you shall tell me all about it.'

The choir of angels was singing in my head.

'*Can* we? Sweetheart, we can and will. Choose; for the world is yours.'

'I choose Rosherville' she said.

'Rosherville? Why?'

'When we get there, I'll tell you. Now take me outside and kiss me.'

In the darkness of Park Street I kissed my little love, and she clung so furiously I had some ado to keep my head. The fever past, we went decorously on our way.

IV

Tuesday was a perfect April day – a soft clear sequel to a daylong shower. The sky was a pale rain-washed blue, the sunlight had the gentle warmth of a young girl's smile. We stood by the rail of the little steamer as it fussed down London River, watching the docks and warehouses and tottering rows of tenements, delighting in them all because of one another.

There were very few passengers and we could move from side to side at our ease. Except for 'Oh, Harry, look at that!': 'Quick, Fanny, or you'll miss this' and similar excited exclamations of two children on holiday, we said little. Arrived at Rosherville we wandered hand in hand past flower-beds, and in the cliff-side found a sort of very shallow cave, where was a seat and a wide prospect over the gardens and the river.

We sat down and she held my hand more tightly.

'Look at me, Harry. I have something important – fearfully important – to ask you, and when you look at me it gives me courage. Are you still *quite quite* sure that what you said the other night is what you meant? I have wondered since whether perhaps you were just sorry for me, and in your dear generous way were trying to comfort me. You see – no, don't interrupt me, please; I want to say my say – I am nothing, nothing at all, compared to you and your life. I do not matter except in so far as I can serve you and give you pleasure. For me, of course, there is no one in the world but you; but that is different, for I have nothing else and want nothing else. But I implore you, Harry, if you were just being kind and trying to cheer me up, say so *now*. I think I can bear it now; but if I am to go on seeing you and being with you and then realize that it was pity only – I shall have to die. And I don't want to die, Harry – while there is ever so tiny a bit of loving you to live for. . . .'

Her voice trembled, and I felt myself near enough to tears to make speech difficult. In order to gain a few seconds and take myself in hand, I got up and stood in front of her. Leaning forward I put my hands on her shoulders and spoke to her wide pleading eyes, which gazed at me with the courage of desperation, and almost spoke their pitiful message of mingled hope and dread.

'Little love' I said 'I have already sworn on your dear hand that I love you, and I will not swear again. I'll just ask you to believe that you are to me what I did not believe a woman could be to a man – the very texture of my existence. I have not thought a private thought these last months but what you were part of it. I have not spent an hour between our meetings without looking forward to the next. My heart and my mind are full of you; you are the blood in my veins and the breath in my lungs. And now that I have got you yourself, as well as the dream of you, I shall not let you go – no, not even if you want to go. It is now too late.'

She gave a long deep sigh, let her head fall back against the rail of the seat and closed her eyes. I looked down at her, and the face seemed smoothed of its little lines of trouble. Her shoulders quivered under my hands. Stooping I pressed my lips to hers, in a lingering but gentle kiss.

*   *   *

Fanny's story did not take very long in the telling, because, whenever she dwelt in detail on other people, I brought her back to herself. 'I don't want to know about so and so' I would say. 'I want to know about *you*. What were *you* doing?' When, however, we got back to the subject of Clive Seymore's divorce, we had to be practical. First I must find out where he was; then how matters were at Aughton; then we would decide what to do.

As evening fell we went to the main dining-room to get some food. The place was not very crowded and we got a quiet corner table. She left me to tidy herself up, while I ordered dinner. I demanded some champagne immediately, and straight off the ice. When she returned, I filled our glasses and gave her a toast:

'To my darling Fanny, and may she never be lonely or un-happy again.'

She smiled and blushed and drank the toast, and her sweet little face was lovely with tenderness and trust.

I had put down my glass and was just looking at her in a daze of incredulous delight, when I noticed that she had pinned to her dress a brooch which I had not seen before.

'What is that pretty brooch, sweetheart? You were not wear-ing it this afternoon?'

'No. I had it in my bag. I decided I would put it on after I

had told you about Mr Seymore. *He* gave it me, you see —
when I was quite a little girl. I have never worn it. I wanted to
wear it for the first time when something really lovely happened to me; but nothing did — till you came, Harry, and
wanted me.'

I could not jump up and kiss her as I longed to do; so I
stretched across and squeezed her little hand as it lay beside
her glass.

'May I look at it?'

She unpinned the brooch without a word and handed it to
me. As I held it under the light, rich changing gleams of blue
and green shone in the large central stone. A delicate border of
diamonds, crowned with fleurs-de-lis, flashed like a fringe of
sparks ringing a deep clear pool of water.

'Oh, Fanny, it's lovely! And so right for you — deep and
calm, but radiant and sparkling. What is it?'

'It is a zircon.'

'I never heard of it.'

'Nor I naturally. But I managed to find out. The Clara
Williams I told you of has an uncle who is a jeweller, and he
was most interested. He said this stone is very, very unusual.
Zircons are not uncommon — smaller and shallower and of
much paler colour; but he had never even heard tell of one of
the size and purity and rich colouring of this. You must see it
in sunlight. It is almost too beautiful to be borne.'

'How clever of Seymore to choose it — no, more than clever.
Did he say why?'

She was pinning her brooch on again and did not answer
immediately.

'Yes' she said at last. 'You won't laugh at me, if I tell you?
No; I didn't mean that. Of course you won't. I'm a bit shy,
that's all. He chose it because it reminded him of sunshine on a
pool of sea-water which lay in a cleft of rock in a cove on the
Yorkshire coast. When he loved my mother they were in that
cove — by the side of that pool. My name is Vandra, really —
which means "water-girl" or "water-sprite". Fanny is just for
short.'

'And for very sweet, angel. What a touching little story. I wonder if I shall ever stop finding out sad, lovely little things about you. "Vandra" – that is beautiful, too, and "water-sprite" is perfect. But I shall stick to "Fanny" – sweetest of sprites – until I change my mind.'

As dinner progressed I told myself that I must now definitely raise the question of our future, a problem which during the ecstatic hours of the afternoon I had purposely ignored. My mind was working in a direction which surprised even myself. For us to be lovers she was clearly as eager as I. I knew that I had only to find some discreet and convenient refuge, and she would move into it forthwith. But somehow the prospect did not please me. In the early days of our acquaintance I had been scrupulously careful not to force the pace, just because the milieu in which she worked might seem to invite me to do so. Now her utter solitariness and the confiding ardour with which she would have come to me, made me hanker after the very regularity she would neither demand nor expect.

When the coffee was on the table and the waiter had gone away, the moment had clearly come.

'Fanny' I said, hoping to hide my nervousness under a cloak of brusque authority. 'We will now decide how soon we can get married.'

She did not answer at once, but smiled quietly across the table.

'We are not going to get married' she replied.

This brought me up with a jerk.

'Not going to —! Fanny, you're joking.'

'No, my dearest, I am not joking.'

'But – but – what did you think —'

'Oh, I knew you meant that and were going to suggest it; if only I could, I would love you more than ever for doing so. But we won't – not yet at any rate.'

'Then what – and why, Fanny?'

'Let's pay for dinner and go outside. I'll try to explain under the trees.'

The gardens twinkled with little lamps, which seemed to throw the winding paths and alleys into deeper shade. It was warm and windless. She tucked an arm through mine, and slipping her hand into my coat-pocket, held my hand there.

'I wonder if I can make you understand' she began. 'I have told you about myself – who I am, what I have done and seen and known. You have told me who you are – though' (with a low ripple of laughter) 'I am afraid I was not listening very carefully, because it does not matter who or what you are, except that you are *you*, and love me. But you have your career and your friends, and I do not belong to your public life at all. I am only a nobody, without importance to anyone but you, and my importance to you is private to the two of us. Love – just the love of one man and one girl – is no business of the world's. The world only comes into it when the girl can help her man with the people he has to meet and the work he has to do. I cannot do either of these things for you; I can only love you – give you all there is of me – be somewhere waiting for you when you are tired or feel you want me. I should be frightened to be your wife, Harry, but I want – oh, how I want – to be your love-girl!'

I made a brusque movement as though about to speak, but she hurried on:

'And that is why, on our first holiday together, I wanted to come here. I came here once before with Chunks (I told you about him – or tried to – but you wouldn't attend) and as we were walking toward the gate in the evening – it was warm and dark and lovely, as it is now – I saw a man and a girl making love in a kind of summer-house. I only had a momentary glimpse; but there was a lost-to-the-worldness about them which thrilled me right through. I believe I grew up in that moment. I have never forgotten the complete absorption of those two in themselves; and I made up my mind that, if ever I was lucky enough to have a real lover of my own, I would get him to bring me here and love me as that girl was being loved. So please, Harry; I want you to love me, *now*.'

While she had been speaking, the marvel of my having

found and won this enchanting creature made me almost dizzy. The pathos and pride of her, the wildness of her surrender and the simple sweetness of her humility filled me with triumph and reverence. With her last urgent words, I managed to find my voice:

'Oh, Fanny, Fanny. There are no words to say what I would like to say, no words worthy to answer you as you deserve. But I am not going to do what you ask and love you now, for somewhat the same reason as you give for saying you will not marry me. If you and I are to have a secret love-story because our happiness is our concern only, our first coming together shall be secret also. I thank heaven for Rosherville because of what it did to you, and for my own unbelievable fortune in reaping the result; but when I take my love-girl, it shall be with ceremony and beauty and behind friendly walls.'

She stood silent, her eyes on the ground. At last she murmured:

'I expect you are right, darling. Let it be so. But make it soon, Harry, very very soon. . . .'

LITTLE WELBECK STREET

I

LITTLE WELBECK STREET had several claims to distinction. In the first place, although it had all the characteristics of a mews, it was not itself a mews at all but merely the approach to one. In the second place, it had houses on one side only, the other consisting of the blank house and garden walls of dwellings facing on to Welbeck and Wimpole Streets. In the third place, its single residential terrace was built in the best style of eighteenth century London – with severe, well-proportioned façades, delicate fanlights over simple front doors, brickwork smartly pointed in white, and elegant railings enclosing areas cleanly white-washed to lighten the basements to the utmost. In the fourth place, number five was occupied by Mrs Muggleton.

This last recommendation was personal to myself for Mrs Muggleton – though doubtless held in respect and affection by many other people – was a very special friend of mine. The widow of a man who had been my father's coachman for many years, she had been a beloved figure of my childhood, an ally and confidante during my school-days, and ever since I had grown up a loved and local sympathizer. When my father died – ten years previously – my mother, who had never liked Muggleton or his wife, declared she could not afford to keep a carriage and would hire at need from the Livery Stables. The ex-coachman thereupon took a lease of Five Little Welbeck Street, and started a one-man hire-business. He was doing very nicely (there was plenty of emergency work in that district for a really smart brougham with a sober and skilful coachman) when, kept waiting one bitter night some way from his stable, he took off his own cape and coat and put them over his precious horse. The horse was none the worse; but Muggleton went down with a bad chill and never left his bed again.

I was able in several ways to help poor Mrs Muggleton in the distress and difficulties of her first months of widowhood, and for a week or two actually lodged in her house, so as to be able to spend more time getting her affairs in order. She decided so to arrange and refurnish her home as to provide accommodation for two sets of lodgers on her upper floors, herself retaining ground floor and basement. In this also I was able to help her, and introduced her first tenant – a barrister named Julian Carteret, who although some years my senior was perhaps my most intimate friend. Since then I paid her regular visits, remembered her birthday, brought her quaint things from holidays abroad and generally did what I could to repay all the kindness and affection she had shown me in my youth.

When it was decided that Fanny and I set up an unofficial establishment, I thought immediately of Muggsy. The house was centrally situated, and Fanny (who was determined to go on with her job) could as easily continue to work for Kitty Cairns from there as from Marylebone Road. Muggsy herself had all the good-natured Cockney's fondness for lovers; and I was confident that her attachment to me and her dislike of my mother and sister would reconcile her to connivance at my irregular union.

I was perfectly candid with her. We were sitting over some very strong tea in her neat basement kitchen, when I made my considered speech:

'Muggsy, I have fallen in love with the most adorable creature alive. There are reasons why we shall not marry – at any rate immediately – but we are going to live together, and that as soon as possible. I want Miss Hooper to come and lodge with you, and I shall be in and out as often as I possibly can. It's no good saying that you've no room, because the card is in your front window and Mr Carteret told me yesterday the top floor was vacant. And don't try to look shocked, because you won't do it well and I shan't believe you.'

She stirred her tea, watching me with shrewd and amused

eyes. 'You're a cool one and no mistake' she said. 'Does your ma know anything of this?'

'Not at the moment, But she will, I daresay. Anyway she's bound to smell a rat. I don't care. I don't care about anything but my Fanny; and, if they don't like it, they can lump it. As a matter of fact, she and my sister go for their annual visit to Scotland in two or three weeks and won't be in London again till September. When they leave I shall move to the Club as usual. But this time I shall not return to Kensington in the autumn. I am not going to live at home any more. I am going to live here.'

'Ho! You'll live here too? Then will you be wanting the young lady to have a double room? Or is it two singles?'

'Muggsy, you're being a goose. I've told you as plainly as I can that we shall be living as man and wife. Two singles indeed! You'll be wanting to sleep with us yourself, as chaperon, in a minute!'

'There now, Mr Harry, there's no call to be indelicate!' The old dear was trying hard to stifle her laughter. 'And what accommodation would Miss – er – Miss —'

'Miss *Hooper* – Christian name Fanny – and an angel out of heaven.'

'What accommodation beyond a double room will Miss Angel require?'

'She must have a really nice sitting-room, and, if there is a little extra room near by for odds and ends, I'd like her to have that also —'

'Odds and ends?' she queried, slanting her eyes at me. 'Not yet awhile, surely?'

I jumped up and kissed the top of her head:

"Now who's being indelicate! You are an old darling, Muggsy, and we'll go upstairs and view the premises.'

*   *   *

Of the first months of my life with Fanny I will only say that their sweetness – and hers – exceeded even my most extravagant hopes. As she gradually lost the conviction of her

own solitariness – a conviction which, I am sure, had dominated her adolescence and, though patiently accepted, shadowed
it – her capacity for enjoying every moment of her day
blossomed like a flower. She was always cheerful, always busy;
but her gaiety was never strident nor her housewifery a bustle.
As for her gallantry in love, I could only give thanks to the
good angel who strengthened me against her first passionate
appeal, and helped me to insist that friendly walls, instead of
the scented groves of Rosherville, enclose our first embrace.
The walls of Muggsy's house were more than friendly. Possibly they were grateful for the beauty and harmony which
Fanny brought to them.

So far, in fact, as Little Welbeck Street was concerned, life
was unblemished happiness. Muggsy adored her lodger (as I
knew she would); gave us much too much to eat, and threw
herself with enormous zeal into the whole conspiracy of stolen
bliss. But outside there were times of trial, of which the most
serious involved my family. Some time in July, after she had
been in Scotland five or six weeks (and Fanny in Little Welbeck Street about a month), I wrote from the Club to my
mother a careful and, I hope, dutiful letter, saying that I had
decided not to live at home in future. I promised I would come
and see her regularly, but said candidly that the social duties
of Kensington bored me and that I believed she and Kate, no
less than I, would really be happier apart. I got no answer.
Then one day, more than a fortnight later, an office-keeper
informed me with shocked respect that a lady was asking for
me. Unsuspecting I went downstairs to the waiting-room, and
found Kate. She was tight and white and evidently in a mood
of repressive pugnacity. She asked with dangerous civility
whether I could spare her half an hour for a private conversation. I fetched my hat, and we went into the dusty August
doldrums of St James's Park.

I was fairly prepared for what was to happen and waited for
Kate to speak.

'You wrote to mamma two weeks ago. She showed me the
letter and I told her not to reply to it.'

'Really?' I said mildly. 'Why did you do that?'

'Because I wished to make some inquiries.'

'Inquiries. What about?'

'About the real reason for your extraordinary attempt to break up our home.'

'Aren't you being a little extravagant, Kate?' I said. 'I hardly think for a man of thirty, who has lived with his mother more or less all his life, to say he is going to live somewhere else in easy reach of her, is quite equivalent to breaking up a home. Besides – forgive my saying so – is it altogether your affair?'

She tossed her head.

'Anything which concerns mamma is my affair, and you can be as oily and sarcastic as you like, you won't frighten me. I made up my mind to find out what was at the back of all this, and I've done so.'

She proceeded to let me have it good and strong. I listened without resentment, feeling she was only saying her piece and had to get through with it. But I knew that any moment she would go too far and permit herself to say something impermissible. So, when she paused for breath, I put in a word of warning:

'Kate, please! I don't want us to quarrel, and I beg you not to say anything which might lead us to do so. I don't mind what you have been saying about me. It is not for you to admit or deny my right to be independent, and you are at liberty to call me names for an hour if it helps your conscience. But I warn you that there are things I will not tolerate —'

She had worked herself up into a real frenzy of indignation, and interrupted me with deliberate insolence:

'So we are not to quarrel? That's charming! Mamma is to submit to your abominable selfishness – cry a little privately, perhaps, but accept her son's decision and tell her friends that the poor boy is "bored with Kensington" – while you wallow about with your filthy harlot, whom you have the impudence to put in lodgings with an old servant of the family! Oh —'

I had taken hold of her wrist, and my fingers are fairly strong. She stopped her ranting and began to whimper:

'Harry! You are hurting me!'

'No' I said. 'I am not hurting you at all, much as I should like to. I am merely stopping your nasty mind escaping through your mouth. You have chosen to insult the woman I love. All right. Then go back to mother and tell her that so long as I am liable to meet, or even *see* you in Phillimore Gardens, I shall not come there. You have succeeded in parting your mother from her son, and I hope you are satisfied. Now leave me, before I do you a mischief.'

I flung her arm back at her, and stood digging my nails into my palms, while hatred of her struggled with traditions of decency. She skipped out of reach and almost spat at me.

'You low disgusting beast! I never want to see you again.'

The tension relaxed. As before, I did not mind what Kate said of *me*.

'The wish is reciprocal' I said. 'But you had better give mother my message, for in three days I shall write it to her.'

That evening I found my little love sewing busily by the fireside. She jumped up with a cry of welcome and ran to kiss me. But with her hands already on my shoulders, her expression changed and she drew away:

'Harry! My poor darling! What is the matter?'

'The matter, sweetheart? Nothing. Why? Am I bleeding or something?'

'No, no. Nothing like that. But something has happened to make you unhappy or angry. I can tell, just by looking at your eyes. What is it, dear heart? Tell me what it is.'

I took her in my arms, and kissed her rich resilient eyebrows and her absurd little nose and the moist enchantment of her lips.

'Something good in the long run, sweetness. You have refused to come into my world, so I am coming into yours. Henceforth it is you and I, and Nanny and poor Seymore (if we can find them), and Julian and one or two more – and all of

Kensington can go to hell. But always you and I, Fanny; swear to me it is for always – you and I!'

I then told her briefly of my beastly encounter with Kate. She said nothing and turned the conversation. Late that night, as she lay with her head on my shoulder and the scent of her hair was lulling me to sleep, she whispered:

'When you want to go back ... back to your own people – you will go, won't you, Harry? I shall be all right; really I shall.'

The arm which crushed her against me forgot its strength. Also, in my half dream, anger against Kate had once more laid hold of me and I had dimly thought the yielding body was my sister's.

'Oh, Harry!' she moaned. 'Are you killing me?'

Her stifled cry brought me instantly to wakefulness.

'I am just a clumsy brute, Fanny' I said into her ear. 'But God knows I love you!'

*   *   *

The second 'outside complication' caused by my new way of life may be thought hardly to deserve the name, but to have been merely a pale reflection of the first. Actually it was infinitely more disagreeable, partly because it lasted much longer, partly because I could not say a word about it to my darling, who would have blamed herself, and been unhappy to the depths of her humble sensitive little soul.

Among the men I knew – colleagues in the office and casual friends made socially – were some who saw fit to drop my acquaintance when it gradually leaked out that I was living in lodgings with a girl from nowhere. However little I might care for their good opinion or their amity (which was very little indeed), I found the formation period of our estrangement a severe nervous strain. I had to force myself to go to the Club with reasonable regularity, and frankly dreaded the inevitable sudden encounters with men I used to know quite well, but who might now treat me to a blank stare or look through me as though I were not there at all. Gradually the enemy declared themselves; and once I knew where I was, I learnt how to cut an ex-acquaintance with the best of them. But it was a slow process and a hateful one.

In compensation I had the warming experience of continued friendship with other men, who either considered the affair none of their business or actually approved it. Chief among the latter was Julian Carteret, who had been in the secret from the beginning, to whom I had introduced Fanny at the earliest possible moment, and who now was a staunch and affectionate ally of us both. I would have liked to be able to tell him in words how deeply I appreciated the delicacy of his championship, at the time when the extent of my ostracism was still undefined. He went out of his way to be seen with me in places where unexpected and doubtful contacts were liable to be made; he seemed to know by instinct who was likely to be crudely insulting to me, who would funk outright discourtesy but exchange a few apparently civil words and then creep away to blather behind my back, who liked me well enough for myself (or was sufficiently well-bred) to be content for me to manage my own private life without his approval or otherwise. Nor was this ostentatious fidelity the only service he rendered. More than once he restrained me from taking violent revenge on some unusually offensive detractor. 'Don't be a fool, Harry' he would say firmly. 'Of course you can thrash the swine with one hand; but it won't do any good. Let them spill their venom and be damned. The real kindness to Fanny is to keep quiet. It will all pass over.' Of course he was right; and, as I say, I wish I could have thanked him outright for all his help. But men find it hard to say things of the kind to one another; and I got no further than looking my gratitude and acting it. I expect he understood.

*   *   *

There was one other major problem – external to Little Welbeck Street yet closely concerning it – which required as prompt a solution as possible, and that was the problem of Clive Seymore. Once again Julian was implicated, because once again his help was needed. Fanny and I agreed that it was hardly for us to tell him that she was Seymore's daughter; but we explained our anxiety to find out what had become of Seymore by stressing the long-standing relationship between his family and that of Fanny's mother, with my having known him thrown in as make-weight.

Julian was well placed for getting information as to what had transpired after the divorce had been granted in the early summer. We did not feel in need of details of the case itself which, even though undefended, had attracted the notice of some of the sensation mongering papers. During what I liked to call our 'courting days' Fanny and I had studied a few of these reports hoping to be able to read between the lines. But after writing up the family connections and social prominence of the parties, the reporters had found themselves sadly short of spicy material and soon decided that the Seymore case was a *fumier manqué*. Consequently 'between the lines' was as devoid of sense as the lines themselves, and as the lurid emptiness only caused Fanny distress without telling her anything of value, we read no further.

Soon after the beginning of the autumn term, Julian came to our sitting-room one evening and announced that he had got what information there was.

'Seymore is living at his Yorkshire home – by the way he is "Sir Clive" now; you knew the old man had died? Almost the entire estate has been sold or is up for sale and he must be finding things very difficult. No one sees him and apparently he never goes outside his own grounds.'

'Oh dear!' sighed Fanny 'I wonder who looks after him. Some of the old servants *must* be there.'

'I'm afraid I can't tell you that, Mrs Harry' said Julian (he always called her 'Mrs Harry' – a sort of compromise between personal friendship and the observance of correct terminology so important to the legal mind). 'The fellow who told me the little I know was sitting in court while the case was on and, although Seymore did not appear, felt sympathetic with him and took pains to inquire what became of him. I gather the lady made a bad impression. Oh, yes – there was one little thing he told me which might interest you. You remember she accused her husband of smuggling a left-handed child of his own into the house —'

Fanny was sewing, and I felt rather than saw her start violently. She gave a faint cry and next moment was sucking her finger, very red in the face and suspiciously bright in the eyes. Julian stopped short.

'What's happened, darling?' I asked, though I knew well enough.

She had control of herself now, removed the finger and excused herself with charming confusion.

'I am so sorry, Mr Carteret. Like a clumsy thing I pricked my finger rather badly. It's all right now. Please go on – about the girl in the house.'

He gave her a quick appraising look.

'Ah, yes. Did I say she was a girl? Well, she was; and the judge inquires how Mrs Seymore – no, she was Lady Something, wasn't she? no matter – how the plaintiff knew this girl was the defendant's daughter. The question seems to shake Lady – er —' ("Alicia" I put in) '— of course, thanks – to shake Lady Alicia up a bit. She makes out that, as soon as she saw the child, she felt there was something familiar about her, *and*' (he was now looking rather hard at Fanny, with just a gleam of mischief at the back of his impassive legal face) 'when she heard her voice – her *voice*, mind you – she was quite certain. Certain of what? That the child was like her husband. The judge isn't at all satisfied with this. "Come, come" he says, "you are not asking the Court to believe that an apparent likeness in appearance and voice between a girl of fourteen and a man of forty proves the former to be the latter's daughter? Is this all the evidence you had before bringing this gratuitous extra charge against your husband?" Very reluctantly the lady has to admit that she had previously sent a confidential agent to her husband's home neighbourhood to collect any private information he could find. "What sort of information" asks his lordship. "To Mr Seymore's credit or otherwise?" No; not exactly to his credit. About any early love affairs and so on. "I see" says the judge. "You wanted to pry into his past just in case you might be forced in the future to come to the Court to heal your poor broken heart. Very prudent. And what did your 'confidential agent' find out?" That Mr Seymore, as a young man, *had* had an affair with a farmer's daughter, and that a girl child had been born. The incident seems to have been known to several people in the neighbourhood, who took it quite calmly. "A pity their example has not been more generally followed" says his lordship dryly. And lets her go.'

Watching Julian as he talked, I had come to realize that he knew Fanny was the girl in the case, and had adopted this indirect means of telling us so. I was wondering how best to turn the subject and keep the conversation on general lines until I had an opportunity of talking to him (and to her) alone, when to my surprise she said in her low clear voice, without looking up from her work:

'Mr Carteret, Harry told me that at one time Lady Alicia also accused her husband of setting this child of his to spy on her. Was anything said in court about that?'

'No. Nothing about that.'

Fanny laid her sewing in her lap and stared into the fire.

'Was it wise of Mr Seymore not to defend?' she asked.

'Mrs Harry' he said gently 'no outsider can say in delicate matters of this sort what a man should or should not have done. From a purely material point of view he would have done better to defend; for it is an open secret she was more guilty than he was, and he would have saved the alimony, which I gather he can ill afford. But he may have shrunk from the publicity – perhaps on his own account, more likely on account of his daughter, who would have been a leading witness: and who has the right to blame him? As things turned out, his policy saved her not only from having to appear, but from being even mentioned by name. My friend told me it was almost noticeable how the girl's name was never revealed. The judge actually stopped Lady Alicia at one moment, when it

seemed that she was going to say it. There can be no doubt
that that was one of the conditions made by Seymore's lawyers
and accepted by the petitioners. Rather touching, I thought.
And successful – for nobody knows her name.'

He got up from his chair and crossed the room to take his
leave of Fanny. She looked up at him as he stood by her side,
and smiled a little wistful smile.

'Yet you know it, Mr Carteret, don't you?'

He bowed over her hand:

'Yes, my dear. I know it – and, I am proud to say, its owner
also. Goodnight and God bless you both.'

II

From the doorway of the Plough Inn at Aughton Seymore I
watched Fanny's dogged little figure start on its solitary way
to visit her father. It was the third week of a golden October.
There was colour in the trees, in the rich soil, in the chickens
scuttering across the road, in the walls and roofs of the humble
but mellow buildings which lined the village street. Only in her
dear cheeks, when she left me, was no colour. She was frightened for him and racked with worry. Incongruous on her plain
tight-bodied dress and emphasizing the pallor of her face, her
beautiful zircon brooch glowed blue and green on her bosom. I
had fingered it, questioningly. 'In case he does not recognize
me' she had said, with a fleeting smile, 'or is suspicious. I
daresay he suspects everyone, just at present.'

We had arrived the night before. In London Fanny had
written a letter to Seymore, but had torn it up. 'Better he
should have no chance to hide' she said. 'In his mood, the
nearest intruders are the most to be feared.' In the train to
York I had seen a grand opportunity to raise once more the
question of marriage. 'You say I must not come with you when
you go to Aughton; that Sir Clive may be in no mood to know
that his daughter is living with a man, and especially one from
the very office he has had to leave. May she not even be engaged to such a man?'

'Oh darling!' she cried, putting my arm round her and curling herself against me. 'Don't make it harder. I only want to spare you both until I see how things are. If all goes well, you shall come with me the second time.'

'But, sweetheart – your father apart, why not marriage soon? I am free of the things which you thought stood in the way. I am just the other half of you; and no one cares what either of us do – except me.'

'*And* me, Harry! I do care. Indeed I care about nothing else. But – oh, I don't know how to put it – I am an *outside* person. I always have been, and I am too proud to come *inside* – at any rate at present. If being your wife could be any lovelier than being what I am now, I might be tempted. But it couldn't; nothing could. And to have this happiness, and still be "outside", gives me a sort of extra delight in what has happened.' Wriggling round, she peered anxiously into my face: 'You aren't angry with me?'

'Silly child! I doubt if I could be, except on your own account. Will you promise me this – that after you have been "outside" for another six months; all right, another year – you will do what I want?'

She considered my question carefully and answered with another:

'Will you trust me to say on my own when I want it too?' I nodded.

'Leave it like that then, Harry. Please! It may be in three weeks or six months or longer. I don't know. But I will own up . . . truly.'

*   *   *

The slight figure climbed a stile on the left and was lost to sight. I lit my pipe and started for a walk in the other direction. What will she find, I wondered. Will she be happy when she comes back, or in despair? I wished I could have seen her safely to the house at least. But she had refused to hear of it. 'No. I should know my way in the dark. It is only just over two years since I was there. Besides I may meet someone who knows me.' So I had let her go, and was now walking nowhere in particular, just to kill time.

I had been back at the inn for an hour when she returned. She shut the door of our little parlour behind her, threw her bonnet on to the settee and ran into my arms. I had a glimpse of a tremulous mouth and of tears seeping through her lashes as she buried her head on my chest. I stood a few moments holding her close. She was absolutely still. She is not crying for grief, I told myself: she is shocked or exhausted. At last I gathered her up – a featherweight absurdity to hold my great carcase in her thrall – and sat in the big chair, with her body, limp as that of a kitten, crumpled against me. She began to speak into my waistcoat, her voice without a tremor but her face still hidden.

'I saw him, Harry. He is so aged and beaten – that gentle, proud man whose boots they were unworthy to lick. How do the ungodly flourish – isn't that right? It's near enough. And she is peacocking about London, beast that she is, while he sits there behind the shutters with his heart broken and his life in ashes. Oh, Harry – what can I *do*, what can I *do*?'

I held her more tightly and rocked her gently to and fro.

'Never mind at present, little love. Just lie there safely and rest. Remember you are not alone any more.'

For a while she was silent, snuggling against me till I felt the warmth of her stir my senses. After a few minutes she spoke again:

'I told him about you. He seemed glad. But I am not sure whether he remembered you or connected the name with the office. I did not mention the office – merely that I had a lover now and was safe and happy. He would like to see you to-morrow. Will you come and see him?'

'Of course, if you both wish it.'

'Nanny is with him' she went on, talking in a low monotone as though reciting to herself rather than reporting to another. 'That is one comfort. But she is getting old, and what happens when she goes? Someone *must* be with him and there is no one – no one but me.'

'Do not meet troubles halfway, sweetheart. When need arises we will see what can be done. Now you are going to lie down and rest. Sleep, if you can.'

I carried her to the low cottagey bedroom, with its small window almost on the floor and its irregular sloping ceiling, laid her on the big feather bed, took off her shoes and coat, and wrapped her in a rug. She submitted passively and said no word. When I came back from filling our travelling foot-warmer with hot water and put it at her feet, she was lying perfectly still, with her long dark lashes asleep upon her cheeks.

*   *   *

Next morning we walked across the fields toward the Hall. I looked forward with some dread to the coming interview, for the relationship in which I stood to Seymore was dually deli-cate. I had no idea how, if he recognized me, the thought that I had known him in his days of glory would fuse with the realization that I was now his daughter's lover. But I kept my forebodings to myself and tried to talk naturally to Fanny of the countryside and the final splendours of the dying year. We came in sight of the house some little while before we reached it for it stood on the crest of a low hill and we were crossing the levels over which it faced. The October sun lit the long stone façade to a soft grey, and I looked with interest at the building which Fanny had often described to me. Certainly the great stone birds were very curious, and I was wondering whether they were not also likely to be dangerous (for they were manifestly over-sized, and a strong gale might bring one crashing down if the stonework were at all perished) when I was struck by a lack of symmetry in their disposal. Surely one was missing? Was there always a gap in the birds on the right? I asked. She looked up toward the house and stopped short. 'Indeed no! I did not notice yesterday. It must have fallen.' We looked at one another, but said nothing more.

I was relieved to find no signs of actual neglect or desolation in the outbuildings through which we had to pass to reach the

house-door. The place was silent, certainly; and the only
human being I saw was a stable lad, who came out of the barn
with a loaded hay-fork and slouched past us without even raising his eyes. But the gravel of the drive was clear of weeds and
only a few blades of grass pushed up between the setts of the
large paved yard. Fanny rang the bell and an old butler in
rusty black came to the door. He smiled a cordial greeting.

'Come in, Miss Fanny, come in. And we hope you come
often. Your visit did the master real good yesterday.'

'I am very glad, Mr Tyas. This is Mr Somerford, come to
call on Sir Clive; Harry, Mr Tyas has been here many many
years and I doubt if Aughton could get on without him.'

The old man bowed respectfully.

'Ay, it is a long time, sir' he said 'and may be a bit longer
yet before my time is up. Let me take your coat and hat, sir.
Miss Fanny, will you go through or shall I tell Sir Clive you
are here?'

'Better tell him. We will find Mrs Heaviside first and be
with him in five minutes.'

Once again I had the experience of seeing for myself something Fanny had frequently described – this time the square
surface-grim figure of the former housekeeper at Upper Belgrave Street. I think she was probably as shy as I was, for she
received Fanny's introduction with stiff formality; but she was
also curious, and I was uneasily conscious of being shrewdly
and critically measured up. We exchanged a few awkward sentences; and then Fanny, with the briskness of embarrassment,
suggested we go in search of the master.

'Goodbye for the moment, Nanny. I'll see you again before
we go.'

The old woman merely nodded.

'Rather alarming' I whispered to Fanny as we went down
the passage.

She squeezed my hand.

'It is the watch-dog in her. She is afraid for her adored
Clive. She will accept you soon, and then love you for my sake
as she now loves me for his.'

Fanny knocked on a door to the left of a wide irregular hall, which we reached through a baize-door at the back. There seemed to be no principal entrance or front door to this hall, though I could tell from the shape of the windows that it lay just behind the main façade of the house. Next moment we were in the presence of Clive Seymore. He was sitting close to a bright fire, in an upright armchair with a rug over his knees. He was pale, and the look he gave us as we entered was listless and dull, but apart from a suggestion of sagging in his cheeks, he was less changed than I had feared. He made no attempt to rise. Fanny ran to him and kissed him, and a flicker of welcome passed across his face. Holding his hand she stepped aside for me to approach:

'Andrew, this is Harry Somerford, whom you wanted to see. Harry, my father.'

He looked at me with a lack of expression in his eyes which I found grievous and unnerving.

'How do you do, sir?'

There was nothing else to say.

A wan smile just touched his lips.

'I am very glad to see you, Mr Somerford' he said, in the dusky voice which I remembered from the past and now loved dearly as part of my darling's inheritance. 'You must forgive an invalid remaining seated; but I am not strong these days. Still, seeing my little girl again has put some heart into me, and to know that she is happy is the best news you can bring.'

'I hope she is happy, Sir Clive' I said. 'She deserves to be, if ever a woman did.'

Fanny stretched out her other hand to me.

'Dear Harry! I deserve very little of the good life you have given me.'

She made no pretence of being other than loverlike, and I concluded she had been quite open with her father as to how things were with us. Perhaps this made the position easier; but I was not at all sure.

'Vannchen' said Seymore (and the pet-name caught my

attention and pleased me) 'will you be very kind and go and
ask Nanny to make me some tea now, and have the sherry sent
in for yourself and Mr Somerford. I am sure you would both
like a glass and a piece of cake after your walk.'

She went at once. As the door closed behind her, Seymore
pointed to a chair. He seemed suddenly more vigorous.

'Please sit down, Somerford. It is strange our meeting again
in these circumstances. How are things in the office?'

I managed not to appear taken aback and to play up to his
sudden mood of realism. I told him a few general items of
office news and at the end ventured to say:

'We all miss you, sir, and were distressed to hear of your
bad illness. There are several others who could better have
been spared, if someone's health had to break down.'

He smiled almost with animation, and I was glad to see a
little colour had come into his cheeks.

'That is very handsomely put, and I thank you. I need
hardly say that for me the break was a disaster. To have been
busy and interested and then to have nothing to do – nothing –
that is terrible. Indeed I thought I should not be able to bear it
at first. But no man can die when he wants to, except he kill
himself; and I should be ashamed to do that. So I relapsed
into the state in which you see me – perhaps I should say
"would have seen me two days ago", for first Vandra coming,
and then you, has given me something but myself to think
about. Do you want to talk to me about Vandra? It is for you
to say; for I did little enough for her while I could and now
there is nothing I can do.'

'I would like to talk about her for hours, Sir Clive. But my
song in Fanny's honour must wait a better opportunity. She
will be here any moment. May I say one thing – at the risk of
seeming absurd? It is this. I want her to marry me; but she
will not – not yet. Can you persuade her....'

His eyes were no longer dead, but astir with intelligence and
quiet irony.

'This situation is becoming more and more bizarre' he said.
'It is most unusual for a suitor to ask a parent's help in regu-

larizing his daughter's union. Maybe it is even more unusual for the parent to say that he sees the daughter's point of view. I should be proud to think of you two as man and wife; but I can sympathize with Vanny's non-conformity and – well, I have some reason for not regarding marriage as the element in a love-affair which is made in Heaven. Heaven's work comes at an earlier stage – if it comes at all. Be patient, Somerford, and you will get your way. Meantime love her and take care of her; and know that you have, for what little it is worth, the blessing of one who has made a sad mess of things, but really knew better – yes, I assure you, really knew better.'

I had walked to the window while he was speaking, instinctively, I think, to save embarrassment for both of us. I found myself looking out on a weed-grown gravel terrace, scattered over which – just in front of my eyes – were the broken pieces of a huge bird, carved in stone. Nervously anxious to change the subject I said, when he had finished:

'One of your great heraldic birds has fallen, I see. That is very sad. How did it happen?'

'I had it levered off the cornice when my father died' he replied quietly. 'A sort of totemism, I suppose. Silly, wasn't it?'

III

We stayed a week at Aughton Seymore, seeing Fanny's father daily and rejoicing to observe a slow healing of his wounded mind and a gradual return of bodily energy after the apathy into which he had sunk. I had in due course been admitted to Nanny's good graces; and, as we were perfectly content to tell one another Fanny's virtues – she, as bringing credit on the Seymore family; I, as proving that my ladylove was the sweetest of her sex – we got along famously.

Then came our visit to Gowthorpe.

'You had better get it all over at once, Harry' Fanny said laughing. 'I'm sorry for you; though in the circumstances running the gauntlet of the girl's parents is not so bad as it might be. And thank your stars I haven't a lot of brothers and sisters!'

As things turned out, the experience was disagreeable. Mrs Hopwood proved much more of an ordeal than Sir Clive. Her father – Fanny's Grandfather Hooper – was dead, and she now kept house for her brothers. They greeted me without interest and I only saw them for a few minutes; but Mrs Hopwood was at once possessive toward Fanny and only too clearly resentful of me. After the first shock of feeling disliked, I was able to appreciate the difficulty of the situation. Mrs Hopwood's own love-story had ended in stultification. She had a daughter to whom she was devoted, but seldom saw. Her former lover, in view of their difference in standing, was the more separated from her for living near at hand; and the catastrophe which had befallen him, by driving him into brooding retirement, had made matters worse. She could hardly welcome the prospect of an irregular union for Fanny also, which she would naturally parallel with her own. It was beyond the scope of her experience to realize how different her daughter was from what she had been at the same age – how much more on equal terms with the world and how unaffected, in the intermediate society to which she belonged, by class distinctions. In her eyes, Fanny was the victim of a casual amour and liable any day to be cast aside. That she and not I resisted marriage; that I had broken with my family to be with her; and that our association could not be understood without knowledge of its background, were things impossible to explain. I had, therefore, to endure two very unpleasant hours, while Fanny strove to include me in her affectionate chatter to her mother and Mrs Hopwood deliberately shut me out.

I bore the poor woman no grudge. To her I was not an individual; I was just *wrong* and unlikely to do her daughter any good. I had only to imagine how my own mother would receive Fanny, if ill-luck ever brought them together, and I was safe from blaming Mrs Hopwood for doing me any personal injustice. But I could see that the atmosphere caused Fanny increasing distress, and for that reason I hated it.

When at last we could decently take leave, climb into the dog-cart and start on our drive back to the village, Fanny faced up to the visit's failure.

'I am so sorry, Harry' she said. 'That was horrible for you. I was a fool not to have known it would be. You see she has lost touch – in the sense of intimacy – with Andrew, and her fondness for me is all that remains to her of an experience she never wants to forget. In a way, the fact that she and I and he and I are two pairs of close friends only divides the three of us the more completely. Then you come along, and she sees another pair – this time you and I. She is jealous for her share in me, poor mamma, and I ought to have guessed it.'

'Never mind, sweetheart. It can't be helped. You must stay friends with her, for you are all she has. I will keep out of sight in future.'

Next time she went to Gowthorpe, she went alone. It was a consolation that at least at Aughton we were both of us welcome.

I was glad to realize that extreme poverty was, as applied to Aughton Hall, a relative phrase. Undeniably the Hall's activity as a 'big house' was finished. The staff, inside and out, had been reduced to a strict minimum; the only vehicle kept was a small one-horse wagonette; the few remaining fields were almost empty of stock. But Sir Clive had sufficient income left to feed and clothe himself and his household; to carry out the necessary repairs and renewals, and to lead the solitary studious life which was all he wanted.

'Come back soon' he said, when we took leave. 'You will find me here always. And next time you must stay in the house. Simple doings – but no worse than the Plough, I daresay, and more room for your clothes.'

IV

The months which followed our return to London passed with a level quietness ideal to lovers. Fanny and I had grown into that best sort of intimacy which has its own nonsense, almost its own language. We needed no company, although it was sometimes pleasant to see special friends or go to a music-hall or, as spring came round, to make an expedition to Kew or Richmond or down the river to Greenwich or Rosherville. Once a week we played whist with Julian and Muggsy – a game involving a technique of its own, as the latter invariably trumped her partner's aces, which had therefore either to be played third hand or counted a total loss. It was, I suppose, what many would call a monotonous life, and it would certainly make for monotonous telling.

Early in December I felt a twinge of conscience about my family. It seemed that I ought to make a gesture of affection toward my mother, even one of reconciliation toward Kate Accordingly I wrote to my mother, saying that I was sorry to have parted from Kate in anger and in so doing have separated myself from my old home; that at this season disputes should be forgotten, and would they, so far as our personal relationship was concerned, let bygones be bygones. She replied cordially enough, inviting me to take Christmas dinner with them and maintain at least that tradition unbroken. Not even the most indirect reference was made to Fanny, and I soon realized that, purposely or otherwise, the invitation put me in a quandary. To leave my darling for the first Christmas we were together was in itself unpleasant and might in its implications seem almost brutal. On the other hand, I knew my family well enough to be sure that these were their terms of armistice and that, if I refused or made an alternative proposal, war would go on. I worried for a while, and then told Fanny what my mother had suggested and that I believed it was my duty to go. She was clearly disappointed, and I thought at one moment she was going to show resentment – a prospect which terrified me, for I had never seen her anything but tractable in moments of social dilemma and doubted how I should handle her in an affronted mood. When I got back in the evening, she had evidently decided either to forget her hurt or to conceal it; for she broached the question at once, and with brisk common-sense.

'I was taken by surprise about Christmas, Harry, and probably seemed out of temper. I'm sorry. Of course you must go; and I will keep a tradition going also, and have my dinner with Chunks and Polly as I did last year. I've written to ask if I may, but it's sure to be all right.'

Greatly relieved I declared the plan an excellent one, but insisted on her hiring a cab for the journey and told her to stay there until I came for her.

'I badly want to meet Chunks' I said 'and it will be easier on his own ground and at a time of general good fellowship.'

*   *   *

Christmas dinner at Phillimore Gardens had the surface amiability and the basic dullness of any artificial reunion. It is curious that one can be quite fond of people, yet find their company utterly tedious. Inevitably there was a bond between my mother, Kate and myself, inevitably it was agreeable for the three of us to find ourselves together again. But, for my part, once these satisfactions had been registered, only boredom remained. To begin with, after we had exchanged tiresome presents, there was really nothing to talk about. What mattered in my new existence – the jokes, the quick interplay of two similar senses of humour; the delight in just being *with* someone, which made the silliest remark or incident a moment of gay harmony – was automatically excluded, being outside the consciousness of my mother and sister and the two or three odd cousins who made up the party. In the second place, because of the six months' break in our common experience, conversation was mostly that much out of date and in consequence tedious. Finally, although my mother was clearly trying to be conciliatory, Kate was not. She made several references to things which had occurred during the autumn, and put a quick sting in their tail with 'Oh, no, of course, you weren't here' or 'How stupid! I'd forgotten you were away.' I was determined not to be drawn, and toiled on with civil commonplace and meaningless palaver, sinking every minute into a deeper dejection. After the meal we sat in the drawing-room, looking (in my judgement) the dullest collection of fools imaginable, while a nice twaddling cousin sang nice twaddling songs. At last I could bear it no longer and rose to go. My mother asked me to come to her room to see a water-colour she had been given for Christmas. I was suspicious, but could not refuse. It was a deplorable water-colour – pretty enough, but as vacant as this whole lamentable party – and I grinned a vague appreciation and murmured that I must really be off. I could feel my mother gathering herself together:

'Harry dear' she said 'how long is this going on?'

No use pretending not to understand.

'So far as I'm concerned, for ever' I replied.

She raised her eyebrows.

'Ever is a long time.'

'Is it?' I replied brutally, for the sneer behind the eyebrows angered me. 'Not so long in some places as in others.'

'What do you mean, Harry?'

My temper had ebbed again and I was a little ashamed.

'Forgive me, I should not speak to you like that. But I must be allowed to manage my own affairs. After all, I only proposed to stop living at home. I had intended coming here often; but Kate made that impossible.'

Her eyes were at once obstinate and appealing. Outraged conventionality, personal offence and fondness of a mother for an only son struggled in her mind.

'I wish I understood better' she said hesitatingly. 'Kate was wrong to do as she did; but it was a shock to her – and to me.'

'Why a shock, mother? I have fallen in love. Is that so shocking?'

'You are quibbling' she replied sharply. 'You know quite well what I mean – your father's son, hiding away with a kept woman like some common rake. . . .'

'You are talking rather nonsense, dear. Nothing so lurid is happening. I am not hiding away, as you call it, and as for being a rake, surely to deserve that name a man must be more enterprising and catholic than I?'

She sank down into a chair and stared across the room, working her hands nervously together.

'It is so difficult to explain your not being here' she faltered tearfully. 'I know you pretend to despise my friends and not to care what they think; but these last months have been horribly embarrassing for us. Why has it got to be like this, that is what I cannot understand?'

'Forgive me, mother' I said gently 'I ought to have thought more of your having to account for my absence. I am very sorry.'

'It's all very well to be sorry, Harry; but if this – this girl is all that you think her, why wasn't she introduced to your mother and, if everything was satisfactory, the two of you properly engaged?'

The bland assumption that Fanny ought to have been produced for my family's approval stung me, and I nearly let my temper once more out of control. But the basic reason for my mother's bewilderment was too genuine and understandable to be side-tracked in recrimination, and even in anger I realized that she intended no offence. To claim the right to endorse her son's choice was instinctive and a part of her social training. She could no more help doing so than she would be able to see why it infuriated me.

So I forgot my irritation, put a hand on her shoulder and spoke with careful moderation.

'You must believe me, mother, when I say that, until you know Fanny's story, you cannot begin to understand why things are as they are at present. I am confident that this is only a temporary state of affairs, and that before long we shall be as regulation a couple as you could meet anywhere. But at the moment it's not possible to do otherwise than we have done.'

'Is there a husband, then?' she asked quickly.

'Oh, dear, no! Nothing so simple as that. It is a complicated business, with pride and humility and foreground and background all mixed together, which I could never explain to you unless you knew Fanny. And Kate's behaviour that day in

the park made your knowing Fanny impossible. That you must
see.'

She shook her head impatiently.

'No! I don't see anything about it, or that all your talk has
any meaning. That Kate spoke ill-advisedly is no reason for
putting an insult on your mother. As for your own position no
really nice girl would dream of consenting to the sort of
arrangement which you now seem to prefer – as I daresay
you'll find out soon enough.'

I felt a momentary wry amusement at this vision of myself
tricked by a heedless wanton into an amourette; then sadly
accepted the inevitable. It was hopeless. She was not only incapable of understanding, she did not even want to.

'I'm truly sorry, dear' I said. 'You've got it all wrong. But
there is no good in our discussing the matter further. I will say
goodnight and be off.'

I kissed her on the cheek and left her there, twisting her
fingers together and torn between anger and distress.

An unwilling hansom drove me to Islington. It was a cold
dry night, with a moon in its third quarter high in the sky. We
kept running into crowds of merrymakers with flares and
lanterns, and out of them again into the black and silver spaces
of deserted streets and squares. The mingled fret and weari-
ness of the detestable evening in Kensington gradually yielded
to the soothing beauty of the night, to anticipation of being
with Fanny again, and to satisfaction in the thought that
Christmas Day was likely at least to end in an atmosphere of
genuine jollity.

I paid off the cab at Islington Green and plunged into the
narrows of River Row. Demolition had already begun and one
side of the street was a fence of planks. Over this low barrier
the moon shone brightly and I could stride along without fear
of stumbling. That the Bargee was indeed jolly became evident some distance away; and when I pushed open the saloon
door and surveyed the scene inside, I could have laughed
aloud, so perfect was the contrast to the genteel sham of the
party I had left. Sitting on the actual bar, swinging their legs

and beating time with their heels against the woodwork, were
Fanny, a golden-haired bundle of a woman who was certainly
Polly, and a buxom wench wearing a waterman's hat and a
beautiful black shawl embroidered with brilliant flowers. The
noise was so terrific that no one heard the door open nor
immediately noticed that a stranger was present. I had therefore a few seconds in which to take in the presence of a large
purple-faced man in an armchair near the bright coal fire, a
piano set crosswise in one corner and vigorously pounded by a
faded individual with sweat dripping off his whiskers, several
other men standing or seated, and the dense pall of tobacco-
smoke which hung over the whole bar. Then Fanny saw me.
She jumped off the bar, and shouting 'Here's Harry! Hooray!'
rushed across the room and flung her arms round my neck.
There was an immediate silence. I picked Fanny up and carried her into the middle of the floor.

'Evening, everybody' I said. 'Merry Christmas!'

The purple man struggled to his feet and came slowly forward, grinning as he came. I put Fanny back on the bar and
turned to greet him. Simultaneously:

'Mister Box, I'm sure.'

'Mister Somerford, ain't it?'

We shook hands with much solemnity. He looked me up and
down.

'Fine big feller too' he said, as though reporting to an invisible audience. 'Looks like e'd be andy with the dooks....
Come along, Fannikins, do the honours, and then we'll get
your friend somethin to drink.'

I was presented to Polly, to the other young woman (whose
name was Ada and seemed to belong to a man called Nobbs),
to the pianist (who belonged to Polly), to Nobbs, and to the
rest of the company. Chunks then provided me with a glass of
hot rum-punch and a cigar, made me sit at his side and
shouted to the pianist to tickle the ivories once more.

As I looked round I could see that the company was well-
liquored. Even Fanny was flushed and noisy, and when I
thought back to the muted sprightliness of my mother's

drawing-room, I loved her the better for being a little drunk under the flaring gaslights of an Islington pub. I finished my drink and asked for more. There was leeway to make up.

We were soon dancing waltzes and polkas and singing as we danced. We played blind-man's buff and postman's knock. More music followed. Chunks struck up 'Camptown Races', and we all 'do-dahd' till the glasses rang. The pianist played and sang 'The Laird o' Cockpen', followed by 'Paddle Your Own Canoe', followed by some increasingly bawdy songs of his own composition. Ada, who had once had a walking-on part at the Royal Surrey, gave a spirited rendering of a scene from 'Rose Mortimer or the Ballet Girl's Revenge', in which, with great virtuosity, she impersonated not only Blanche Baverini and Lottie Chepstow, but also the wicked Earl of Sloeford. Polly recited 'Beautiful Sally or the Harlot's Progress'; and I did my imitation of Queen Victoria, wearing the black embroidered shawl to complete the illusion. It was childish and rowdy and very alcoholic; but it was grand fun, and I understood for the first time what the Christmas spirit ought to be.

At twelve o'clock I bade Fanny prepare to come home. When she reappeared wearing the sealskin jacket, cap and muff which I had given her that morning, and looking like a bacchante packed in fur, we all sang 'Auld Lang Syne' and had another drink.

'Ow will ye get ome?' asked Chunks.

'Walk' I said. 'We'll pick up a cab somewhere.'

He gave Fanny a humorous glance.

'Ardly in walkin trim, is she?'

She put out her tongue at him.

'Can walk miles, you horrid thing. Miles and miles and miles —'

'Plenty, my dear' I said. 'There and back again. Come along, and, if you are tired, I'll carry you.'

We took affecting leave of everyone present; and as Polly and her pianist were going toward the Angel, the four of us started off in company. I found myself supporting the not inconsiderable weight of the genial barmaid, whose legs were a little unsteady but her conversation no less fluent for being slightly confused.

'I like you, Arry' she said. 'You're a man that's what you are and there's plenty as aint for all their long moustaches and their tight trousers, as I ought to know as well as the girl next door. And I like yer little Fanny too. She's a first chop good girl, and no Brummagem. And aint she mashed on you! My word, it's Arry this and Arry that and wait till you see my Arry, till I could've bust me stays keepin a straight face. But she means it awri, and now I *ave* seen yer I don't wonder at er. Tell me, I says, ow does e – you *know*? And she goes all pink, the little dear, and whispers —'

She pulled herself together and went on with tremendous dignity.

'You must reely excuse me, Mister Summerfield – Mister Arry, I should say – but I'm not quite meself and I do run on something shockin, once me stomach is disordered.'

'Please, Polly, I like it. Tell me some more. Tell me about your friend. He's slap-up on the piano.'

'Oh, im! Es all right. Quiet sort of feller. I must ave someone to worry about, you see, else I'd be thinkin of meself all the time; and, though there's plenty of me, I'm a bit samey. So I worry about Fred.' Her voice dropped to a note of extreme caution. 'Es fond of is drop, pore man. That's all e cares for. Dont smoke, dont swear, dont it is girl about, dont do nuffin like an ordinary man, except lift is at when e meets a lady and is elbow when e meets a pub.' She giggled suddenly and dug me in the ribs. 'Lot o' use to a girl a man oo only lifts his at and is elbow I dont think. You oughta ave three of everything as the man said to the pawnbroker oo complained is eggs wouldn't atch and it turned out e'd forgot the rooster.'

We were now near the point where Fred and Polly turned into Pentonville, so waited till Fanny and her escort caught us up. After more fervent leave-taking, Fanny and I walked on to the Angel. Halfway down Pentonville Road we found a decrepit growler and reached home at one o'clock.

The fluctuations of the evening's atmosphere, the rum-punch, the songs and knockabout, and the shameless good humour of Polly's monologue had inflamed my blood and my imagination.

In the sitting-room I took Fanny by the shoulders and kissed her soundly. She was drowsy and clinging, in the reckless aftermath of drink and excitement.

'Angel' I said 'you are even lovelier drunk than sober. But not, I gather, very discreet. You have been telling secrets to Polly – curtain secrets. Now go and get ready for bed and you shall have something fresh for next time.'

But she cheated me; for when ten minutes later I followed her, I found her flung like a scarf across the bed – ivory-naked under swathes of her rich brown hair, and fast asleep.

v

One morning toward the end of April Fanny exclaimed over a letter which the postman had just brought.

'My word, Harry! Lucy has got to the Gaiety. We *must* go and see her.'

For one reason and another I had not yet met Lucy Beckett. Fanny had shown no particular anxiety to introduce us and I could still recall the unreasonable jealousy I had felt toward her on that evening in Park Street when I first told Fanny of my love. But the two girls had seen one another once or twice, and I had a fair idea of Lucy's history.

Under the influence of some man or other she had thrown up a job at a smart dressmaker's and had decided to go on the stage. Her first attempt got her no nearer than behind the long buffet, whose picked attendants were the main feature of 'The Spittoon' – a dilapidated theatre in Upper Street, with the baptismal but almost forgotten name of 'Philharmonic'. From there she migrated to the Canterbury in Westminster Bridge Road; and this time on to the professional side of the footlights. As the Canterbury had seen the début of Louie Crouch (who became Cora Pearl and gave parties in St John's Wood, wearing nothing but some clusters of diamonds), it may have suggested to Lucy a future more glorious than its rather dingy present. But nothing promising occurred; and late in 1875 she had transferred to the Opera Comique, which for all its jerry-built discomfort was at least in the Strand and therefore West End. Unfortunately she struck a bad period even for this traditionally unlucky house. Throughout 1876 she dawdled hopelessly through poor quality Opera Bouffe; but in the winter her luck turned. The enterprising Hollingshead (flushed with his Gaiety triumphs) took over the management, brought there for a short season in December his new burlesque company, and produced *The Bohemian Gyurl*. He roped in a few of the Op. Com. chorus girls, among them Lucy, who quickly took the fancy of a Gaiety frequenter.

This man, it now appeared, knew Hollingshead, and persuaded him to transfer so beautiful a show-girl to the Gaiety itself. In consequence Miss Lucy was now playing under Kate Vaughan, Nellie Farren and Edward Terry in *Our Babes in the Wood*, the second item in the current Gaiety bill.

I undertook to get a box for a convenient evening, and looked forward to making the acquaintance of one who had been intimate with Fanny nearly all her life.

We arrived in good time for the first piece, and from our box near the stage in the first circle amused ourselves watching the house fill up, and spotting oddities. The stalls were soon crowded with Guards officers, mashers in evening dress and old men with opera glasses. The pit and gallery were loud with talk and scraping feet. I then observed that the Stage Box, virtually opposite to and a tier below our own, was occupied by so strange a party that I drew Fanny's attention to them.

The most prominent figure was a big man, in full evening dress and wearing a silk hat, who stood with a cigar in his hand, talking to a woman seated in the corner farthest from the stage. He was a formidable looking fellow, with a heavy dark moustache and side-whiskers, an eyeglass, and a gold chain and fob dangling from his waistcoat. The woman to whom he was speaking, and her companion in the other corner of the

box, were manifest half-world. Dressed in an exaggeration of
fashion, with hats of the most outré and busts forced up by
tight-lacing into bulging shelves, they lounged in their chairs
and stared about them brazenly. One was smoking a cigarette,
the other wore a corded monocle which she kept dropping
from her eye and replacing. Each time it fell it chinked against
crystal buttons, two circles of which, each with a central
button, were sewn on to her bodice over her breasts in the most
suggestive manner possible. On the ledge of the box were
champagne glasses, which the big man filled from a bottle
standing against the wall behind him. There was another man
in the background; but I could not see his face, as he stood
back in the shadow.

'There's a rum show' I said. 'Almost too obvious for this
place, I should have thought.'

Fanny was giggling at the women's clothes.

'Did you ever see such frights! I wish Miss Cairns could see
them. She'd have a fit. Surely they don't have to get up like
that in order to get over?'

The house was now full and the audience settled in its seats;
very soon the curtain rose. The piece was a comic drama and
rather bored me, so that I was glad when lights went up for the
interval, and we could take a turn in the foyer and promenoir.
As we rose to go I noticed that the persons opposite were also
leaving their box, and for a moment I had a glimpse of the
second man.

'Why, that looks like Sir William' I said. 'Yet I can hardly
believe he'd come out in public with that circus.'

'Who is he?' she asked.

'Sir William Ferraby – a friend of my father's who is
always nice to me when we meet. He is one of those quiet
elderly men-about-town, who have known everyone and been
everywhere, but like to keep themselves in the background.
The perfect onlooker, but shrewd and kindly.'

We wandered along the corridor. The bar was a remarkable
sight, solidly hedged with members of the crutch-and-tooth-
pick brigade. On the promenade walls were portraits and

caricatures, and a number of pictures of the famous Gaiety chorus, whose sparkling eyes and dazzling charms kept alight what the mischievous Hollingshead called the 'Sacred Lamp of Burlesque'. There was no sign of the big man or his companions.

Back in our box we waited impatiently for the piece we had come to see. Almost as soon as the curtain rose on the opening chorus Fanny saw her friend, and only a few yards distant.

'There's Lucy, Harry; the fourth from this end in the front row.'

I saw a tall beautifully-made girl, with very fair hair and an air of dreamy indifference to her surroundings which struck me as slightly over-cultivated. Though she was not my type, I could see that in the regulation way she was lovely – oval face, regular features, full curving lips. Her legs were slim and straight, and if ever a girl had a front-row chorus figure, Lucy had. But to my taste her very perfection was expressionless, her languid aloofness a tiresome affectation and her hands and feet too large. Glancing sideways at my companion, with her angular elfin little face, her tiny hands and the perpetual shimmer of interest in her eyes and smile, I told myself that here was all I wanted of fascination and feminine grace, and that what's more I had got it.

The show was a good one – with catchy tunes, the Gaiety Quartet in form, and the various desiderata in burlesque (from a handsome, under-dressed chorus downward) adequately supplied.

When the performance was over we walked round to the Stage Door, Fanny having written Lucy a note to say we would await her there. For some reason or other – I suppose because (rightly) I never regarded myself as one of the gilded young – this was my first sight of the Stage Door of the Gaiety after the evening show. I had been in the rough and tumble of Wych Street outside the Olympic; I had run the gauntlet of the hooligans of Drury Lane when the Middlesex came out at midnight; I had 'done' the East End Halls – Foresters,

Wiltons, Lusby's and the Cambridge – and seen misery
pickled in gin to give it a taste of happiness. But never before
had I witnessed the amazing spectacle of grey hairs, dun-
drearies, shirt fronts, fur collars, eyeglasses, gold-knobbed
canes and gleaming hats, waiting outside the Gaiety for the
girls they had sized up within. It was an incredible sight. The
spring evening being mild and still, the younger men carried
their coats on their arms, and stood there in the contortions of
masherdom only possible in a dress-coat, some holding
bouquets, all leaning on their sticks and looking vacantly about
them through plain-glass monocles. The older men – and there
were plenty, a few actually decrepit – wore fur or astrakhan,
and also leant on their sticks, but with the stiff forward bend of
Pantaloon. On the fringe of this crowd of half-wits and lechers
was a struggling mass of urchins, counter-jumpers, pedlars,
'kebbsir' boys and street walkers, with here and there the
unobtrusive stealthy ruffians who move with such surprising
speed and silence through any gathering where pockets are
likely to be worth the picking.

The chorus were beginning to trickle out. Over the door a
lamp in an iron bracket threw a light on to the threshold. A
few of the girls were immediately claimed by an expectant
cavalier; others paused for a moment under the light, until
anything from one to a dozen men surged forward to greet
them. It was a lesson in cynicism to watch a girl with several
courtiers look them over, treat the unprofitable to a cut direct,
but tease two or three of the more promising toward the
shadows of the kerb. There, I presume, she made her choice;
but I could not follow any negotiation to an end, as we had to
watch the door for Lucy. Out of the corner of my eye, I saw a
girl standing with an amused smile behind a young man and
an egg-shaped ancient, who were almost at blows over her,
while a hansom waited grinning at the kerb. At another place
what must have been surely the colonel of the crutch-and-
toothpicks stood dismayed to find himself solemnly introduced
by a lovely girl to a fierce old harridan in a bonnet. I could

almost hear the charmer: 'Lord Fitznoodle, my mother.' 'Mother' was good; business-manager more likely.

The spectacle gave cruel point to another of Hollingshead's defiant quips. When some moralist reproved him for using the stage as a market for the display of feminine beauty and asked if he felt no responsibility for the girls in his employ, he replied: 'None at all. Why should I? I am a manager, not a governess. The moment a girl passes out over the threshold of my theatre, she becomes her own mistress – or someone else's.' It was evident that truth at least was on his side.

At last Lucy came. To such as knew this to be her first Gaiety season, the haste with she darted into the street was a sure – and rather engaging – sign of the novice. There was no poising on the threshold; just a girl coming out of a door. Fanny ran forward and the two kissed affectionately. Arm in arm they came to where I stood. The light was dim, and Lucy greeted me civilly but without curiosity.

We walked through Covent Garden to Evans's Supper Rooms, where a table was already engaged.

The correct thing was to deplore the disrepute into which Evans's had fallen, and mourn the good old days when Thackeray and Lemon and Jerrold and Gilbert à Beckett supped there nightly and scintillated wit and taste. I could not bring myself to share this nostalgia. In my opinion there was more justification for harlots to show off in public (how else can they live?), than for intellectuals to do so (who are already paid to work in private). Also, though the traffic at Evans's was now all too obvious and the company very mixed indeed, the place was uncritical and unashamed. Finally, damaged goods which admit themselves damaged are surely more genuine merchandise than stale jokes labelled new? I had consulted Fanny about going to Evans's, and she said she had long wanted to see what it was like. And Lucy? I asked. Fanny was inclined to think that Lucy would not mind going there either.

So to Evans's we went. The place was a babel of voices, and

over-heated for the sudden spell of warmth. On entering you found yourself in a large open saloon brilliantly lit with gasoliers and walled with mirrors and gilding. A bar ran the whole of the hall's inner length. From the bar to the street, dividing the space into two, was fixed a wooden partition about four feet high, in the centre of which was a small gate. The right-hand and much smaller space was reserved for un-attended ladies, the left-hand and larger space for gentlemen and their lady friends. Do not misunderstand 'reserved'. Communication from one part to the other was as easy as if the partition were not there; and any lady could accept a gentleman's invitation and join him in the left-hand section. On the giving and accepting of such invitations the prosperity and popularity of Evans's depended. Scattered about the men's section were small tables and chairs. Waiters scurried to and fro with trays of drinks, sandwiches and cigars. There was continual movement and noise – scuffling of feet, scraping of chairs, popping of corks. In the women's section (the entrance to which cost five shillings) ladies of varying age and attraction sat quietly waiting. Each kept her eyes on the milling crowd beyond the partition, watching for a man to raise his glass or give some other sign of a wish to be acquainted. Both would move toward the boundary fence and exchange a few words. Then the lady probably passed through the wicket-gate and joined her new friend.

Behind these 'contact-areas' were the Supper Rooms; and the usual procedure was for a couple who had made acquaintance and drunk together in the front to pass through to the back for their sit-down meal. What happened after that was no business of Evans.

We went straight to our table; I had ordered clear soup, chicken and mushrooms, ices and Stilton cheese. The champagne was already cooling in the bucket. When we were settled in our chairs, Lucy treated me to deliberate and unembarrassed scrutiny.

'Will I do?' I asked.

She smiled a slow beautiful smile; and I had to admit that

Fanny had not over-stated her friend's physical attractions. She did not move me in the least; but she was undeniably lovely and her colouring was exquisite. She gave me a lingering and provocative glance and looked away.

'You'll do, Harry' she said, with a self-possession which took all character from her familiarity. 'I wonder how Fanny did it?'

One of my sudden rages took hold of me. The insolence of this conceited doll, treating my darling as a Cinderella – and in her presence too! But, as I opened my mouth eternally to blast my reputation for hospitality, I felt Fanny's little hand on my knee. It gripped tight. 'Shut up' it said. 'I don't mind, so please don't you.' With an effort I achieved what must have been more a grimace than a smile.

'She didn't do it, Lucy' I said. 'I did.'

Fanny broke in with a cheerful demand for all Lucy's news since their last meeting. It was obvious that to be the centre of any stage was the young lady's desire, for, invited to talk about herself, she proceeded to do so.

As she told her story, I could see Fanny watching her with a mixture of amusement and admiration. Oh, Vannchen, I thought, what an enchanting thing you are! You know this *papier-mâché* Venus has no more talent than a dressmaker's dummy; you know she has got to where she is by lying on her back; you know she despises you for a plain Jane who by a lucky fluke has landed a lover. Yet you are so generous and so uncensorious that you do not mind her patronage, do not even envy her beauty, but are happy to see her happy.

'Where are you living now, Lucy?' Fanny asked.

'In North Bank – do you know it? – near Lord's Cricket Ground. Such a sweet little house with a garden backing on to the Canal. You must both come and see me.'

I saw Fanny drop her eyelids, and wondered why. This address means something, I told myself. But nothing more was said, and I filled up their glasses and hoped for more.

At this moment came an interruption. In one corner of the big supper-room was a small stage, on which a desultory variety entertainment was in progress. No one seemed to take much notice of the turns, which were so short in themselves, and separated by such long intervals, that even the performers cannot have had much faith in them. We were at some distance from the stage, and hitherto I had only been conscious of a little more noise when a turn began and a little less when it ended. I had just registered that a song was finished, when loud hand-clapping and shouts of Bravo! and Encore! came from the doorway leading in from the saloon which was opposite to where I sat. There, to my surprise, I saw the big man who had been in the Stage Box at the theatre, and behind him the small plump figure of Sir William Ferraby. The big man was still shouting and clapping; Ferraby looked embarrassed; and I concluded that this noisy approval of the latest performer was drunken exuberance rather than critical appreciation. Wishing the silly disturbance was over but realizing it was no business of mine, I gave attention to my two guests. Miss Lucy was becoming more human under the influence of the champagne. She was forgetting to strike attitudes, behaving like an ordinary young girl on the spree, and actually showing some interest in Fanny's recent doings. I was telling myself that the party would be a success after all, when I became aware of a large figure immediately behind Lucy's chair.

'Ha! Ha! It *is* the charmer with the silver hair! I *thought* I should know those shoulders again and that fine straight back. What luck to find you here! I'd like to talk to you, my beauty, and so I will in a minute or two. Just got to see some friends in the inside room. Don't run away, pretty one. I'll only be a moment.'

The creature lurched off toward the inner room. He had both hands in his pockets and was still wearing his hat. Before I could begin to consider how best to handle the situation which threatened, I felt a touch on my shoulder. It was Ferraby.

'Hullo, Sir William! Delighted to see you. Let me introduce

Miss Hooper, Miss Beckett – Sir William Ferraby. Sit down and have a drink.'

'No, no' he said hastily. 'I can't now, my boy, thanks all the same. Could I speak to you a moment in private? Ladies, I beg you to forgive my interrupting like this, but it is important I should have a word with Mr Somerford.'

He was so agitated that I followed him without further demur, wondering what in the world was the matter. Once we were out of hearing, he began almost breathlessly:

'Harry, you must get those girls away before Manderstoke comes back. He's badly scammered, and out for women. I'm trying to keep him out of mischief, but' – with a wistful smile – 'I'm hardly up to his weight if he turns nasty. He insisted on coming here from the Gaiety, though I urged him to come to the Club after we were shot of those ghastly molls. He had his eye on the fair girl you've got there right through the show. So be a sensible fellow and clear out.'

'But, Sir William, we're not halfway through supper yet, and I don't fancy being driven from a public eating-house by anyone. It's very good of you to warn me, but I think I can manage your outsize dolly-mopper, if he does interfere with us. Probably he's so tight he's forgotten all about us. What did you say his name was?'

Poor little Ferraby almost wrung his hands.

'Pray God he has! That's Gerry Manderstoke. I thought everyone knew him only too well. But anyway, if you won't go, you won't; and I hope you don't mind my —'

'Not a bit, sir. Most kind of you. So that's Manderstoke, is it? I've heard tell of him once or twice, but never seen him. Not exactly a nice-mannered cove. Well, I'll be getting back to my party. And don't worry. We'll be all right.'

When I returned to my place, Fanny merely smiled a welcome. There was a gleam of anxiety in her eyes, but she asked no questions. I decided I must make some mention of the impertinent accosting of Lucy, so I asked her if she knew who the man was. She tossed her head, though I could see the incident had frightened her, and said:

'No, indeed! I'm surprised cads like that are allowed in here at all.'

'A handle to your name opens most doors' I said. 'He's a lord, that fellow, and his name is Manderstoke.'

I heard Fanny catch her breath.

'What name, Harry?' she faltered.

I repeated it, and she set her lips in a tight line. Then she looked at me with fear and pleading.

'Be careful, Harry darling! Promise me you will be careful. He's a bad man.'

'I promise you, dearest. Watch me and see. Aha, here he comes.'

The ugly brute came straight to our table.

'Here I am again, true to me word. Always keep me word with lovely ladies. Now, popsy, let you and I get better acquainted.'

He pulled up a chair from another table, set it between the two girls, and sprawled forward with his elbow on the table-cloth and his head on his hand. His back and shoulders were turned on Fanny, and he craned over to look into Lucy's face, who shrank back in confusion and alarm. I had a vague impression of the people at neighbouring tables, already twittering with excitement and agog to see a row. It was noticeable that every waiter within reach had vanished. I leant across the table, tapped Manderstoke sharply on the wrist and said:

'You'll excuse me, sir, but this table is engaged.'

As he took no notice, I jabbed him sharply in the hand with a fork and repeated:

'This table is engaged. Please go away.'

The fork hurt him and he swung quickly round and glared at me.

'Who the hell are you?'

'That – like this table and these ladies – is my business. Now get out.'

He gave a short hoarse laugh.

'Now get out' he mimicked. 'That's very good. And suppose I don't get out – what then, Mr Counter-Jumper?'

'I put you out' I said, and said it very loudly so that persons nearby could hear. I suppose he realized this, for he dropped his heavy irony and spoke in a low voice, throttled with anger.

'I'd like to see you. Do you know who I am?'

'I know your name, and the only thing I like less is your company. I give you one more chance – are you going or am I taking you?'

We both rose simultaneously, and at that moment a flustered head-waiter came hurrying forward.

'Gentlemen, gentlemen! I beg you to calm yourselves. There are ladies present and —'

'Go to hell, you!' shouted Manderstoke, and the wretched man shrank away as though expecting a blow.

'Just one moment, please' I called to him. 'Would you kindly ask Mr Amor to come here?' To Fanny over my shoulder, I said quickly: 'Take Lucy to the Ladies Room: hurry.' Then I turned to Manderstoke. 'If you will stand there quietly until the proprietor comes, I will not touch you. He shall decide how and where this is to be settled. But if you try any tricks, I'll knock you into a cocked hat.'

The girls had gone, and only the disordered table and Lucy's empty chair stood between us. He glared at me, muttering to himself, and seemed to be debating my quality as an opponent. Suddenly little Ferraby appeared at his side and seized him by the arm:

'For God's sake, Gerry! Not in here. Don't be a fool, man: they've sent for the police already! Gerry —'

I could see that Manderstoke was wavering, and though he shook his arm free of Ferraby's hands, he seemed to have heard what was said.

'Police? Don't want them. But got to settle this flashy spark. He's insulted me.'

Ferraby, from behind the brute's back, raised his eyebrows in query and gestured with his fists. I nodded. He spoke soothingly to Manderstoke.

'Yes, yes. Of course you have, Gerry. But not in here. Come

outside and fight him there – round the corner in the Piazza –
they are used to fights under the arches.'

I saw Mr Amor approaching in a stately fashion. The
treacle of his unction flowed over us:

'Good evening, my lord; good evening, Mr Somerford.
What is this? A little disagreement? Surely two gentlemen
would not wish to bring my house into disrepute and themselves into the cells for a mere tiff? Come, come, gentlemen!
A breath of cool night air, a few moments of re-consideration –
and you will be friends again.'

'Mr Amor' I said. 'I asked you to come because this man
has broken up my supper-party and thrust his attentions on one
of my guests. I do not want to have trouble in here, but I mean
to have trouble somewhere. So please get the fellow outside,
and I will deal with him.'

This suited Amor to perfection. He joined his urgings to
Ferraby's, and Manderstoke went growling through the outer
saloon. Fanny must have been watching from the Ladies
Room, for she was at my side the moment he disappeared.

'What's happening, Harry? Oh, do take care! Come away,
dearest. Leave him. He's a terror, Harry. I know he is.'

'Listen, my darling! You will get a cab, take Lucy home,
and drive on home yourself. Here is some money. I shall not
be very long, but that mobsman needs a lesson and I am going
to give him one. No! Don't argue – and don't worry. Goodnight for the present, sweetheart, and apologize to Lucy for her
dismal party.'

The dear little soul just looked at me for a moment and
obeyed. As she rounded the corner on her way to rejoin
Lucy, she blew me a kiss. I collected my coat and hat, signed
the bill and went out into the street. Two policemen were
standing near the door. I walked quickly past them and
round the corner to the left. In the dim light of the Piazza
Manderstoke was waiting, with Ferraby at his side. The
latter trotted forward as soon as he saw me and began to talk
feverishly:

'Harry, I have been telling Manderstoke who you are and that your father was a dear friend of mine. I have made him see that he behaved in a way of which he will be ashamed tomorrow. He is prepared to let bygones be bygones. So I implore you to shake hands, like a good fellow, and accept my apologies on Gerry's behalf.'

I moved a few steps nearer to the enemy, and, when I was sure he could hear me, replied:

'If Lord Manderstoke will himself offer me an apology for his disgraceful behaviour, I will consider accepting it. Otherwise I shall knock him down.'

The big man came scowling towards me.

'Apology be damned! I've never apologized in my life.'

'Then I recommend your making a start' I snapped, handed him a beauty just under the chin and sent him flying. He lay for a few moments while I stood over him, then began lumbering to his feet. I took him by the lapels of his coat and held him at arm's length. The blow had driven the fumes of alcohol from his head to his legs, and he was sagging at the knees.

'That's enough for now' I said to him, slowly and clearly. 'If you can't behave when drunk, stay sober; if you can't stay sober, keep clear of me; if you can't do that, look out for yourself.'

I let go suddenly and he subsided on to the pavement.

'Sorry, Sir William' I said to the hapless chaperon, who was hopping from one foot to the other in the near background. 'It had to be done. Goodnight.'

I walked quickly up James Street to Long Acre and so to Regent Circus and home.

*   *   *

We were engaged the following evening to drink mulled claret with Julian, and I told him of the trouble at Evans's. He smiled a little grimly over the final scene, then shook his head.

'Good for you, Harry; but I doubt if you've heard the last of it. He's a nasty customer is Gerry Manderstoke.'

'If yesterday's behaviour is a fair sample, I'm sure he is. Tell me some more about him. This time yesterday he was only a name to me, and now he's little more than a bruised knuckle.' (This was not literally true, I fear, for Fanny had told me that very morning a strange and terrible story about the tavern in Panton Street over which she had lived as a child, and the tragic fate of the man her mother had married; but I wanted to hear Julian on Manderstoke and admittedly the Warrior episode was the purest guesswork.)

'Tell you about him? Well, in one capacity he's a swash-buckling rowdy, who'd have been laid by the heels long ago if he weren't a lord and a damned rich one too. He prides himself on playing the Mohawk a century too late, and relies on swagger and violence and powerful connections and plenty of backsheesh to get him through. But there's another side to him, which I happen to know more about, for his place in the country is near my father's. The guvnor has known him since he was quite a boy. He came into the title when he was a minor, and weak trustees gave him his head. But he's a big man down there now and popular with the common folk. He's a keen sportsman, free with his money, keeps a big establishment and, as they say, does a lot for the district. The more straitlaced among the gentry look down their noses and keep out of his way, but the farmers and local tradesmen like him. They don't care a farthing about his carryings-on in town or his drinking or his noisy parties at the Castle. He's clever enough to leave their wives and daughters alone and never to meddle with the maidservants in his own house. So to them he is just a good spender, a fine horseman and a prime shot, who brings others like him to the neighbourhood.'

'I see' I said. 'A sort of two-headed Janus. Well, the Mohawk head is welcome to keep an eye on me, but I imagine it has more important things to worry about. Perhaps he'll summon me for assault.'

'No, I don't think he'll do that. He would cut a poor figure himself when the facts were known. But he's a revengeful fellow and a dangerous wire-puller. If it were only a question of a stand-up fight between the two of you, I shouldn't worry, but — '

He paused. Fanny, who sat quietly sewing in the corner of the sofa, looked up quickly.

'But what, Mr Carteret?'

He smiled and shrugged his shoulders.

'That's the trouble. I don't know. But I advise Harry to hug the shore for a bit.'

I proceeded to tell him Fanny's tale about Hopwood's Hades. He listened without interruption, asked a few questions and then sat back and frowned at the fire.

'What a dreadful thing . . . I can't believe even Gerry would be such a savage. In any event there's no evidence, Harry. Not a scrap. And such a long while ago.'

'Chunks said he was practically certain!' broke in Fanny excitedly.

'Chunks?' queried Julian politely.

She blushed and laughed.

'I'm sorry to be so silly. Please explain Chunks, Harry.'

I did so.

'Well, maybe Chunks is right' said Julian. 'But knowledge is one thing and proof another. Much more than the piecemeal certainties of Chunks and his friend would be needed in a court of law, especially as it would have to be a public prosecution. The AG wouldn't intervene without cast-iron evidence, and even with it there would be all sorts of influence brought to bear against provoking so terrific a sensation. Why, it would be jam for the Radicals – criminal debauchery of the rich – innocent sacrificed to save vicious lord – down with the aristocracy! The authorities would not say so, but their private attitude would be that there is plenty of unrest already without feeding it with old scandals. No, no, Mrs Harry, I fear Chunks won't get anywhere with his case on legal lines.'

This seemed to settle it, and talk turned to other things.

VI

A few weeks later, when I had forgotten all about Manderstoke, I was reminded of him by meeting Sir William Ferraby at dinner with Kitty Cairns. This dinner was a special one and was apparently given more or less in honour of Fanny and myself. Perhaps 'in honour of' is too majestic; let me say that we were its excuse.

During the preceding autumn she and I had had a tussle over her continuing to work at Florizel. She put forward several arguments in favour of doing so and generally talked a lot of nonsense, but I was determined to have my way and at last she yielded. We agreed that she should remain at her job until Christmas; but since then, although she had called on Kitty several times and the three of us were good friends, she had no longer been in an employment which I regarded as unsuitable for a girl who, to all intents and purposes, was my wife. Kitty had accepted the resignation with an amused shrug, and I think her dinner-party was a sort of gesture to show there were no hard feelings.

It was a purely private affair, and besides ourselves were present only Ferraby and a man called Ridsdale with his wife, who had been one of Kitty's girls and married him from Florizel Thirteen. They seemed an agreeable and cheerful couple. I gathered he was an engineer of some sort and had presumably a good practice, for they lived in Hyde Park Terrace and kept their own brougham. But I was at a loss to understand why we had been brought together.

The question was soon answered. Introducing us to the Ridsdales, Kitty said:

'You four should know one another, for Fanny has to all intents and purposes married from here, just as Agnes did, and I take a parental interest in my *sous-ménages*.'

This jarred on me. I disliked the bracketing of Fanny and Agnes Ridsdale, nice girl though she was, and the fact that I was a friend of Kitty's and had visited her house did not seem to me to justify her setting the same trademark on one of her many girls and my only one, who had never been hers at all, and was now not even connected with her place of business. But at the moment I was her guest and must behave as such, even though it involved keeping an unwelcome conversation going.

'How many are there now?' I asked.

'Alas, only your two. There were two more not long ago, but poor Nellie died and that little fool Joan played about with the groom who went riding with her and was thrown out. Quite right too. She always was an idiot, that girl; but I really hoped a place of her own might settle her.'

'What has become of her?' Mrs Ridsdale enquired.

Kitty shrugged.

'I've no idea. The Argyll, I should think. She never showed her face here again, though I would have tried to help her for old times' sake.'

At this point dinner was announced, and when we had taken our places, Ridsdale said:

'You mentioned the Argyll just now, Kitty. I hear it is unlikely to last another winter, the agitation against it is so strong.'

'Good riddance' she replied. 'It's a terrible place now, especially to anyone who remembers what the "Duke's" used to be. I made a sort of sentimental pilgrimage there not long ago with Stokesay, and such a collection of flash cads and draggle-tails I never saw.'

'What do the agitators want to do?' Fanny asked Ridsdale.

'They want the magistrates to refuse to renew the dancing licence. Without that the Rooms could not remain open.'

'Isn't it ridiculous' said Kitty 'this solemn pretence about dancing? A precious lot that rabble care about dancing, until jig-jig time comes round.'

The meal went cheerfully on its way. When we were done with food and were sitting over brandy and cigars (there was rightly no suggestion that the ladies withdraw – a convention out of keeping with the traditions of Florizel Thirteen) the

talk turned on London night-life in general and the changes
seen within quite recent memory.

'I can't *imagine* what it was like' cried Agnes Ridsdale
(though facts were against her, she affected the virginal bright-
ness of a *jeune fille* in a drawing-room comedy) 'with no
Florizel and no proper pavements and mud splashed all over
you and hardly a theatre one could go to except dingy old opera
or Shakespeare without being bruised and bothered by old
women selling apples and oranges and butter-scotch. It must
have been fearfully dull.'

'You must ask Sir William' said Kitty. 'He can tell you, if
anyone can – and if he will.'

Ferraby smiled at the pretty nit-wit. The little man had
dined well; food and wine had dispelled the shyness which
usually kept him in the background of general conversation.

'Not dull, my dear; London was a rough and noisy and
often dangerous place when I was a young man, but it was
certainly not dull. You go to the Hyperion sometimes, I
expect?'

She nodded.

'Well, twenty-five years ago the correspondingly popular
West End night tavern was the Piccadilly Saloon. All the little
ladies from round about went there, and the rackety young
officers and the sporting men – very mixed but very gay, and a
pleasant change after the ponderous drawing-rooms of May-
fair. One night a quarrel started between two men over a girl.
They were all well-known characters there, and the crowded
place took sides. In ten minutes it was Bedlam – Bedlam and
nothing less. Bottles were hurled across the room, smashing
mirrors and heads, cham squirted all over the girls' hats and
dresses; tables were kicked over, with oysters and kidneys and
turtle-soup swilling the floor; there was a great chandelier in
the ceiling and several men swung on this and brought it down
in splinters of glass, showers of melted tallow and clouds of
ceiling plaster. All the time a free fight was going on with
fists, sticks and fingernails. I don't say the Piccadilly Saloon
Riot was an ordinary occurrence, for the peelers walked in at

last and there was the devil to pay. But such a flare-up would be quite inconceivable in the Hyperion of today, even as an exception.'

Agnes shuddered prettily.

'Yes, indeed, and I'm thankful it would! Were you there, Sir William?'

'Oh, yes: I was there – unluckily.'

'Did you get hurt?'

He laughed.

'No. In those days I was a young shrimp and even smaller than the old shrimp I am now. I usually managed to squeeze out of a rough and tumble without serious damage. But I was fleeced for compensation along with every other man present, and it wasn't *my* quarrel. I didn't care who had the girl. I'd got one of my own.'

'Oh, tell us about *her*, Sir William!' the little Ridsdale screamed delicately.

He pursed his lips and sat for a moment looking at the table-cloth. Then shook his head.

"No, no. Please excuse me. I am old-fashioned, I know, but I have my secrets.'

Kitty came to the rescue.

'Go on, William. Let us have more of what London used to be. You know you are an encyclopaedia, once your pages are opened, and I'm sure everyone would be interested.'

We murmured assent; but he pretended confusion and appealed to his hostess.

'But what sort of thing, Kitty? I'm not sure I remember anything but what everyone knows. I've seen Skittles – dined with her, as a matter of fact; I knew what they called the Vinegar Road off City Road; I went to Kate's. But they don't want to hear about places like that.'

'Try them with Kate's, my dear William. But remember that to these children you must talk in words of more than one syllable. Simply "Kate's" means nothing to them.'

'I beg your pardon!' he beamed round the table. 'I was referring to the once notorious Kate Hamilton's – just at the corner of James and Oxendon Streets. Which reminds me! Towards the end of Kate's time, a still finer place was opened by – almost next door in fact – I must tell you about that. It was called Hopwood's Hades. . . .'

I felt it was my turn to play – and urgently.

'I have always wanted to know about Kate Hamilton, Sir William. Do tell us.'

I suppose I must have been looking toward Fanny as I spoke; for Ferraby flashed me a glance, then one at her, and with a quick tact which was one of his many endearing qualities, took the cue:

'Kate? . . . Kate was a detestable marvel. Our dear Kitty here is an adorable marvel, and we shall never see her like again. But Kate . . . well, you'll judge for yourselves. Here is her story.

'She came to London from somewhere in the provinces. Whether she had really studied painting at an art school or whether it was all my eye, I don't know. Anyway Art was her opening gambit. Presumably some man brought her to town and she got some money somehow. She started what she called The Royal Academy of Life. This institution (it was somewhere in Chelsea) was a mixture of genuine *atelier* and private theatre. A class of young women, supported by men both young and otherwise, copied Old Masters – principally Rubens and other experts in the nude. When painting palled they adjourned to act what they had painted. A dance followed, and the affair (as you can easily imagine) became an orgy.

'When she tired of this – or perhaps to get nearer the centre of things – Kate opened a cigar-shop opposite the Olympic. Probably you infants do not understand the significance of a "cigar-shop". In those days it was a euphemism for a cheap drum. The front shop sold cigars, so-called "sporty" books and periodicals. But at the back of the shop were other rooms – and girls.

'It seems a queerly modest venture for a woman of Kate's imagination; but I suspect there was more behind it. You see

Vestris was managing the Olympic at this time and a crowd of dubious little shops and cafés sprang up in the neighbourhood, which must have had – well, an understanding with the theatre. Such understandings were not uncommon. The AI Hotel, for instance, in Tottenham Court Road, had one with the Oxford Music Hall. The arrangement gave the theatres all the advantages of an off-licence – 'we supply the goods but please consume elsewhere.'

'Eventually Kate's cigar-shop – and most of its nearby competitors – got into trouble. There was a temporary clearance of Catherine Street, Newcastle Court, Wellington Street and so on, and Kate also disappeared for a time. When she cropped up again, it was in Charlotte Street – you know it as an untidy street lined with flat grim houses, but it was more fashionable then – where she opened a Reception House for the Copulative Conjunctive —'

'Sir William, you are inventing!' I broke in.

'I am not, Harry, I assure you. Kate had a grandiloquent taste in names, and this was one of her best. Well, the Reception House was, I have been told, very receptive indeed. There were baths and tableaux and all sorts. But it must have been conducted with discretion, for it lasted three years before the authorities became inquisitive. When they began asking really awkward questions, Kate did a moonlight flit to – of all places – Littlehampton. A brief period of winkles and bathing-huts and innocent holiday fun, and she returned to London – this time to the house I spoke of – just off the Haymarket. There for nearly fifteen years she ruled like a bloated empress over an empire of debauchery. She was now enormously fat, and sat on a high throne at the end of the great saloon. Tables, sofas, palms covered the main floor, and lovely girls sat about waiting for a friend or, having met one, taking refreshment with him before going upstairs. The main saloon was also used as a luxury tavern by a few of the kings of the underworld. More than once I saw the great Belasco there – a monster, if ever there was one – talking closely to a bully, or hatching a plot with one of the madams he had in his employ.

'When you came to Kate's you were announced by a flunkey: you advanced to the throne and kissed the imperial hand. If you were – shall I say lucky? – you were commanded to buy her Majesty champagne (not very good champagne either, and deuced expensive) and had to stand talking to her while she drank it. Otherwise, after paying homage, you were free to walk about and join any charmer who took your fancy.'

'Was Kate's place very magnificent?' I asked.

'Not by present standards. It ran to plush and gilded ornament and deplorable paintings of nudes – very large and in tremendous frames. But it had a warm-water swimming bath, which was a sensation in those days. Also all manner of horrid contraptions which appealed to certain tastes. She was an abomination, as I have said – a cruel gloating lump of beastliness – but she knew life and how to make it pay.'

'Is she dead?' from someone.

'I think so. The '65 Act killed her shop as it killed all the places which lived by burning gas all night: and, as there was nothing left for her except to die, I expect it killed her too.'

'And her house?'

'I am *told* – this is pure hearsay, mind you, for I have got past that sort of thing – that it is still accommodating. But ordinary, quite ordinary. Shuts at one am, and so on. They'll be sending us to bed at nine o'clock in another twenty years – when, thank heaven, it won't affect me.'

'There were a lot of all-night houses, then, in those days?'

'Lord bless you, yes: hundreds of 'em! Not on Kate's scale, you know, or with her attractions; but popular cribs for clerks and shopmen. They used to call themselves "Coffee Shops", had coloured lights over the door and a little placard "Bedrooms to Let". They stuck up a Bill of Fare and every third item was "Mutton" or "Greens" or "Jam", written twice as black as anything else. They got going about midnight, and you could take a girl and a bottle of gin any hour till morning and pay nothing except the room-rent.'

'Not licensed, I suppose?'

'No indeed, nor pretending to be. But there were so-called Supper Houses – every second house in Bow Street and Brydges Street and Phoenix Alley was one – which were unlicensed yet sold drinks freely. They used to pay some Free Vintner to paint his name over the door, and then, if ordered to show a licence, said they were employed by such and such a Free Vintner and need not have one. But they've all gone this many a year.'

'Do go on, Sir William' said Fanny suddenly. 'This is the sort of thing one never hears about.'

He looked at her with kindly admiration.

'Why bother your pretty ears with dead history, Miss Fanny? The present is for the young and lovely, not the past.'

She blushed, and I knew what was in her mind.

'It interests me' she said simply. 'I like to imagine vanished streets and know what goes on behind blank walls – particularly walls I have known. . . .'

'Where shall I take you then?' he asked good-humouredly. 'To Ratcliff Highway; or to a dance-hall in Bluegate; or to a Thieves' Kitchen in St Giles; or to the notorious Brunswick Hotel in Bow Street? They have all disappeared or changed their coats – and in their place we have a brand new Royal Aquarium, which for all its tanks of fish and concert-rooms and other educational facilities, already shows signs – so I am told – of teaching little except the oldest lesson of all.'

Fanny gave him one of her twinkling smiles.

'We cannot cover all that ground tonight. Sometime I would like to visit several of those places – at a safe distance.'

Kitty rose from her seat.

'Shall we all meet in the drawing-room in a few minutes?' Ferraby held the door for her.

'I must apologize, Kitty' he said. 'I have been an old bore.'

She gave him a little smile. 'Dear William' she said.

*   *   *

A little later Sir William found an opportunity to draw me aside.

'Harry, that's a charming little girl of yours! I haven't been so attracted for years. Tell me, was the mention of Hopwood's place a *gaffe*?'

'You were wonderful to take the hint so quickly' I replied. 'Not a *gaffe* exactly, but Fanny was mixed up with Mr and Mrs Hopwood, and the trouble he got into distressed her very much. That is all. I didn't want her to be startled and embarrassed.'

He looked at me shrewdly.

'I see' he said. 'Well, I'm glad you stopped me. I would not like to give pain to Miss Fanny. By the way' he continued. 'I don't know if it interests you, but Manderstoke is on the track of that fair girl who was with you two at Evans's.'

'The devil he is! How's that?'

'He found out who's keeping her and where, and will either buy or batter the fellow out.'

'Well, I can't do anything' I said. 'The girl is an old friend of Fanny's, but almost a stranger to me and none of our business. How is it you keep in with Manderstoke, Sir William? He seems to be nothing but a worry to you.'

The little man sighed.

'He is indeed. But I promised his mother before she died to do what I could to control him: and because he was really fond of his mother, he never turns on me, though he takes no particular notice of what I say.'

'That's bad news about Lucy' I said. 'For Fanny's sake I'd like to keep her out of his clutches. Do you mind if we consult our hostess?'

Kitty listened to the story with her cold half-smile.

'Did you actually see Harry lay him out?' she asked Ferraby.

'Rather! It was a prime ferricadouzer.'

'Well done, Harry. Serve the brute right. I hate that man and he hates me. I won't have him here at any price, and at last he seems to have given up trying to get in. But about Fanny's little friend . . . Who is keeping her now?'

'A fellow called Barclay Pippin – a stockbroker or something who dabbles in the theatre. He got her to the Gaiety, I presume; perhaps bought her in.'

Kitty shook her head.

'It's very difficult. I suppose the silly thing is stage-struck, and once a girl takes the taste for showing herself off in the theatre she is anyone's game. Let me think it over. We must cheat Manderstoke if we can. I'll invite Fanny to tea tomorrow and ask her a few things about the girl.'

VII

'I am going to have tea with Lucy' Fanny said to me one morning shortly after the Florizel dinner. 'Miss Cairns has been asking me about her and says I ought to warn her against Lord Manderstoke.'

'I should have thought the man himself was the best warning' I replied. 'One look should be enough for anyone but a lunatic.'

Fanny seemed embarrassed, and I realized she had more to say and did not like saying it.

'You see, Harry, Miss Cairns wants Lucy got away from London, out of the man's way – and suggests you might be able to back me up with this Mr Barclay Pippin – convince him she ought to disappear for a while. I don't see why you should, I must say. . . .'

'But does Kitty think Lucy will need any persuading?'

'That's the worst of it; she does. She says Lord Manderstoke has a sort of fascination for some women – dominates them despite themselves – and that Lucy, though she was angry and frightened that night at supper, probably plays with the idea of seeing more of him.'

'I see – beauty hoping to subdue the beast. Well, Kitty is no fool on that sort of subject. But I can't see where I come in.'

'Nor can I; and I said so. But she insisted I could not frighten Mr Pippin into doing something, but you could.'

I was not going to have poor little Fanny tackle this job on her own, and she said frankly that she must do anything she could. So naturally I agreed to support her and call at the house in North Bank at about half past five.

Lucy's villa was exactly right. Built about fifty years earlier in the elegant rustic style of that period, it had a creeper-covered veranda and vases on either side of the pathway, from gate to front door. The little garden was half-screened from the road behind a plaster wall, and shrubs, with a laburnum, a may-tree and a copper-beech, completed its privacy. A neat maid admitted me, and led me to a sitting-room facing south, from the long window of which could be seen a small lawn which sloped to an ornamental wall overlooking the canal.

Lucy and Fanny rose to greet me, and during a few minutes of general commonplace I was able to observe the sort of interior which Mr Pippin had provided for his mistress. His taste was that of a wealthy business man of twenty years earlier. The walls were covered with a dark-red paper, over which sprawled honeysuckle flowers in salmon, shading into cream. At suitable places *étagères* were fixed to the walls, covered in bright-blue velvet and set out with ornamental china.

From the centre of the ceiling hung an ornate moderator-lamp, deeply fringed with red silk. The curtains were of deep crimson, edged with gold cord and crowned with pelmets of similar design. Amid the welter of furniture I noticed a sofa, two or three padded easy chairs, an upright canterbury, a piano, several stools, occasional tables and chairs, and two jardinières carrying ferns. The upholstery carried out the general colour scheme of crimson, salmon and bright blue.

I had just concluded that Mr Pippin was neither austere nor a skin-flint, when Fanny abruptly brought the conservation to the business in hand.

'I have been talking to Lucy like a governess, Harry – you know what about. She must go away for a time; there are no two ways about it. It means giving up the Gaiety and it's a bad wrench for her. She thinks I ought to mind my own business. Will you join your persuasion to mine?'

I turned to Lucy, whom in entering the room I had thought looking pale and tired. I now saw a mutinous twist in the set of her lips.

'I can sympathize' I said. 'It must sound a lot of nonsense to you. But the gentleman won't leave you alone, so long as you are in sight. Is he increasingly troublesome?'

'Well, he sends me notes and flowers and invitations, and comes night after night to the theatre and watches me through glasses. A girl ought not to be persecuted like that – even though it *is* complimentary, I suppose, in a way.'

('You like it' I said to myself. 'It excites you. What worries you is that Pippin may find out, before you've landed your new fish.')

Aloud I said:

'Do you come across him after the theatre – when you are with your friend?'

She looked a little sulky:

'Mr Pippin doesn't care for going out. He likes just being here. Says he's too tired to range about the town till all hours.'

'Does he fetch you from the theatre?'

'Sometimes. Usually my maid comes for me. As a rule he comes round about this time and after tea takes me to the theatre. Then he goes to his Club or somewhere, and I often find him waiting here when I get back.'

'Does he know about Manderstoke?'

She was frankly indignant.

'Certainly not! And he mustn't know – at any price.'

There was a short silence; then Fanny went over to her friend and crouched on the floor beside her chair.

'Lucy dear' she said softly. 'I know you feel I am an interfering little fool; but I have risked that in order to save you from this horrible man. You must believe it when Harry and I tell you that he is a cruel brute. He is all flattery and honey when getting his girl; but once he's got her ... well, you saw how he behaved when he was drunk at Evans's. Imagine being at the mercy of such a man! Oh, Lucy, don't give him a chance; go away, I implore you!'

The beautiful face was almost ugly, as Lucy turned and looked down at Fanny.

'I don't know what you are trying to gain by this' she said nastily. 'But, whatever it is you are aiming at, you won't get it with my help. I can look after myself, as I always have done. Now I think you had better go.'

Fanny scrambled to her feet and stood a moment in sorrowful silence.

'Very well, Lucy' she said at last. 'If you won't listen you won't. I've done my best. Goodbye.'

I held the door for Fanny, passed out immediately behind her, and at her side walked down the path to the garden-gate. We had just stepped into the street and I was opening my mouth to say something of what I felt, when a medium-sized middle-aged rather fleshy man, with a beard cut in the style of the Prince of Wales, almost collided with us. He stared at us a moment and then with a pleasant smile said:

'Are you friends of Miss Beckett? I see you have just left her house. If so, you must allow me to add my welcome to hers. My name is Pippin – Barclay Pippin. Perhaps she has spoken of me?'

'She has indeed, Mr Pippin' I replied, suddenly decided on a plan of action. 'Permit me to introduce Miss Hooper. My name is Somerford.'

He beamed at us.

'Well, well, this is a pleasure! How do you do, Miss Hooper! How do you do, Mr Somerford! I know your names quite well. Lucy told me a few weeks ago of that unpleasant experience at supper somewhere – a drunken man – I am grateful to you for taking such good care of my little girl.'

'It was nothing, Mr Pippin' I said. 'I was only sorry for the ladies. But will you grant me what may no doubt seem an odd request. If you can spare me a few minutes – we might stroll up the road – I should like to tell you, for her sake and your own, why we have been to call on Miss Beckett.'

He gave me a searching and slightly nervous look. Perhaps he thought I was contemplating blackmail. But Fanny broke in:

'Mr Pippin, please, please listen to Harry! It is really important. Lucy is such an old friend that I should not ask such a thing without good reason. She is in danger. . . .'

'Danger! Heavens above, what sort of danger?'

We had fallen into line and were walking slowly along the road. In as few words as possible I outlined the position. He listened without interrupting; then shook his head.

'Manderstoke . . . Manderstoke . . . I just know the name. But she would have told me if anything like this were seriously threatening. Are you not perhaps – forgive me; please don't think I do not appreciate your motive – making much of little? A girl cannot be the loveliest creature on the Gaiety stage without getting notes and flowers. I'm sorry for the poor chap, wasting time and money for nothing; but after all it is his affair.'

'Mr Pippin' I said earnestly. 'I know enough about this man to assure you solemnly that he is no ordinary masher. He is rich and powerful and used to getting what he wants. If you or Lucy opposes him, he will have no mercy. The only thing is to get her right away. I am serious, Mr Pippin. There is danger for both of you in trifling with this matter.'

He threw up his hands in mock despair.

'But my dear sir, girls are not abducted these days! It's all nonsense. Anyway, what does Lucy herself say? Is she frightened?'

'No' I admitted. 'She is annoyed at what she considers our interference.'

He considered this for a moment.

'Oh, she is annoyed, is she?' he said slowly, swinging round toward the villa again. 'I think we will go and ask her why. It seems a poor return for all your kindness.'

His tone made me uneasy. But there was nothing for it but to follow him back to the charming villa, up the path and in at the front door.

Lucy met us in the little hall. For a moment wild fear

looked out of her eyes, but she managed with remarkable strength of mind to keep her composure.

'Barclay!' she cried. 'How lovely!'

He was no less the actor.

'And how is my silver swan?' he asked gaily, kissing her on the cheek. 'By great good fortune I met your friends and persuaded them to return with me. A little drink, poppet, would not come amiss. Port, perhaps, for Miss Hooper and yourself; brandy and soda for us. Brandy suit you, Mr Somerford, or have you a preference?'

He had shepherded us into the drawing-room while he was talking, and I could not but admire his spirited self-possession. Lucy rang the bell and gave instructions to the maid, who returned with a tray. Mr Pippin kept up a flow of cheerful small talk.

'Very pleasant out here, after the dust and heat of the city! I was lucky to find this house, which is almost worthy of its occupant. There are plenty of little ladies hereabouts, but none so lovely as my Lucy. Is she not lovely, Mr Somerford?' He looked at her with his head on one side, as though she were a painting. 'And as sweet as she is beautiful. Well, here is good health and good luck to all of us!'

We drank the toast with mixed feelings. Lucy was serene and smiling, but I knew she was wondering desperately what had been said outside. For myself I was trying to guess Pippin's next move. He was evidently no fool, and as evidently in command of the situation.

Suddenly he turned to me:

'Mr Somerford, I would like a word with you in the next room. Would you be so kind? Bring your drink with you. Au revoir, ladies; in a very few minutes.'

As the door closed behind us, his bustling good humour changed to gravity.

'I am inclined to believe you, Somerford. The thing is preposterous, but I have been in business long enough to know that even the preposterous can happen. Also I am not too sure of Lucy. She is not yet stuck on him – that I am confident; but she has never mentioned him to me by name (which is significant), she has resented your warning her against him, and she is now all on edge.'

'Mr Pippin, it is no disrespect to Lucy to say that a woman can be taken by storm, even against her will. It is obvious that you give her everything she could want and treat her kindly. But a girl can feel too safe and want adventure. Once she is sure of something, she is apt to hanker after something else. And there is a flame in Manderstoke which draws the moths.'

He scratched his head carefully.

'I am a peaceful man' he said 'and thought I lived in a peaceful age. What am I to do? You say this fellow may just snatch her away. How can I stop him if she wants to go?'

'You have influence in the theatre, I believe' I ventured. 'Could you get her a part – a *real* part – in something well away from London? Even abroad? That would soften the blow; for her resistance is a good deal due to pride in her Gaiety work and not wanting to lose the progress she has made. If she disappeared for long enough, Manderstoke will find another interest. . . .'

He still havered and hummed, tapping one foot on the ground, his eyes flickering nervously from side to side. At last, impatient with the whole imbroglio, I spoke sharply:

'Don't you understand, man, that this fellow is a beater? Do you know what that means to your lovely Lucy? Even if I exaggerate Manderstoke's chances of getting her, I don't exaggerate what she will suffer if he does. Nor will he spare you, if you stand up against him. For her sake and your own you *must* act.'

He gave me a scared look and tried to brace his plump round shoulders.

'Very well' he said meekly. 'I will take your advice. But it is hard on me. I shall miss her so.'

He looked utterly dejected and the simplicity of his last words was moving. I patted him on the shoulder.

'Good man! It's wretched for both of you; but in a few

months the threat will have passed and then you can be all the happier.'

*   *   *

As we walked home, I said to Fanny:

'Barclay Pippin is really quite a good chap, you know. He's soft and "City" and not much to look at; but a gentle soul and devoted to Lucy. Perhaps it's an ill wind ... If this hadn't happened, I'd be afraid she might in time have got bored. It's a very domestic life for a girl who likes to be seen and looked at.'

Fanny nodded.

'I'm sure she is bored already, and that alarms me. She adores being admired, and though at the moment she is a little scared and unwilling to lose the bird in the hand, she could easily cheat herself into believing that with a rackety lord who is on the town night after night she will be able to queen it in public places and become a sort of Mabel Grey.'

'In fact poor Pippin is as good as finished in any case?'

'Likely enough. But the alternative must not be Manderstoke. That's what concerns us.'

I sighed. 'I wish none of it did. I don't want anything to concern us except ourselves.'

She squeezed my arm.

'Nothing else does – *really*.'

PART THREE

Told by Fanny Hooper

LES YVELINES AND PARIS

I

LATE IN MAY 1878 I more than suspected that I was going to have a baby. The emotions of a woman believing for the first time that she is carrying the child of the man she loves have been so often described (and so much better than I could ever describe them) that I shall not attempt a version of my own. It is enough to say that I held the mere idea close against my heart, as I longed to hold the new-born child and as I had so often held its father.

The prospect of motherhood had, however, practical as well as emotional significance, for it changed the whole position as regards my relationship to Harry. He had more than once pressed me to marry him, but from a sort of perverse pride (as well as from an only too vivid prevision of the treatment I should get from his mother and sister and of the vexations they would cause him), I had refused. Finally I had promised faithfully to tell him when I changed my mind; and since the promise was given he had never – like the faithful trusting soul he was – said another word.

Now, of course, everything was different. While there were just the two of us, the pleasure we had of one another, where we lived and with whom we associated, were no concern of anyone else. But a child must have a name and a home and a background of which it need not be ashamed. I must, therefore, tell Harry that my silly mood of defiance had passed; and that I now wanted, as utterly as till now I had been his in secret, to be his before the world. You may think that a woman who had handled a situation of the kind with such naïveté

deserved humiliation. To such as take the conventional feminine view of masculine selfishness, it will probably seem a frank
invitation to disaster to have lived as a man's mistress for
nearly two years, steadfastly refusing his offers of marriage,
and then – the moment a child is on the way – to expect him
to renew them. Good luck to you, with your worldly wisdom. It
is, however, beside the point, because you did not know Harry
Somerford and, I suspect, because you are unable to imagine
what mutual confidence can be, between two people who love
one another more than they love themselves.

That Harry would not only honour his earlier pledge but
exult in doing so, I had not the smallest doubt. The only question to be decided was when I should tell him. During the
winter he had talked of taking his annual leave (and, he hoped,
some owing from the previous year) in the early summer, so
that before the middle of June we could go away for our first
long holiday. Why not keep my secret until that holiday were
over? Let us have one more period of enchanted freedom, and
then face up to marriage-lines and domesticity and parent-
hood. The idea of giving a last fling to my secrecy-mania delighted me. So it should be. Until we were back in London I
would say nothing.

II

It seems extraordinary that Harry and I should have lived
nearly two years in Little Welbeck Street, and yet, when I try
to think how we spent our time, that I find hardly anything to
record. It is true that everything happened – and went on
happening – which to me meant life. I had my lover; and from
the moment of waking, when I felt him beside me with his arm
across me, to the delicious minutes during which we both sank
into the peace of sleep, he was the sum, substance and justification of my existence. But if I try to express in terms of
incident my daily sense of completeness, the result is a bleak
record of routine.

For the first few months I continued to work at Florizel,
although from October onwards I was, as it were, under

notice. The notice was given by me, and at about three months' range so as to cause Miss Cairns as little inconvenience as possible.

It was all Harry's doing. He said bluntly that I must stop working there, as he did not wish me to be part of a brothel. I explained to him that, for the concern I had with the kind of business we were doing, I might as well be in a hotel or helping to run a private house. He said he understood that well enough, but that my being in any way connected with this particular traffic offended him. I asked him how I was to spend my time, with him away most of the day and nothing to do but keep three rooms in order, give Muggsy a hand and mend his socks. This flummoxed him rather, but he said airily that I could amuse myself going about, or could lie in bed, or visit the few friends I had. I declared I should get so desperately bored that I would probably take to drink or drugs, or at best wander wildly through the streets, a prey to designing men.

I knew I should have to give way in the end, and was secretly touched and delighted that he wanted me that much more for himself. But he looked so sweet when he could not answer my objections but only mutter at me in obstinate bewilderment, that I wanted to tease him a little longer. So I began an extravagant argument in defence of the Florizels of this world and to prove that women were realists at heart, and men sentimental old frauds. I told him he must try to realize that the idea of making money by selling your body to strangers was not nearly so horrific to many women as men liked to think, and therefore as all women made out. Admittedly it was not my line, and I should hate to follow it. But that others did it was perfectly understandable; and I should no more have thought of shying away from the girls at Florizel or despising them for what they did than of jumping over the moon.

I went on like this for some time, intoxicated with my own eloquence. At last he burst out laughing at me, and said I looked so fierce and fanatical that I ought to take up Women's Rights; and I said that was exactly what I was doing; and he said what about Men's Rights; and I said come and take them.

When we got back to the subject of Florizel, Harry went all gruff and throaty again. He said I could talk for a week, but he wouldn't have his Fanny even remotely labelled as a market-girl; that she was *his* girl; and that before anyone else could have her, he must get past *him*, which (though he said it as shouldn't) would take a bit of doing.

He was altogether adorable in his mood of fierce possessive-ness, and partly for this reason, partly because I did not want to make him even the tiniest bit angry, I surrendered. He was so pleased that he made no difficulty over the three months' notice, which would at least give Miss Cairns the chance of finding a successor.

*   *   *

Throughout the autumn of 1876, therefore, my life followed a dual course and, I confess, kept me almost too continuously on the go.

After breakfast, when Harry went off to his office, I would do the rooms, take the tray downstairs, help Muggsy with her washing-up, probably stay and talk to her, while she made her marketing list or checked the laundry or mixed bread for baking or bottled fruit or declaimed against the dishonesty or incompetence of local tradespeople. At about half past eleven I walked up to York Gate, cut across the park and was at Florizel Thirteen by noon. After an hour and a half with letters and accounts came the simple midday meal, at which all the girls as well as Miss Cairns were present. They chattered inces-santly, but almost entirely about clothes and what they had done on their free evening and the beauty of the Princess of Wales and her four children and the latest gossip concerning HRH. 'Shop' was tacitly avoided, although now and again some unusual incident of the previous day could not be passed over.

All the afternoon I was busy with multifarious jobs, mostly indoors but frequently involving expeditions to one or other of the house's suppliers. As a general rule I left about seven o'clock, except on Saturdays when my hours were ten to one. It was like Miss Cairns to observe the Saturday half day which had become almost general in offices and workshops during the recent years. She played the business woman so determinedly that for her secretarial staff to conform to business practice was, so to speak, part of her make-up. The girls, of course, had to be organized differently; but by a carefully worked out system of free evenings, by being daily off duty from noon to five pm and on Saturdays from noon to eleven pm they got an equivalent share of leisure.

On Thursdays, when Miss Cairns was At Home, I helped entertain callers in the drawing-room if desired to do so. Her orders in this respect were very erratic and seemingly given on the impulse of the moment. Often I have shuddered to think how easily I might not have been instructed to attend on that wonderful afternoon when I first saw Harry. Just a word unspoken, and I should never never have met him; nor he even have known that I existed. I plucked up courage once and tried to thank Miss Cairns for the whim which had brought me such happiness. She was the least sentimental person in the world, and I was afraid I might be badly snubbed. But she smiled her tight little smile and said:

'Foolish Fanny! There are plenty of men. It would have been another, if it hadn't been Harry.'

But it would not. I told her so; and she actually laughed.

With 1877 I became a lady of leisure. At first the sense of release was agreeable; but after some weeks I began to miss my regular employment. I had not the heart, however, to let Harry guess that I regretted Florizel. He was pathetically pleased to have done with it, and began coming home for his lunch two or three times a week (I am sure at considerable inconvenience) just to prove that I was there to share it with him.

But he was far from being the simple adoring swain which he sometimes liked to pretend; and at last I realized (with something of a shock at my own obtuseness) that there had been another motive besides high-mindedness in his determination to remove me from Florizel. He began making casual references to a possible home of our own. He would throw out opinions on this or that neighbourhood; pass a remark as to the

advantage of a small garden; even complain half-humorously
of Muggsy's stairs – as though a pair of stairs could bother a
big man like him! For a while I suspected nothing; but
allusions to an independent ménage kept cropping up in his
conversation, and all of a sudden I guessed what he was up to.
He was trying to force my hand on the marriage issue. We had
agreed from the first not to set up house on our present basis.
He, in his dear funny way, refused to do the conventional
thing and add another 'kept woman' to the tolerant population
of St John's Wood; I was frankly afraid of having to face up
to neighbours in the guise of a housewife while really nothing
of the sort. And now, with a craftiness which had completely
deceived me, he had manoeuvred me out of my job, knowing I
should be at a loose end without it, and therefore more easily
persuaded to marry him in order to have a day-long woman's
work to do.

I loved him the more for his ingenuity, but was not going to
be beaten too easily. So I gave no sign of having fathomed his
little plot, and kept on my guard against making even the
slightest admission that time hung on my hands. This diplomatic duel became in itself an occupation and helped to occupy
my mind. So time passed, with both sides on the qui-vive and
completely happy.

*   *   *

We emerged rarely enough from the seclusion of Little
Welbeck Street. Twice we went to Yorkshire to visit Andrew,
the second time staying in his house and happy to find him
more or less reconciled to the restricted and retired life which
was all he could hope for. He had revived an old interest in
Italian history, and was writing a book about the Gonzaga
family, surrounded by books which might possibly have some
bearing on the subject. Between my mother and Harry it was
evident that no real cordiality could exist. She had been
jealous of him from the first: and I could not find it in my
heart to blame her, bearing in mind the sad dislocation of her
own life and the tangle of frustration in which she was now
caught. I spent all the time I could with her, and we retrieved

almost our old footing of affection and trust; but it was better for Harry to stay behind with Andrew, and my divided loyalties kept me continuously on the move.

The two Christmas days we spent at the Jolly Bargee, and I am afraid the revelry was too unrestrained to be altogether genteel. Everyone got drunk and made a maximum of noise; Polly grew steadily more outrageous; and Harry became a sort of idol to Chunks and the bargemen present, because he was phenomenally strong and did lifting and wrestling tricks which set them roaring with delight. We two were in a grand state by the time we got home; and Muggsy winked and gurgled and nudged me for days afterwards, whenever the most remote reference was possible to our homecoming in the small hours and to what went on between then and our dazed reappearance well after noon next day.

My only serious anxiety during this time of tranquil happiness arose from one of our very rare evening outings. We had gone to the Gaiety Theatre to see Lucy Beckett, who was now in the chorus there and very pleased with herself, and had taken her to supper at Evans's after the show. About halfway through the meal an unpleasant thing happened. A drunken bully of a man forced himself on Lucy, and poor Harry was driven to deal with him. To my horror – a horror more due to actual fear than I wished to admit – the creature turned out to be none other than Lord Manderstoke, who seven years before had caused a violent scene in Hopwood's Hades, and whom Chunks suspected of having planned in revenge the frightful discovery of the child's body in a cupboard at the Warrior. I could not get out of my head that if this dreadful man were to turn vindictive against Harry, he might do him serious harm. I had no idea how; and kept telling myself not to be a fool. But the uneasiness remained, and was deepened when Mr Carteret, to whom Harry described the incident, expressed the same fear. He did not suggest anything definite, but advised Harry to keep a weather eye open. Harry, of course, made light of the whole affair; and I was careful to say nothing more about it. But I went on worrying.

Just on chance that something might be done, we had told Mr Carteret the Warrior story; but though he was much interested, he was very discouraging about the possibilities of proof. Worse still, he said that even if proof existed, the affair would be smothered, as it would encourage revolutionary feeling. Without telling Harry, I wrote to Chunks and asked him to meet me one morning at York Gate. As we walked across the Park I told him what Mr Carteret had said, and that there was absolutely no hope of his bringing Manderstoke to book. 'Aint there, Fannikins?' he asked, after brooding for a few moments over my report. 'I wonder.' Then he dropped the subject, and said no more about it.

A very nice little man – an old friend of Harry's – called Sir William Ferraby had been with Manderstoke on the occasion of the row, seen Harry knock him flat, and approved him for doing so. Then, some time afterward, we met him at dinner at Florizel Thirteen, and he warned Harry that the brute was still after Lucy. He seemed to expect poor Harry to do something to rescue her. It was no business of Harry's; and when he told me of Ferraby's half-appeal, I begged him to keep out of it, which he was quite willing to do. But the next day Miss Cairns asked me to tea and tackled me about Lucy. What did I know of her? What was she like? I told her of our long-standing friendship, of Lucy's leaving home and going first to Henderson and then to Neldé, and that my having applied for my job at Florizel was really her doing. I added that I had seen very little of her during the last twelve months and, until the night when I saw her at the Gaiety, only knew she had left Neldé and gone on the stage. As for what she was like, I spoke of her extraordinary beauty, and stated truly that I had always got on excellently with her, not minding in the least being treated as an unpretending foil to her startling loveliness. 'She is a delightfully simple girl at heart' I said, 'but very vain – and no wonder.' 'Extravagant?' asked Miss Cairns. 'Probably – if she had money to spend.'

A few days later I was again invited to call and Miss Cairns said:

'Fanny, I've been thinking about your friend Lucy. I know a good deal about girls who live by their looks, whether at a place like Neldé or as show-girls on the stage. I also know enough about Manderstoke to want any friend of yours to keep away from him. But what you tell me about Lucy Beckett makes me fairly sure she will knuckle down to him, if she gets a chance. He can be dazzling to a certain kind of woman – with his strength, his title, his money, his lavish compliments paid with masterful familiarity, and the Pasha-like splendour with which he promises presents and pin-money and excitement – and she is just the type to be dazzled. If you want to help her – to save her from herself (for that's what it amounts to, in my judgement) – you must get her right away. Oh, I know it's difficult! She'll resist and hate you for pressing her. She'll say she loathes Manderstoke and has no intention of having anything to do with him. She'll probably be petty enough to accuse you of envying her success and working up this scare in order to spoil it; that's the kind of hysterical silliness to which vanity drives a girl of her sort. But there's no other way. If Manderstoke wants her enough, he'll get her. The hope is that he never wants any one thing very long; and if she's out of sight, she will soon be out of mind. Try influencing the man who's keeping her. Send Harry to frighten him.'

'Miss Cairns, must Harry be mixed up in this?'

'He needn't appear in it after the one interview. Once, between you, you have convinced Lucy and her friend, they will arrange for her to disappear and the whole trouble will be over.'

With the utmost reluctance I reported the scheme to Harry. I could see he didn't relish taking part in it, and – to my private relief – I was on the point of telling him I would find some other way, when he asked me point-blank whether, if he held off, I would promise to do the same. This embarrassed me, and I tried to be evasive.

'It's no good, Vannchen; you're hedging. If I don't come with you, you will go alone to try to get Lucy away. Now, own up!'

'I can't just do nothing, Harry' I pleaded. 'She is such an
old friend.'

'Then I go too. Let me know when and where; and I and
my pippin will do battle with Lucy and hers.'

The upshot of it all was that Mr Barclay Pippin – for that
was the name of Lucy's lover – got her an engagement to play
chorus-lead and central figure on the tableaux with a company taking a musical extravaganza to Canada for an ex-
tended tour. It was sad for him, poor man, and he acted most
creditably. He adored Lucy; had established her in a pretty
little house in North Bank (the sort of place which she had
once described to me as the height of her ambition), and would
clearly be lost without her. She, I am afraid, felt no wrench at
all. Once she was assured that her part in the travelling show
was more important than that at the Gaiety and that Mr
Pippin would continue her allowance throughout the tour, she
seemed to welcome the prospect of a change. She said she
would at any rate see something of the world, which there was
little opportunity of doing from a back street in St John's
Wood. Lucy could be very ungrateful when she liked.

Nevertheless, though I was shocked by her selfishness and
very sorry for Pippin, I was too relieved on Harry's account to
be other than delighted that the matter was settled, and that
Lucy could now be considered secure from Manderstoke.
During the months which followed my dread of him gradually
faded; and by the Spring of 1878 – my mind becoming first
preoccupied and then wholly absorbed with the tremendous
prospect of motherhood – I had forgotten all about him.

III

We had been three days in Versailles, and I was still dazed
with the novelty of everything about me. The smallest incident
of daily life was as exciting (and as exhausting) as the vast
palace, with its park, terraces and fountains. From the moment
of our leaving London I had been absorbing unimagined sights,
collecting fresh experience. Though every day brought the thrill

of discovery and I was deliriously happy to know myself lost with Harry in the crowded wilderness of a foreign land, I felt almost battered by the continual impact of new impressions.

'Please, Harry' I said, 'may we go somewhere in the country before we go to Chartres? I just can't sight-see any more at present; and you will be disappointed with me, because I shall be stupid and dull.'

'My poor sweetheart, of course we will! I am a selfish brute to drag you round as I have done. I tell you what, we'll hire a carriage and drive in the direction of Chartres and if we come to a little place we like, we'll stay there for as long as you want.'

About noon next day we set off in an ancient landau, drawn by two dejected horses. Our luggage was piled on the front seat and we sat opposite to it, my head and shoulders only just appearing above the high built side of the carriage. 'We look like a very large King and a very small Queen, going into exile from a very unimportant kingdom' said Harry. 'I shall have to perch you up on a hold-all or something; otherwise your sorrowing subjects – if any of them *should* turn up – will hardly be able to see even the tip of your ridiculous nose.'

I've no doubt we looked comical enough, and there was certainly no dash about our rate of progress. But that was all the better. The old landau was well sprung and very comfortable, and no slowness of movement could be too slow for me. The hotel proprietor at Versailles had recommended – seeing that Madame was fatigued and wished to drive leisurely along quiet roads – that, instead of taking the high road through Rambouillet and Maintenon, we make a détour to northward and break our journey at the town of Houdan, which was a quaint mediaeval place, with the remains of a fortress, a number of picturesque old houses and an inn well-spoken of for its cooking. The next day we could go on to Dreux (where we must at all costs visit the magnificent mausoleum of the family of Orleans) and thence strike south to Chartres. Our driver estimated the distance to Houdan as over forty-five kilometres, and boldly declared that we should cover that distance in three hours. His optimism was unconvincing from the first, and when we found that our speed was unlikely to average more than seven miles an hour, it had to be wholly discounted. But it did not matter. There was no hurry.

We had gone about twenty miles and taken three hours to do so, when instead of gently undulating tillage, small woods, and scattered farms, there rose on our left a tree-crowned ridge which, in contrast to the open country through which we had passed, seemed high and almost precipitous. The road meandered nearer and nearer to the foot of this ridge, and we saw that it was a regular escarpment, with outcrops of rock and bracken-covered slopes falling steeply to the level plain. A little further, and sight of the lofty range was suddenly cut off. We were passing through a region of orchards brilliant with flowering fruit trees, and masses of pink and white blossom walled us in. We rounded a corner and came abruptly to a wide space lined with neat low houses. There was a stream in the middle and a pond surrounded by lime trees. Beyond the trees was the apse of a church. The Landau swayed pompously along the side of the church, turned slightly to the left at its western end, and clattered on to the stone setts of a narrow irregular street, which looked as it must have looked for a hundred years at least, so old and undisturbed were the buildings on each side of it.

'What is this place, Harry?'

He prodded the driver in the back, who drew in his willing horses and said we had reached Les Yvelines. Another hour and we should be at Houdan.

With the cessation of the noise made by our own wheels, the extraordinary peace of the little town flowed over me. It was mid-afternoon, the sun was still high and the air warm and still. No one was about. The place seemed wrapped in greyness and sleep.

'Is there an inn here, I wonder?' I said to myself.

Harry heard me. 'I think that's one a little further up on the right. I'll go and see. You stay here.'

He got out of the carriage and went up the street. The

driver turned round on his box and made me quite a long
speech, of which I understood no single word. I smiled and
shook my head. Harry returned. There was a hotel and it
looked clean. Was I hungry? We had better stop for an hour
and eat something.

'I'd like to stop more than an hour' I said. 'This is a nice
place. I feel it. And so lovely and quiet – and hidden away.
Could we stay here, Harry, just for a day or two?'

We stayed for four weeks.

*   *   *

Is it from after-knowledge of what followed that I now
think of our sojourn in Les Yvelines as at once a magical
interlude in my life and the climax of it? Partly, no doubt; yet
not altogether. I can remember telling myself every day –
several times a day indeed – that this was the perfection of
human happiness; and I should not have done that (seeing how
happy I was before), had there not been some special enchantment in the remote solitude which enfolded us.

And there was; I knew instantly that there was. Thanks to
poor crippled Mr Clements I had an instinct for places; thanks
to Harry I was in love. Thus doubly aware, I did not find it
hard to realize that Les Yvelines was deliciously bewitched. If
I say that there are many little towns in France more beautiful
than Les Yvelines and with as much of age and tranquillity,
but that no one that I have visited has had the same capacity
for blending this world and the next, you will smile tolerantly
and reply that a girl in love sees dandelions as fairy-gold. Yet
my being in love was not all of it. With its drowsy contentment, modest industry, outward shabbiness and inward distinction the little town belonged to this world. But its serenity
of spirit, which transcended any quality a mere visitor could
wish for it, was on a different plane; and any who came under
its spell found access to another world altogether.

To describe what that other world was like is almost impossible. Perhaps if I say that those four weeks were weeks
with love and companionship in the foreground and no back-

ground at all, I shall say something of what I mean. But only
something. The secret lay in the sweet loneliness of us two;
and only such of you as have been one of two (or both) will
know how precious is that secret, and how unshareable.

*   *   *

The spell of Les Yvelines worked rapidly. The intention of
staying a day or two and moving on was soon abandoned. In
its place came a plan to use the little town as a centre of
excursions, leaving our bulky luggage and driving here and
there on overnight visits to more sensational places. But after
seeing the beauties of Chartres and the grandiose horrors of
the Chapelle Royale at Dreux, we gave up the excursion idea
also, and just stayed where we were.

From the crest of the ridge, southward and eastward,
stretched miles of forest. Rough tracks wound through oak and
birch and pine, past thickets of thorn and bramble, across
clearings where heather and bracken smelt sweet and warm in
the sunshine. Here and there a marshy pond lay in a hollow; a
little further and there would be a stretch of sandy soil, with
sand so white and fine that an open space seen ahead through
the thinning tree-trunks, gleamed like a pool of silver. For
hours on end we wandered through these woodland solitudes,
with a little food in a knapsack and all day to walk or lie in the
heather or sit under a great tree, while Harry smoked and I
sewed or knitted. Tired and hungry, we would come down the
hill in the falling dusk, to the friendly streets and alleys of Les
Yvelines. Lamps were already glimmering in the windows;
people moved slowly up and down or sat at their open doors
gossiping; children ran and shouted in the roadway. Back at the
inn, it was heaven to find our room again; to light the lamp and
draw the curtains; to luxuriate in slow removal of dusty boots
and sweaty clothes; relaxed and naked to sponge away fatigue
and heat; to dress again in cool clean linen and, shamelessly
eager for quantities of food and drink, to go downstairs to
supper. After the meal we sat in the old untidy garden behind
the inn, or strolled up the street to the café opposite the

church, or when the moon was up, walked at random to the edges of the town – they were near at hand, for it was a tiny place – and gazed over the shimmer and shadow of the silent fields. By ten o'clock we were in bed, and behind the soft ramparts of mattress and pillows found our ultimate privacy.

Of sights in the accepted sense Les Yvelines had only three – a church, an abandoned cloister and a huge quarry in the hillside. On the last-named the little town largely depended for its simple livelihood, and must have done so for generations, seeing that the place's full name was Les Yvelines-la-Carrière. Men were at work in the quarry from early morning until twilight. Somtimes the noise of blasting would reach us in the forest; usually one heard nothing until near at hand, when the rattle of stone, the sound of pick or chisel or the scrunch of waggon-wheels told of active toil. The quarry itself was a vast and rather terrifying place, so sheer was the inner cliff and so many the piles of stone and pits and caves and sudden deep pools which broke its wide arena. The quarried stone was half-worked on the spot and then transported to a big yard near the church, along two sides of which ran the old cloister. This was in semi-ruinous condition; but the vaulting was sound enough to shelter benches and toolracks from the rain, and the place might, I suppose, have been put to greater degradation than to serve the purposes of masonry. The church of Les Yvelines was only a little less decayed than the cloister. The façade had been badly damaged in the Revolution and the broken carvings had never been replaced. The gaps had merely been filled in with plaster, so that the once elaborate west-front had a curiously blotchy appearance, as though permanently spattered with mud. By a miracle, however, the stained glass windows of the interior had escaped destruction, and very remarkable windows they were. One in particular, which depicted Adam and Eve and proclaimed that bodily love played its part in the happy days before the Fall, became for us a treasured place of pilgrimage and a treasured impropriety. 'Let's go and look at us' we would say, and hurry to the church and back again. We called the figures Harry and Fanny, drew odious comparisons, and generally made silly lovely fun, as doubtless generations of lovers in Les Yvelines had done before. But we gave no thought to them, having none to spare from one another.

* * *

Then one brilliant morning in July Harry said:

'Little love, I must be back at work in a week's time.'

'But, darling, we've only been here —'

'Four whole weeks, sweetness, four mortal weeks. And wonderful weeks too. Indeed they have been so wonderful that I feel we must break the descent to normal life, and have a few days of modified honeymoon in a place where crowds will remind us that there are other people in the world. Shall we leave here the day after tomorrow, and go to Paris for four days?'

Of course I agreed. Anything he wanted, I wanted. But it was grievous to leave Les Yvelines, and a round of farewell visits to our favourite places kept me on the edge of tears. But he said we would come again next year, and was so full of plans and so gentle with me that I had not the heart to tell him, then and there, why in twelve months' time a foreign holiday would have its complications. It was an ideal opportunity for telling him; and I let it slip.

We went a last walk in the forest, stood for the last time under the towering rocks of the quarry, ate our last supper in the quiet dining-room. The next evening we were in Paris, in a hotel behind the Madeleine.

There followed two busy and enjoyable days. Now and again I thought wistfully of the calm and seclusion of Les Yvelines – of the cool clean air at night, and of the scent of fruit blossom and resin and damp earth which marked the sunlit hours – for Paris was noisy, dusty and hot. But shops and a chance to buy some clothes; the elegant crowds in the Champs Élysées; the fine streets and buildings; the evening gaiety in casino or public garden – these and other distractions left little time for vain regrets. One afternoon we went out to the gardens at Asnières; one evening danced with the students and their girls at the Closerie des Lilas; the next sat in fashionable state at Mabille, watching the professional dancers and listening to the excellent orchestra. The third evening, said Harry, we must go to a theatre; and in order to see something different from what could be seen in London and to minimize the drawback of my not understanding French, proposed that we choose a theatre staging musical extravaganza. Enquiry at our hotel brought automatic recommendation of a production at the Bouffes Parisiennes – the principal house for shows of this kind – but also a tentative suggestion that Monsieur and Madame might be wiser to see the really startling performance at a smaller theatre called Les Menus Plaisirs. This, it appeared, introduced an amazing water-ballet – featuring a beautiful French Canadian actress supported by nymphs, elves and water-sprites – which was a delight to the eye as well as a *tour de force* in theatrical engineering. Harry clapped his hands together:

'Oh, Menus Plaisirs of course! My little Vandra *must* see the rival water-sprites; and they shall have their noses put out of joint by the loveliest of their kind. That'll learn them to go nymphing about.'

In due course we tipped our way into a loge at the Menus Plaisirs.

The show opened gaily and with a riot of colour. There were some tuneful songs, comedians whose jokes were evidently outrageous but, alas, beyond my understanding, dance-numbers and the miscellanea usual to a musical medley of the kind. Everything was a little quicker and more extreme than in England. The tunes were livelier or dreamier, the cross-talk more rapid, the show-girls more numerous and more flimsily attired. The great water-scene – suggestively entitled 'Née-nuephar' – was billed for the end of the first half of the programme, and when it was due the curtain was lowered to allow preparation to be made. For two or three minutes the audience sat in a darkened theatre listening to exciting and mysterious noises beyond the curtain – the whirring of wheels, the gurgle of water, creaking and thumps. Then the curtain rose again.

The stage had been transformed into a woodland pool. In the centre of the stage was a picturesque pond of real water on which floated a few water-lilies; round it were rocks and moss and a glade of fresh green grass; over it drooped trailing boughs of trees. The scene was the prettiest imaginable, and the spectators shouted their applause. The orchestra began a trilling elfin melody, and little gnomes and sprites came flitting on and off. Then older girls, costumed as flowers or lightly swathed in long strips of green material like water-weed, did a graceful dance on the grassy glade. A nymph came running from the wings, pursued by a satyr. They danced a duet, a passionate sequence of solicitation and recoil. The music was now gradually gathering force. It caught the house and held it in suspense. A climax was approaching, and we all sat forward in our seats, eyes fixed on the scene. We hardly dared to breathe, lest we lose a moment of the mounting excitement with which by now the very air was quivering. On the stage elves and sprites, nymph and satyr began scurrying to and fro, tucking themselves one by one behind the rocks or trees. At last, when the stage looked empty, there was a stirring of the surface of the pool. Slowly there rose from the water the head, the shoulders, the body of a girl. She had her back to the audience, and a more perfect body I never saw. For a moment she stood with the water to her knees; then stepped gracefully on to the grassy edge of the pool, where the glade sloped gently to its bank. Lazily she stretched her arms above her head, and with an insolent languor turned to face the auditorium.

Completely naked, save for a spangled triangle on a chain about her hips, she stood there gently swaying, while the water trickled down her flawless skin. With an abrupt gesture she pulled a tight gleaming cap from her head and her silver-gold hair fell in pale brilliance over her glistening shoulders. Then she began to dance.

Involuntarily, the moment I saw her, I had put my hand on Harry's leg. Now I discovered that I was digging my nails into his thigh.

'What's the matter, Vannchen?' he whispered patiently. 'You will tear me to bits if you hold on so tightly.'

'Don't you see who she is?'

He raised his glasses.

'By George! You're right! But it can't be!'

Astonishment kept us dumb until the dance was over, the curtain had fallen and the lights had gone up.

During the interval we debated what to do. It was undoubtedly Lucy, although in the programme she was Clotilde de Lannoy. She was billed to appear once more in the final tableau, so must remain in the theatre till the show was over. I scribbled her a note, which we sent behind. 'How lovely!' she wrote back. 'After the show will you drive me to the Château Rouge, where I have to meet a friend? I'll come to the foyer.'

I thought she was genuinely glad to see us. In the fiacre she gave us her adventures in a few sentences. The Canadian tour had proved unbearably provincial (I smiled to hear Lucy in the role of world-weary metropolitan), and after some months a chance meeting with a French Marquis on a visit to Quebec had given her an opportunity of escape. She had thrown up her part, to the delight of her understudy, and sailed with the Marquis to France. For a while she had lived in luxurious idleness in Nice; but the call of her Art proved too strong, and she felt that the Theatre had need of her. So she had come to Paris and mixed with a theatrical crowd. One of them had designed a water-ballet, of which she should be the most prominent figure. A number of managers had demurred, thinking the venture too extreme, quite apart from the heavy cost of production. But at last the Director of the Menus Plaisirs had shown himself a man of discernment and enterprise. From the first night the daring spectacle had conquered the town. Meantime she had made a new friend – a rich Englishman. We should see him before long and (with a mischievous smile) envy her good fortune.

The cab climbed the Rue Cadet, crossed the boulevard into the Chaussée Clignancourt and drew up at the lighted entrance of the Château Rouge. This popular resort was a mixture of garden, dance-hall and cabaret. On a fine summer evening (such as this), the open-air stage was in use; and before a crowd of spectators – seated at little tables, drinking and smoking – comedians did their turns, and groups of girl-dancers gave exhibitions of high kicking or presented one of the innumerable versions of the Can-Can. The night was deliciously cool; and as we settled at a prominent table – specially reserved for Mademoiselle de Lannoy (who was received with extravagant homage) – I felt that fate had played a kindly trick in thus throwing us across Lucy's path. I looked forward to seeing the latest 'protector', wondered what had become of the Marquis and whether his name were 'de Lannoy'. I doubted it; as I doubted some of the links in Lucy's story. But uncertainty made the whole affair the more intriguing. The situation struck me as piquant, and full of delightful possibilities.

We were eating salmon-mayonnaise and drinking champagne, and I was giving Lucy such news as I could of London and its doings, when she started up, gazed over my shoulder, waved her hand and cried:

'Here's my friend.'

A man was standing behind me; Lucy and Harry were both on their feet; I half-turned and, looking upward, saw Lord Manderstoke.

* * *

Lucy was making the introductions.

'Gerry, these are Miss Hooper and Mr Somerford. You have heard me speak of them. Fanny: Mr Somerford – Lord Manderstoke.'

He stared hard at Harry for a moment, and I saw him throw a look of astonished inquiry at Lucy. But she was smiling complacently round, delighted to be the centre of so prominent a group, with two big men to set off her graceful beauty. Manderstoke then bent over my hand, bowed politely to Harry, and stroked Lucy's cheek with a negligent finger. He made no further sign of recognition, but took his seat and looked about for a waiter with the unconcern of any man joining a party in a café-garden.

'Another bottle of the same, I think' he said. 'I am sorry to have been delayed, and so have compelled Mr Somerford to act host in my place.'

I looked at him curiously. It was only the second time I had seen him, and the first occasion had hardly favoured scrutiny. He was a very big man – bigger than Harry. His heavy torso and long arms must have been out of proportion to his legs, for when he was sitting he towered above the table. He wore bushy eyebrows, a heavy moustache and sideburns, and this profusion of dark brown hair accentuated the pallor of his face. His eyes were black, with heavy drooping lids; though the moustache concealed his mouth, I got the impression that it was long and straight and, from the line of his jaw, slightly underhung. While covertly studying the man whose very name had for so long haunted me, I happened to surprise a momentary savage gleam in his sleepy eyes. It was as though a fire were smouldering behind them and had suddenly spurted into flame, throwing a flash of hatred across the table.

A stab of fear pierced me like a knife-thrust, so that I almost cried out. Anguish of mind came fast on the heels of physical pain. I felt myself shaking with terror and fury, but gripped the sides of my chair, set my teeth and said over and over again to myself 'Oh, God, warn Harry. Make him be careful! *Please*, God, warn Harry to be careful'.

The two men were smoking and talking in desultory fashion. To all appearances we were an amicable quartet of casual acquaintances, exchanging commonplaces over a glass of wine. The first shock of realizing that we were sitting on a volcano had passed. I regained sufficient self-control to answer a trival question of Manderstoke's and turn to Harry for confirmation. To my relief I saw that he was at least on his guard. I knew his every movement and attitude, and one glance told me that he sat taut and free-limbed on his chair, ready at any moment to move and to move quickly. In awful suspense I waited for something to happen.

The party had fallen silent. Manderstoke rested an elbow on the table, took his cigar from his lips and blew a fine plume of smoke into the air. Then, with a new edge to his voice, he began to speak:

'Mr Somerford, this is a fortunate meeting, because it has taken place sooner rather than later and has come about easily and naturally. But you and I had to meet sometime, because you have twice chosen to interfere with me, and I do not allow interference from strangers.'

Lucy, her face suddenly pale with alarm, leant quickly forward and grasped his arm.

'Gerry, please! I beg of you – don't start a quarrel here—'

He flung her hand away and snarled at her:

'Hold your tongue, you! Whores should be seen and not heard.'

She shrank back in her chair and held both hands to her trembling lips. Manderstoke turned back to Harry and, still speaking with bitter formality, said:

'On the first occasion we met face to face, and you chose the honourable course of assaulting a drunken man. (You see I make no bones about being drunk that night at Evans's. Why should I?) On the second occasion we did not meet, because you went behind my back and scared that flabby coward Pippin into sending his girl away so that she should not be mine. I frightened Mr Pippin still more and he told me the whole story. I got on the girl's track and finally caught her – as you see. Now we meet again – I think on equal terms – and it gives me much satisfaction to tell you that you are a low blackguard whose face needs washing.'

With the last words he flung the contents of his glass straight at Harry's eyes.

But the wine struck no higher than the shoulder, for Harry had leapt to his feet a split second before the throw. Next moment he vaulted the table and hurled himself at Manderstoke, who fell backward on to the ground with Harry on top of him. Lucy and I both screamed. Men came running from every direction, and dragged the combatants apart. They were now on their feet, glaring at one another, with a knot of waiters and gate-keepers hanging on to their arms and coats. There appeared an agitated man in a frock-coat, clearly the manager or proprietor of the Château Rouge. The little crowd of restraining men fell back leaving the principals to confront authority.

'Gentlemen, gentlemen! You will bring the police! Permit me to attempt a reconciliation ... perhaps Monsieur will state his case?'

To this request for an explanation of what had occurred, Harry said sharply that it was a private quarrel. Manderstoke, with a sneer, declared that he had offered a recognized provocation, but instead of a challenge (as would have come automatically from a gentleman) had received a direct assault. The manager thereupon addressed Harry. I could not understand much of what he said, but his manner was faintly contemptuous and it was clear that he sided with the enemy.

Harry listened, shrugged his shoulders and came over to me.

'Vannchen' he said. 'I shall have to call this fellow out. If I don't, they'll brand me for a cad. It's all pompous nonsense, but he knows the ropes here and I don't. The difficulty is —'

He looked round uncertainly, and a man stepped forward from the circle of onlookers. He was a pleasant-looking Frenchman, who said in excellent English:

'If I can be of any service, Monsieur, pray command me. It is possible that you are a stranger here and know of no friend on whom to call. In that case I shall be delighted to act for you. My card, Monsieur.'

Harry glanced at the card and thanked the stranger for his offer.

'I shall be most glad of your help' he said. 'I know very little of the procedure in cases of this kind.'

The other bowed.

'If you will tell me where you are staying – and your name —'

Supplied with these details, he approached Manderstoke

who, I suppose, gave him the name of some friend, for he wrote something down and returned to Harry.

'I will call on you tomorrow morning, Monsieur Somerford, by which time all will be arranged. Madame – Monsieur —' He bowed to us in turn and went briskly away.

All this time I had hardly moved. I felt numb with the shock of what had occurred. That this horror should have come crashing through the shell of our peaceful holiday froze me to a sort of helpless lump. I was watching, almost without seeing them, the various persons move to and fro, when an arm was thrown round my shoulders and I heard Lucy's broken whisper in my ear:

'Oh, Fanny, what have I done? It is frightful. Stop it; for God's sake, stop it! Get Harry away at once. Gerry is a crack shot. I —'

'Chérie, it is time to go. Allow me to escort you.'

At the sound of Manderstoke's voice – he had spoken loudly and in French – she started away from me as though lashed with a whip. I saw her hasten to her lover, take his arm and, acknowledging the obsequious salutes of manager and staff with the gracious smile of a notorious stage beauty, move toward the gates.

IV

'Gerry is a crack shot' – Lucy's final words beat about my brain, which seemed to be choking in a fog of terror and impotent rage. Suppose anything *should* happen to Harry... Nothing would, of course; the very thought was absurd; but all the same, if there were the faintest possibility... 'Get Harry away' she had said. That must be tried forthwith. He must refuse the challenge.

But, when I began to speak, he was almost rough with me:

'Don't talk nonsense, sweet. I can't do a thing like that. I should have expected you to know it was impossible!'

With tears in my eyes, I begged and implored him:

'Let us go home tomorrow – early! If he wants to find you

in London, he can – and get a good thrashing. Harry, I beseech you to listen to me. If you never do what I want again, do this for me!'

'Please, Fanny. I have said no and I mean it.'

I lay awake far into the night, hot-eyed and frightened, and turning over and over in my mind the gravest problem of all. Was it my duty to tell him about his child now, or still to say nothing? I listened to his quiet breathing. At least he could sleep. So, partly from timidity, partly from fatigue, I persuaded myself that it would be wrong to rouse him and that the decision whether or not to break the news should wait over till morning. Thus, though I could not have known it, the final opportunity was lost.

During the forenoon following, Harry seemed preoccupied, and I could not bring myself to open the subject. He wrote a letter to Mr Carteret and another to Sir William Ferraby, not showing them to me but merely saying he wished to let them know what had happened. About noon the French gentleman called, and had a brief conversation with Harry alone. I wanted to be present, but was bidden to remain upstairs in the bedroom. After he had gone, Harry said the meeting was arranged for eight o'clock next morning. I asked him where, but he would not tell me. In the afternoon, he went out, saying he had business to attend to and must see to it alone. He had not been gone long when a messenger brought a note which he insisted on putting into my hand. The flap of the envelope was endorsed: 'If undeliverable return without fail to Clotilde de Lannoy'. I opened it with shaking fingers.

Fanny darling, [wrote Lucy in her flamboyant scrawl]. I won't ask you to forgive me, for I don't think you ever can. But I *must* tell you how utterly ashamed I am of bringing this shocking thing to pass. I had no idea in the world except to surprise you both and score a stupid little triumph of my own. I was annoyed with you, that day in North Bank, when you and Harry cornered Pippin. I thought you were handing me about like a parcel; and the very fact that you wanted to get me away from Gerry made me more curious about him. Then he got on my track and finally traced me to Paris. But by then I had forgotten all my irritation with you; I swear I had. Up to last night, everything had gone smoothly. He's rough as a lover and frightens me – which I rather liked. Now I see what a silly little fool I have been – too late.

That Gerry had thought twice of Harry's opposition to him never occurred to me; and that he should break out like that was horrifying. I do pray you have left Paris and that this note comes back to me. I daren't say a word to Gerry. I thought he was going to strike me last night, he was so cold and savage.

Goodbye, Fanny. I suppose you'll never want to see me again. Your miserable friend, Lucy.

This unhelpful though rather pathetic outburst had the effect of reviving my worst fears. Sitting alone, I fought a last fight with the forebodings which were slowly overwhelming me. Every hour the crisis which faced my lover looked more grim; every hour I was being more thoroughly excluded from it. When at last Harry returned, my control had broken. I threw myself into his arms and in an abandonment of tears blurted out my secret. Instantly he was his old tender self. Full of delight and excitement, I believe that for a while he actually forgot the cloud which hung over us. But when I said, quite simply, that I was ready to marry him as soon as he wanted, he gave me a look of startled dismay and slid forthwith from gay enthusiasm into distraught reproach:

'Oh, God!' he cried. 'Why, in Heaven's name, Fanny, didn't you tell me sooner? Even yesterday. We ought to be married instantly – and now it is too late.'

Hastily he corrected himself.

'Too late for today, I mean. I would have liked it done today. Now it must wait till tomorrow.'

But I knew what he meant, and sat in a daze of misery, cursing myself for a coward and a bungler.

About ten o'clock, after a supper I could not eat and an hour and a half of restless tormented silence in the uncomfortable little salon, he bade me go to bed. He would follow in twenty minutes. When he came into the room, I was in bed, lying rigidly on my back and staring at the ceiling, which seemed to billow and twist as it does to one in fever. Sitting on the bed, he took me in his arms and holding me very close said gently:

'Sweetheart, you are having a terrible time and I am deeply, deeply sorry. But everything will be all right to-morrow. I want you to be patient just a little longer. This is my affair and I *have* to keep you out. Now go to sleep if you can; and, when next we meet, all will be happiness again.'

In wild alarm I wriggled out of his arms, knelt up in bed and clutched him by the coat.

'Where are you going, Harry?' I cried. 'You are not leaving me now? You can't!'

'I must, darling. I shall go to another hotel nearer to – well, more convenient for my appointment. My second has to be with me, you see. He is awaiting me there. Please be brave, little love – just for these next few hours. I will come straight back to you.'

My heart seemed to fall in on itself and my whole body to crumple. I slumped forward on to his shoulder and lost consciousness. When I came to myself I was back in bed, with the clothes carefully tucked round me. Harry had gone.

v

It was not yet afternoon on the day of the duel. At ten o'clock the French gentleman had called on me at our hotel. With embarrassed courtesy, he had regretfully informed me that my husband had received a bullet wound in the right arm which had broken the humerus, had been taken back immediately to the hotel in the Rue de la Roquette and that, on the instructions of his principal, he had the honour to hand me a letter, written the night before and entrusted to his care for delivery in case of accident. He bowed, and had turned to leave the salon, when he swung round and stood rigidly at

attention, heels together and hat held at arm's length against
his leg.

'Madame' he said. 'I ask permission to express my respectful condolences. Your husband is a man of honour and deserved better fortune. You may, however, be assured that the
duel was fought with perfect correctness. I may add that every
precaution has been taken to conceal the fact that there has
been a meeting. The people at the hotel will hold their
tongues. Madame, your servant.'

He left me holding Harry's letter in my hand and staring
through a haze of panic at the door through which he had
disappeared.

With an effort I pulled myself together, ordered a cab and
hurried upstairs for hat and coat. In the fiacre I read my letter.

12.30 pm

Fanny darling. I am leaving this letter with M. Bourdon,
just in case anything should happen to me later in the day.
Our hotel proprietor has money in his charge which is to be
handed to you when required. I have made a will and de-
posited it with the British Consul. If you call at his office
with a passport, it will be given to you. As you know, I have
already written to Julian and Ferraby, and either of them
will give you any help you may need. I did not, however,
write to my mother; and, though I am sure it will be unnecessary, I must ask you to advise her by telegraph if
things go amiss. Her address is . . . Phillimore Gardens.

All this sounds very tragic; but as it is only one chance in
a hundred that you ever get this letter, no matter. It shall at
any rate end on a different note.

I love you, Fanny, if not as much as you deserve, as much
as it is in me to do. You have given me two years of such
happiness as falls to the lot of few men. And now there is to
be a little Fanny, to enrich and share that happiness and
make it last a life-time. Thank you, my sweetheart, just for
being you.

Goodnight, and God be with you.

H.

They took me straight to his bedside. He lay pale as death, and the hint of shadows creeping about his eyes caught me in the throat and nearly choked me. When I touched his hand, he raised his eyelids and, I think, recognized me, for his fingers just moved beneath mine. Every now and again the muscles in his face contracted and relaxed and a little shiver of pain ran down his body. I sat a few minutes until he had sunk into an apparent coma. Then I crept out of the room and demanded to see the doctor.

* * *

The old doctor waved his hands and made soothing noises. He was a snuffy, watery-eyed old man and inspired no confidence. We were in the bleak corridor of the hotel in which Harry had spent the previous night, to which he had now been carried back. The doctor knew no English, and a middle-aged nurse, recommended by the hotel-people, was acting as interpreter.

'The medicine e say not to agitate yourself, madame. Monsieur will be better for repose and e give im something to make dorm. E think all will go well.'

'But he is desperately ill' I insisted. 'I can see he is!'

'Ill, yes' she agreed after repeating my words to the doctor — 'A gunned one is always ill. But they often become well once more and so will im.'

The vague, leisurely optimism of the doctor and nurse sent me from the hotel in rage and despair. At the corner of the street was a quiet café. Regardless of convention, I went inside and ordered some brandy. Re-reading Harry's letter, I forced my mind to the composition of a telegram to his mother. I decided to telegraph also to Mr Carteret. To the former I finally drafted this message:

Harry dangerously ill Hôtel des Acacias Rue de la Roquette Paris result of serious accident Julian Carteret will confirm.

and left it unsigned. To Mr Carteret I would say:

Harry seriously hurt can you come immediately Fanny

and add the address of my own hotel.

With the brandy lying like a tepid blanket over the bitter lump of grief and dread which had settled in the pit of my stomach, I sought a Telegraph Office and sent my messages. Then I went miserably back to the Rue de la Roquette.

All that afternoon till late at night and all the next day I hung about the hateful building, in which my love lay prostrate and in pain. They let me sit with him; but there was nothing I could do, save watch his dear face and wipe the sweat from his forehead and now and again touch that hand, once so cool and dry and firm, now so limp and hot. The arm had been badly shattered and he had lost a lot of blood: so much I extracted by persistent questioning. But what was being *done*? Ought there not to be an operation? The doctor was manifestly out of his depth; he teetered and shrugged and spoke of opiates and nature finding a way.

I wanted to storm at them all and demand a second opinion. But I was not too distracted to realize that, if the affair were to be kept secret, I was in their hands. So I kept silent, waiting for some reply from Julian, and even gave the hotel proprietor a hundred francs which helped him to appreciate the need for discretion.

My own helplessness almost drove me mad. I knew no single soul in Paris – save the two who had wrecked my lover, and was condemned to sit and watch the most precious life in the world virtually left to look after itself – sit and do *nothing*, because there was nothing I could do.

Next day in the early afternoon I returned to my hotel. I had been in and near the sick-room all night, and was bemused with lack of sleep and the torture of growing anxiety. I would have a wash and a short rest, and resume my useless, powerless vigil. As I groped my way to the desk to get the key, a figure rose from a chair in the vestibule and a familiar voice cried:

'Fanny, at last! How is he?'

'Oh, Julian' I gasped. 'Thank God you've come!'

He caught me as I swayed and carried me into the salon. There, after a few moments, I found my wits again and poured out the story, with all my fears and all my conviction that something further should, and must, be done. He was splendidly calm:

'My poor child. You are worn out. I will now take you to your room and you must go to bed. I shall go straight round to Harry's hotel and see for myself. Then we will beat up all the greatest doctors in Paris. Come along like a good girl, and don't worry any more.'

Dear Julian! He more or less carried me upstairs and laid me on the bed. The very fact of having someone on my side lulled me to a momentary peace. I believe I was asleep almost before he left the room.

*　　*　　*

About nine o'clock in the evening he returned, in company with a small bearded Jew, who looked at me searchingly through gold-rimmed spectacles when Julian introduced us.

'Fanny, this is Doctor Loewenthal; Monsieur Loewenthal – Mademoiselle Hooper, the friend of M. Somerford. We have just come from the Acacias, Fanny, and the Doctor has made an examination. The various people I had time to consult all agreed that he is the best man possible and has worked miracles. He will now tell you his opinion.'

The little man led me to a sofa and, sitting at my side, laid his delicate white fingers on my wrist. Then in precise but correct English he made his report. The condition of the patient was undeniably serious. The haemorrhage had not been properly checked; and though the injury might have meant the loss of an arm, it need not have produced so extreme an over-all weakness. But he had bled . . . bled dreadfully.

Even now, however, we must not despair. M. Somerford had a wonderful constitution and his strength had kept up far better than anyone could have expected. In his opinion it was not too late to operate. There was naturally a grave risk; but at least a reasonable hope of success. Whereas if no operation were attempted – he gave a little shrug and shook his head. It was for Madame to decide. That was his advice, and (if I did him the honour of putting the case in his charge) he would do everything possible to prepare the patient to withstand the further strain.

I would have liked to go on my knees and pour out my heart to him; but I could only sit by his side throttled with terror and trembling all over. He went on stroking my wrist very gently and slowly the ague subsided. I found my voice, and seizing his hands cried:

'Save him for me, Doctor! Do anything – anything. You are in absolute control. Only save him!'

He raised my hands, which still clutched both of his, and brushed them with his lips.

'I shall do my best' he replied. 'I thank you for your confidence. It will help me to know that my patient has one who loves him near at hand, and that she will be thinking of him and joining the strength of her hopes to mine. And now, madame, I become for a moment your doctor also. You will go to bed, and I will give you a little draught – see, I have it here in my bag. Tomorrow, when we shall both need all our courage and all our faith, you will be strong and rested.'

'And when may I see him again?'

He gazed at me thoughtfully.

'If you will come to the Hotel des Acacias at midday tomorrow, I hope you will be able to see him for a few minutes. I am going back there now to install a good nurse. We must take every care of him during the coming night. If things go as I hope, he will be as strong as we can make him by the middle of the day. Then we shall go into battle and – God willing – win our victory.'

*   *   *

Doctor Loewenthal's draught did its work, and I awoke refreshed and ready to endure the day's ordeal. Julian called for me and insisted on our taking a walk in the sunshine before going to the Rue de la Roquette. He had himself been there early in the morning and seen the doctor for a few moments. Things were, it appeared, proceeding as satisfactorily as could be hoped.

At last we arrived at the gloomy building in which I now felt I had spent years of my life. As we climbed the steps to the front entrance, I was surprised to see the bearded face of the little doctor peering through the half-glass doors. Surprise turned to alarm when on our entering the vestibule, he seized Julian by the arm, drew him away into a corner, and made a rapid speech in French, pointing upward and gesticulating excitedly.

Julian came slowly back across the hall. He kept his eyes on the ground, and was frowning either in perplexity or embarrassment. He came to a halt immediately in front of me, and, without raising his eyes, began to fumble for words:

'Er – Fanny – er . . .'

'What is it, Julian? What's happened. For God's sake tell me the truth. Is he . . . ?'

The relief of being able to deny the worst restored some ease of speech.

'Oh, no, my dear. He is better in himself. But an awkward thing has happened. His sister is here.'

Thinking only of Harry, I did not at once see the significance of this news.

'It was good of her to come so quickly! Harry asked me to telegraph to his mother, and I did, when I telegraphed to you. I gave the address of this hotel, so Miss Somerford will have come straight here.'

'Yes, yes, Fanny; but don't you understand? She has taken charge now, and – and . . .'

'Taken charge? How? Doctor Loewenthal is in charge!'

He looked wretchedly embarrassed.

'On your instructions, Fanny dear, which are no longer valid – in her view.'

'But, Julian – she can't interfere at this vital moment! She can't!'

'I'm afraid she can' he said miserably. 'I don't say she *will*, mark you – to the extent of repudiating the doctor altogether. But she has already taken a step which has upset Loewenthal very much. She – she has refused to let you see Harry. He is fully conscious and has been asking for you; and Loewenthal was counting on your visit to do him just that bit of spiritual good— But now...'

His uneasy halting speech was suddenly overswept by a torrent of anger.

'Damn her to hell!' he burst out, 'and damnation take the rotten hypocritical world which produced her! What *are* we to do, Fanny? She is technically within her rights – her smug abominable rights – and — Oh, God, Almighty, what a mess!'

He swung away and returned to the little doctor, who was pacing nervously up and down against the far wall. They exchanged a few words, and Julian came quickly back to me.

'I am going up to see her' he said curt and grim, 'and taking Loewenthal with me. Perhaps if he puts the case strongly enough she will yield. Please wait here.'

For quarter of an hour I stood in a corner of the vestibule, sunk once again into the numb despair of two or three days ago. The hatred Miss Somerford must feel for me was shocking enough; but it mattered nothing beside her wicked interference with the doctor's plans. Over and over again I repeated to myself: 'She *must* let me see him: she *must*!' And then Julian came slowly downstairs, and I could see from his face that it was hopeless.

He took my arm and walked me down the steps and along the street.

'No good, Fanny' he said at last, in a voice flat with the exhaustion of rage. 'No good. There she is, and there she means to stay. I have quarrelled with her, if that's any consolation. I pleaded and implored and she as good as told me to mind my own business. Then I lost my temper and let her have it. She enjoyed that, and I was a fool to do it. God! I'd like to choke the life out of her!'

'And Harry?' I whispered. 'How is he?'

'I fear a little over-excited. They had words – at least to the extent possible to the poor fellow, and the haemorrhage started again. Loewenthal was with him while I was fighting that woman in the passage, and came out as I was leaving. He looked grave, but asked me to tell you he was still hopeful, though this business has not improved matters.'

I put my hands to my forehead.

'I believe I shall go mad' I said unsteadily 'or faint or something.'

We were passing the café in which I had composed the telegrams summoning friend and enemy to Paris. He guided me in, and ordered sherry-cobblers. The cold clean drink checked the whirling in my head, and left me blank and limp.

'What shall I do now?' I asked dully.

'For the moment stay here. I am going back to find out what is to happen – about – about the operation. I will come and tell you.'

While he was away I sat propped in my chair like a bundle of clothes. There was no feeling in my limbs; and inside I was a hollow thing, emptied of all emotion. I do not know how long he had been gone, before I became conscious of him standing over me.

'Loewenthal will operate' he said. 'He says it is the only hope. If he throws up the case now and nothing is done, it is the end. So he will swallow the insults which have been offered him, and do his best. "Tell the little lady" he said "that I do this for her sake. I would like to give her back her lover because she deserves him. But tell her also that I may fail, for her man is very near the edge".'

*   *   *

Harry died under chloroform at two-fifty-five in the afternoon. The date was the twelfth of July, 1878 – almost exactly two years after he and I began our life together in Little Welbeck Street, and five months before, at Gowthorpe in Yorkshire, his daughter came into the world.

LONDON AND GOWTHORPE

I

THOSE FIVE MONTHS – a desolate hiatus between Harry's last breath and my baby's first – only remain with me as a scatter of disjointed memories. They buried my darling in the cemetery of Père Lachaise under a sweltering July sun. On one side of his grave stood Miss Somerford; on the other Julian Carteret, Doctor Loewenthal and I. I could not help admiring – even while hating it – the granite inflexibility of the woman, who in the name of righteousness had killed her brother.

Her convictions were cruel and fanatical, but she had courage; and although she must have known that the three of us standing opposite held her for little less than a murderess, she gave no inch to embarrassment or conciliation. Passing out of the cemetery, she acknowledged Julian's bow with a curt nod; but as she walked by me to her cab, she never gave me a glance – merely with marked emphasis gathered her skirts about her.

I could not even cry, as the long box containing all that was left of Harry Somerford slid finally out of sight. Ever since I knew for certain that I had lost him, my whole being had dried into a parched stupor. I had no will to anything, but in a sort of daze did whatever Julian and the doctor bade me.

I have no words to describe the unfailing kindness of those two good friends. Julian went to the Consulate for Harry's will, and made all arrangements for the journey home. Jointly they extracted from the Hôtel des Acacias details of the funeral as arranged by Miss Somerford, threatening to expose the whole affair to the police, but at the same time adding cash inducement to a promise of secrecy, in return for the information Harry's sister sought to keep from us. In addition the little doctor came constantly to see me, watching for signs of strain, unobtrusively prescribing for sleeplessness or lack of

appetite or the spiritless melancholy which set me brooding by
the hour. On what was to be his last visit (Julian and I were
leaving Paris in the morning), he took my hands and twinkled
at me through his glasses.

'Ma petite' he said 'you are a true woman; and here in
France we value women more delicately than your clumsy
Englishmen. It has been a privilege for an old French doctor
to see the gallantry of a young English girl in the most terrible
experience which could befall her – and all the time perform-
ing a woman's highest duty. You will at least have a living
token of your dead lover. Take care of yourself, for its sake.'

I stared at him, too astonished to feel embarrassment.

'So you knew, doctor?'

'Oh, I knew. The first time I saw you, I knew. Your eyes
alone would have told me. A lucky child, to have parents so
much in love and a mother so gentle and so strong. The blessing of an old man on you and your baby, my dear. Will you
write to me, when she is born? I think she will be a girl, when
I think of him and look at you. But I should like to hear that
all goes well.'

I could only nod and squeezing his hands kiss his scrubby
cheek. I was unable to say a word, for his tenderness had
released my tears at last.

*   *   *

I suppose the crowded worries of the last days in Paris and
the cares of the journey home so occupied my mind, that until
I was once again in Little Welbeck Street I did not face up to
any conception of what life would be without Harry. Then,
however, with sudden horror I saw myself on the threshold of
desolation. The empty rooms in which we had been so happy;
Muggsy setting the table in gloomy silence, instead of exchanging jokes and news with him sitting by the fire, or with
me tidying my hair in the bedroom and calling through the
door; waking in the morning after uneasy sleep, and finding
myself alone and the other half of the bed cold and void, his
pipes on the mantelpiece, his walking-stick in the corner, his

old hat on a peg on the landing, his tail-coat and evening suit in the wardrobe, his shoes in the rack, his shaving soap and hair-oil on the marble washstand – every moment, every corner had its intolerable reminder of what had been and was no more. If I had yielded to impulse, I should have run upstairs whenever Julian was in and begged to sit with him, if only to escape the ghosts which flocked round Harry's empty chair. But I had sense enough to do no such thing. Poor Julian! He had had trouble and to spare on my account.

On the third evening after our return, he knocked punctiliously at the sitting-room door. Ever since we stepped out of the train on to Charing Cross platform he had become once more the lawyer – grave, cautious, considered in his judgements. It was hard to believe that this same man had broken out savagely against Miss Somerford in the dreary hallway of the Hôtel des Acacias. Even his manner toward me had changed. I became once again 'Mrs Harry' (was it in part a delicate wish to credit me with at least my lover's Christian name?); so he, of course, had to be 'Mr Carteret'.

Bidden to enter, he greeted me with his usual courtesy.

'Mrs Harry, I think you should know the terms of our friend's will – of which (I hope you will not object) I am sole executor.'

I grew suddenly impatient of his scrupulous formality.

'Dear Julian, for mercy's sake treat me like a human being, even if I am a client! You have been lovelier to me than any man could; and I cannot – and will not – go on calling you Mr Carteret.'

He coughed.

'I beg your pardon – and incidentally thank you. I will begin again. Fanny, here is Harry's will. He leaves everything to you. It isn't a great deal. There's the balance at his bank – about two hundred pounds; also the money he inherited from his father, a decent little capital sum invested in Consols and bringing in about eighty pounds a year: also of course, all his personal belongings in these rooms. But that is not all. Attached to the will was a letter to his executor, and among his papers at the hotel I found a codicil to the will, executed apparently the evening before the duel, properly witnessed and in an envelope addressed to me.

'Let us take this codicil first. From it I learn that – er – forgive me if I have to intrude on a very private matter, but lawyers can keep their counsel – that – that in due course you expect to become...'

The poor man was so embarrassed that I summoned a reserve of cheerfulness to help him through his difficulty.

'Yes, indeed. Isn't it wonderful? It is the only thing to live for now – that, if all goes well, I shall hold his baby in my arms before the year is out.'

'Dear Fanny' he said softly. 'I am very glad. All will go well, never fear. All *shall* go well.'

Resuming his professional manner he went on:

'This codicil appoints in trust for Harry's child his share of his father's estate, which is vested in Mrs Somerford for life. Harry's father gave his property to his wife for life and, after her death, to such of his children as his wife should appoint. Some time ago his mother made a deed – there is a copy with Harry's papers – in which she appointed the money equally between her two children, and this would normally pass to them on her death. You ought, therefore, in due course to be able to reckon on the use of the income from Harry's appointed share to spend for the benefit of the child.'

'I think I understand' I said. 'It sounds fair and sensible, as he always was.'

'Yes' he agreed. 'It makes the best of a not very good job.'

He sat a moment fiddling with his papers and once more looking uncomfortable.

'What is the matter, Julian? Don't be afraid of speaking frankly. What is not a good job?'

'Well, you see, my dear, although there has hitherto been every reason to expect that the deed signed by Mrs Somerford will make everything all right, it *can* be revoked; and there is a danger, now Harry is dead, that she may revoke it. I am bound to recognize that the breach which opened between poor

Harry and his family may affect the situation to the disadvantage of – er – Harry's child – and its mother.'

He looked at me gravely, and I could only hang my head and yet again bitterly reproach myself for having kept silent until too late.

'You realize' Julian went on 'that Mrs Somerford is bound to learn of the terms of her son's will. She is, I am thankful to say, a more accessible person than her daughter and, as Harry's mother, will naturally feel more tenderly toward him than his sister might do. I hope, therefore, that with Mrs Somerford maternal love and human kindness will overcome the moral disapproval. But I cannot be sure; and it is necessary for you to understand that the child's future, which lies absolutely in the grandmother's hands, may be much worse provided for than Harry anticipated.'

I nodded.

'I understand. Except that Harry wished his child to have some of his father's money, I would far far rather it were all squandered and gone. I shall work for my baby and we will both come through.'

'I am sure you will' he said warmly 'and – let me say this now – any help I can give you at any time is yours for the asking, and not only for Harry's sake either.'

I tried to speak, but he hurried on:

'Please! There is still the letter. I will read you a portion of it.

'With regard to the rooms at Little Welbeck Street, I paid them up to the end of September. It seemed a foolish precaution at the time, but is one for which I am now thankful. At least Fanny will be able to stay on while she makes her plans. I do not believe she will want to continue there. I know I shouldn't, if she were gone. But she and Muggsy and I were such good friends that, in the remote event of Fanny being left there alone, I rejoice to think that for a while at least no money need pass between the survivors of the trio.'

'Stop, Julian! I can't bear it!'

Tears were streaming down my cheeks. I could not control them, so made no attempt to hide them. He sat silent, pretending to read his papers, until the outburst was over.

'I'm sorry' I sniffed. 'It took me unawares. Go on.'

He went on reading in a level voice, as though there had been no interruption.

'The only other thing I can leave my darling is my Life Insurance of five hundred pounds. I had always intended to leave one hundred of this to the Working Men's College in Great Ormond Street. Not only do I think it a grand undertaking, but thanks to it – and to Tom Hughes – I was able to meet her on those precious Thursday evenings. I owe to the College the opportunity to tell her that I loved her; and you know what that has led to – to my being divinely happy every moment of every day and every night — '

Julian's voice broke, then failed altogether. I was now sobbing unashamedly. At last I managed to say:

'Of *course* the College . . . of *course* . . .'

He pretended to make some notes to give us both time to recover; then, after a short pause, collected his papers and rose to go:

'Come upstairs and let us make some tea, and talk' he said. 'The professional interview is over, and we go to another floor and become a social gathering. There is an admirable Madeira cake. You have the details clear? In the bank, two hundred; from Consols, eighty per annum; all but a hundred of the Life Insurance, four hundred — It's not much, Fanny.'

'I don't mind' I said. 'It's enough for me – anything's enough, without him.'

II

Harry's death was not reported in the English papers, apart from a formal notice inserted by his mother in *The Times* obituary column. This described him as having 'died abroad after a short illness'.

There were just a few people, who, in my opinion, ought to know the truth; and I forced myself to the effort of letter-writing. Actually, when I got started, I found comfort in doing so. My days were now empty and purposeless. Going through my darling's things and deciding what to do with them, was a task so hateful that I could not bear it for more than a few minutes at a time. I would begin on the contents of a drawer. All at once spirit would fail me, and I would leave everything strewn about or hastily pack it away again, flop on to a chair and stare into the past. At least writing about him kept my mind active for a little while, and gave an excuse for living over again our last weeks together.

I wrote fully to Andrew and to Sir William Ferraby; less fully to Chunks and to Miss Cairns, and at length but on more personal lines to my mother. To her I explained that I was expecting a baby in December and hoped for her advice and help.

Andrew replied with an urgent invitation to come to Aughton at once and remain there. He wrote with moving sincerity about Harry, was deeply sympathetic with my grief and hoped we should be able to console one another. My mother responded nearly as quickly. She was grieved by my ill-fortune, but keenly interested in the prospect of a grandchild, who must of course be born at Gowthorpe under her supervision. About Harry she said nothing. The other three to whom I had written replied in person. The first to arrive was Chunks. I had not told him many details – merely that Harry had fought a duel and been fatally wounded. When he had patted my hands till they were almost bruised, and blown his nose like a trumpeter, and muttered vague threats against everyone who had had the smallest share in depriving his Fannikins of her man, he demanded the whole story. I told it, as fairly as I could. He listened in silence, twisting his brown billycock between his knees and scowling at the floor. When I had finished:

'That blackguard again!' he muttered. 'It's the finger of Providence; no less.' Rather wistfully he added: 'no ope uv yer coming back to us, I suppose? Always welcome, ye know, at the Bargee.'

I decided to tell him.

'I'm going to have a baby, Chunks, and shall go north to my mother. But I've very little money and will probably come to London again in the spring. May I invite myself when I know my plans?'

His great face creased into a thousand wrinkles.

'A little un? That's prime! And won't e be a nipper and a arf! Polly'll be besides herself when I tell er. You come, Fannikins, as and when you want, and bring the ole family. The more the merrier, that's the motto at the old Bargee.'

'I'm afraid there will only be two of us' I said sadly.

'Ho! And ow do you know? What about twins, hey? – one for you and one for im?'

This made me laugh, and we parted with surface cheerfulness.

The next visitor was Sir William Ferraby. He had come up specially from Gloucestershire.

'My poor little girl' he said. 'I would rather anything but this had happened. You knew Harry had written to me before the fight? I am ashamed to say that, though the news distressed me, it never occurred to me he would come to harm. Such a grand fighter. But duelling is not fighting, as the English understand it. I was very fond of Harry, my dear; and, if you will allow me to be, I would like to be very fond of the girl he loved. We do not know one another very well as yet; but that can be remedied. I want you to promise that if ever you want the sort of help I can give, you will ask for it. I am getting on, and shall not be here for ever. But I've some years yet, and a lonely old man asks for nothing better than to be of service to someone he likes. Will you promise Fanny (forgive my calling you that, but I have always thought of you as Fanny), promise to come to old William Ferraby at any time? He is at your service.'

'Thank you from my heart, Sir William. Indeed I promise....'

And finally Miss Cairns. She drove up in a shining Victoria with two men on the box, and her clothes – black touched with white – were impeccable.

'I am not a kisser, Fanny' she said 'but I am going to kiss you. There! I haven't done that for years. What a funny feeling. I wonder why it is so popular? No, I don't; I know. Now let me look at you. You poor little thing, so pinched and white! And, unless I'm a worse judge than I think, there's a baby on the way too. I thought so. When is it?'

Rather confused I told her. Her eyes softened and, looking as I had never seen her look before:

'I do believe I shall envy you that baby' she murmured. The next moment she was her old self again.

'Now then, let us be practical – and no false pride, please. Have you any money? If one woman can't help another in a tight corner, it's a pity; so I'm your banker when you need one.'

'I'm all right at present, Miss Cairns, and very very grateful for your kindness. When I'm about again, I must think seriously what to do, and may badly want your advice. But till then I shall go into the woods, and wait for my baby.'

'Very well, my dear. I've said what I came to say, and I mean it. Take care of yourself and don't mope. Write to me when the youngster has made his bow; and if after that you want me, you know where to find me.'

I went downstairs to the door with her and watched her step into her carriage. The footman climbed into his place beside the coachman, Miss Cairns waved a beautifully-gloved hand, and the gleaming turn-out drew smoothly away. As the horses turned northward into Wimpole Street I had a last glimpse of her, a slim proud figure in a black gown, with a white parasol slanted gracefully toward the sun.

III

My baby was born on the fourth of December at eight o'clock in the morning. It was an easy birth, and the child was perfect. My mother had made every possible preparation and took complete charge of me from the moment of my arrival at Gowthorpe. Now there was no pain, only a drowsy weakness. Gradually my mind began to clear. It was over. The tiny girl was born and breathing. Another woman's life had begun.

As I lay there exhausted but at ease, with Harry's daughter in the bend of my arm, watching through the window the winter sunshine sparkling on the rime-covered twigs of the big walnut tree, I felt for the first time since my lover had been taken from me a stirring of interest in what the future might have in store.

The morsel of humanity stirred and sputtered and nuzzled against my side. I thought of Doctor Loewenthal and his prophecy of a baby girl. But from the rest of Paris memory swerved away, finding a refuge only a few days farther back in the carefree happiness of Les Yvelines. In that moment I made the decision. She should be christened Evelyn.

WARBECK AND FANNY

WARBECK turned the final sheet of typescript, pushed the pile of paper away from him and sat back in his chair. He stretched his arms above his head and yawned.

'There!' he said aloud, though the room was empty. 'That's the best I can make of it.'

He picked up the typescript again and turned the sections over with professional neatness and speed. Selecting a typical page he counted the words in four or five consecutive lines and did a little sum in pencil on the margin of his blotter.

'Hundred and fifty thousand' he said to himself. 'Rather more. Five thousand at least, at eight and six.'

He wondered whether, from the point of view of his profit and loss account, it were three hundred pounds' worth, plus cost of manufacture and advertising. To him personally the whole adventure had been cheap at the price. 'Warbeck Ltd. shan't lose' he decided, 'even if I have to sell my Cézanne drawing.'

Next morning he put the typescript in his bag and set out for his office. One of the advantages of being an author-publisher – perhaps the only one – was that a book written was a book accepted. He would get a cast-off and specimen pages forthwith.

*   *   *

The previous year Warbeck's summer holiday had been more than twice as long as usual. Early in June he had in his customary way departed from his office, leaving no address and saying he would be back in three weeks' time. But a day or two before he was due to reappear, his manager and co-director had been astonished to receive a letter, written from a place in France called Les Yvelines, saying that Warbeck had got on to a likely book and would be busy fixing it up for another three weeks at least. The letter went on to say that the equivalent of three hundred pounds in French francs was to be paid immediately into the head office in Paris of the Société Générale for the credit of Madame Hooper, Hôtel de la Boule d'Or, Les Yvelines-la-Carrière, S. et O. The office must carry on as well as possible, and this would be his continuing address, in case they wanted to get at him. There followed various special instructions and an apology for upsetting normal routine.

The manager and the senior members of Warbeck's staff shook their heads over this unprecedented irregularity. The publicity man, who was addicted to the more lurid type of society novel, made them mark his words there was more in this than met the eye. This 'Madame Hooper' was one of those casino-sirens, or a crystal-gazer which was equally as bad. Warbeck's secretary tossed her head and said Mr Warbeck was not that kind of man at all; didn't they remember how he'd put that illustrator-woman in her place, when she set her cap at him? The manager called them to order. He was less concerned to reject the suggestion that the guvnor had fallen for an adventuress and was paying his footing, than to deny that anyone who knew him as well as they should think he'd be fool enough to court the maximum of publicity by drawing a cheque on the firm's account. 'She's the author of the book' said the manager sagely, 'and wants her advance right away. That's what it is. He'll send us the terms for the contract in a day or two, you'll see.'

Meantime, out in Les Yvelines, Warbeck was working far harder than if he were back in his office in Garrick Street. Old Mrs Hooper, once she had consented to talk of her life, talked with a vengeance. While she was actually speaking he made as few notes as possible, for he had a retentive memory and the sound of her voice was a delight. But after every session he sat down to record what she had said, often writing into the small hours rather than risk forgetting some tiny but vivid detail which gave character to a person or a place.

The days went by and the pile of notes grew and grew.

At last the old lady reached the end of her store of recollections.

'That is all I can tell you, Mr Warbeck. No doubt, when you let me see what you have made of my chatter, I shall think of a fresh point here and there. But it will only be revision now; the story is over. Are you repenting of your bargain?'

'Not in the least. I shrink a little from the job of writing you into shape and of finding suitable equivalents for the real names. But it is marvellous material; and I shall always be grateful for what you have given me to think about and remember.'

The night before his departure for London they took their coffee as usual in the hotel garden.

'I shall miss you sadly, Mr Warbeck' she said. 'I had grown accustomed to being alone; but now for six weeks I have had a companion and shared a common interest with a man I like. To return to aimless solitude will seem very hard at first; but I shall settle down again. At least I need not worry about money. It was very sporting of you to treat me like that. Please believe I am deeply grateful. And I can look forward to reading what you have written. That will be an excitement for me.'

'I only hope it won't prove a tragic disillusionment' he laughed. Then after a pause: 'May I ask you two questions?'

'Of course you may.'

'Is this hotel the same building to which you came with Mr Somerford, all those years ago?'

'Yes' she said softly. 'This was the one. No Madame Bonnet, of course, and no veranda there on the garden. The salle à manger was smaller and the whole place more primitive. But externally it looked very much as it does now. I had to die somewhere, and decided some years ago that I would like to spend my last bit of life where I had spent my happiest bit, and then go finally to sleep – not at Harry's side, but – near enough to – to know – he is not far away. . . .'

Her voice trailed into a silence which Warbeck made no immediate attempt to break.

*   *   *

A minute or two later he put his second question:

'There's one thing I would like to know about your daughter, if it's not impertinent to ask. What finally happened over Mrs Somerford's money?'

'Did I not say? How stupid — seeing that it was almost the only pleasant episode in our relations with Harry's family. Pleasant at the time, anyway. I told you how Evelyn got a scholarship, went to High School and Training College and how, when she first became a teacher, we had those quiet and delightful years together in Oxford. Well, when Evelyn was about twenty-five, Julian Carteret came down to see her. Mrs Somerford had sent for him. She was in bad health, and wished to put her affairs in order. You will remember that she had it in her power to revoke a deed which left Harry a share of his father's money, and dispose of it elsewhere. Well, she now offered to leave the money to Harry's daughter on two conditions — that she take the name of Somerford, and undertake to break off all relations with her mother. It was implied that if either of these conditions were refused, the money would go to a hospital.'

Mrs Hooper paused a moment, then said:

'I thought it was rather unkind to put the girl in such a position. Almost vindictive. Don't you think so, Mr Warbeck?'

'More than almost' he replied quietly. 'And did Evelyn accept?'

'She went straight up to London to see her grandmother, sweeping poor Julian along with her, so that he could obtain the interview she wanted. She never told me in detail what happened; but I gather she refused absolutely to be severed from her mother, though perfectly willing to change her name. She must have managed the conversation very skilfully, for the old lady asked her to come back in two days' time. She did so, and Mrs Somerford said she had decided to waive her second condition. She lived to a great age and the money only came to Evelyn just before the War. It enabled her to give up her teaching and go out with the Friends' Ambulance Unit to

Serbia, where, as you know, she died. So the money did me grievous harm and Evelyn little good, as I had always felt it would. But it was to Mrs Somerford's credit that her heart warmed toward Harry's daughter. That has always comforted me a little.'

'Mrs Somerford never asked to see *you*?'

'Oh, no; nor mentioned me, when Evelyn went to see her. How anyone can go on hating a stranger as she and Kate went on hating me, I cannot understand. But then I am a bad hater. I did not mind, really, except for the awkwardness it must have caused for Evelyn.'

'And Kate?'

'Kate had married – a clergyman, I believe – and gone to the other end of nowhere on missionary work. If she had been home I doubt if Harry's mother would have relented as she did. But she was lonely, poor soul, and after all Evelyn was her granddaughter.'

'So Evelyn never saw Kate at all?'

She shook her head.

'Lucky for Evelyn . . .' said Warbeck.

She made a little face.

'But I can't help feeling sorry for the poor heathen' she added.

*   *   *

The task of writing up his notes proved an even more formidable one than Warbeck had anticipated. They had first of all to be given a chronology. Although Mrs Hooper had kept roughly to the main sequence of her life, she was often confused or erratic; and he found numerous examples of incidents manifestly misplaced, of assumptions which could not possibly have been made until a year or two later, of cause postdating effect, and similar derangements. Only when the mass of jottings and memoranda had been got into order could the writing start. To make matters worse, for some while after his return to London the time at his disposal was limited and scrappy. There were arrears of office-work to be made up, and for weeks he found it impossible to secure the few consecutive days necessary to recapture the spirit of the past which, while Mrs Hooper had been talking, had seemed to crowd in upon them, and become almost tangible. At last, early in October, he managed to take ten days at home and doggedly settled to the planning of his book.

His original idea was to cover the whole of the old lady's long life in one narrative; but he had not plotted very far into her childhood, when he realized that this was out of the question. The result would be impossibly unwieldy, hopeless from the market point of view, and probably tedious. He must find a division, but preferred not to prejudice where it should fall. As writing progressed, a suitable break would show itself.

The next problem was the handling of the material and the method of narration. Her personality had become very familiar to him during their protracted companionship, and he wanted, if in any way possible, to tell the story as though she were telling it. But there were aspects of events and people – in particular aspects of herself, as she appeared to others – of which she could not possibly have been conscious, but were nevertheless of vital importance, if the tale were to have its third-dimension and not be merely a flat tapestry of one individual's experience. He hit on the device of making Harry Somerford the recorder of the all-important epoch in Fanny Hooper's life when they two were together. This device, he argued defensively, was a favourite with certain famous novelists of the Victorian period, and could therefore suitably be revived for a book with a Victorian setting.

Finally he had to steer a way between pedantic observance of period-detail and reckless commission of anachronisms. He decided that when he was not writing conversations – not, that is to say, purporting to record words actually spoken sixty years earlier – he would write freely and in his own manner; but that when characters were speaking, they must so far as possible speak as they would have spoken. It went without saying that details of life and environment must be strictly in period. He realized, when he had written these desiderata on a piece of paper, that he had taken on a real job; and several times, waking in the middle of the night, his heart failed him, and he cursed the easy optimism into which, like a sentimental fool, he had allowed the enchantment of Les Yvelines to lure him.

Throughout the winter (with two clear weeks after Christmas) he toiled at his book. Every moment of his free time was given to it. He went nowhere except to the office; saw no one except his small staff and such callers as could not be denied. The manuscript grew slowly but steadily. And then one morning at his flat he got a letter from Madame Bonnet to say Madame Oupère was dead.

She must have died peacefully in her sleep; for Léontine had seen her comfortably into bed about midnight, and when she went to have a few words with her at six o'clock next morning (the old lady always woke early and liked to see her friendly helper as soon as the hotel was astir) she found her cold. The bedclothes were not disarranged; Madame's book and spectacles were on the night-table as usual; the reading lamp had been extinguished. Her face was calm and happy.

*   *   *

Warbeck sat with the letter in his hand, feeling as though something had hit him on the head and half-stunned him. As his wits slowly returned, he realized that he was more than shocked – he was profoundly grieved. He had corresponded with her at intervals during the winter months, and she had regularly replied to his questions with intelligence and care. Now she was gone. She would never see the book she had so longed to see.

'Poor lonely unlucky Fanny!' he thought. 'All your life things have happened just wrong for you. And it had to be *me* – who, now that I know your story, admire and love you for the gallant unselfish little woman you were – who dealt you your last disappointment, by not getting finished in time.'

He groaned aloud and buried his head in his hands. 'I couldn't help it, Fanny' he whispered. 'Really I couldn't help it.'

He pulled himself together. There was an enclosure in Madame Bonnet's letter. He must look at that. Then he must pack a bag and go immediately to Les Yvelines. Unavoidably he had failed her while she was still alive; he was not going to fail her now that she was dead.

The enclosure was a sealed envelope, addressed to himself in Mrs Hooper's hand. He tore it open and saw to his astonishment that it bore a date in the August of the previous year.

Dear Mr Warbeck,

It is a fortnight or more since you left here, and I know that I cannot for long endure the loneliness and uselessness of my life. I have tried to get back to the nothing-matters-so-why-worry condition in which I have passed the last few years. But it is no good. I suppose that talking to you, reliving things I thought I had forgotten, has stirred up feelings which were better asleep. Please do not think I regret our rummaging in the cupboards of the past. The experience gave me a few weeks of life as I once knew it – an adventure, a thrill on waking (what will happen today?), a lovely recalling of times when I was *part* of something – a cog, if nothing more, in the wheel of existence. But I have lost the secret of indifference. I *do* care now what becomes of me – and nothing can become of me, except a corpse. So I am sure I shall not last very long. I hope it will be long enough to see what you have written. You will be as quick as you can, I am sure, for you are a man of sensibility, and have treated an old woman with courtesy and consideration. But just in case ... I want to write this letter and leave it with dear Madame Bonnet, to be sent to you when I go.

No one cares whether I live or die – except the kind people here and – dare I hope? – my friend Mr Warbeck. I want, therefore, to make some return for their friendship while I am still able to do so. I would like *you* to have my adored zircon brooch – given me by my father, admired by Harry, and hardly ever worn since he died. Perhaps you will love someone well enough to give it her. I hope so – and that she is worthy of you. Of money I have practically none, save what you paid me. If any of this is left when I am dead (and something will be, I am sure; for it cannot be long now) I would like almost all of it to go to Madame Bonnet and Léontine, as a small reward for their patient kindness to a troublesome and often ailing old pensionnaire. I know Madame Bonnet has long wanted to make certain improvements and renewals in her hotel, and Léontine, with an addition to her *dot*, may find it easier to get the husband she deserves.

I said 'Almost all' of whatsoever I leave behind. Is it selfish to want to spent just a fraction on myself? I would like to be buried in or near this beloved place, in a tiny patch of ground bought outright and dedicated to Harry and to me.

This brings me to my last request. Will you, dear Mr Warbeck, see to this for me? There is no one else I can ask, and there could be no one I would more readily trust. In return, the book you are making of my memories – the book you have already paid for so generously (so that I have been able to send back all my 'compensation-money') will belong to you, absolutely and for always.

Now goodbye; and thank you for the last time for your forbearance and friendliness toward a forlorn – and I daresay ridiculous – relic of a time before you were even thought of.

Fanny Hooper.

*   *   *

A telegram to Madame Bonnet announced his arrival with plans for the funeral. He took the ten o'clock plane, and was in Paris for lunch. The head-office of the Société Générale, after peering at his credentials and flicking through several unnecessary card-indexes, unwillingly admitted that Madame Hooper had a credit balance of nearly twenty thousand francs. Hiring a fast car he was at Les Yvelines by three o'clock. Rapidly he explained the position to Madame Bonnet and her niece. The body must go instantly to the mortuary at Dreux. They threw up their hands at intervals, and oh'd and ah'd, and finally cried unrestrainedly.

But when he raised the problem of the grave, the widow dried her eyes and said with dignified simplicity:

'But, monsieur, where else should she lie but in the garden of the Boule d'Or? The land is mine. Choose any part of it you think she would have liked, and it is hers for always.'

* * *

The formalities so dear to officialdom were completed. A monumental mason had done his work. At last, in a sunny corner of the quiet garden of Madame Bonnet's hotel, Fanny Hooper lay in her last resting-place. The headstone read:

HERE LIES
VANDRA (FANNY) HOOPER
ONLY DAUGHTER OF
CLIVE SEYMORE
OF AUGHTON SEYMORE, YORKSHIRE
AND
CHÈRE AMIE OF
HARRY SOMERFORD

BORN 1857 . DIED 1933

*'Il n'y a pas de silence plus docile
que le silence de l'amour.
Croyez-vous que j'ai soif d'une parole sublime,
lorsque je sens
qu'une âme me regarde dans l'âme?'*

MORE ABOUT PENGUINS
AND PELICANS

For further information about books available from Penguins please write to Dept EP, Penguin Books Ltd, Harmondsworth, Middlesex UB7 0DA.

In the U.S.A.: For a complete list of books available from Penguins in the United States write to Dept CS, Penguin Books, 625 Madison Avenue, New York, New York 10022.

In Canada: For a complete list of books available from Penguins in Canada write to Penguin Books Canada Ltd, 2801 John Street, Markham, Ontario L3R 1B4.

In Australia: For a complete list of books available from Penguins in Australia write to the Marketing Department, Penguin Books Australia Ltd, P.O. Box 257, Ringwood, Victoria 3134.

In New Zealand: For a complete list of books available from Penguins in New Zealand write to the Marketing Department, Penguin Books (N.Z.) Ltd, P.O. Box 4019, Auckland 10.